D0130328

WHITE MARE, RED STALLION

Druith filled the bowl with water once more.

"Behold the sacred water of the Goddess, Her milk and Her blood. As it becomes part of us, may we become part of Her . . ." Druith lifted the bowl, lips moving in silent prayer, drank, then passed it on.

When the bowl came to her, Maira held it a moment, wondering what to ask for. A husband and children? She was sure that was what the other girls desired – and so did she, but there must be something more. *Lady*, she said silently at last, *You choose for me*.

And then she drank. At first the water tasted bitter, then oddly salty, then sweet, Maira's ears buzzed; she felt as if the stones beneath her had shifted suddenly. Blindly she held the bowl out to the girl girl beside her. After a time she heard the others talking softly, the soft splashing as they waded back to shore.

Do they feel nothing? she wondered, *or has this come only to me?*

White Mare, Red Stallion

Diana L. Paxson

NEW ENGLISH LIBRARY
Hodder and Stoughton

First published in the United States of America in 1986 by Berkley Books

First published in Great Britain in 1988 by New English Library Paperbacks

British Library C.I.P.

Paxson, Diana L.
  White mare, red stallion.
  I. Title
  813'.54[F]

ISBN 0 450 43054 5

Printed and bound in Great Britain for Hodder and Stoughton Paperbacks, a division of Hodder and Stoughton Ltd., Mill Road, Dunton Green, Sevenoaks, Kent TN13 2YA.
(Editorial Office: 47 Bedford Square, London WC1B 3DP) by
Cox & Wyman Ltd., Reading.

Acknowledgments

I would like to acknowledge my debt to Alexei Kondratiev of the Celtic League in New York City for advising me on second century Brythonic linguistic forms and details of culture; Sharon Folsom and Dr. James Duran of the Institute for Celtic Studies in Oakland, California, for insights into the interpretation of folkloric survivals; Jack Langley of the Butser Ancient Farm near Portsmouth, Britain, for explaining the work and findings of the Iron Age farm project to me; and Mrs. Stone of Scaur Cottage for letting me climb Tynron Doon and showing me the countryside, and to all the other kind souls in the Celtic edges of Britain who helped me with advice, information, and hospitality. To them should go much of the credit for what is good in this work—the mistakes I claim for my own.

Contents

Principal Characters

Novantae tribesmen of the White Horse Clan

Conmor map Ycuit, *lord of Rath Uath and chieftain of the White Horse Clan*

Druith merch Gutuator, *his wife*

Maira merch Conmor, *his daughter, later Lady of Din Rhun and chieftain of the White Horse Clan*

Temella, *Maira's friend*

Eoc map Conmor, *her brother*

Beth, *Eoc's wife*

Gutuator, *the Speaker, a Druid of unknown age and powers*

Tadhg, *a harper of Eirinn in Conmor's service*

Ness, *a serving woman of the old race*

Urr, Lod, Petric, Kitto, and Caw, *clansmen sworn to Maira*

Rosic, Kenow, Dumnoric, *clansmen sworn to Eoc*

Maelscuit map Bituit, *Conmor's cousin*

Maelor, Waric, Neithon, *principal men of the White Horse Clan*

Selgovae tribesmen of Din Carn

Carric map Cador, *son and tanist to the chieftain of Din Carn*

Trost and Conon, *his sword brothers*

Romans and others

Tiberius Flavius Pintamus, *an Iberian Decurion commanding a troop of Brigante scouts on detached duty*

Lucius Ostorius Rufus, *Prefect of the Ala Petriana and officer commanding the Wall*

Antiochus Callidus, *a Syrian trader*

ONE

The Black Pool

A HORSE WHINNIED, the sound sweet and distant as the call of a bird. Maira stood up in the dark water, listening, but the echoes were lost in the whisper of wind in birch trees and women's laughter. One of their own ponies, scenting the wind, she thought then. It must be . . .

They had left a lad to guard the horses, wide-eyed at the thought of remaining so near the women's ritual. Forbidden to approach the lake, still he could have cried out any danger. And what danger could there be? The Selgovae knew well that this was Novantae land, and the Clan of the White Horse could be as deadly as any folk in Alba to those who threatened them.

Maira sighed and let tension drain from her body into the dark water. She saw her white limbs elongated as if drawn there by an artist of her tribe, so unlike the stolid images the Romans made—long legs trained to the curve of a horse's back rippled into the water, arms whose grace hid the hours she had labored with lance and sword. Her hair, water-darkened from red gold to carnelian, clung in ringlets to her breast.

For a moment Maira saw her reflection and the round of dark pool and sky as a unity. *Like the circle of the Goddess*. Then water splashed cold against her skin, shattering the image. Maira whirled, crouching defensively as she shook back her long hair.

"Hai! Maira—what warrior do you dream of?" Laughter echoed the question as ripples spread from the drops of water that had fallen back into the pool. Recognizing the voice, Maira straightened. Beth, her brother's wife, saw the change in

1

her expression and laughed. Maira felt the hot flush of color beneath her fair skin, but she held her tongue. Beth's belly was still flaccid from the birth of the child for which they had come here to purify her, her breasts blue-veined and swollen with milk. Beth was sacred today.

"Oh, she dreams of no human lover," said dark-haired Temella, laughing. "Of the herd-stallion, maybe!"

Maira's grey eyes turned to her friend. It was not so long since Temella had been as eager as any to help break the young horses or race through the hills. With no quiver in mouth or brow to signal her intention, Maira dove toward the other girl. Her strong hands closed on smooth flesh and she swept Temella's legs from under her. For a moment the water frothed, then Temella gasped her surrender and Maira let go.

"For shame, Maira—remember where you are!" Druith, her mother, spoke from the shore.

Maira stared back at her, feeling her hot gaze deflected by her mother's monumental calm. Temella was eyeing them both warily, rubbing the red mark on her arm where Maira had gripped her.

"She should not have provoked me." Maira shivered, wondering if she had offended the spirit of the pool. She sent a swift glance around her, but the only ripples on the black water had been made by Beth and the five maidens who stood with her there.

Then Temella grinned, grasped Maira's hand and pulled herself upright. "Forgive me. I did not know you would take it so."

"I will marry when my time comes," Maira said patiently. "I know what I owe the clan." Her father led the Vindomarci —the people of the White Horse who held the eastern marches of the Novantae tribal lands, and her brother Eoc would likely follow him. But there were some in the clan who held that succession from brother to sister's son was the better way, and in any case, healthy children strengthened the clan.

Unwillingly her gaze went to the red-faced infant cradled in his grandmother's arms. They had named him Arminoric after the ancestor who led them to this land, but had taken to calling him "Acorn" until he should grow into a warrior's name.

Acorn . . . her nephew. They had let Maira hold him. Even now her fingers remembered the grip of that tiny hand, and abruptly she wondered how it would feel to have a child of her own. *I will bear heroes,* she promised herself. *But who will father them?*

"I am only a year older than you, and I have a son," said Beth smugly. "What are you waiting for?"

"Perhaps for some prince of all Alba to drive the Romans away!" laughed Beth's friend Onn, a girl from her home village down the river Nova on the brushy ridge of Din Prys.

"Oh, the Red Crests are all hiding behind their great wall!" Temella said scornfully. "Their forts in the north are abandoned. They will trouble us no more. *I* think that Maira is waiting for Carric of Din Carn to win as many cows as she owns so that he can offer—"

Maira turned on her. "He is of the Selgovae! Think you I'll lie down by my enemy?"

"When the enemy is so fair a man as Carric, you might at least dream!" retorted her friend. "If I were not promised to Dumnoric I would not mind joining the tanist of Din Carn in the Lughnasa Dance. . . ."

"There has been peace so long." Beth glanced apprehensively at her small son, still sleeping obliviously in his grandmother's arms. "Surely the Selgovae are no longer our enemies."

Maira shrugged. "It is the Peace of Rome, and if Rome falls, who will make them keep it? You cannot have it both ways." Maira saw a sudden pallor in Beth's face and was sorry she had spoken. This was not the time or place to talk of such things, even though what she had said was true.

Is that why I have continued to train with the warriors when most of my friends prefer the spindle to the spear? she wondered then. Her mother was the child of the Druid, Gutuator. Perhaps his prophetic spirit spoke in his granddaughter now. Maira shuddered and forced her awareness back to the white bodies of the women around her, mirrored like the birch trunks in the still pool.

"It is time," came a stern voice from the shore. Druith had given the baby to one of the other mothers to hold and was standing with arms uplifted at the water's edge. Her mantle of deep blue wool had fallen back; the golden armlets shone against the whiteness of her strong arms.

Silent now, the five young women moved through the cool water to circle Beth. Now Druith entered the pool as well and drew from the breast of her gown a shallow bowl carved from a single piece of jet, polished by age and the touch of many hands.

"Behold the vessel from which life's waters flow. . . ." She bent, let the dark water cover the bowl, then raised it, overflowing, so that sparkling droplets of water cascaded back into the pool.

"The Goddess of the sweet waters beholds Her daughters, suppliant here. As our mothers before us, as their mothers before *them*, we have come to seek Her blessing for one who has brought new life into the world. . . ."

She paused, her eyes unfocused as if she were listening. Maira saw the surface of the waters ruffled suddenly, flashing back the light of the westering sun in a thousand glimmering stars, and the hair lifted on her arms and neck, for she had felt no breath of wind. The air seemed heavier, weighted with the Presence her mother was invoking now.

"As the waters of the womb nourish the life it bears, so Her sweet waters are the life of the land. Let the Lady bless Her daughter! Let Her waters cleanse and heal her so that she may raise her child to manhood and bear others to honor the Goddess and to defend the clan."

Druith stepped forward, dipped water from the black bowl and touched it to Beth's belly and her breasts, then poured the rest over her. Maira blinked—for a moment the water had looked red, and she remembered vividly how Beth had lain in the strawbed, white and exhausted from her labor, with the birthblood smearing her thighs. Later, Maira had helped Druith take away the afterbirth and bury it under a young oak tree.

Druith passed the bowl to Temella, who dipped, poured, then handed the bowl to Onn. When it came to Maira she found herself trembling. She gripped the sacred vessel tightly, scooped up more water and stared down into it, waiting for the surface to still so that she could breathe her blessing into it. The bowl felt warm despite the coolness of the water within it. Somehow it must be retaining the warmth of the other women's hands.

The water rippled, and Maira forced herself to stillness again. There—there—now she could see a reflection forming in the ripples. It steadied, and her breath caught—for she was not looking at her own familiar features—fair and freckled with the round grey eyes of her people, but at another face, thinner and browner of skin, framed by long, black hair. This woman wore a necklace of carved jet and amber and pendant earrings of pierced bone.

Was it one of her foremothers, or perhaps a face she had worn in a previous life? Maira did not know. But the woman in the mirror was smiling at her—she seemed about to speak, and Maira knew that her words would answer questions that Maira did not yet know how to ask.

Then a dragonfly hummed by her ear; a flicker of iridescence caught her eye, and the vision was gone.

Maira stood still a moment longer, her eyes blurring with tears. Then she blessed Beth and poured the water over her, feeling as if she had given the other girl a part of her soul.

When they were all finished, Druith filled the bowl with water once more.

"Behold the sacred water of the Goddess, Her milk and Her blood. As it becomes part of us, may we become part of Her. . . ." Druith lifted the bowl, lips moving in silent prayer, drank, then passed it on.

When the bowl came to her, Maira held it a moment, wondering what to ask for. A husband and children? She was sure that was what the other girls desired—and so did she, but there must be something more. *Lady*, she said silently at last, *You choose for me*.

And then she drank. At first the water tasted bitter, then oddly salty, then sweet. Maira's ears buzzed; she felt as if the stones beneath her had shifted suddenly. Blindly she held the bowl out to the girl beside her. After a time she heard the others talking softly, the soft splashing as they waded back to shore.

Do they feel nothing? she wondered, *or has this come only to me?* She sank breast-deep into the water and cautiously opened her eyes. But she saw only the trees, and the pool, and the other girls' white bodies as they rubbed themselves dry.

And yet there was a difference, for everything seemed edged with radiance. Abruptly, Maira knew that the Otherworld was very close now. If she stilled her spirit just a little more, she would see. . . .

"Maira, are you coming?" called Temella. "We must start homeward soon."

"Yes, I know it. Give me only a little longer here." Shaken, Maira took a long breath and sank farther down into the water, trying to master her emotions. But the others were still too close. She moved deeper into the water, nearly went under as the stones beneath her fell away to the unknown depths in the midst of the pool, then began to make her way around the edge, holding onto overhanging branches when the water deepened.

From the far bank Temella watched her anxiously. Maira took a firm grip on a projecting root and waved back reassuringly. Then she turned and went forward again, blinking as she caught the full glare of the westering sun. For a moment she was half-blinded. Flame and darkness danced in her vision; then the stark shapes of the trees steadied, and among those black silhouettes she saw something which was not a tree, though it stood as still as they.

Heart pounding, Maira grasped a handful of rushes and pulled herself forward until her feet found bottom where the lakebed shelved into the shore. She stood up, blinking as the shimmer of sunlight on the water that beaded her body clothed her in jewels. But her attention was fixed on the figure she had seen among the trees—there, she found it again—a man's shape, surely, broad-shouldered with muscles in sharp outline against the glare. But she could not see his face. Maira took another step forward and he moved, and then her breath stopped, for above the shadows that hid his face she saw forked antlers curve.

She knew Him—surely she knew Him, and her blood burned. He was the progenitor and the destroyer. He was the Lordly One, and something previously unawakened within her began to tremble.

Maira stared, and her skin chilled as the blood drained inward; the glare of light and darkness whirled and fused. Her legs lost their power to hold her and she sank gently backward into the dark waters from which she had emerged.

The cold water shocked her back to consciousness. Spluttering, she broke the surface, wiping her eyes and trying to see. But the angle of the sunlight had altered, and she saw only trees there now.

Temella called to her once more. Maira turned, breathing hard as if she had just run a race, and saw the other girls still dressing. Her vision had seemed to last half a lifetime, but to them hardly a moment had gone by. The Druids taught that there was another world, to which this one fitted close as a glove to the hand. But to mortal eyes it was invisible—only for a moment her own sight had shifted, and she had Seen.

Somehow Maira managed to get back across the pool. By

the time she had dried herself and pulled on a tunic she had woven herself in squares of lichen-dyed golden wool and natural grey, her vision was assuming the dimly-remembered splendor of a dream. The other women were already threading down the hill through the trees. Fumbling with the laces, Maira pulled on her braies and tied the thongs of her slippers and hurried after them.

The horses were well-rested, and they had grazed freely on the rich grass of the meadow. Reluctant to leave it, they sidled and pranced as the women tried to mount them. Maira slapped Roud's roan neck in warning, and the mare butted her playfully, then she shortened the reins and vaulted into the padded saddle. The mare quivered beneath her, and suddenly Maira shared her excitement.

She forced herself to hold the mare to a walk as they passed the others, checking instinctively to make sure everyone's gear was fastened properly and none of the horses were lame. Temella smiled and offered her the sacred rowan branch hung with silver bells, but she shook her head.

"Roud is too frisky; she wants to run. Goddess, *I* want to run!" Maira laughed. "I will wait for you down where the path joins the road."

They were coming through the last of the tangle of birch and alders that enclosed the pool now. Roud's ears pricked at the sight of the more open country ahead of them and Maira eased her pressure on the rein.

"Now, my lass, my lovely one—*now!*" she whispered, and like a bird taking flight, the mare sprang into her speed. The path blurred, and the steep slopes to either side were a glimmer of varicolored green. Maira felt Roud's muscles bunch and release beneath her and kept the grip of her long legs light, riding on balance. She had outrun her companions, was she trying to outrun the confusion of vision as well? She dug her heels into Roud's sides. The whipping mane stung her face, and for a few moments she knew only the release of swift flight.

Then, from somewhere ahead came a horse's neigh. Roud's head came up and she slowed, her first burst of excitement replaced by curiosity. Maira brought her to a halt and sat still, listening. The air was still warm, and at the height of summer, the light of the vanishing sun would remain for half the night.

The year had been dry, and already the grass in field and meadow was ripening into gold. Through the hardpacked earth hoofbeats vibrated like distant thunder.

Most likely the riders were her own clansmen, perhaps men of Lys Speiat coming out to see what had taken their women-folk so long. Then, clear in the stillness, Maira heard the thrice-repeated call of a wren. The bird had been on her left, and she tried to remember what that would mean. If the call had come from the south it could foretell evil, but this music had been from the east. It was people coming then, or tidings, if she remembered her grandfather's teachings right. The bird called once more, close by, then flicked into the safety of a hazel copse. That had another meaning, but she could not remember it. Maira sat still on Roud's back, listening to the music of the women's voices as they came down the trail behind her, and the other hoofbeats that grew ever louder as they came toward her over the rise.

Beyond that last hill the ground sloped down toward Scaur Water and the valley of the River Nova into which it flowed. East of the river rose the bare-topped mountains of the Selgovae lands. The hills to the west were gentler, except for the perfect peak of the *dun*. Maira had been born in its shadow, but she still found it wonderful, pointing like a spearhead at the sky. Perhaps that was why they called it the Lance Fort—Din Rhun.

Even as she assessed the country around her, Maira had been tracking the progress of the horses before and behind. She took up her reins and held up a warning hand as the Novantae women trotted up behind her at the same time as another group of riders swept toward them over the hill.

A touch of Maira's toe shifted the mare sideways across the road; the knife that was always at her side flicked into her hand. She knew who was coming. Even in the first glance, when they were only blurred shapes against the trees, she knew those shaggy hill-ponies and the Roman cloth of the cloaks their riders wore—it was Carric of Din Carn and his friends.

"It's a fine night for riding, but you're far from your own hunting runs," she called as they swirled to a stop before her. A quick check showed them all armed with bows and lances. One pony bore the carcass of a buck deer.

"Ah, but doesn't it depend on what we're after?" Carric laughed, head thrown back to display the strong column of his neck. His bronze-brown hair had come free of its bindings, and beneath the cloak pinned at one shoulder, his torso was bare. Maira noted with a perverse satisfaction the flush of sunburn on his fair skin.

"Not when you are hunting in my land!" she said grimly.

The other women had drawn their mounts up close behind her now. She heard a spurt of soft laughter, quickly suppressed, and then the sweet shimmer of silver bells. Some of Carric's men saw the rowan branch and lost their high color, but Carric did not appear to see, or hear.

A deft twitch on the reins set his bay horse to rearing, pivoting on his hind legs so that Carric faced Maira from the other side now. He swayed and came upright again as the animal halted, blowing gustily. It had been a pretty display of horsemanship, and the bay stallion was a fine beast, big enough to carry his rider easily, with good legs and an intelligent eye. But Maira kept her face still. Carric had not yet explained what he was doing on Vindomarci land.

"Oh, but we're all friends now, surely?" The brown-haired burly man, Trost, had come up upon Carric's right side, while his other sword-brother, Conon, flanked the left. "One family beneath the benevolent roof of Rome. . . . Why not pay a visit to our dearly loved kin?" He grinned sideways at Carric, who seemed suddenly redder than could be accounted for by the sunburn. They all seemed a bit rosy, now that she considered it, with a glitter in their eyes that could come from excitement, or possibly from the leathern bottles slung by their sides. Beth and Onn giggled appreciatively, and Maira felt a spurt of anger. Beth would not have laughed in just that way if Eoc had been here. Eyes narrowing, she urged Roud forward.

"Not so close as to need no invitation!" she said softly, "Nor so beloved as to claim one unasked!"

The flushed faces before her darkened with anger, then sobered abruptly. Trost and Conon backed their mounts to form the balanced fighting triangle of the *trimarcisia*, supporting their lord. Their eyes were fixed on something behind her.

Maira looked over her shoulder, and saw her mother sitting quietly on her grey mare. But Druith had taken the rowan branch from Temella, and held it in her outstretched hand.

"Enough," Druith said. "It is not proper for you to be here. If you have words for Conmor, my husband will listen to your spokesman. If you have words for my daughter, you may see her at the Feast of Lughnasa. But we may neither speak with you nor offer you hospitality now." She gave the branch a twitch that set its bells chiming, and the Selgovae horses tossed their heads as their riders jerked on the reins. "We come from serving the Lady, and there lies the only male who may lawfully be in our company. . . ." Druith pointed to the baby held against his mother's breast by her knotted shawl. "Now you have been warned, so be gone!"

Carric's high-boned face had gone first red, then pale. His gaze moved from Maira to the other women, who watched him with little cat smiles. For one confused moment Maira wanted to defend him.

"Come away, Carric," called Conon then. "There's better sport at home. We'll get Illic to let us sample his new batch of heather beer!" The bravado in Conon's voice wavered a little as his eyes flicked from his leader to Druith's stern face and back again.

Carric looked impatient. His gaze returned to Maira and he nodded.

"Yes, I will see you at Lughnasa. . . ." Finally, his eyes met hers. But the light was too dim now to tell if he was uncertain or was mocking her. Angered, Maira looked away. She had had the situation in hand—why did her mother have to interfere? Roud pawed at the hard ground and Maira pulled her up severely.

Carric straightened and yes, he *was* grinning now. He hauled the stallion back on its haunches and turned it, then sent the horse pounding back down the road. Abruptly they were all in motion, a confusion of plunging horses and flying cloaks whose colors glowed dimly in the fading light.

Maira watched them hurtle down the road, half-hidden as they rounded the hazel-copse, then reappearing as a moving darkness upon the white road. Then they were climbing the next hill. For a moment she saw them in sharp silhouette against the amethyst glow of the sky, then they were gone.

By the time they set their horses up the track that followed Scaur Water up into the hills, the western sky had the pale lucency of a seashell. The hawthorn hedge that gave Lys Speiat its name was a dim tangle of branches, starred with the last white flowers; the conical thatched roofs of the buildings inside, dark silhouettes against the steep slope of the step-hill that linked the vale to the greater height of Din Rhun. The wind was blowing toward them, welcoming them with the familiar scents of cattle and wood-smoke.

Roud broke into a trot unurged, and Maira did not restrain her. Too much had happened today. She wanted to be home. Druith and Beth quickened their pace to keep up with her. The other women had already turned off to their own homes in raths and farmsteads scattered through the hills.

The milking cattle lowed from the home pasture as she went by—only a few of them now, for the greater herds were still out on the hills. With a mental reminder to ride out soon to check on her own beasts and the men who herded them, Maira turned the mare through the open gateway of the housestead and rode in.

Something large and brightly colored loomed up against the shed and Roud shied. As Maira righted herself and got the mare under control she sorted confused impressions—blood on the ground and a stained sheepskin tacked against a wall, women bending over the firepit, from which a wonderful smell of roasting meat was being carried by the changing wind, and dominating them all, the big, gaily-colored wagon with its two white mules.

Her eyes widened, and she turned in her saddle. "Mother, Beth! Look—it's Antiochus' wagon. The trader is here!"

She slipped from Roud's back and led her toward her pen, stopping a moment to remind her father's fosterling, Coll, to unhitch and feed the mules and to make sure that all the horses that had been out that day were fed and rubbed down. She tended Roud herself, and only when the mare was eating eagerly did she allow herself to move toward the blaze of firelight that shone from the open house door.

"So the Red Crests have posted a new Decurion to lead Scouts from the Petriana?" Maira's father lifted his cup, drained it, and set it down. He gave her a quick, complicit smile as she eased past him toward her own bed-box on the Women's Side, then turned to his guest again.

Antiochus laughed, teeth flashing white against the black luxuriance of his beard. That beard had always fascinated Maira, for the tribesmen shaved their chins and left only their moustaches to grow, while the Romans she had seen shaved beard and moustache and all.

"Ho—Conmor—" The trader's voice was a gravelly rumble, oddly accented, though he spoke the British tongue quite well. "What will you give me for the news?"

"More beer?" the chieftain grinned, twisting the spout on

the oak cask to fill his cup again. His hair was corn yellow in
the firelight, and Maira thought that the lines in his face only
made it look stronger. For all the strains of his nearly sixty
years, Conmor of Lys Speiat was still a handsome man.

Maira bent to enter her compartment where the roof sloped
steeply between the supporting pillars of the house and the
outer wall. The space was just big enough for a box bed and the
chest where she kept her clothes. She gave a swift twitch to the
curtain to hide the tumble in which she had left things that
morning, hung her cloak on its hook, and began to struggle
with the tangle of her hair.

"Well, it is good beer—" she heard Antiochus' voice
through the curtain. "I would buy some, but to whom would I
sell it? Your folk brew all they need. I am getting old, my
friend, and these northern winters chill my bones. I dream of a
grove of date-palms beneath a desert sun, but to live in comfort
in my homeland I must return with much gold. If I cannot sell
beer I must sell news, so I ask you, is this beer of yours a fair
trade for this news of mine, eh? That's what I want to know!"

Conmor laughed, and Maira heard other voices as her
mother and Beth came in with Eoc, who was teasing his wife
and making silly noises at the child. For a moment a ripple of
notes from Tadhg's harp stilled them, but he was only tuning,
and the conversation went on.

A strange little man, Tadhg was, Maira thought as she began
to rebraid her hair, with a head as black as any Roman's, and
eyes like new-turned earth. He had fled to Alba from some war
in Eirinn, and even Segovis the High King did not have a
harper of such skill, for it was Conmor who had found the man
dying in the streets of Carbantorigum and nursed him back to
health and brought him home. Tadhg never spoke of who or
what he had been, but his eyes followed Conmor as the eyes of
a good dog will track his master about a room.

Maira flipped her braids back over her shoulders, straightened her tunic, and slipped past her curtain back to the group
around the hearth. Conmor smiled and gestured, and she eased
down into the bracken beside her father's bench. The golden
torque at his neck caught the firelight as he turned back to
Antiochus.

"Come now, tell me the name of the puppy they've set to
watch us—you know I will learn it soon enough, and Rome has
not moved against us since Clodius Albinus took half their
strength from the Wall three years ago to fight for the Imperial

Purple in Gaul. Twelve years ago it might have mattered which lad they posted where, when Ulpius Marcellus was in command. But surely not now. . . .''

Antiochus lifted his hands like a gladiator acknowledging a fair hit and laughed.

Eoc joined in the laughter and reached across to fill his own cup from the cask, a thin, gangling young man whose frame held only the promise of his father's power. Immediately, Conmor struck his hand away.

"*You* can wait, boy—or shall we let Antiochus go back to report me a niggard at my own fire?'' Conmor plucked the polished wood cup from the trader's hand, refilled it and handed it back again. Flushing angrily, Eoc filled his own cup, drained it almost in one swallow, and filled it again. Maira found her own cup of polished oak banded with silver, drew some beer for herself and sat back, sipping quietly.

"No indeed.'' Antiochus chuckled. "How can I repay such generosity? So I'll tell you—the new lad's name is Tiberius Flavius Pintamus, posted here from Iberia. He's camping out in what's left of the old fort at Blatobulgium. He looks competent—I saw him when I passed through Luguvalium. But he'll have a frustrating time down there with nothing to do but watch the grass growing on the hills. These young men don't know when they are well off!'' His heavy-lidded glance rested for a moment on Eoc, who flushed and filled his cup again.

Maira sighed. Antiochus had been coming to them every summer for as long as she could remember, and Eoc should have known better than to react to his needling. The trader was a friend, but as a strange beast brought from a far land might be a friend—to wonder at, to use, but not to trust.

Conmor squeezed his daughter's shoulder, and she laid her hand over his. This had been her place ever since she could toddle from the Women's Side to take it. Sitting here, all her anger and confusion of the afternoon misted away.

The rich scent of roast mutton drove all other thoughts out as Ness and the other servants brought in the young sheep that had been baking in the firepit outside. They laid the long wooden platter by the hearth, and Druith's terse orders set everyone bustling to bring in platters of brown bread with plenty of cheese and butter, boiled sweet beans, and "fat hen'' greens with wild onion to join the meat by the fire.

Carved hardwood plates were filled and passed around—

Maira noticed without surprise that her mother had contrived to give the best portion to Eoc—and for a little while conversation surrendered to consumption. Maira took the first edge off her hunger and leaned against her father's side, confirming her content with the sight of the woven hangings, the weapons hanging from the house pillars, the joints of meat suspended high under the roof-wheel where the woodsmoke percolated out through the thatch, her mother's loom, and all the other impedimenta of everyday.

With eyes half-closed, she watched Tadhg's face as he cradled the open curve of his harp. He was plucking the gut strings very softly—this was no time for the Great Music, but for something ornamental and undemanding to season the mood of the evening as Ness had added herbs to the roast.

"But what about this one? The lass has been growing," rumbled Antiochus. With a start, Maira realized that the trader was talking about *her*. She sat up, watching him with her chin resting on her father's knee.

"She'll be wanting women's gauds now, to catch a young man's eye! I've an amber necklet that would be just the thing for her—big, clear pieces with a golden glow that would set off her bright hair!"

Maira blushed with a mixture of irritation and pleasure. She loved the liquid sunlight of amber, but surely she could wear it for that reason, not to please some man!

"Save it for me until next year." She smiled sweetly at Antiochus. "My cattle are prospering. Likely I'll have the price of it for you by then!"

"Why not buy it for me?" Beth said petulantly. "I've given a son to this family. Should I not receive some reward?"

"That is true." Conmor smiled at her and at the sleeping child in her arms. "Well, lass, let us see how the harvest goes, and the trading at Lughnasa Fair."

But as Maira watched him, it seemed to her that there was some trouble in his eyes. Abruptly she realized how much silver had frosted his fair hair. She shivered, as if there were a draft in the crowded room, or as if a raven had called from the left, prophesying some doom.

Roud's hooves beat out the one-two-three, one-two-three rhythm of festival drumming, faster and faster as she carried Maira down the hill. The shaggy black backs of the cattle bounced before her. They lowed with the same bitter music the pipes made, singing of war.

Maira forced herself to rein Roud down, to rein in the war cry that trembled on her lips. It was only a cattle drive, not a battle, she was charging into, and she did not want to stampede the herd down the glen.

Just beyond the copse of hazel trees she saw the peeled poles of the holding pen. A knee pressed to the mare's side eased her off to the right, where the slope was gentler.

"Sa, sa, my lovely—gently now. . . ." she murmured, straightening in the saddle.

Suddenly two heifers saw the opening and swerved toward her. Maira's heels drummed against Roud's sides and the little mare leaped forward. Maira's hazel switch hissed and snapped against the first heifer's side. Eyes rolling, the frantic cow wheeled again, back, then up the hill, dodging nimbly, her brindle coat flashing in and out of visibility in the shadows of the trees. The other cow, the spotted one, took advantage of the distraction to dash straight across the hillside.

Teeth bared, the mare cut off the brindle heifer's rush, the little cow snorted in frustration, and giving up the duel, lolloped back to the herd. Maira looked over her shoulder. The spotted cow was disappearing over the rim of the hill, tail lifted in triumph. Maira began to turn Roud after her, but another half dozen animals were coming down the slope— better to get them in now and go after the escapee afterward.

Determined not to let any more beasts get away from her, she followed almost on their heels until they hurtled into the pen like rocks tumbled in a flooding stream. Maira pulled up among the hazels, wincing as the supple branches slapped her bare arms. Time slowed and the blurred world steadied around her and became solid once more.

As the pounding pulse in her ears faded, Maira became aware of the cries of the other riders bringing the rest of the herd along—Petric and Caw and little Kitto and behind them the three sons of Urr, and finally Urr himself, riding a sturdy pony so short that his legs nearly dragged on the ground.

They had kept the cattle well this year, both her cattle and their own, even though the lack of rain had sucked vigor from the grass. None had been lost to illness or accident, and no reivers from across the river had driven any of them away.

Except for the heifer that had run off, the herd was intact.

Maira frowned. The spotted heifer was a granddaughter of the black cow her father had given her when she was thirteen. She could have had a golden bracelet, but cattle were a better kind of wealth than gold or amber, for they bred more. That first milch-cow had given Maira many calves to raise or exchange for the service of her men.

Maira's grin broadened and she counted them as she had counted the cows—seven men here and three more over in the glen of the wildcat—two less than her brother Eoc had oathed to him, and he was two years older than she! It was a good start for a following. Carric of Din Carn would have to stretch himself to offer for her on equal terms. . . .

Maira realized what she was thinking and swore softly. What matter how much wealth Cárric had? If he asked for her in marriage she would refuse him. The shadow of Rome discouraged open warfare, but the Nova had been a bloody boundary, and there were too many old scores still unsettled between the two tribes.

Perspiration stung her eyes and Maira used the skirt of her tunic to mop her brow. The hazels screened her from the sun, but the air was hot and still. The season her people called Iuchar was truly upon them—the hot days at the end of the summer, just before Lughnasa. Her cheeks were burning, and she did not know if it was from thoughts of Carric or the sun.

Urr and his little pony hurtled down the hill. He waved his arms and screeched at the last bunch of cattle, and with tails up and eyes bulging they clattered into the pen. Quickly Caw and Kitto ran the withy gate across the opening and leaned against it, panting, as the cattle swirled around and around inside.

Urr trotted past the pen and up to Maira. "Heugh! Hot work!" He ran stubby fingers through his sun-streaked brown hair, then turned to look at the cattle again. "Eh, then, Lady—there they be. A wild lot they look now, but they'll settle soon."

"I know. They've run free on the hills since Beltane. Three months with scarcely the smell of a man—no wonder if they're lively!"

Urr grinned, showing the gap where his front teeth used to be. "Aye, Lady, and I remember when it was you out on the hills herding them—very near as wild as they!"

His eyes met hers and sobered. She knew he remembered the day he had gone seeking a strayed ewe and slipped among the rocks of Corrie Cathal. It was Maira who had found him, unconscious and bleeding, and who all alone got him onto her pony and home.

When he was able to speak again, he had sworn to serve her. It was a binding more potent than any oath in exchange for cattle, for he was a man of the older race who had held these hills before ever the Novantae left their home in the lands across the narrow sea. His folk counted themselves as part of the White Horse clan now, but Urr had never oathed to any of its lords. The support of men of Gallic blood like Petric and Caw might bring Maira more standing in the councils of the clan, but there was no price for the loyalty of a man like Urr.

"I hope I've not forgotten my tracking," she said with a smile. "That spotted heifer got away from me, and I'll have to go after her soon. In the meantime, we should be thinking which animals we want to winter in the vale, and which ones to market at the fair at Lyn Mapon."

Urr nodded and sighed. "There's some that'll not last the winter here. We should sell them if we can."

"That is what my father has said. Think you the cold will come early this year?" Maira's gaze sought the hilltops, the color of a dun pony's hide above the trees. Southward, the tip of Din Rhun shimmered in the heat-haze. She tried to remember the bitterness of snow.

Urr shook his head, shaggy as the pelt of one of his own ewes. "Not early, but hard when it does come. There will be little grass."

Bits jingled as Roud shook her head and sidled impatiently.

"Are you rested already?" Maira patted the mare's damp neck and took up her reins. "We'll do what we can when winter comes," she said to Urr. "Now I had better be off after that wretched heifer, and you had best water the other beasts before the heat kills them all!"

TWO

The Harvest Sacrifice

THE SPOTTED HEIFER'S tracks led straight downhill toward Scaur Water. From their depth and placing, it appeared that the creature had continued her all-out scramble away from the cattle drive, but Maira kept Roud to a jog, knowing that the cow could not continue such a pace for long. She was surprised that the heifer had managed to keep it up as far as the stream; usually cattle forgot why they were running as soon as the first fright was past. But she must remember that this particular beast came of canny stock and was probably motivated by the pure, perverse desire to drive any human following her to distraction!

Maira began to frown when the tracks led down into the water and then up the other side. She had not intended to spend the rest of the day trailing one spotted cow, and the afternoon was drawing on. Grimly, she slapped Roud's neck for more speed and urged the mare up the slope.

I should have gone after her immediately, she thought in exasperation, *but who would have thought the wretched animal would be so determined? She wasn't even one of those to be sold at the Fair, but by the Mothers, if she puts me to much more trouble she will be!*

By the time Maira had followed the heifer over the hills between the Scaur and the Nova and down along the river toward the ford, she was becoming seriously concerned. It was late afternoon now, but that was not what worried her—she would trust Roud to find her way home by night or by day. But they were on the edge of Selgovae territory, and if the cow

18

strayed across the river she would be easy prey. Maira did not think she could bear to beg one of those arrogant Selgovae bastards to return her property, even if there were a chance he would do it. It was hard enough to hold on to cattle when they stayed safely in your own pastures, and strays were fair game for anyone who happened along.

The sun was dipping toward the western hills when she reached the ford and saw hoof marks which had become all too familiar fresh in the mud on the other side. But the heifer could not have crossed long ago. Suppressing her own uneasiness at venturing into the land of her enemies alone, Maira kicked Roud across the rocky ford.

The countryside was the same mix of hazel and oakwood mixed with moor that she had left behind, but the farther Maira went, the stranger she found each shadow. In her own country, she knew every rock and tree, but here, any bend in the road could hide danger. She rode more and more slowly, listening as intently as any hunted doe, and presently her caution was rewarded, for she heard the sounds of men's voices and horses' hooves.

Swiftly, she reined Roud up a deer trail that led through the trees. Torn between the needs for haste and silence she urged the mare on and held her back so unpredictably that Roud tossed her head and blew through her nostrils in frustration. And at that moment she heard a shout from below and knew that she had been seen.

"Ho, lass, don't go away—are you looking for me?" came the call.

Maira gritted her teeth and kicked Roud across a patch of meadow, seeking a way over the hill. Unfortunately this brought her for a moment into clear view of her pursuers.

"It's that red-headed girl of Conmor's—I recognize the mare!" someone cried, and the troop erupted in catcalls and whistles.

"Where's Carric? Oh, Carric, watch out—she's come for you! A filly in her first heat—you know what they are—she'll wear him out. Maybe he'd better run!"

"If he gets tired, I'll be glad to service her," came another voice.

Maira felt the hot blood redden her cheeks and bent over Roud's neck to hide her face. Was Carric with them? She peered through the branches, trying to see. He must be laughing too hard to reply—she knew just how he would look, laughing at her!

"Oh, she wouldn't come after Carric," someone said with lazy mockery. "You heard how she talked to him last week! She's likely come to lift some of our cattle in exchange for that buck we took in Scaur Vale!" There was more laughter.

"A reiver! Oh, we'll know how to deal with her!"

Maira heard brush crashing as if in their eagerness they could no longer keep to the trail. There had been an odd quiver in the last man's voice, and Maira felt a chill. She was a chieftain's daughter—she told herself that surely even if they caught her she would suffer no more than a little mockery. But she could not be sure. Everyone knew that Carric's friends were a wild lot—worse even than the young bloods her brother Eoc led. If they got too excited they might rape her. Nobody knew she had come here—what else might they feel impelled to do to hide what they had done?

As she drummed her heels into Roud's sides she heard another voice rise above the laughter, shaking with suppressed fury.

"You crazy louts, what are you doing, going this way?"

"But Carric," someone protested, "there's a girl up there— that Vindomarci wench you're always mooning after. In a moment we'll catch up with her, and then—"

"I don't care if it's Epona Herself on a grey mare." Carric's voice deepened to a roar. "In case you've forgotten, we've another search on now, and dusk is falling fast!"

"What if she steals a cow?" said someone in a somewhat chastened tone.

"Let her! I think it's highly unlikely, but if there's any loss I'll repay it from my own herd!" he replied.

"But shouldn't we at least find out what she's doing here?" came a last, plaintive objection.

"The Mor-Rigan take you, I don't *care* what she's doing here! We have work to do! Now get back down to the trail!"

Leather cracked, and from the sudden crashing in the undergrowth, Maira suspected that Carric had slashed someone's mount with his rein. She pulled Roud to a halt and peered back down the hill. It seemed to her that from the shadows eyes gleamed, but she could not be sure, and then the sounds of horses crashing through underbrush faded, and they were gone.

By the time her pulse stopped pounding, the last sunlight

had left the sky, though the long northern twilight would remain for quite a while. She looked around her, trying to see the road, but she could not even make out the deer trail up which she had come. If she had not been able to see the familiar silhouette of Scaur ridge against the western sky, she would not even have been sure which direction was home.

With the loss of the sunlight the air was growing cold. Maira unstrapped her chequered cloak from behind the saddle and wrapped it around her, then took up the reins again.

"Well, lass, I hope you can find us a way back to the river," she told the horse, nudging her with one toe. "I don't want to spend the night here."

Roud shook her head as if in agreement and began to pick her way down the slope. Maira leaned back in the saddle to balance, ears alert to all the small sounds around her as the nocturnal life of the land began to awaken. Two bats flittered overhead in crazy spirals, agitated silhouettes against the luminous evening sky. They disappeared for a moment as a larger shape, perhaps an early owl, sailed silently above them, and then returned to their hunting. In the damp hollows she could hear frogs tuning up for their nightly concert, and crickets in the grass.

Despite her uncertain position, she began to relax. These were the same sounds with which night fell in her own country—the Selgovae land was not so different from hers after all.

Then she heard a sound that made her stiffen in the saddle, battling thoughts of bogles and the spirits that old Ness said haunted the hills. She halted Roud and listened, motionless, waiting until the noise came again.

It was a whimpering, not quite the sound a trapped hare makes, but similar—like some small animal in pain. Then the creature snuffled, and she heard, quite clearly.

"Mama—please, Mama, take me home! I won't do it again!"

Relief brought beads of perspiration to Maira's forehead. She dropped the reins on Roud's neck and stared around her. But she could only see shadows, and the small voice had fallen silent when Roud snorted her impatience to go on.

"Child, where are you?" she called finally. "Are you all right? I have a lovely horse here to carry you home . . ."

"You're not a bogle?" came a frightened whisper.

"No." Maira smiled, remembering her own fears. "I'm a mortal woman, and my horse is a very pretty mare called Roud. Don't you want to see her?"

There was a rustle in the bushes almost at their feet, and Roud threw up her head and danced backward. Maira peered at the small figure that had appeared in the path before them. It was a girl child, perhaps four or five years old, dressed in a single garment of coarse linen liberally smudged with berry-stains. Speaking sternly to the mare, she slid down and bent over the child.

"You're not hurt?" she asked anxiously.

"Mama hit me 'cause I tipped over the cau'dron and I ran 'way," the small figure explained. "An' I ate a lot of berries and then I took a nap 'cause I didna feel well. But now I'm hungry again and I want to go home!" The small face turned up to hers trustingly.

"Who are your people, and where do you live?" Maira asked belatedly.

"My papa is Cadros and we live by Taran's oak tree," said the girl.

Maira nodded in the darkness. She knew of the man, and recalled passing his steading on a visit to Din Carn long ago. It lay on the main road—wherever that was—and probably not too far away.

"Come on, Roud," she said as she vaulted into the saddle and pulled the child up in front of her, "you'll have to find the road for us now."

Eager for her dinner, the mare found her way through the woods to the pale glimmer of the road with little difficulty, and made only a token protest when Maira turned her eastward instead of toward home. It was only then that Maira remembered why she had left the road in the first place, and began to wonder what would happen when she rode into Cadros' housestead. Would they attack her as Carric's friends had done?

It would be so much simpler to set the little girl down in the road and turn Roud's head toward the river and safety.

But the child had already fallen asleep against her breast, and if the forest held no bogles, it might well harbor a wild cat or a wolf who would find a human this size quite an acceptable meal. Something within her made it impossible to abandon the child. Without having made a conscious decision, Maira realized that she had kicked Roud into a trot up the hill.

It was full dark by the time she reached Cadros' steading. The great branches of the oak that was its pride glowed in the torchlight, and the place was bustling with what looked like half the fighting strength of the clan. Maira drew rein in the gate, gathering her courage to ride in, and had been staring for several minutes before anyone noticed her. But then there was enough uproar to set Roud plunging, and the girl-child was not only awake but laughing excitedly by the time Maira got the mare calmed again.

With considerable relief she handed the child down to her mother.

"Yes, she's not hurt at all, beyond a little tummy-ache from too many berries," she assured her. "And since she's safe, I'll be on my way now." Maira shortened her reins.

"Oh, but can't I reward you?" cried the woman, wrenching at the jet bracelet she wore. "May the gods bless you, lady! She is the only one of my children who has lived!"

"Please, I did nothing, and I must leave. I have a long way to go," said Maira, embarrassed.

"A long way to go, and a long way to come," said Trost nastily, sauntering up as the woman carried her child into the house. "Did you find what you were looking for?"

Maira straightened. "I did not have to come here," she spat back. "Would you rather I had left the child in the road?"

"Why *did* you come here, Maira merch Conmor?" Carric came out from the house and stood beside his friend, eyeing her hopefully. "It is far from your own hunting runs!" He added in gentle mockery of her words to him the month before.

"It is not you I will answer to!" She glared at him. "If you have any control over these hounds of yours, call them off and let me go!"

"Are we stopping you?" laughed Trost before Carric could shut him up.

"No, by the Mother, nor will you!" she exclaimed, yanking back on the reins so that Roud half-reared, and on-lookers scattered from before the flailing hooves. The mare pivoted in place, and then Maira was lashing her into a gallop down the road.

Too angry to think of the dangers of racing down a strange road in the dark, Maira let Roud run until her pace slackened of itself. She could feel foam on the mare's neck and shook her head ruefully. Fortunately the night was mild; if she kept the horse going till she cooled she should come to no harm. But the spring had left Roud's step. It had been a hard day.

And Maira found that she had outrun her own anger as well. What did it matter what Trost, a Selgovae, said to her! She would go home and forget him. But despite her resolve, she could not help remembering his malicious grin in the torchlight —no, it was not his face that stuck in her memory, but Carric's. And what she had seen in Carric's eyes had not been hostility.

She was still trying to understand what she *had* seen there when she heard hoofbeats behind her for the second time that day. She knew that Roud couldn't run anymore, but it was only one horse coming, by the sound. She halted the mare and drew her dagger.

Seeing her blocking the road, her pursuer pulled up. Maira peered at the dim silhouette against the stars, somehow recognizing it even before he spoke to her.

"Well, have you come to taunt me some more?" she said into his silence.

"I've come to apologize," Carric said in a low voice. "And to offer you an escort home."

She stared at him. "Considering that your own men are my greatest danger, I suppose I should accept it." she said, but his mildness took most of the force from her answer. She turned Roud and started her moving again.

For a time they rode without speaking. Maira sensed an unaccustomed constraint in Carric, but she found his silent companionship surprisingly welcome. In the darkness, she felt as if they had left the ordinary world of feud and fear behind.

"That was a good thing you did, bringing home the little girl," he said finally. "The Selgovae are in your debt. We were all looking for her when we surprised you, before."

"What else could I have done?"

"You could have just left her, after what we said to you," Carric said bitterly.

That was too true for denial. Maira sighed. "One of these days your friend Trost is going to open his mouth once too often and someone will ram a spear down his throat!" she said instead.

Carric shook his head. "Trost is a good man, really. He's been a loyal friend."

That did not make him any less dangerous, thought Maira,

but she supposed that if Carric had not defended his sword-brother she would have had less respect for him.

"Why *were* you riding in these hills?" Carric asked her then.

Startled by the question, Maira realized she had forgotten all about the heifer. She gave an exasperated laugh.

"I was chasing a stupid spotted cow, a young heifer with a crooked horn. I suppose she's gone for good, now."

"Well, would you return a stray that came over from our side of the river?" Carric asked reasonably.

Maira suppressed a grin, aware that both of them knew the answer to that question only too well.

The rest of the ride was nearly as silent as the first part had been, but somehow the constraint between them had disappeared. After a time, Carric began whistling, an odd, minor melody that sounded like the song of the stars.

The month that the Romans had named for their deified Julius drew to a close. The moon that the Druids called after the oak tree shrank and the moon of the flowering holly tree began to swell in the sky. In the turmoil of gentling the wild cattle and driving them to their new pastures no one had realized that Maira had not guested with some other family the night of her encounter with the Selgovae, and she was grateful that the lack of communication between the two tribes had kept the story from crossing the border. Now the vale of the Scaur was noisy with the lowing of cattle and the shouts of herdboys trying to keep them out of the fields of ripening grain.

But now they could draw breath a space, for it was time for the Feast of the First Fruits, when every farm and steading honored the Lady of the Harvest and thanked the land. When it was over, many would gather their saleable cattle and drive them to the Fair at Lyn Mapon, but everyone celebrated the Feast of the Mother at Lughnasa.

Maira sat, impatiently turning her wristlets of gilded bronze round and round while Ness combed out her long hair. She could hear her father humming outside, and the long scrape of the sickle blade against the grinding stone. The scent of roasting meat drifted tantalizingly from the firepit on the hillside, promising revelry. But first they had to perform the ceremony.

She twitched nervously and felt the sharp pain as the comb hit a snarl.

"Be still, child—how can I comb your hair smooth if you do not sit still?" Ness complained. "Your hair has grown longer this summer, and I'm sure that's a wonder, with you snarling it like a mare's tail, running the hills. Red gold it is, too, like the headpiece of a Queen. . . ."

"Oh Ness, there's no need to flatter me. Just be done with it—it must be nearly noon!" said Maira.

"Ness! Where is my belt? The red leather belt Eoc gave me?" Beth's call stopped the comb in mid-pull.

"I'm sure it was hanging on its peg, mistress. Perhaps it fell down?"

"You shouldn't let her order you about," whispered Maira. "You've been a part of this family far longer than she." She heard the old woman grunt, and the comb resumed pulling at her hair.

"Ah, a spoiled child, that one, but she's mothered a fine boy just the same," said Ness equably. "I'll not have her milk soured by lack of a soft answer." She smoothed the last strand of Maira's hair, then held the bronze mirror so that she could set the silver circlet on.

Beth emerged from her compartment, fastening the red belt, and Maira grimaced. *The mother of that fine boy!* indeed. But it was true, nor was she herself immune to the sweetness of that small sleeping face, or the grip of that tiny hand. But what was any infant, however promising, compared to a trained warrior? One did not sell a foal for the price a war pony would bring. . . .

"Maira, do you have the pail of milk?" Her mother's call startled the thing she had almost understood away. She stood up as her mother came through the door. "Well, *get* it!" Druith's voice snapped her into motion.

She treats me like a child. Resentment curdled in Maira's belly as she went around the house to the shed. *She would not even let me explain!*

The sun had nearly reached its zenith, and Maira's woolen gown was sticking to her back already. It was chequered in soft crimson and a blue that had taken many dippings in woad. It was her best gown, but a torment to wear in this sun. She could almost long for a gown of the fine eastern cotton that the Roman ladies wore.

She filled the little pail from the larger one and carried it carefully back to the yard, where the rest of the household was gathering now. Maelor of Lys Corenn down the vale set the reed of his pipe to his lips and began huffing air into the pig's bladder below, belaboring it until it squealed as if the pig were being killed again. And then, of a sudden, it steadied, and a fine, melodious skirling split the hot air. Eoc lifted the bodhran and bones and as the piper found his rhythm the drum galloped into a beat that supported it.

Conmor nodded and strode up the path. Involuntarily Maira's feet began to dance and she made herself slow, afraid the milk would spill. The line thinned and lengthened as they toiled up the first slopes and around the hill.

Now Lys Speiat was hidden, and they saw the outbuildings of Lys Corenn below. Again the path turned, and now there was only the peak of Din Rhun against the blue sky.

Maira stared up at the sharp, still line of the hill, then gasped as a flicker of vision showed her darkness and red torchlight on a rampart of stones. Ness nudged her and she started forward again, blinking the vision away—no, not vision, but memory, for she had been ten the last time the weak ones of the clan sought refuge here while the warriors rode against Rome.

And now the stones of the ramparts were tumbled along the hill in obedience to the victorious Romans' law. But no decree of the Red Crests could change the size and position of the peak, and Din Rhun was a strong place still.

They passed through the empty gateway of the outer rampart and picked their way among the stones to the Lady's well. After so dry a year scarcely a trickle of water sparkled in the little stream, but the spring itself had never entirely failed. As they formed a semicircle around the well, Beth handed Acorn to Ness and began to bind the green branches and wildflowers she had gathered to the poles and roof of the little wicker shed that protected the well. When she was finished, she stepped aside so that Druith could kneel on the platform of dressed stones.

"Lady, we hail Thee! Like a spring of sweet water is Thy bounty; for the health of the harvest we invoke Thy blessing; Lady, hear us now!"

"Lady, hear us!" came the echo from two dozen throats. Druith sat back on her heels with upraised arms. Her eyes were closed, she was trembling.

It is only my mother. . . . Maira's grip on the milk pail tightened, for this was not her mother, but the Druid's daughter, a priestess in communion with her gods. The hairs lifted on her arms despite the heat, and angry at her own fear, she looked away.

"It is She Who gives the harvest!" Druith proclaimed. Her voice vibrated in the earth of the hill.

"She is Lady of the harvest!" the response echoed from hill to hill.

"By Her breasts heavy with milk, by Her womb ever fertile, She will bless you; by Her shining eyes and flowing hair, by Her holy head She will bless you." By repeated affirmation, the priestess claimed the power of the Goddess for the people who were worshipping Her.

Then Druith rose, heavily, as if the plate of curd-cheese pressed from this morning's milking was almost too great a weight to bear. Slowly she circled sunwise around the well, nine times she circled it, and each time she cast another piece of cheese into the water in offering. Her lips moved, but they were not meant to hear the words.

One last time she bowed, then straightened and took her place beside Conmor again. He took her arm to steady her as the power of the Goddess drained out of her, then led the way up the hill. As they moved off, it seemed to Maira that the voice of the stream behind them grew louder.

They passed through another gateway and up the hill to the third rampart. The slope was very steep now; steps had been cut into the path. The procession turned off on the built-up surface behind what had been the rampart and circled the hill, for the slope itself, covered with slippery grass, was here too steep for anyone to stand.

The younger girls climbed the steps carved into the hill and laid down their garlands of summer flowers. Maira's heart beat like the festival drum and she tried to steady her breathing. It was her turn now. She kilted up the skirts of her gown, took a firmer grip on the milk pail, and balancing carefully, began the climb.

Far too soon her legs were aching. Until this year Druith had performed this part of the ceremony too; Maira wondered how she had managed it. But the physical strain was the least of the burden.

I have to speak for the Goddess, but if She truly enters me, what will I do? The instruction they have given me is not enough! she thought desperately. But if the Goddess did not come, what use would it be to make an offering?

She felt a grudging respect for her mother. This required a different kind of courage than she had ever needed before. *It is for the family,* she told herself, *for the clan, for Din Rhun!* It did not matter what happened to her.

Then, suddenly, she reached the summit. For a moment the wonder of the view distracted her from her fears. To the east a ridge rose above Scaur Water, and beyond it the higher curves of the hills beyond the Nova—Selgovae land. To the south she could see down the valley to Din Prys and a distant blue glitter that was the Salmaes Firth. The west was lost in a misty distance of wooded ridges and glens that stretched to the lowlands by the sea, the territory of the Novantae tribe.

Only to the northwest did a spur of the mountains block the view, rising mountains, that hid among their folds the dark and caverned eminence of Craig Duw where the seven crones reigned. The thought sent her gaze back down to the people below. Maelor's old mother was watching her with bright eyes, next to ancient Idha from down the vale. Even her own dear Ness seemed one of them, standing there—one of the terrible old women of the tribe.

But the mountain protected her. The hags had nothing to do with the terror she faced here. Maira tried to remember what Druith had told her. There must be an inner stillness, an attention of the spirit, as one strained to hear the first notes of a nightingale, and then, the form of the Goddess would build up behind you, and fill you, and your own consciousness would be swallowed up in a greater one.

They were all watching her. *I will say something. I will make the offering, and if they are only my own words, who will know?*

"You will know . . ." came an inner answer. *"The Goddess will know, and if disaster strikes the clan this year it will be your fault."*

Very carefully, Maira set down the vessel of milk and knelt, flattening her palms against the short grass that crowned the hill.

"Lady, listen to me," she whispered. "I will give whatever Thou dost ask, only come to me! Not for my own pride," she went on, "but for the Vindomarci, for the clan!"

For a moment, she heard only the whistling of the wind. A strand of hair blinded her, then whipped back. Maira pressed her hands against the earth as if she could set her prints into the turf and squeezed shut her eyes. The wind was so strong! She clutched at the slippery grass, afraid the wind would pluck her from her perch and whirl her away.

Then a voice, distant and amused, spoke in the darkness of her soul.

What do you offer, maiden of the White Horse Clan?

Maira was a chieftain's daughter, and from birth she had known the price a sovereign must be willing to pay for the people and the land. She forced her lips to move.

"My life's blood if Thou dost desire it, Holy One . . ."

Not your life's blood, but your life, maiden—remember well! The Voice in her head grew louder, louder, until it drove out all other sound. *Now, let Me in!* Maira felt a sense of Presence as if Something too great for vision were hovering over her. With a gasp, she bowed her head, and summoned up from somewhere the courage to make the last and greatest offering—the surrender of her own body's control.

As if from a distance, she was aware of rising, of speaking the ritual words of offering and pouring the milk out upon the top of the hill. Then she stood with her arms outstretched in blessing upon the land, but the voice that spoke was not her voice, and the blessing given was not in her words.

Then the power flowed out of her, and she sank down, aware only of the sun's heat upon her back and the whisper of the wind. After a time she found the strength to climb back down to the parapet. Her father put out strong arms to catch her and she clung to him gratefully. But over her shoulder she saw her mother's bitter smile.

Conmor stood at the edge of the wheatfield, hefting the sickle he had sharpened so carefully. Maira watched him, wondering what he was feeling now. With the earth solid beneath her feet and the scent of roasting beef coming from the housestead, it was hard to believe that the Goddess had spoken to her. She had never had the gift of vision, not like Druith, or the children the Druids took to train. Could her desire for something to happen have made her imagine it all?

And if she had imagined it, could everyone else be pretending too? The thought made her dizzy, and she gripped Ness's arm.

"Sa, sa, lass, be still. It's food you need now, and you shall have it as soon as this is done!" the old woman whispered.

Conmor took a deep breath. Then, treading carefully to

avoid crushing the grain, he made his way to the center of the field. It was the long field on the southern slope of the *dun*, where the grain ripened first. In a wet year they might be hard put to find a head of grain ripe enough for harvesting at Lughnasa, but this summer had been so warm and dry the wheat had ripened early. The ears were small and parched, but at least they would be able to begin the full harvest as soon as they returned from Lyn Mapon.

Maira forced her scattering thoughts to still, watching her father's arms lifting, the moon-shaped blade of the sickle flashing fire back at the sun.

> "On the first day of Lughnasa, day of blessings,
>   I will curve my sickle around the corn;"

Conmor's voice deepened as he spoke the traditional words.

> "I will grasp the first cut quickly
>   And draw it three times round my head.
>   This spell shall I say with my back to the north
>   And my face to the fair sun of power."

The sickle flashed down; he gripped, slashed, and the cut sheaf was in his hand. Quickly he lifted it, drew it sunwise around his head three times.

> "Goddess, bless Thou Thyself my reaping:
>   Each ridge, and plain, and field;
>   Each sickle, curved, shapely, hard,
>   Each ear and handful in the sheaf!"

Cheering buffeted the air like thunder, and the pipes spoke with an exultant skirl. Colors swirled in Maira's vision—golden grain waving against an azure sky, and a splash of crimson—

Consciousness snapped into focus and she saw blood on Conmor's hand. But no one else seemed to have noticed it; perhaps she was the only one standing where she could see. The red flow was welling freely now and beginning to wind down his arm. He must have slashed his own flesh when he cut the sheaf of grain, but how? Conmor had harvested every year since he was old enough to hold a sickle in his hand. . . .

His hand moved in blessing—did he not feel it? Did no one else see?

Then Conmor's face changed. His grey glance flicked downward; his eyes widened with knowledge, and perhaps with pain. Hastily he thrust the sickle through his belt and pulled down his sleeve to hide his hand.

But the movement flicked a spatter of crimson outward, and the blood of her father fell like rain upon the thirsty ground.

"My life's blood if Thou dost desire it—" memory repeated her own words of not so long ago. *My own blood!* she shrieked silently. *My blood, dear Goddess, not his!*

She tensed to run to him, then saw that Conmor had wedged his hand against his body with the sleeve covering it and was trying to smile. Abruptly she understood—the people must not know what had happened. She held herself still, biting her lip, watching him.

Carefully the chieftain retraced his path through the field. Color came and went in his face as he mastered the shock and the pain. Then he reached the edge of the field and held out the sheaf to Druith with his right hand.

"Behold the bounty of the Mother. She preserves us; Her bounty will sustain us now and in the coming year!" His voice was strong, but harshened by pain.

Druith's eyes flicked from the hand he held pressed against his side to his face and back again. Her lips opened, then closed as she read the message in Conmor's eyes.

Maira took a step forward—why didn't her mother do something? But Druith's strong features showed no sign. She cleared her throat and spoke the ritual answer.

"As Lady of this steading I accept the gift of the Lady of the Land. As She provides for us, may we ever serve Her!" She took the sheaf of grain from her husband, then stepped quickly to his left side so that the bulk of her body hid his arm.

She knows something is wrong! thought Maira. *Why are they walking so slowly? She should hurry him back to the house and take care of him!*

But the two heads—silver-threaded red and faded fair— moved on at the same steady pace and the procession fell into place behind them. Maelor massaged his pipes into life again and began to play.

The ten minute walk between the fields and the steading had never taken so long. Then, suddenly, they were home, and Druith was disappearing into the house for the ritual grinding of the grain. Maira tried to push her way through the crowd to her father's side.

She heard him laughing, talking about getting more wood, and slipped around the house just as he reached the woodpile. The axe flashed and fell and he swore loudly, clapping his left hand against his side. Then he held it up so that everyone could see the bright blood on his hand.

"Father, are you hurt?" cried Maira, throwing her arms around him.

"This cursed axe has gashed my hand." Conmor forced a laugh.

"Then we had better make sure the blade has blood on it!" she hissed, snatching up the axe while her body was still between Conmor and the others who were hastening toward them. She wiped the bright blade on the blood-soaked cloth of her father's sleeve, and threw it into the woodpile.

He straightened and stared at her. "You saw?"

She nodded angrily. "What do you think you are doing? We must get that gash bound and cleaned quickly, and—"

Conmor forced a smile. "Yes, we can do that now. But Maira—be silent! The others must not know!"

"But—" Maira's lips closed again. The fragile barrier of concern for his wound was broken by awareness of the worse thing which Conmor had immediately seen. For the Goddess to take the chieftain's blood when he cut the harvest sheaf was an omen of the gravest kind.

"Please—" he said in a low voice. "I have had dreams of fire and blood staining the ground, and the harvest will be so scanty this year . . . I wanted the ritual to be a perfect offering. But if a price must be paid, it is best that the blood be mine."

"It was an accident!" Maira's words crossed his. The others were close now. She gripped his hand with all her strength, holding the edges of the wound together, pressing hard to check the bleeding. In a low voice she added, "You did all that was required!"

Then Ness shouldered her aside, clucking in exasperation, and Maira surrendered him to the old woman's care. He smiled at her, but beneath his bitter amusement she saw another expression—the bewildered stare of a trapped beast that suffers without understanding why.

Ness's efficient nursing soon had Conmor in his place at the head of the long planked table they had set up in the yard. He was a little pale, but he seemed his usual self to anyone who was not, like Maira, watching his eyes.

Her mother watched him too, looking up from the wheat she was grinding in the stone quern, from the bowl in which she mixed the flour with egg and milk and honey, from the sheepskin on which she kneaded it and formed it into a bannock which could be toasted on the rowan-twig fire. It baked quickly. Druith broke it into fragments for everyone, and then at last they could begin the feasting.

Maira sat through the meal in sullen silence, scarcely tasting the succulent beef, the curded cheese and bannock, or the bilberries that the children had gathered on the slopes above the stream. She was just licking the last grease from her fingers when Coll came running through the gate to tell her that one of her cows was loose in the road.

Swearing under her breath, she got up and went out to deal with it, wondering which animal it was, and how on earth it had escaped from the pens. Then she saw the beast and stopped short, recognizing the spotted hide and twisted horn. Looking oddly chastened, the heifer mooed plaintively and lowered her head to be scratched.

Maira took a firm grip on the rope around the beast's neck and looked quickly up the road. There was no one in sight, but she thought she glimpsed a haze of dust down the Vale. Then she began to laugh. If Carric had ridden up to their gates with the heifer in tow he would have had to explain where he had found the beast and how he knew to whom it belonged. Neither of them wanted what had happened to become the gossip of the Nova Valley.

But to get the cow all the way from his own land to the heart of Vindomarci territory and leave it here in broad daylight without discovery was surely a greater feat than the usual midnight raid. Carric must have made the last distance while they were all involved in the ritual, and stayed hidden with the heifer until they were settled down to feasting. What a pity it was that the story could not be told, she thought ruefully, for surely it belonged among the great raiding tales.

How her father would enjoy it—At the thought, Maira

realized abruptly that Carric's deed had distracted her from remembering Conmor's wound. But her brief escape from anxiety was ended. Frowning, she hurried the heifer into a pen and went back to the feast.

Conmor grew more cheerful as the afternoon faded into evening. They had broken out a new cask of beer—apparently a potent brewing. Eoc got drunk very quickly and had to be carried to his bed, and the chieftain's pale face reddened. Maira drank milk and scowled at them all.

Later that night, when the curtains before each sleeping compartment were pulled tight, she heard her parents whispering.

And for certain it is time—perhaps now she will take care of him!

Maira knew that, constrained by the ritual, her mother could not have intervened and helped Conmor. But her heart did not believe it. Her mother was the priestess, the Druid's daughter, the strong presence always there to settle quarrels, make decisions, tend wounds. She should have prevented the disaster, and if she could not, thought Maira, then she must make sure there were no consequences. . . .

Maira was falling asleep when she heard her brother wake, still half-drunk, and in a voice that no protests from Beth could make him lower, began talking love to her. Maira could not help overhearing them—she wondered that they did not awaken the whole house with their murmurings and the rhythmic rustle of bedstraw. She tried not to listen or to visualize just what they were doing in the close darkness with the baby asleep in his trucklebed nearby. But she ached with emotions for which she had no words. She twisted and turned in her narrow bed.

Eoc would be touching Beth's full breasts now . . . Maira's hand went to her own breasts, developed enough that she found it more comfortable to bind them when she fought or rode. Tentatively she fingered one nipple, then the other, squirming as a teasing tickle of sensation ran from her breasts to the secret place between her thighs.

Now she heard Eoc's deep grunting, and Beth moaned. What was it like, she wondered? What made the mare stand beneath the assault of the stallion; what made a woman take a man's weight upon her and allow him entry to her innermost mysteries?

As if they belonged to someone else her fingers moved lower. But it should not be her own hand touching, exploring, there. Maira tried to imagine the strength of a lover pinning her, caressing until she opened to him. Her hand moved faster and after a few moments she quivered in a faint echo of Beth's exultant cry.

Eoc and Beth were quiet after that, and soon Maira slept too.

But she did not sleep soundly. In her dreams she relived the moment when her father's blood had fallen to the ground. Only in her dream, she ran to him and cradled him in her arms. He grew heavier and heavier, and when she turned him she saw in horror that the life had left his eyes.

No! she cried out, *It cannot be this way!* She forced herself to relive the beginning of the dream again. And finally, as she kissed the still lips of the man she held, his arms tightened around her and he turned and pressed her down in the midst of the grain. And as he moved upon her Maira stared up and saw that it was not her father, but Carric of Din Carn.

THREE

---•❦•---

Lughnasa

MAIRA STRODE DOWN the path to the lake of Maponus, kicking up dust with every footfall. Her mother's voice faded behind her, still loudly ordering men and maids to weave more branches into the bothies they had built for shelter during the festival, or to gather more wood for the cooking fires. Maira was hot, and she would have lashed back like a wounded wolf if her mother had nagged at her one more time. She took a deep breath, trying to anticipate the coolness of clean water on her skin.

Men stood arguing by the cattle pens. She heard Conmor's voice and her step faltered. His wounded hand had healed quickly, and after being sworn at a few times, Maira had learned not to hover about trying to help. Finally he had ordered her off to take charge of gathering the cattle for the drive to Lyn Mapon.

And now, after three slow days of dust and the stink of cattle, they were here by the triple lake nestled among sheltering hills that echoed with the noise of the cattle and the assembled tribes. The smoke of hundreds of cookfires stained the pale late-summer sky.

"And still I think you were wrong to bring that bull here to market, Conmor—" a harsh voice answered her father's and Maira stopped. But it was only Maelscuit; she should have known his pompous tone. He was her father's cousin—the only other man of that generation remaining of the chiefly kin, and he had never quite understood why Conmor had been elected chieftain instead of him.

"He is old, cousin," said Conmor soothingly. "He's lost muscle in the flanks already. But with luck I'll find a buyer who can't read the signs."

"We need new blood for the health of the herd!" exclaimed Eoc, and Maira felt something twist in her belly at the words.

But her father did not appear to have noticed. He looked up, saw Maira and smiled conspiratorially, as if he wished he could leave the dust and the argument and go with her to the lake. Her heart unaccountably lightened, Maira continued on her way.

The touch of the cool water calmed her. She eased gratefully beneath the surface, letting all her tensions wash away with the dust of the road, and the laughter of the other women blended with the whisper of wind in the reeds.

By the time she returned to her clan's encampment, the construction of the chieftain's bothy was finished. The white horse tail on its pole stirred in the breeze over the Vindomarci encampment. Druith had finished arranging their possessions and laid out Maira's festival gown. She recognized it as a gesture of reconciliation, and feeling a little ashamed, put it on.

Druith was already dressed for the festival. Her gown was striped in broad bands of dull red and cream, drawn up at the belt to show the heather-colored undertunic. She was wearing her gold torque and the heavy armlets, and despite the heat, her deep blue cloak with the tablet-woven banding around its hem.

Maira stared at her, thinking that despite her mother's fifty years, the loss of three children in the great sickness and the birth of two more when she was already by most accounting old, Druith was an impressive figure. Her thickened body looked strong, not soft, and though silver glinted in the chestnut of her hair, it was still thick, braided and twisted now into a shining crown.

"Come with me to the market, Maira. We'll see what the Greeks have brought this year, and if the cattle sales go well, perhaps we will be able to buy."

Maira nodded and grinned. "I will go with you, if only to provide protection. You'll need it, looking so fine!"

Her mother colored with pleasure, picked up the comb and began to struggle with Maira's tangled hair. Maira gritted her teeth but said nothing, dimly understanding that her mother did not know how to respond to her compliment in any other way. But it had not been quite the truth—no man would dare to insult a woman with the kind of beauty Druith had now. She looked every inch a chieftain's wife and a Druid's daughter— the Lady of her clan.

Maira's scalp was sore and stinging by the time her mother was done, but as they walked through the encampment Maira found herself glad she had endured it, for every woman there, and most of the men, were loaded with all the finery they had. Gowns and tunics were striped and chequered in every shade the dyestuffs of the hills could produce, trimmed with braid or embroidery and adorned with jewelry of silver and bronze or gold.

Temella, walking half a step behind her, wore a dress of crimson that set off her dark hair, and the other women who attended them had put on every bit of jewelry they owned. Maira smoothed the red and blue of her festival gown. It was still too hot, but she did not mind, now.

"Needles and pins! Fine needles of iron to last a lifetime, lady!" The shrill cry startled her and Maira bumped into her mother, who had stopped in front of one of the booths. Sunlight filtered through the woven branches to dapple the cloth in which the merchant had displayed his wares and strike sparks from the needles and pins stuck there.

Druith plucked one free, tested the point with her finger, and thrust it into the cloth again.

"Perhaps we should get some of these," she said thoughtfully. "I have broken one of mine, and you will be needing your own sewing gear when you marry. . . ."

Maira stiffened and looked at her mother suspiciously, wondering if she had somehow found out about the return of the spotted cow, but Druith's face showed only a placid interest in the pack-man's wares. He was a little, eager man with carroty hair and a Gaullish accent. She supposed there was scarcely a real Greek among the traders, but men of that nation had been the first to come to her people, and now all traders were called by their name.

In the next row she saw Antiochus' bright wagon. Maira could not help wondering if he still had the amber he had showed her at home. If she got a good price for the two heifers she was selling here she might be able to buy it this year instead of waiting. Druith was immersed in comparing two cloth-knives, and the other women were examining cloak pins. Quietly Maira made her way around the booth and over to the Syrian trader's wagon.

"Ah lady—it brightens my day to see you!" Antiochus held up one hand as if to shield his eyes from the sun, and Maira laughed. "Have you come to look at the amber then? See here it is, sun's gold, fit for a Queen—or a bride!" he added slyly. He opened the leather case and spilled out a necklace of chunks of northern amber which had been polished just enough to bring out their full clarity.

Maira felt her face grow hot, and hoped it was from the sunlight that was filling the pieces of amber with golden light.

"Try it on, try it on," urged Antiochus. "Ah," he added as she draped it across her breast. "I was right—do you see?" he handed her a mirror of polished bronze. "But such beauty is too powerful for me," he went on. "It needs a young man to appreciate it, a young man who rides a bay horse, perhaps, and who for a short time owned a certain spotted cow. . . ."

Maira started and eyed him warily. Antiochus grinned and stroked his ebony beard.

"Ah Lady, you needn't look at me like a cornered vixen—your secret is safe with me! But Antiochus goes everywhere, talks to everyone! And in the land of the Selgovae men were talking of the price young Carric had paid to buy a certain strayed heifer from one of his clansmen, and wondering what he had done with it. The description reminded me of a beast I had seen in your cow-pens—and now you are turning that lovely rose-color again, and so I know that I have guessed correctly!" He chuckled as Maira stiffened, and shook his head.

"Did Carric tell you to say this to me?" she asked in a low voice.

"Ah mistress—old Antiochus sees things, he hears things—he doesn't need to be told! What memories I will have when I sit beneath my date-palm tree!"

"But did he speak to you?" she could not help asking. Antiochus was outside the tangle of clan loyalties; there was a curious relief in talking to him, especially since he already seemed to know everything she had been trying to conceal.

"Did Carric map Cador speak?" the black eyes sparkled. "No—why should he? He could not guess I would have the chance to talk to you. But it is true that if someone wished to send a message without having it discussed by all the tribes, Antiochus could carry it. . . ." He looked at her expectantly.

"Well, don't be expecting to carry any message for me!" Maira exclaimed. She pulled the amber necklace over her head and handed it back to him, beginning to feel like the hunted vixen he had likened her to.

"I think then that you are wise," Antiochus nodded soberly. "For if Carric did not speak of you, there were others who have not forgotten your escapade. They are still wondering why you were skulking in the Selgovae hills. They talk of spying, Lady, or make rude comments about your interest in young Carric which I will not repeat to you. . . ."

Maira stiffened. How *dare* they? She would have expected them to feel at least a little gratitude! She should have left Cadros' brat in the forest, she told herself, and as for having any interest in Carric, what should she feel for him beyond a certain gratitude, which was rapidly being eroded by his people's churlishness? She would as soon consider allying herself with a nest of vipers as with Selgovae!

"I have no wish to hear it!" she snapped back at him, "and indeed I have wasted too much time here. My people will be missing me!" With as much dignity as she could muster she stalked back to where her mother was still looking at sewing gear.

They moved on, admiring cloak pins and glass bangles from Rome, bright ribbons, lengths of wool and linen and little twisted flagons of pale-blue Roman glass filled with perfume. Some things they passed with no more than an admiring glance. At other booths they paused to finger the merchandise, even to haggle for a few moments or try the look of an ornament against fair skin or bright hair, even though both the women and the traders knew they would not be buying until after the cattle were sold.

But now and again Druith would say something that set Maira's nerves twitching. A joke about managing a household, about babies, about what Maira would need when—when—when!

"Oh, I do not think we need worry, Mother—even if not a horned beast sells!" she retorted finally. "I will not be furnishing my own house this year. . . ."

Druith turned to look at her, her earrings swinging, and raised one eyebrow. Maira stared back at her defiantly, and after a moment Druith shrugged and moved on. Maira followed slowly, feeling she had failed to make her point somehow.

Now they were passing the weapons booths. Maira wanted to stop and try the balance of some of the shining blades, but her mother was striding determinedly along with the other women straggling out behind her like a line of heifers following the bell-leader to the stream.

I will come back here, later, when I am alone, she promised silently. Reason told her she would have more use for linen and needles than for a sword, but something in her lusted after the sleek beauty of those blades with their grips of twisted bronze. She had spent many hours wielding the wooden practice sword, but an iron blade was an investment. Eoc had been given his at his manhood ceremony; only if great danger threatened would they think it worthwhile to give her a sword. Perhaps she could take one in battle, she thought grimly. But no, the suffering of her people was not worth the joy of a blade in her hand.

But war might come, no matter what she desired. She stood still a moment, eyeing the swordsmith's customers. There were two groups of them: some northern warriors with their brightly woven cloaks thrown back nonchalantly to display the warrior tattoos on their broad chests; and a party of Romans whose dull red military cloaks covered corselets of hardened leather over tunics of grey wool.

Maira moved a little to see the patterns of the northern cloaks and nodded. They were Venicones and Caledonii, as she had expected. She had seen a surprising number of them at the Fair, and even heard a little of what they said: *"The south is rich and Rome is weakened now . . . the time is coming for us to join together and overrun the Wall. . . ."*

Her gaze went back to the soldiers. They looked British—auxiliaries from the Brigante country, probably, sent across the hills from the Castra Exploratorum to keep an eye on the festival. Two of the men moved back to let their commander look at the weapons, and she saw a middle-sized man with a very tanned face and dusty brown hair. His polished breastplate gleamed in the sun. She thought it must be hot to wear, but he did not appear to notice the heat. He had a lean, intent face, focused now on the swords, and she could not see his eyes.

Then Temella came running back to fetch her, and she had to move on, still wondering if the Romans knew what the Caledonii warriors were trying to do. . . .

They had made a field for the competitions just where the ground began to rise toward the hills. Maira followed her mother to the benches on the Women's Side, almost full now with clan and kinfolk of the men who were to wrestle today. Druith paused to salute the women of Din Carn—Carric's mother, Ailm, and Ura his sister, with their attendants. Maira tried to pretend she did not see, furiously aware of their knowing expressions and whispered comments as they looked at her.

There was a murmur of expectation as the first wrestlers came out onto the field. Maira strained to look over the heads of the women in front of her, then stood so that she could see. The men fought stripped to their clouts, their bodies oiled so that each muscle shone. Maira frowned, watching them, remembering how she and Eoc had wrestled in the days before her breasts began to grow.

They had made a wrestling ring with piled brush. Three pairs were fighting, with the sticklers hovering about them to ensure fair play. As she watched, one of the combatants threw his man and stood, chest heaving and arms up in triumph. By his tattoos she knew him for a man of the Damnonii, the tribe with whom they shared the northern border. She saw that the man he had beaten was a Selgovae, and smiled.

Two Novantae—a man from Carbantorigum and another from one of the coastal clans—were still struggling; beyond them a Selgovan fought a man of the Votadini from the east coast of Alba. He was a long way from home too, but Maira recognized him as a champion wrestler who rotated his appearances among all the festivals year by year. He had no need to fear tribal animosities—festival grounds were sacred space, and even those traveling to and from the great fairs were protected.

In a moment he had his opponent flat on his back in the grass, and he grinned, having saved his reputation for another round. The Novantae pair were still straining, and all attention was focused upon them now.

"Young Conbrit is doing well, don't you think?" Maira's mother spoke almost in her ear. "He's grown into a fine man, and wealthy too, as I hear."

"And he has no wife, I suppose?" Maira laughed scornfully. "Are you trying to get rid of me?"

Druith tried to look unconcerned. "It would do us no harm to make an alliance with the clan of the High King. . . ."

"I won't marry down on the coast. There are no hills there,

and I don't like the damp sea wind.'' Maira closed her eyes, seeing vividly the sharp peak of Din Rhun against a sunset sky, and shivered with a sudden longing to be home.

"Very well," her mother answered equably. "But you will have to choose sometime, and you will rarely see the men so admirably displayed as they are here!"

Maira's eyes flew open and she turned on her mother. "Oh indeed, and shall I go squeeze their muscles as if they were bulls I wanted to buy? Is that how you chose my father, then?"

She was gratified to see the quick color rise in Druith's face.

"Daughter, it is my duty to see you settled!" Heads turned as Druith spoke, and she lowered her voice. "Any other girl would be grateful. . . ."

Maira bit her lip. The women of Din Carn were watching, hiding small, amused, smiles.

"A filly in her first heat. . . ." came the whisper, and Maira, glancing quickly around in a vain attempt to see who had spoken, felt her face flame. It seemed to be a common Selgovae gibe.

Three more pairs of wrestlers had entered the ring. Urr's eldest son Lod was clasping arms with a young Selgovae. With his shaggy brown head and tanned skin he looked sturdy as a tree next to his taller, fairer, opponent.

Maira pushed her way to the railing of saplings at the front of the enclosure, and stopped short as the next pair moved past her. It was Carric! She started to retreat to the benches and he turned and saw her and grinned.

Maira cursed silently. He must have seen her moving and assumed she wanted a better look at *him*. But the damage was done. She might as well stay and cheer Lod on.

Only, as the signal was given for the combat's beginning, she found her attention wavering from her own man to Carric and his opponent, a burly man from Anant. Well—that was not surprising—she already knew how Lod fought. Patient and steady, he was outwaiting his foe, and minutes might pass before either of them moved.

But Carric and the Anant man had already grappled and parted three times without either finding a hold. Carric's hair was bound into a fighter's knot atop his head. His body shone with oil—his back and arms rosy where the sun had kissed them and the skin of his legs milky fair.

She watched the muscles slide and tighten beneath that pale skin as he crouched and leaped at his foe. The other man reached for him; he twisted deftly and suddenly gripped the thick shoulders of the Anant man, took a quick step with his left foot and pivoted, then thrust his right leg inside the other's left, crooked and lifted it.

For a moment the two men, both balanced on one foot only, strained and swayed. Carric was trying to shift his grip so that he could draw the other man into a fore crook, but the Anant man got his hand around and began to push. Carric tried to counter by slipping from the crook into position for a fore hip throw, but his opponent's shoulders bunched, released, and suddenly Carric was flying through the air, twisting, by some miracle landing on his feet a short distance away.

From all around the ring came a gasp, and then a cheer. Carric managed to straighten, though his chest was still heaving, glistening now with sweat as well as oil. She saw the fuzz of red-gold hair there glint in the afternoon sun.

The stickler motioned to them to continue. After a last glance around him, Carric's attention focused on his foe. But he was smiling, his blue eyes alight with something more than eagerness to come to grips with his opponent again.

Maira bit her lip. He had seen her looking at him—there was no way to deny it now—and the Goddess knew what he must think. The Goddess only knew what *she* was thinking, for that matter, for her pulse leaped as if she were about to do battle too.

Both fighters were warmed up now. The Anant man stalked forward, his big hands open and ready. Carric's long, lean strength put him at a disadvantage with a more solid man whose center of balance was nearer to the ground.

They closed, there was a flicker of movement and the slap of flesh against flesh as Carric's hand and forearm came up to block his opponent's grab. Then Carric darted in, gripped, strained, and was thrown off again.

It continued. The other combatants finished and left the ring. Maira was vaguely aware that Lod had won his fight and managed to smile and wave as he went by, but she did not really see him.

Carric should not have been matched against this man. The Anant wrestler was older, heavier, obviously more experienced. But Carric was staying with him gamely, making a supple agility do duty for pure strength. Still, after a time he began to slow. He must end it soon, or the other man would break him in two.

Maira, watching, saw Carric's expression change. It was an inward focusing, as when Tadhg tuned a harpstring or her father sighted on a deer and drew back his lance for the throw.

For a moment it was as if a mask had been peeled from Carric's face and beneath his usual off-hand humor she saw another man, with the glimmer of a terrible beauty about him like the blade of a sword. The man from Anant had seen it too, but he was only beginning to brace himself when Carric sprang at him, gripped, then ducked under the other man's right arm, reached across the front of his body with his left arm and heaved.

Taken by surprise, the Anant man's feet went out from under him, and Maira saw the heavy body wheeling, up and up and over, and then Carric released his grip and dropped his opponent neatly onto the grass. They heard the 'ouf' of expelled air, and like an echo, a kind of collective sigh from the benches.

"An under-heave!" said Carric's sister.

"And very well done, too!" one of the other women replied. Then everyone began to cheer.

Carric stood still, head bent, chest shaking as he fought for air. Maira saw a muscle along his arm jump and quiver with releasing tension, then grow still. After a few minutes his breathing grew easier. The Anant man had finally opened his eyes and was staring up at the sky.

He is probably wondering how Lugh's thunderbolt could strike him from a cloudless sky! thought Maira wryly.

Carric took a careful step toward him, walking as if he wondered if all his muscles still worked, then bent and held out his hand. The Anant man blinked, grasped it, and with a groan let Carric pull him to his feet. The cheering grew louder.

Carric's face had gone very pale, but now the color was coming back. He looked around him, waved at the friends who were shouting from the Men's Side of the ring. He continued to turn, saw Maira and stopped.

She was not cheering. Mute, she stared back at him. Something within her protested like a netted bird, but she could not look away. Finally he took a deep breath, nodded, and turned.

The pulse fluttered in Maira's throat as if she had been running. *He did not grin,* she thought, *at least he did not laugh at me!*

"So—he is a fighter after all!" Druith took her arm.

"Perhaps if he drives his cattle through our gate you should listen to him."

"No!" Maira pulled her arm away. "I was only watching a fight—is that a declaration? You are so eager to marry me off—do you fear I'll outshine Beth, or you, now that I'm grown?" She barely saw the blur as her mother's arm moved, but the open-palmed slap to her ear cracked like thunder and nearly knocked her into the ring. She scraped her hand on the brush, righting herself, then managed to stand, blinking to restore her vision, trying to hear through the ringing in her ears.

"Or is there another reason?" she whispered viciously, hardly knowing what she said. "Do you wish to establish me with some other man because you fear something will happen to father and Eoc and Beth won't want me at home?"

She waited for her mother's second blow and rocked with it, wondering if the bruise would show. Carric and she had both been beaten today.

When she could see again her mother was already disappearing through the crowd. The other White Horse women averted their eyes and whispered behind their hands. But old Ailm of Din Carn watched her with pity in her gaze, and that was the hardest to bear.

Maira blinked, then stared hard at them all until everyone had to look away. Then, though her eyes were beginning to water as her face started to sting, she marched through them with head high.

Of course the gossips would be buzzing as soon as she was out of earshot, but at least they would not be able to peck to pieces the quarrel's true cause, for now that she thought about it, Maira herself was not sure what it had been.

When the light had faded from the sky they lit the torches, and suddenly the plain of Lyn Mapon was a meadow filled with flowers of fire. From the promontory on which the shrine lay hid came the deep throb of drums.

Ness had arranged Maira's hair so that the heavy locks hanging on either side of her face hid the red marks of her mother's blows. As the pulsing of the drums grew louder she draped her cloak across her shoulders and went out to join the others. Her mother gave her a long look, but said nothing, and Maira, who found it easier not to move the muscles of her face at all, did not try to speak to her.

I will not be first to break the silence, she thought. *If it pains her to be at war with her only daughter, let Druith be the one to offer terms.*

But there was pain in her father's eyes when he looked at her, and that was harder to bear. She wondered what her mother had said to him. Then she remembered what she had said to her mother and something in her breast twisted with fear.

But that was only anger speaking! It isn't true!

The drumbeat grew clearer. The drummers had dispersed to each quarter of the encampment, calling the people to witness the sacred rite. Maira took her place behind Eoc as they moved out, family by family, clan by clan, and tribe by tribe, and the scattered light-flowers became a river of fire.

The earth transmitted the vibration of countless feet; Maira's body quivered with the beat of the drum. Her heartbeat steadied, matching it, and a measure of peace filled her for the first time that day. The crowds met, swirled, and merged, intermingling friend and foe. But it did not matter. It was not the prohibition against bloodshed but the beat of the drum that bound them together now. The sky arched above them like the belly of a great cauldron, riveted with stars, reflected by the massed torches of the people below.

The promontory into the lake was crowned with alder trees. The shrine lay on the hill at its point; from there the ground sloped down the neck of land that joined it to the shore. A platform had been built there, against the backdrop of the trees, and the multitude surged up to face it and spread out to either side, so that the reflected torchlight surrounded the point with a crescent of fire.

The throbbing of the drums rolled unhindered across the still waters. Then a white-robed figure appeared on the platform and the beat abruptly stopped. The crackling of torches and the lapping of water along the shore seemed loud in the stillness that followed.

Then gold flashed in the torchlight. A harsh blaring split the still air as the Druid lifted a boar-headed *carynx* of gilded bronze. Three times he blew, and the people answered him with a wordless cry.

The echoes faded, and suddenly the platform bore a line of white figures. Maira peered at them across the water, trying to make out their features. That one on the left, with the silver beard, was that her grandfather? She had not seen him for over a year, for old as he was, Gutuator still moved from steading to steading as he was needed, teaching and counseling.

Now one of the tallest of the Druids stepped forward and lifted his hands. His voice had the curious quality of seeming nearby no matter where one stood. His words vibrated in the air.

> *"For behold, the new moon's sickle harvests summer stars;*
> *The womb of the Mother swells; She gives birth, She*
>   *gives birth!*
> *Her children arise and flourish in the land!"*

Maira took a deep breath, and, exhaling, joined her voice to the people's low murmur of assent. The sound was taken up by the Druids and transformed into a deep, harmonic humming that vibrated through the earth as easily as through the air. Her skin prickled. *Druid magic*, she thought; *now it begins. If those Romans are not safely hid, then let them beware!*

Once more the priest spoke.

> *"I climbed the hill and slept, and in the night I dreamed:*
> *I saw a white cow, giving her milk;*
> *A red cow whose meat is endlessly renewed;*
> *A black bull that tramples the fields . . ."*

Beneath the voice of the Druid the humming shifted a half step up in pitch.

> *"I climbed the hill and slept, and in the night I dreamed:*
> *I saw the white horse of abundance;*
> *I saw the red horse of courage;*
> *I saw the black horse of death.*
> *I climbed the hill and slept, and in the night I dreamed:*
> *I saw a field white with daisies,*
> *I saw a field red with poppies,*
> *I saw a field blackened by fire."*

With each triad the note of the humming changed, moving step by step up the scale.

> *"If you will climb the hill you will get wisdom:*
> *This is the first truth: the body is mortal;*

> *This is the second truth: the spirit is eternal;*
> *This is the third truth: each life is a garment to be*
>   *outgrown."*

As the chant ended, the underlying vibration reached its highest pitch and intensity. And this note they held, one voice filling in for another seamlessly. The torches burned steadily in the still air, but the surface of the lake was pocked and dimpled as if troubled by the wind.

With such sounds as these the Druids must have moved the sacred stones, she thought, or if not they, then those who taught them their mysteries. Maira struggled to retain self-awareness, wondering.

Then the note became a regular pulse of vibration, and beneath it the drums beat once, twice, again. The Druids seemed to float to either side of the platform, and the leader spoke once more.

> *"For behold, the Mother has given birth, and her Son is*
>   *grown;*
> *Lord of the Spear of Light, the god of the clever hands.*
> *The Son of the Mother arises—"*

White robes lifted like wings as the Druid turned, and there beside him on the platform was a figure costumed in golden straw, plaited to form a mask and helm with a crest of gold, golden tunic and shield and a slender gold-headed spear. He brandished them, scattering light.

Maira shivered, seeing the very image of the deity before her, and for a moment all arguments about the habitation of the gods seemed meaningless. Perhaps their true home was in the Otherworld, or perhaps their country penetrated the world of men for those who had eyes to see. But surely the presence of Lugh shone through the figure on the platform like light through a lantern shade.

> *" 'Make for Me a Festival,' saith the Mother,*
> *'With gold and with silver,*
> *With sweet music, and the strength of man against man*
>   *in joyous contention;*
> *An assembly adorned by knowledge and eloquence;*
> *An assembly of men with no lie or injury,*

Without quarrel or thievery,
Without lawsuit or seizure,
Without escape or capture."

Sweet and sonorous as the playing of harps, the catalogue
went on; the yearly chanting of the Law of the Festival.

"An assembly without anger, without deceit,
Without injury, without shame.
The men shall refrain from the place of the women;
The women shall not go to the place of the fair men,
But each one shall have his place in the company.
Corn and milk on every height,
Peace and fair weather, because of this festival!"

The people sighed, understanding, beyond feud and fighting, their unity. And again the bright figure turned, but this
time there was a darkness behind him, echoing his every
move. The drums thundered. The Druid spoke anew.

"But behold, there was a Shadow behind the bright god,
Like a dark cloud in the heavens, thunder in the air.
Darkness filled the earth; the Black God spoke:
'Lord of the Lightning, shalt Thou deny me?
I am the Shadow at Thy shoulder,
The darkness Thy light casts.
I come from the depths of earth
To devour the children of the day.
All that the Mother bears is meat for me—
The harvest and the cattle that eat it
and the men whose life the cattle are.'"

The Black God stalked across the stage, menacing the Son,
who lifted shield and spear to keep him at bay. He was
grotesque, horrible, a humped shape beneath a black cloak
with branching, distorted horns.

" 'Behold my champion,' says the Black God,
'Who shall trample your lives to dust!'"

The black cloak spread like wings. The drums thundered,
overwhelming all other sounds. And when the cloak closed

again a black bull stood beside it—a real animal, old, with the
scars of his battles pale upon his dark hide.

The bull lowered his head, snuffling at the platform, then
lifted it again. His coat had been brushed and oiled until it
shone; the heavy neck muscles rippled as he turned his head.
He had not been drugged. Maira wondered how they had got
him onto the platform. Perhaps by singing, she thought; but
they were not singing to him now. The great head with its horn
crown came up alertly; dark eyes caught the glitter of the fires.

> " 'Then I shall slay him,' cries the Bright God;
>   The Black God replies,
>   'Behold the Black Bull in his power!' "

The bull began to move. Red metal caught the torchlight.
The golden god had exchanged shield and spear for a bronze
axe with a butterfly blade.

"Hai!" shouted the priests. The bull quivered, and pawed at
the platform. Again they shouted, and the beast's answering
bellow seemed to rise from the earth below. Maira's pulse
pounded in her ears. She could hardly breathe.

A third time the Druids shouted, louder, and the axe flamed
up and down in a lightning stroke that cleft the bull's spine.
The breath that men had not known they held was released in a
single sigh.

With head half severed from its body, the bull reared
upward, blood falling like rain. The white robes of the Druids
were jeweled with crimson. The black bull fell, its great body
still denying its death. The axe struck twice more, and blood
washed across the platform as the severed head was pulled
free. Two of the Druids wrestled it onto a pole and levered it
upright next to the platform. The Black God had disappeared.

There was silence while the pole with its grisly standard
ceased to sway. Red blood twined down it like red ribbons, and
the bull's eyes, only now beginning to dull, stared down at the
white, upturned faces of the assembly.

> "Thus saith the Bright God: 'Behold, the monster is slain.
>   Now there shall be no shadow on our celebration;
>   The Bull's blood buys your lives. . . .' "

Drums rumbled softly, supporting the deep thrumming
from the gut strings of a dozen great angled harps, shoulder

high with sound-boxes resting on the ground, arched like multi-strung bows.

The people moved in a slow tide out onto the promontory and back again. Maira was drawn along by the motion, from the northern shore out and down and around again. She could just see the platform where the priests were working swiftly to skin the bull and butcher its carcass. Then the pieces were piled into the already filled iron cauldron, which was winched into place above the unlit fire. Maira felt the blast of heat on her cheeks as they cast the torch onto the pyre.

As the crowd moved forward, the Druids chanted the genealogies of kings and heroes who had made their way halfway across the world to end here in these islands, this time, this ritual.

Then Maira was next to the platform, her nostrils flaring at the reek of blood. She looked up at the head of the bull and felt a wet touch on her forehead as the Druid dipped his finger into a golden basin and marked her.

Dazed, she moved onward and back to the shore again. The odor of blood was replaced by the savor of the bull's flesh boiling, and one by one the chieftains went forward to share the sacred meal.

"This is the first truth: the body is mortal," the Druids sang.

"This is the second truth: the spirit lives on;
This is the third truth: life is a garment to be outgrown."

But Maira, standing in the firelight with the bull's blood drying on her brow, wondered, Why must there always be the sacrifice?

FOUR

The Fire Dance

AT DAWN ON THE Festival's second day the White Horse clan drove its stock down to the lake for the ritual bathing. Like the others, Maira had stripped to her clout; the early morning air was chill, but by the time they had gotten the protesting cattle fully into the water she was warm enough to welcome the cold bath.

When all the cattle were in the lake Maira urged Roud in after them. The mare shied and snorted, but she had done this before, and a determined kick to the ribs got her to go on. Maira gasped as the icy water closed over her, then reached out to splash the mare's tossing head. "There, my lass—every inch of you must be wet for you to have the protection!"

Roud snorted disgustedly and Maira laughed, then urged her farther out so that she could splash the heads of the cattle as well. The light grew brighter. They let the wet cattle turn back toward the shore. Still laughing, Maira scooped a last handful of water across a heifer's rump, then let Roud have her head to follow them.

The mare gathered herself to scramble up the bank and Maira clutched at the wet mane. A faint, musical bawling echoed the noise her own herd had made and she turned to look, water still streaming off her bare skin.

Another herd was coming down for its dipping, escorted by yelling riders. All but one. . . . Maira squinted into the rising sun, trying to make out the features of the horseman who was coming toward her. Then he passed in front of a tree, she turned, and recognized Carric.

Suddenly she forgot her resentment of Selgovae suspicions. He looked at her uncertainly, and she nudged Roud forward.

"I got my heifer back," she said, smiling. "I wanted to thank you. That was a clever piece of work—I hope you never come raiding us, Carric, we would have no defense against you!"

He looked up at her and then quickly away again. "You wouldn't take a reward for finding the child," he said in a low voice. "I thought that at least we owed you your cow. . . ."

But you didn't have to spend your own gold to buy her. The words died unspoken, because if Maira told him how she knew that, she would have to tell him what else Antiochus had told her, and she didn't want to remember that now. Why wouldn't he look at her?

A shout from his herd brought Carric's head up. He looked back, waved, and then his gaze met hers. For a moment he allowed his eyes to travel over her body. Abruptly conscious of her own near-nakedness, Maira pulled back on Roud's rein. She knew that she was flushing. She could not speak.

"I'll see you at the dancing," said Carric a little desperately as his friends called to him again.

Still wordless, Maira nodded, wrenched Roud's head around, and kicked her into a canter back to the camp.

By the time the cattle were all safely penned and Maira was dry and dressed again, the sun was high. She came out from behind the curtain in the Women's bothy, suddenly aware that she had eaten nothing but a bannock since dawn. Her mother should have some stew simmering; she took a wooden bowl and started toward the fire.

"Divitiac slept last night in the bull-skin, but it takes time to interpret a dream. . . ." Someone was speaking in Latin nearby; a slow deep voice, and familiar.

Maira turned quickly, and saw her grandfather Gutuator sitting with her father in front of the Men's House on the other side of the fire. Sunlight burned like silver fire in his beard. But the sight of a red cloak beyond him distracted her—it was the Roman she had seen at the swordmaker's booth the day before.

Well, at least that explained why they were speaking Latin. Still watching them covertly, Maira continued on to the fire and began to ladle out stew. She had been taught enough of the Roman tongue to follow the conversation, though she had little practice in speaking it. She wondered what the Roman was doing here.

"I have heard rumors in the camp already. . . ." Conmor's voice had an edge to it, but only someone who knew him well would have heard the note of strain. "Evil omens . . . blood on the land."

"Any event may be interpreted in many ways," said Gutuator calmly. "One must look at the context to perceive the pattern."

The Roman cleared his throat. "That is true, surely. Sometimes the priests who take the auspices for the Legions argue like magpies over what the marks on the entrails mean."

"You see, Flavius Pintamus, we are not so different after all." Gutuator smiled oddly. "What did you think of the ceremony?"

Maira suppressed a start of surprise and saw that the Roman's face had betrayed his own chagrin. Holding her bowl carefully, she moved toward them and sat down on a convenient log.

"You knew?" Pintamus managed to keep his voice steady.

"Of course. But from your hiding place you could not interfere. We rather welcomed the chance to demonstrate that our rituals are not so barbaric as your Roman writers have said. . . ."

"You mean Caesar." The Roman had the grace to look embarrassed. "Educated men understand that some of Caesar's writings were inspired more by the muse of politics than by that of history."

"Tell that to the dead of Mona!" said Conmor bitterly.

"The dead are dead, my son, and understand all," said the Druid. "But you Romans must know by now that when Suetonius Paulinus massacred our priesthood on the isle of Mona he wounded our Order badly, yet it was not destroyed."

"Not while you flourish unhindered in Alba and Ivernia!" Pintamus agreed wryly.

"That is not the only reason. Our tradition is very old, and its structure has been transformed many times. The soul of a man may undergo many incarnations, but its essence remains the same. So it is with our wisdom. There may come a day when the name of Druid is forgotten in Britain, but the truth that we have served will endure. . . ."

Maira looked at her grandfather's calm face and shivered. He had not altered since she could remember, and she could not imagine a world without him, or the Order of Druids to which he belonged. She gripped the horn handle of her spoon as if she could hold the whole world still, and thought, *If I had my will, nothing at all would change!* A bird called softly from the left and she shivered again, not wanting to know what it might mean.

"But as for the ceremony, indeed I found nothing there to disturb me," Pintamus continued after a short silence. "It was surprisingly familiar. In the mountains of my homeland there is a bull-ritual, but there the man goes alone into the ring to face the beast, armed only with a sword."

"You know the bull-sacrifice also from another ritual," said Gutuator. He touched his forehead respectfully and stared at Pintamus. Maira, following his gaze, saw the brand of Mithras between the Roman's brows.

An expression of consternation passed across the Decurion's face. His lips opened, then closed again. Gutuator smiled.

"I know that you are sworn to silence, but at the beginning of things the Magi of your religion were one with the Wise Men of ours. We know the story of the Light-Bearer who slays the Bull from whose flesh the gifts of life come."

Flavius Pintamus stared at him. "I should like to see a meeting between you and my priest someday." He lifted his mug and drained it, then set it down.

Conmor reached for the pitcher, looked into it, then held it out to Maira. "Come bring us some more beer, lass," he said in British, "lest we shame our hospitality."

She nodded, took the pitcher and filled it from the cask, then bore it carefully back to them.

"This is your daughter?" the Roman asked Conmor. "Greetings, Domina, and my thanks to you. Talking is thirsty work!"

Maira looked down at him, smiling a little rigidly while she tried to frame a proper Latin reply.

Mistaking her hesitation for lack of comprehension, Pintamus repeated his compliment in British, and she answered in the same tongue. Conmor and Gutuator exchanged amused glances and Maira suppressed her first impulse to explain. Her Latin was clumsy at best, and she did not wish to make a fool of herself in front of this foreigner.

"You speak our language well," she answered instead. And it was true that although his accent was odd, he spoke quite fluently.

"I have need to. My scouts are Brigante tribesmen from near Eboracum—very nearly your cousins, as I understand."

"Close enough," said Conmor. "We fight among ourselves like wolf-cubs from the same litter, but we are all one pack in the end."

"Are you?" Flavius Pintamus did not seem offended by the challenge in those words. "Forgive me," he went on, "but if your British wolves had stood together I would not be here today."

Conmor grinned, looking rather wolfish himself. "That was the south. We had some good hunting in these hills ten years ago."

"Which Ulpius Marcellus ended," countered the Roman. For a moment the two men's glances met and clashed.

He has courage to say that, thought Maira, remembering the day her father had returned from that last rising of the northern tribes. He still bore scars from that fighting. But she knew that even if this very Roman had made them, still he would have been safe drinking her father's beer at her father's hearth.

Conmor shrugged. "Perhaps, but today your soldiers have gone back to guarding the Wall."

"Most of them," said Flavius Pintamus blandly. "But I hope for authority to rebuild Blatobulgium." His glance sought the southeast as if he could see across the hills to the tumbled stones of a fort which had already been torn down, rebuilt, and dismantled again, a victim of changing Roman policies.

"Too much independence among one's warriors can be a problem," said Conmor agreeably, "and so can too rigid a discipline. But we have one advantage—it is our land, and even our women and children will fight for it."

Pintamus smiled, apparently undisturbed, and looked over at Maira.

"And you, Lady," he asked, "are you a warrior too?"

"I ride, and I am learning to use the sword. It is a tradition among our people that a woman should be able to defend her home."

"She rides very well," said Conmor. "She will be running her roan mare in the Women's Race this afternoon."

"Ah." The Roman nodded and smiled again. His tanned face really looked quite pleasant once one got used to it. "Then I shall be sure to watch for you. . . ."

Roud ran well that afternoon, but she came in a nose behind a rangy black gelding ridden by a Selgovan girl, and both of them were a length after a sleek bay that the niece of the Novantan High King rode.

Afterward, Maira led the sweating mare back to their camp, smiling determinedly and patting her for comfort. Roud was only a hill pony, after all, and the Carbantorigum horse was one of the big, long-striding beasts they bred in Southern Gaul. She was sure that neither of the other two racers was as clever with the cattle as Roud.

She spent the evening close to her own campfire, receiving condolences and congratulations, too, for third was a respectable placing, after all. And later she went off with the other girls to hear the harping, and Tadhg took the prize for it, so the Clan had some honor that day.

The third day of the Festival dawned with an undercurrent of tension. The individual sports had been exciting, but the faction-fighting had all the advantages of a good battle without its drawbacks: an exciting combat without casualties, though there was always the threat of injury to spice the contest; and no houses burned or cattle carried away.

The Druids said that the battle was a fight between good and evil, though neither side was identified with one or the other. It released spiritual tensions and ensured prosperity in the coming year. The old women shook their heads and hoped that if the men fought for sport at Lughnasa they would have less need for real warfare later on. The men told each other it would give them a chance to assess the young warriors, and it would give the young men themselves some seasoning. It seemed to Maira that the reason they conducted their mock-war so religiously was because they enjoyed it.

Women did not participate in the fighting. Their involvement would have trespassed against the strict separation of the sexes during the Festival; and there was another reason that Maira understood, even as she enviously watched her brother getting ready to fight. Men might battle for the fun of it, but women carried the future of the clan, and when a woman took up weapons it was real. Perhaps when one trained with practice weapons it was different; but there were tales of women who ran battle-mad against imagined enemies, and certainly the women were the most terrifying fighters in real war. No one desired to hear the beating of the raven's dark wings. The

Mor-Rigan was not the face of the Goddess they invoked at this Festival.

I could keep a rein on my passions, Maira thought as she strapped the leather wrist guards tight around her brother's arms. *I would like to try my skill against some of these champions.*

She imagined herself circling and striking at someone who hid behind a long leather shield; someone tall and swift, but not as swift as she. She knocked his shield aside and saw Carric's laughing face. Maira shook her head to clear it of the vision, knowing this was only a fancy. But she was breathing hard as if she had been fighting in reality.

Eoc had stripped to the waist and tied up his hair so that it tossed like a horse's tail. In addition to the wrist guards, he had a broad leather belt to protect his stomach, an oblong cowhide and wicker shield and a stout length of blackthorn to do duty as a sword. He was wearing his braies, but some of the other men wore short fighting kilts or had stripped to their clouts for the fray. The Novantae and Selgovae fielded by far the greatest numbers of men at this Festival, and the Damnonii who had come fought with their southern neighbors, while the eastern Votadini joined forces with the Selgovae.

As Maira took her place on the women's benches she hoped it would do some good for them to fight this way. If the Novantae warriors trounced their foes thoroughly with wood, the Selgovae might think twice about coming against them with steel. She saw Ailm and Ura and the other Din Carn women nearby, chattering like blackbirds and eyeing her curiously. Carric's mother met her gaze directly and smiled, and Maira wondered, *What has he said to her?*

Then the two forces moved out onto the field, focusing all attention.

"Look at Eoc!" whispered Druith. "Like a warrior from a legend, with the sun like gold on his hair! Conmor looked like that when he was young. . . ."

Conmor is still twice the warrior that any of those could be! thought Maira loyally, but now Eoc's sword-brothers Rosic and Kenow were following him, and behind them came some of her own men—Caw and Kitto and the three sons of Urr. The men continued to march past, brandishing swords and grinning at their womenfolk. Drych of Din Prys waved to his sister Onn, Calgac the High King's son walked as if he were already a victor, and still they came—men from the valley of the Nova and the estuary of the Urr, men from the vales of the Tarf and the Cree and the Luce, and all along the coasts that bordered the western sea.

They formed up, chanting with a guttural grunt like the challenge of a wild boar. On the other side Maira glimpsed Carric with Trost and Conon close beside him, and some of the other lads who had been with him when they met on the way back from Lyn Duw. Grinning, stamping out a dull thunder, the two lines of men advanced.

Clouds had begun to move in from the west during the night. Now they banked over the hills like piles of dirty fleece, waiting to overflow into the valley and spill thei load of rain as the two armies waited to strike their blows. It would be hard on the fighters if the storm hit during the combat, but a sign of luck for the Festival.

Very slowly, it seemed to the watchers, the two forces advanced. But they needed the time to let their chanting and battle cries kindle their fury. There was something ominous and inexorable about that steady progress, like some stalking beast of prey.

Beth shifted anxiously on the seat beside Maira. "Eoc won't be hurt, will he?"

"He has taken no harm in the three summers he has fought already," said Maira reasonably. "Except for some bruises and a cracked rib." Beth sighed and Maira suppressed a grin. If Eoc were hurt he would not be much use to her for a night or two, she thought. Or perhaps he would—she had heard that combat made some men amorous.

A shout from the field startled her from her speculations. The fight had started; the two groups were charging simultaneously, striving for as much momentum as possible before they shocked together and the beating began. The object of the battle was not to kill or injure the foe, but only to drive the other force from the field by the weight of bodies or blows, or the strength of the spirit one brought to the fray.

Maira frowned as she saw the right edge of the Selgovae line curling around to take the Novantae from the side and drive them back upon each other so that no one would have fighting room. For a few moments the Novantae gave way, then someone realized what was happening and spearheaded a counter-attack that cut through the Selgovae line, cut off the attackers and drove them to the edge of the field.

"That will change the odds!" shouted Maira. Beth shook

her head, unable to hear over the thunder of wood on wood or flesh or leather shield. If there was thunder from the heavens, no one could hear.

Maira leaned forward, clinging to the edge of the bench, quivering at every blow. There—Eoc's stick rose and fell on someone who screamed in pain. Nearby she saw Carric, striking hard, and laughing. Minutes passed as the line swayed and swirled. Movements became slower as the first fervor wore away; it was becoming a test of endurance now. Even the shouting became more sporadic. Men were saving their breath for their blows.

Then Calgac yelled. The Novantae men formed up behind him and with strength drawn from some reservoir in the spirit ran toward the foe. Back and forth they swayed, and one by one warriors were struck down or fell. But still the Selgovae were pushed back, and back again, though by the time they backed across their line the Novantae had hardly enough fighters left to claim a victory.

The sweet discordance of the carynx horns marked the battle's ending. There was a moment of stillness as combatants and spectators alike caught their breath and looked about to see how everyone had fared. *They held nothing back*, thought Maira. *The gods should be well-satisfied*.

Luckier comrades assisted the fallen to their feet. Many limped or cradled injured arms; some staggered dizzily or hugged themselves to keep damaged ribs still. One expected a certain number of cracked collarbones, sprains and bruises and perhaps a concussion or two, but most of the warriors should be able to dance when night fell.

Beth gave a little sigh and Maira saw Eoc striding across the field, bruised and muddy, but grinning triumphantly. She looked past him, telling herself she only wanted to check on the rest of their men, but her gaze fixed too quickly on a group of Selgovae bent over someone who lay without stirring on the grass.

The women of Din Carn were whispering anxiously, and Maira felt her belly muscles tighten, then release abruptly as Carric emerged from the huddle, gesturing, and the others picked up the fallen man and carried him away. She watched Carric narrowly as he followed them. He was limping, but seemed otherwise unharmed.

Her heart began to pound heavily. He would be at the

dancing, then, and so would she. And then . . . and then . . .
She could follow the thought no more.

The sacrificed bull was reborn.

At sunset they had seen it emerging from the skin of the bull
slain two nights ago like a butterfly from its chrysalis. The
Black God's totem had become the Bull of Blessing, and light
and darkness were reconciled.

Then the platform of sacrifice was dismantled and carried to
the middle of the great field to fuel the bonfire. The deep pulse
of the drums beat from the northern side of the fire, and in the
south the pipers took turns carrying the melody. On the east
side the men waited, watching the women on the other side of
the fire. But around the fire was the space for the dancing.

Maira stood with the other young women, swaying to the
beat of the drums. From time to time she adjusted the folds of
her garment, for like the others she was dressed in the old style
tonight—a single piece of fabric wrapped around her, belted
with her girdle of maidenhood and pinned at the shoulders so
that the long endpiece could be draped over her hair. The men
were garbed similarly, except that the lengths of fabric they
wore were pleated and belted at the waist, and the remainder
drawn across the bare torso and over the shoulder.

Maira fingered the fabric, faded now to a harmonious
chequering of dull red, creamy yellow, and grey-blue, wondering how many women had worn it before. The cloth had been
in her mother's family for generations. It might even have been
made by some women of the old race who were here when her
people came to these isles from Gaul. She had seen folk from
the far north of Alba who wore garments of the same style still.

Now the drums thundered with sudden fervor, then fell
silent. The laughter around her stilled. The crackling of the fire
seemed very loud.

And then the beat resumed, slow and steady as the beat of
marching feet, and the dull sound of bare feet marching echoed
it as the young men of the tribes came onto the dancing floor.

The beat quickened. The line separated into squares that
closed and opened, circled and split as one man after another
leaped forward to demonstrate his strength and agility and
skill.

They were like horses galloping down a hill; like stags
battling in the autumn when the woods kindled like flame; like

the boar, like the eagle, like everything powerful and free. Maira's breath quickened in response. Suddenly she remembered Lyn Duw, and the horned figure she had seen among the trees.

The Antlered One, she named Him; but that had been only a moment of vision. This dance was continuing, a living, moving, manifestation of the thing she had glimpsed before. How could an image capture this dynamic power?

She thought of the fluid strength of the herd-stallion guarding his mares, the explosive beauty of their matings in the spring. That, too, was part of the essential power that the Antlered One personified.

She saw suddenly as one image the Antlered One and the black bull. The Light-Bearer had slain the bull—a god slaying a god, who was then reborn. The drumbeat focused her thought and dispersed it again; only for a moment, she understood the unity. . . .

And then the rhythm took her, and she saw only the lithe bodies of the young men, vying to see who could leap the highest with their multi-colored kilts swirling and their bare chests glistening with sweat in the light of the fire.

Finally the drum beat slowed. Panting, the dancers reformed their double line and began to file back to their side of the fire. With a start, Maira noticed Carric among them and realized she had not seen him dance—or perhaps she had seen all of the men as aspects of him, for looking at him now, she could not remember watching any of the others at all.

The slow drumming continued. The pipes wailed away to silence and a deep thrumming replaced them as the harpers began to play. There were six of them, and despite their skill not all of the strings could be kept precisely in tune. The resulting faint discordance gave their playing an eerie harmony.

That is fitting, thought Maira as the line of maidens stepped out onto the dancing floor. *Let the men remember that there is more than sweetness to a woman's power. . . .*

The Dance of the Maidens began almost lazily. The line of girls swayed into a sinuous circle, then coiled into a spiral and then, like the Lady's serpent, relaxed into a circle again.

Then the circle separated into two equal lines that danced toward each other until their breasts almost touched, then flowed backward again.

The lads were boars and stallions, thought Maira as the line advanced once more, *but what are we? Trees, perhaps—swaying in the wind—or fish slipping through the water, or soaring birds?*

Again and again the lines met and parted, then divided into smaller groups whose ends met in a star. It was a simple gliding step from side to side, but it took concentration to coordinate with the dancers to either side. Yet as the maidens became one with the music they became one with each other as well, until their line undulated like a swimming serpent across the dancing floor. And Maira understood that Carric would not be seeing *her*, either, but the Goddess herself, dancing through the fields of ripening grain.

Pattern after pattern formed and dissolved—the circle, the spiral, the star, the undulating line that coiled back upon itself and the never-ending double circle that required a quick unclasping and clasping of joined hands as each dancer went through the line and came around again.

Then the music quickened. The final circle spun sunwise, collapsed inward and exploded with a shout as the dancers scattered back to stand in an unconnected circle once more. With a chord that shimmered up and down the scale the harps concluded their music. The drums steadied and carried the dancers back to their places.

Maira was sweating lightly, but the dancing had invigorated rather than tired her. Someone struck up a lively pipe tune, double cow horns shrilling as he pumped the bladder-bag, and the drums began to follow it as the babble of conversation burst like an undammed stream. The rigid structure of the celebration dissolved as men and women mingled freely for the first time during the festival.

Great casks had been placed near the fire, filled with water or mead or beer. Maira made her way to them, accepted a dipper of water and drank greedily. Then the rhythm of the dance music drew her back into the circle. For a few moments she nodded to the beat, then she leaped into the center with the others to show off her footwork in a swift, stamping dance.

When the tune ended she was thirsty again and went back to the casks. She closed her eyes, letting the cool water slide down her throat, and nearly dropped the dipper as a strong hand closed on her arm.

"Maira! I did not mean—" Carric broke off, reddening as she half-choked, gulped down the rest of the water, and wiped her mouth on the back of her hand.

"I should have sprayed you for startling me like that!" She
eyed him warily, lifted the dipper again and sipped carefully,
her eyes still holding his. *I ought to be angry,* she thought,
watching the play of emotion on his strong face. *Why do I want
to laugh?*

"I'm sorry," he said with difficulty. "I've been looking for
you. This whole cursed Festival I have been looking *at* you, but
there was no way we could talk!" He coughed, then made a
quick pounce toward the cask of mead and came back with a
dipper in his hand.

"Really?" she said sweetly. "Is there something particular
you were wanting to say?" She stared at him, discovering that
she could make him blush or look away.

I should go. I don't even like him, she told herself, and she
certainly disliked his people. But she saw the mark of a blow
from the stick-fighting red upon his cheekbone and grimacing,
felt a lingering soreness where her mother had struck her.
Emotions she could not understand swirled just beneath the
surface of her awareness. Better to face him, then, and let
reality put an end to her imaginings. Perhaps then she would
have some peace.

"I wanted to tell you—" He looked around, saw two old
women whispering behind their hands, and frowned. "Maira, I
cannot talk to you here. Come up on the hill with me. It will be
quiet there. . . ."

"So that we can gather bilberries?" She had heard that
excuse too often from couples who obviously had something
else in mind.

"Maybe!" Carric grinned suddenly and something tightened in Maira's chest. *I am more agile than he is, and I have
not been drinking mead.* She reassured herself as she would
have calmed Roud when the mare spooked at something
strange in her path. *And I can run like Roud, too, if I want to
get away!*

She shrugged agreement and began to walk toward the
darkness beyond the field, noting with approval that he did not
try to take her hand. Perhaps all Carric had in mind was
talking, after all, but in that case why did she feel just a little
disappointed? *Come, come, my girl,* she told herself, *make up
your mind!*

She knew the hill he meant, a rise in the midst of the plain
just beyond the campground, crowned with oak trees. Still
leading, Maira picked her way among the scattered patches of

broom and found a place that was reasonably level and covered with thick grass.

She stopped, looking around her inquiringly. Carric sighed and carefully lowered himself to the grass, then, with a deeper sigh, stretched out on his back, looking up at the stars. After a moment of indecision, Maira settled herself nearby and sat with her arms clasped around her knees.

"This feels good," he said after several silent moments had passed.

Maira remembered his bruises. "Are you sore from the fighting?"

He grunted agreement. "Not as sore as some. Conon took a head-blow from one of your lads that put him out for three hours, and he's still groggy. I did not notice my own bruises during the dancing, but I'm stiffening up again now. Did you see me?"

"Of course I saw you," she answered tartly, unable to explain what she *had* seen, and then, to forestall further questions, added, "And in the stick-fighting." Unwillingly she remembered the moment when she thought it was Carric who lay still upon the grass. That must have been Conon, then. Quickly she went on, "And when you were wrestling with that Anant man."

"Lord Lugh, that was a hard one." Carric sighed. "I did not think I could take him, but I knew you were watching me."

Maira peered at him through the darkness. Her brother Eoc would never have admitted that.

"What did you wish to say to me?"

"An apology . . . for disturbing you and your women last month. Didn't mean it—we were a little drunk and started daring each other to cross the river, maybe lift a cow or two—it seemed like a good plan at the time."

Maira grunted, but not too angrily. Eoc and his friends had acquired several Selgovae cattle that way; she had had to remind him not to bring any of them to the Festival.

"And then we encountered you, and that was fine," he went on, "but I did not know where you had been. And then the other women came along with the rowan branch, and your mother—Goddess, my men were at me all the way home for fear she'd shrivel their balls!"

Maira laughed. "Sometimes she scares me, too." Her jaw still ached from her mother's blow, but she could not tell him about *that!*

"I am sorry about the horse race," Carric added. "Not fair for that Carbantorigum girl to bring in a foreign horse."

"Especially since your cousin would have won if she had not?" Maira asked a little maliciously.

"Perhaps, but you are a very clever rider." he said calmly. "I noticed that last year, when *you* won."

"You saw me then?" Her question came a little too quickly.

"I saw you then, and in the dancing, and when the chieftains met the Roman Legate at the oath stone at Locus Maporum last Beltane. You had a new cloak then, and a wreath of hawthorn on your hair." Carric's voice was so low she had to strain to hear it. He lay very still, staring up at the sky.

Maira bit her lip. "You were riding your big bay. . . ." The words detached themselves one by one from her memory. "And through your cloakpin you had stuck a spray of broom."

"You were very beautiful tonight, in the dancing, like a willow tree, or a white bird flying—maybe a swan. . . ."

The words seemed unconnected, but Maira was beginning to understand. She looked away to the west where clouds were blotting out the stars. *And to what shall I liken you, my friend?* she wondered then. She had no need to see him to visualize the strength of his shoulders or the sheen of his bronze hair. A blink of lightning slashed the clouds and she jumped. A distant rumble followed; she felt her hair lifted by a cooler breeze.

There was something menacing about those clouds, even though it was supposed to be good luck if it rained on the Festival. She shivered, not entirely from cold.

"Are you chilled? Come here; there is enough of this garment to cover both of us. . . ."

There was no threat in his voice, so why was she trembling? Perhaps she really *was* cold. Maira nodded in the darkness, moved over to him, and carefully lay down at his side. Still without touching her, Carric draped the wool over her. It *was* warmer, out of the wind; or perhaps it was the heat of his body she felt now.

"I remember every time I have seen you during the past two years," he said softly. His breath tickled her ear.

"And I you," she answered, sighing. *He has not forced me,* she thought in wonder. *The defenses and barriers were all my own.*

"Maira," he said then. "I am not your enemy."

"I know. . . ."

"Maira, I love you—"

She could not speak. She reached up to touch his face. The lightning flickered again and his lips found hers; a swift brush at first, and then, as her fingers tightened in his hair, a firm and commanding pressure that took her breath away. And still, only their mouths were touching, meeting and parting, exploring, communicating what they did not know how to say.

It seemed a long time before he drew away, though the wind had driven the clouds only a little way across the sky. He sighed. "Your mouth is like honey-mead."

Maira reached out to grip his shoulder. He turned to her again, but this time his lips traced the line of her cheek, her ear, and moved down her neck till he came to the cloth of her gown. Deftly he unclasped one shoulder-brooch, then the other. With a distant amusement she thought he must have had a lot of practice to do it without stabbing her with the pins, but she did not try to stop him as he pulled the fabric aside and cupped her breast in his hand.

"Your breast is like the breast of a swan," he said wonderingly, and then her breath caught, as his lips explored that softness and her nipple hardened. From one breast to the other he moved. She released her breath and gasped for it again.

His hand moved down to the knot of her girdle and stayed there.

What is he waiting for? Maira tried to control the pounding of her heart. Her skirts were rucked up around her thighs and she wore no clout—the knotted cord around her waist was surely no barrier.

Then she felt his trembling through his hand and realized that the girdle was a symbol more potent than any armor; that he was waiting for her.

"Yes," she whispered. "Yes, my love, you may. . . ."

He fumbled with the knot, but she had tied it well, afraid the dancing would loosen it. After a moment Carric swore and pulled away.

Maira could not help giggling, then she gave him a quick kiss and sat up to undo the knot. *And perhaps it is even better this way,* she thought then. *It is my decision now.* Swiftly she yanked at the cord, then kicked the rest of the fabric away.

She leaned over Carric, her body glimmering in the light of the crescent moon, and kissed him again. "Now, you!"

As he undid the clasps of his wide belt and the pleats of his kilt fell away she saw that he was erect already.

"So soon?" she asked, surprised.

"My dear one," he said ruefully, "I have been this way since the beginning of the Festival!" He pulled her down against him, and she could feel his hardness against her thighs. "I will try not to hurt you—"

"Oh, well, I've done so much riding, I doubt. . . ." She broke off as he kissed her. He would probably know that girls who rode and fought as she did rarely retained a perceptible maidenhead.

She had thought he would reach down and touch her, but he strained her to him. For a few moments Maira lay quite still, growing accustomed to the touch of his bare skin against hers. Then her arms tightened around him. She moved against him, seeking some fuller contact; his grip shifted and they moved together like two wrestlers.

Her hand slipped down his back, feeling the muscles slide beneath his skin. His legs scissored around hers and his heel hooked her ankle, drawing her legs apart. He gripped her buttocks and half lifted her so that suddenly she felt his member rubbing gently between her thighs and gasped.

Carric stilled for a moment, then turned his head to kiss her, gently, then harder, and as Maira's mouth opened beneath his some last resistance melted and he felt it too and entered her.

This was what it was all about, then—but no, when the stallion mounted the mare he thrust into her. . . . Tentatively Maira moved her hips and cried out as Carric pushed further in. It was like the attack and retreat of swordplay, she thought. It was like a dance.

As their movement continued, she began to respond more freely, unleashing her own strength bit by bit against him, knowing that Carric had the power to match hers.

He was not *taking* her—they were taking each other, or perhaps, as the dance went on, giving to each other what neither could gain alone. And then Maira stopped thinking, for her body was mastering her. As Carric's breath began to come in hoarse groans, she rode him as she had ridden her red mare, panting, awareness fixed on an unknown goal.

Then lightning flared above them. She saw his face as it had been when he closed on the other wrestler, shining like a drawn sword. Maira shouted and held on with all her strength as he exploded against her and her own flesh burst into sweet fire.

And then the thunder came.

FIVE

---❦---

The Sacrifice

"Is it always like that?" Maira stirred and turned just enough so that she could see the dim outline of Carric's face.

He laughed softly. "I don't know, love—perhaps it will be for you and me!"

She relaxed and smiled against his shoulder. Of course he had known other women, but it appeared that something about this love-making had been as much of a revelation for him as it had been to her.

"I have twenty-two cows now," he said, "with luck thirty by spring." He kissed her.

"Twenty-five," she answered sweetly, "now. And seven men oathed to me."

"Well!" She could feel him smiling in the darkness. "You're ahead on cattle, but I have more followers. Shall we compromise?"

Maira giggled. "I think my father will agree."

"And then there is the question of where to live," Carric went on. "Would you be willing—"

He stopped speaking, and Maira heard someone crashing through the bushes and swearing as he came. *Someone has had too much mead and is looking for a place to sleep it off*, she thought, and wondered why Carric was listening. Then she realized what he was saying.

"Carric!" The stranger drew breath with a harsh gasp. "Carric, my lord—whoever you have with you up there, you must come!"

Maira stiffened. Suddenly she felt cold despite the warmth of the wool and Carric's arms.

"Carric," the unknown voice wailed, "Conon's dead! That Novantae bastard Eoc's blow has done for him. Carric, you must be here somewhere!"

Maira fell back with a groan. It was not unknown for someone to be killed in the Festival fighting, but for Carric's sword-brother to have fallen by her own brother's hand. . . . She pressed her fist against her mouth to stifle a cry.

Carric still lay face down, swearing softly. His man began to call again, evoking sleepy curses from elsewhere on the hill. Then Carric sat up and answered hoarsely.

"Trost? Is that you? Stay where you are, lad; I'll come." Clumsily he gathered up the unfamiliar length of his garment and after a few frustrating attempts to pleat it, wound it around him and belted it.

Maira lay still, staring up at his darker bulk against the dim sky. *Is he going to leave without a word?* she wondered. *Has he already turned from me?*

Carric threw the end of the fabric over his shoulder, sighed, and leaned over her.

"Maira," he whispered, "I must go now. I know it was no fault of your brother's, but it will take awhile to calm my men. Remember that I love you, whatever you hear. It may take time," he repeated, "but things will come right for us somehow."

Then he straightened, and she heard his footsteps, leaving her.

"By the Black God's balls, I had a time finding you, Carric," she heard Trost say. "Who'd you have up there anyway? I thought you were still mooning after that little Novantae bitch. Well, there's no hope for you in that now, lad, so perhaps it's a good thing you found someone else. . . ."

Maira heard Carric swearing, and Trost's protests; then their voices faded and they were gone.

She pulled her garment close about her and lay there, shivering. She could smell the scent of Carric's body on it, and fancy that some imprint of his body still remained in the grass below. When she was certain they were gone she allowed herself to weep, sobbing soundlessly into the worn wool until her head ached and her eyes stung.

When her tears were finally exhausted she looked up at the lightning-laced sky. "Why don't you rain?" she whispered into the darkness. "I have done my weeping—why don't you?" But there was nothing, only a damp wind to chill her tear-wet skin, and after awhile, the deceptive greyness of the hour before dawn.

Soon the other couples who had spent the night on the hill would wake. She could not bear to have them see her, to laugh, or wonder who had deserted her here. If any of them had heard Trost calling, they would know who her lover had been!

And Maira knew she could not bear to see them waking in each other's arms, smiling in untroubled happiness.

Awkward, her muscles aching from the unaccustomed exercise and the hours spent huddled on the cold ground, Maira got to her feet and pinned her gown around her. For the last time, needing it to hold the garment together, she tied the maiden girdle she no longer had the right to wear.

Quietly she made her way down the hill and across the field, past the embers of the great fire. Looking at those ashes it was hard to imagine last night's blazing splendor—as hard as it was to believe in what had happened on the hill in this bitter dawn.

She went to the Women's Side of the lake and washed quickly, then turned back through the camp, where the first risers were just beginning to stir. By the time the sun lifted above the eastern hills she was wrapped in her own blankets by her mother's fire.

If they ask what is wrong I will say I drank too much and am ill, she thought grimly. And that was not so far from the truth, for she had been drunk on love and her body's awakening, and the aftereffects were bitter indeed.

But with daylight came the news of Conon's death. The camp buzzed with rumors of Selgovae retaliation against Eoc, and no one had attention to spare for Maira's feelings, no matter what their cause. Druith bustled about the camp, giving orders for packing. But Conmor sat by the fire, staring into it with that bleak look he had worn when the sickle gashed his hand.

Maira's knees bent and she scuffed her feet a little to steady her footing, keeping the wooden practice sword poised before her. Then she waited.

"That's right." Eoc squinted at her, then walked around her. She shifted position just a little to keep him in view. "No—don't let your right foot get out of line. You want to keep balanced all the time, like a tree with deep roots."

She grimaced, thinking of all the times she had seen *him* off-balance, but she said nothing. Eoc was doing her a favor, and if his words only echoed what the master at Carbantorigum had taught him, they were all the more valuable for that.

He continued to circle her casually; then suddenly he had dropped into position and leaped toward her. Maira's blade whipped up to parry as his sword cracked against it, and she felt the shock all the way up her arm. She struggled to hold firm, but she did not quite have the strength for it, and gasped as Eoc's blade went on to strike a bruising blow to her forearm.

Eoc pulled back and straightened, shaking his head. "You will have to do something about that, little sister! Either develop more strength in your arms or get out of the way!"

I would have gotten out of the way, you wretch, if you had not told me that this time I must stand fast! With difficulty Maira kept the hot words prisoned. Holding on to one's temper was part of the training too.

"Again," she said shortly.

Eoc shrugged, grinned infuriatingly, then dove at her once more. But this time Maira was ready for him. As the other blade struck hers she twisted, shifting the angle of her sword just enough to deflect his upward, while her own stick continued on to strike the inside of his arm.

Eoc jumped back and stared at her, arm dangling. "You weren't supposed to do that!"

Maira reproduced his own grin. "You were not supposed to let me. Didn't you just finish telling me the body should defend itself without needing to be told?"

"Huh!" His sword came up and Maira knew she was in for it now. She had barely time to get her blade into position before he was on her. For a few moments she let him drive her backward while she collected herself and sought an opening.

There was one blow he had tried three times now—yes, now it was coming—only this time instead of parrying she stepped into his attack, knocked his sword aside and brought hers down on his arm.

But her balance had not been quite true. Her blow was glancing, and Eoc still had the strength to bring his blade around. Maira saw the blur of movement toward her and managed to twist just enough so that it fell not on her neck but on her shoulder and knocked her to the ground.

He could have broken my neck, Maira thought blurrily, her

vision dimmed by more than the fading light of the cloudy sky. *If that blade had been edged I could have lost an arm*. She had practiced throwing the lance until her aim was swift and sure, but she must develop more strength if she was going to use a sword!

She lay in the dust, gasping, while Eoc leaned on his blade, catching his own breath and staring down at her.

"I'm sorry," he said at last. "You made me mad."

Maira sat up and nodded, understanding what must have happened at the Festival. Conon had smacked him somewhere that angered him, and in responding, he had forgotten to pull his blow. But in battle, there would be neither rules nor allowances.

"I asked for it." Her shoulder still throbbed, but she shook her head, reached for her sword, and stood up. As Eoc began to settle into position again, his smile held real respect for the first time.

Maira heard something like distant thunder and felt through the thin leather soles of her slippers a vibration in the ground. As she straightened, the sound grew louder. Now Eoc heard it too, and both of them turned, squinting down the road. Like a temporarily earth-bound, drunken butterfly, Antiochus' brightly painted cart lurched over the rutted road toward the rath.

Maira ran to open the gate for him, wondering if the cart would hold together until he got there. She had never seen the trader in such haste. Others came running as the ungainly vehicle lumbered through the gap in the circle. Maira grasped one of the bridles; the mules halted gratefully, eyes rolling, and the trader dropped the reins and clambered down, wiping his perspiring forehead with the loose sleeve of his gown.

"Thank you, young mistress. Is your father here?"

"I think he is in the south pasture, doctoring a cow," said Eoc. "Shall I get him? What has happened?"

Antiochus looked from him to Maira, then pulled at his beard. "Well, you will learn soon enough in any case. And for this news I ask no payment." The smile died. "Last night Din Carn was raided, and twenty head of cattle taken away."

I hope none of them belonged to Carric! thought Maira. Eoc was grinning.

"You do not understand!" said Antiochus. "The raiders dropped a cloak of Novantae pattern, and the tracks led this way. . . ."

Eoc looked thunderous. "It wasn't me!" he exclaimed. "Do you think I'd be such a fool as to leave that kind of evidence, or lead any man who would do so?"

The trader shrugged expressively. "Young lord, it does not matter, don't you see? They will *think* it was you. They could not claim compensation for that boy, Conon, that you killed at the Festival, but they will take any excuse to come after you, now!"

For a week the sky had been cloudy, with a damp smell in the air that promised rain. Maira took a precise grip on six or seven wheat stalks, severed them neatly, and dropped the heads of grain into the capacious pocket of the leathern apron she wore.

At Lughnasa, when a rainstorm would have signalled good fortune, the skies had held their waters like a cow refusing to let down her milk, Maira thought grimly. But it would be disastrous if it rained now, while they were still getting the harvest in.

Sun and wind and rainfall varied from field to field. For the past week they had waited for this one to be ready, each day biting a grain seed to see if it was hard all the way through. But this was one of the last fields. And though the wheat was parched and withered from the drought of early summer, if they could reap it before the rains came they might get through the winter without too much suffering.

If the rains held off, and the Selgovae calmed down and accepted their losses, she thought grimly. Two weeks had passed since the news of the raid on Din Carn; two weeks of wondering what was going to happen, when their attention should be all on the harvesting.

As hers should be now. . . . The sickle grazed her reaching fingers and Maira forced her attention back to the task at hand. She was peripherally aware of the movement around her as the other reapers bent, straightened, and bent again. Almost everyone had some part in the harvesting—reaping, winnowing, or following the reapers to glean any heads of grain that had been overlooked or had fallen to the ground.

A shadow fell across Maira's hands.

"Daughter, are you thirsty?"

Maira finished her stroke, dropped the grain into the pouch and turned to see her mother holding out a leathern waterskin.

"Barley-water," Druith explained. "It will cool you."

Maira straightened, rubbing at the small of her back, and sighed. The waning of the moon had brought on her bleeding-time. She gave her woman's blood back to the earth with mixed relief and sorrow at the knowledge that she did not carry Carric's child.

Druith handed her the waterskin and Maira set the mouth-piece to her lips and sucked greedily, realizing only as the cool liquid went down her throat how dry she was. The clouds cut off the direct rays of the sun without cooling the air. It was a muggy, damp, sort of heat in which one sweated copiously without understanding why.

"You are doing well," said Druith, looking at the bristling stubble of the half of the field they had done. In a few days, when the grain was threshed and stored, they would come back to cut and stack the straw.

Maira nodded. She and her mother had worked their way back to a careful tolerance since the Festival. There were moments when she wanted to run and lay her head in Druith's ample lap and cry like a little girl. But what if her mother said she should have married Carric sooner and prevented all this, or worse still, told her to stop thinking about the Selgovae warrior?

"Maelor has come back from Carbantorigum," her mother said then.

Maira swallowed too quickly, coughed, and wiped her mouth with the back of her hand. "What does the High King say?"

Druith shrugged. "Since Conon's death was an accident of the Festival, he holds that we owe no honor-price to Din Carn, and he only laughed about the cattle. He has sent messages to King Buan of the Selgovae at Trimontium, but you can guess how long it will take them to get there, or how much good that will do."

Maira spat into the dust. "Segovis is a do-nothing, a fool! How can he expect us to support him if this is all the help he gives? *He* is not living on the Selgovae border! We would get a faster response from Luguvalium!"

"Hah!" Her mother grinned without humor. "We would have to be desperate indeed to call the Red Crests in! But I think we do better to worry about the harvest, now."

Maira nodded, and her mother moved on with the waterskin.

For a moment the girl watched her, then sighed, reached and cut another handful of grain. Eoc moved past her, grasping and snapping the stalks by hand. Every autumn the old men argued about which was the best method for reaping, just as every spring they disputed over the most effective way to yoke oxen to the plough.

Maira thought that doing it by hand was probably quicker, but the harsh stems and sharp ends of the bearded wheat left her fingers scratched and sore by the end of a day. She preferred to trust to her dexterity with the short, right-angled sickle to avoid harvesting her fingers along with the grain.

Her father had always belonged to the faction that favored the sickle, holding that the control it required transferred to skill with a sword. But he was harvesting by hand this year. Maira wondered if anyone had thought to ask him why, and whether he knew himself that he feared to let any more of his blood feed the ground.

Conmor looked older. Maira was sure there was more grey in his hair. Did he doubt his own courage now, or was it the knowledge that his people were threatened and there was nothing he could do? She had heard him in the night, turning restlessly and moaning in his sleep, but she was afraid to ask him what he dreamed.

She knew that somehow this crisis would pass, but other dangers were sure to come. When Cador of Din Carn died Carric was likely to succeed him. If they were married, she would have to help her husband lead his clan. She wished that her father would let her help *him* now!

But what, after all, could any of them do? Her belief that Carric still loved her and was trying to make peace was all that had sustained her since the Festival. She would have gone to him, but the Selgovae could only accept her as a hostage, as things were now. And even if such a relationship were not certain to kill the love growing between her and Carric, she would never allow herself to be used against her people.

Maira's lips set grimly, and she struck at the grain as if it were her enemy.

"Long ago, the Goddess lived on an island with Her two children." Gutuator's deep voice filled the house. He had walked through the gate of Lys Speiat that afternoon, though no one had seen from where he came. "And Her daughter was as fair as a flower, but Her son was the ugliest creature born. . . ."

Maira leaned against her father's knee, watching the Druid, wondering what business had brought him here. The household had drawn close around the fire to hear him, as if they were the last people in a world of darkness, drawing comfort from stories of the gods.

"And She determined that if Her son could not be beautiful, he should be the wisest of men. So She set a cauldron to simmering, and in it She put herbs of great power. And always She was seeking new plants to add to the potion, so She set a little dwarf to tend the fire."

Conmor sighed, and Maira saw his eyes fixed, haunted, as if he heard not the tale the Druid was telling, but some darker history. She shivered and felt him pat her shoulder absently, as he might stroke a dog.

"For a year and a day Gwion tended the cauldron," said Gutuator. He looked around the circle, waiting till he held their eyes. "Then the liquid boiled and three drops burned his hand. Gwion put his fingers in his mouth to soothe them, and suddenly he understood the songs of the birds and the whispers of the trees. Knowledge of all times past and future flooded his memory . . ."

Maira swallowed uneasily, remembering the water of the sacred pool that she had drunk from the black bowl and the knowledge that had teased at her awareness. And that had been only a symbol. . . .

"And then Gwion was afraid. Surely the Goddess would slay him for having tasted Her power! So he fled, and as he had foreseen, the Goddess came after him. Terror pushed him to transformation. He became a hare, but She was the pursuing hound. Then he changed to a fish, but the Goddess became a she-otter, dipping Her swift paw into the stream. Gwion turned into a bird, and She struck as a falcon from the skies. He had been a creature of warm blood, and a creature of the waters, and a creature of air, you see," the Druid explained, "and last he chose to become a creature of earth—a single grain of wheat."

They all nodded, thinking of the harvest just gathered in. How indeed could anyone single out one from a heap of golden grain? Gutuator paused, letting the tension build, then went on.

"But *She* saw him. With one peck She swallowed him, and he lay in Her belly as the herbs had floated in the cauldron, until the time was accomplished and the Goddess bore him as Her child."

There was a kind of uneasy silence. They had heard many stories of the birth of the Son, but this one was disturbing. What kind of a Mother was this, who pursued and then devoured her child? Eoc glanced at Druith with uneasy eyes.

"What happened then?" Beth held Acorn to her breast defensively.

"Then She cast him upon the waters," said Gutuator, "for Her work was done. The stream bore him to a great chieftain, who raised him as his own, and the child grew to be a great bard, and the wisest of men."

Maira cast back through her memory for legends of great bards. "Who was he?" she asked finally. "When did he live?"

"He has lived many times," said Gutuator gently, "and he has had many names. And no doubt, if there is a need for him, he will be born again."

"I don't understand," said Eoc suddenly. "Why did the Goddess go to such trouble to devour him if he still had all Her wisdom in the end?"

"You will only know the answer to that question if you dare to drink from Her cauldron. . . ."

Maira stared at her grandfather, the questions she had wanted to ask dying in her throat. But later, when she lay in her bed and the house was settling to sleep around her, they echoed in her consciousness. She had drunk from the cauldron too, and she was afraid.

Finally she slept, but her dreams were haunted. She was climbing a dark mountain, trying to shield her face from sleet that turned to snow. And then a deeper shadow loomed before her, and within it flickered the mocking light of a fire. Eagerly she hastened toward it, and saw a cauldron heating over the flames.

"She seeks the cauldron," said a voice like a raven's call.

"What she seeks she shall find," another answered her.

And suddenly the flames billowed around her. Coughing, Maira tried to get away, but dark figures cast their cloaks over her. She fought wildly against the cloth that encumbered her and sat up, gasping, her blankets cascading to the floor.

A dream, Maira thought. *It was a dream*. She took a deep

breath, and coughed again. For a moment she held her breath, then, fearfully, she tested the air.

Smoke! Maira stumbled over the bedclothes and yanked open her curtains, staring at the hearth. But any embers still alive there were hidden by ash. Now the smell was stronger. Light flickered and she looked up and saw the thatch kindling as she heard the clattering of hooves outside.

"Fire!" she yelled and grabbed her cloak, Roud's ornamented bridle, and her belt with its sheathed knife. "Wake up and get out, everybody—it's the Selgovae! War! War!" The last words were a shriek. Maira grabbed her lance and sling and dove for the door as the room exploded into motion behind her. Above the yells of the baby her father shouted orders that no one could hear.

Old Ness was struggling to get out of her bed by the door. Maira picked her up and thrust her outside, throwing her blanket after her. Wailing, Beth stumbled forward with the squalling baby in her arms. Maira grabbed her arm and shoved her after Ness, who led her to the relative safety of the water-trough in the yard.

Cattle were lumbering past the gate, and above the heaving backs Maira glimpsed the silhouette of a horseman. She fitted a stone into the belly of her sling and let fly. There was a shout of pain, but the man did not fall.

"Winged him, sister—but it was a good shot all the same!" said Eoc. Maira glanced back and saw that he and her father and Tadhg had their swords.

"Where's mother?" she asked. Conmor jerked his head back toward the house. Most of the thatch had caught now and flame swirled upward. In the doorway she saw movement and another load of goods was tossed into the yard.

"Blessed Goddess!" She dropped her sling and dashed toward the door.

"She wouldn't come!" her father shouted after her, and then, "Eoc—watch out!"

Maira glimpsed a rider at the gate, but the heat of the fire seared her skin. She dodged as the loom came through the door and grabbed her mother's arm. Druith was screaming, trying to get back inside, but Maira would not let go.

Metal clashed from the gate, and suddenly Druith stopped struggling. They both turned, staring at the horseman who had come through it. His pony reared as he turned it. Red fire flared from his sword. Eoc yelled, dancing back and forth as he tried to get in a blow. Conmor grabbed Maira's sling and tried to pick off some of the riders who milled about just outside.

And then Eoc's impatience mastered him and he rushed in just as his enemy turned to face him, and the sword slashed down.

Druith shrieked as the blade came away red. Eoc clutched at his shattered shoulder and fell. Then Conmor roared, going for the Selgovae with his own sword swinging.

"Not my son! It was supposed to be me!" he cried. "Not my only son!"

The enemy warrior jerked back and the Novantae chieftain's sword grazed the top of his thigh and slashed into the horse's flank. The horse, already hysterical from the scent of the fire, trumpeted its anguish and reared as if to shake off the pain.

But it was the rider who came off instead, throwing himself free when he realized he could not control his mount. Grinning, he found his feet and faced Conmor.

Maira followed her mother toward Eoc's body at a run. Druith shoved a rag against the wound. As she tried to tie it Maira caught a momentary glimpse of severed muscles and the white gleam of bone. Then welling blood covered them and Druith pressed the soaked cloth down again. Hooves pounded close by. Maira wrenched around and flapped desperately with her cloak to spook the wounded horse away.

"I am Conmor son of Ycuit, chieftain of the White Horse Clan! Stand and fight, Selgovae dog!" Maira heard her father's shout.

"I can save Eoc," Druith whispered harshly. "We must get him out of the way!"

Maira saw her father stalking his foe, bit her lip and nodded, and got her arms underneath Eoc's long legs, taking as much of his weight as she could while her mother supported him on her breast and at the same time tried to keep pressure on the shoulder wound.

"My name is Trost map Yvi, but it is not you I came to kill," came the voice of the other man. "Eoc slew my brother Conon and now I've avenged him. We're quits now, old man, so hold your blade!"

Maira blinked. The voice had sounded familiar—but it was not Carric. Relief blurred her eyes. Of course it would be Trost, still burning for revenge.

Conmor did not answer. Looking back at him Maira met his bleak gaze, then saw something change in his eyes as he realized what his wife and daughter were doing. One did not move a dead body with such agonizing care. . . .

His face had not changed, but something in his stance drew Trost's attention. The Selgovae began to turn to see and Conmor made a sound like a snarl and attacked.

Inch by inch Maira moved, feeling the dreadful slackness in Eoc's long limbs. He was heavier than she could have imagined, but at least he was still warm. And then they reached the tenuous refuge by the water-trough, and Ness and Beth were struggling to help Druith get Eoc's bleeding under control.

Maira stood up, working her shoulders back and forth to unknot them, straining to see how the fight between Trost and her father had gone. They were still battling. Maira stumbled back toward them, and from somewhere beyond the milling cattle she heard someone calling Trost's name, calling for him to stop, to come back.

Conmor was driving the Selgovae back toward the gate, but Maira wondered why her father had not killed the other man. There—Trost's cut downward left his upper body exposed for just a little too long. Maira moved more quickly, saw her lance where she had dropped it, and grabbed for it. Was Conmor sparing Trost to stop the feud?

And now they were at the gate. Conmor halted, and very deliberately, lowered his sword. Trost, who had been about to flee, wavered, staring at him.

"A life for a life," said Conmor in a soft voice that echoed like thunder in Maira's ears. "If I owe it, then this is the time. . . ."

For a moment more Trost hesitated. Then something like lust came into his eyes and he began to move. Maira drew back her arm. Trost leaped forward, sword raised, and the lance left Maira's hand, but Conmor did not even try to get away.

Like a stooping hawk the lance winged toward its prey, but even as it transfixed him, Trost's arm came down. Maira did not see it. Running, she saw only the bright blade bite and her father's severed head hurtle through the air.

Instinctively she dashed toward it and bore it back to the body. They had saved her brother—perhaps. . . . Maira knew she was not thinking quite clearly. She fell to her knees by the headless body with the corpse of its slayer fallen over it, saw the lance rising from Trost's body like a standard, and looked into the empty eyes of the head cradled in her arms.

"Father—I've killed him. I've avenged you already! Do you see?" Gently she turned the head so that the dulling eyes could see Trost's contorted face.

"Trost!" From some great distance came the voice she had heard before. Hoofbeats echoed the rumble of thunder overhead. Maira took the sword from her father's nerveless hand.

A bay stallion, seeming redder in the firelight, slid to a halt, snorting and shaking its head at the fire. Maira, with her father's sword clenched in her hand and her naked breasts reddened by her father's blood, gazed up into Carric's eyes. She saw his face whiten as he looked at the two bodies, and at her. "Blessed sweet Goddess, you've killed him. . . ."

"The Goddess is not sweet and blessed, Carric," Maira said. "She has a terrible tearing beak, Carric, and great beating wings. Don't you hear them? I do . . . She is coming, and death will be the least of Her gifts to the Selgovae! Do you hear that, my father?" She bent to the head in her lap and it seemed to her that she heard a murmur of assent from not too far away. "Yes," she murmured, "you hear me, and I will not betray you again!"

Carric stared at her.

"Do you think I am mad, Carric?" Slowly Maira got to her feet. The sword was still in her hand, the head cradled in her arm. "Perhaps, but it is *Her* madness. They are *your* men—you should have been able to stop them. Carric, I won't die of this grief . . . *you* will."

She wound her fingers into her father's long hair, and holding the head before her like a talisman and his sword at the guard, she took one step toward Carric, then another, until the stallion, obeying an involuntary tug at the rein or perhaps its own terror, began to tremble and back away.

"Now you begin to understand, and to be afraid!" Maira lifted the sword and the horse, startled by the motion and the scent of blood, made a stiff-legged jump away. Carric wrestled it back to obedience, but more hoofbeats were coming, more riders with shocked faces clustering round.

"Carric, come away! The whole vale is boiling with men—let's take the cattle and be gone!"

"Yes, go, Carric!" cried Maira. "Next time, your kinsmen will not be able to rescue you!"

His face worked with indecision—to fight her, to plead with her, or to flee? Maira could not tell, but suddenly he seemed ridiculous, sitting there. She began to laugh, and one of his men snatched at his reins and hauled him away.

And that was even funnier. Her laughter mingled with the sound of retreating hoofbeats and distant thunder as the rain finally began to fall.

And suddenly she saw folk from the other raths up and down the Scaur Water, getting the Lys Speiat folk to shelter, beating at the fire. Druith was wailing over Conmor's corpse. Someone came to Maira, wanting to reunite the chieftain's head with his body so that they could prepare it for burial.

"No." Maira shook her head, and their shocked expressions almost set her to laughing again. But her mind was clearing a little now, and she knew they would not understand.

"No." More clearly, she said it again. "I killed his slayer—the decision is mine. Conmor led us in life, and his head is too holy a talisman to let go. . . ." She remembered how the head of the slain bull had presided over the Lughnasa Festival. "We will preserve it, as they did in the old days, and he will guide us still."

They stared at her. It was an ancient custom, but they all understood what she was trying to say. They looked at each other doubtfully, and then, with relief, at the white figure who had joined them.

Gutuator. . . . He had finally gotten down to them from the hut he had up the hill. *If he had only come sooner*. Maira stopped the thought, knowing she had no room for 'ifs' anymore. For a long moment she met her grandfather's gaze.

"Yes," he said finally. "It can be done. Give the head to me."

Maira bit her lip, doubting him, but his eyes were steady on hers. The first waves of reaction lapped at her, but her brother was near death and her mother wailing for Conmor. There was so much still to do. . . .

Gutuator came to her and she let him take Conmor's head from her hands. There was a sigh from the crowd as the Druid took the chieftain's head into his keeping, and Maira felt curiously lighter. She took a deep breath, and shook back her wet hair. A face she knew glimmered from the mass of the crowd.

"Maelor," she said, almost steadily. "Did they burn any other dwellings? Who?" Swift question and answer sent him off to see that the homeless had shelter, and then there were others with questions, more orders to be given. Men came and went away with a palpable sense of relief that someone from the chieftain's House was still in charge.

And finally they were all gone, and Maira was alone in the wet dawn beside the smoking timbers of her home. And then, at last, she sat down in the reddened mud and allowed the tears to come.

SIX

Conmor's Head

THE SUN WAS going down in fire and splendor behind the black peak of Din Rhun. But as the fires of daylight faded in the west, another fire flickered, caught, and began to burn on the eastern slope of the hill. Gutuator the Druid stood between the hill and the fire; its light bloodied the white specklings of the goose-wing headdress he wore and the dun bull-hide that cloaked him, and glowed with a dull sheen on the black garments that covered Druith in her place at the northern end of the pyre.

Maira's fingers tightened on the coarse wool of her own black robe, then released. For a moment the fire flared high, veiling the pyre; then it subsided and again she saw the body—cleansed, dressed in all the finery the clan could offer, its missing head represented by Conmor's helm of gilded bronze.

For three days they had watched beside Conmor's body, the women wailing with a sustained ululation that rasped each separate nerve, the men adding the irregular rhythm of their own grunted pain. The dreadful music of it still rang in Maira's memory. But now at last the mourners were silent. Surely Conmor's spirit must be satisfied with the grief they had given him, and eager to be gone.

Gone, thought Maira. *He will leave us alone, and what will we do?* Flame struck a brighter gold from the helmet and Maira stared at it, remembering why it was there. Conmor's cleansed skull was already enshrined in the wicker enclosure that protected the sacred spring. Though the Druid's arts might send the spirit to the Otherworld and Conmor's ghost go below ground, still the chieftain's wisdom would remain to watch over them. Maira clung to the thought as she gripped the cloth of her gown.

"Out of four sacred elements our bodies are compounded. . . ." Gutuator lifted his hands and the murmuring crowd grew still.

Maira saw the fearful faces of the women and the frowns of the warriors. Conmor's old friend Waric stood in the front row, with Maelscuit next to him, resplendent in a crimson cloak and all of his jewelry, as if he were already chief of the clan. Eoc's sword-brothers Rosic and Kenow stood together, looking unhappily at the spot where their lord should have stood. But Eoc still lay in his bed in Maelor's steading, weak as a new calf and muttering with fever, while Beth hovered over him. It should have been Eoc who tossed the first brand into the pyre, but in his absence Maelscuit had claimed that honor as the closest male kin.

Maira's gaze moved on. She saw compassion in Urr's brown eyes and felt her own fill with tears. He and his sons had been like arms and legs to her in the planning for this funeral—they, and Maelor, and the other folk of the vale. And now all the heads of households were gathered here, nearly two hundred strong, the assembled strength of the Vindomarci.

"First, we are earth—our flesh, our bones and the food that builds them. As children of the earth we return our bodies to her keeping when we are done with them. . . ." The Druid bent and pressed his hand against the grass in homage. The people grew quieter, until Maira heard only the whisper of the wind and the crackling of the fire. There were so many people—how could they stay so still? And who would watch over them when Conmor's ashes lay beneath his mound?

"Second, we are air—the wind of the spirit that passes outward with the breath of life and goes we know not where. Listen to the wind, my children, for it bears the spirit home!"

Maira flinched as wind gusted up the hillside and swirled the flames of the pyre over the grass. Was that Conmor's spirit, hovering over the fire in which his body burned? Or was it a wind that Gutuator had summoned to bear the dead chieftain's spirit away?

"Third, we are fire—the fire of life which warms our flesh and in which the other elements combine. As holy fire made this flesh to live among us, fire shall transmute it into its several elements again and free Conmor's spirit to journey where it may be renewed and reborn!''

The heat of the fire stung Maira's skin. She stared into that golden glow, and as the wind shifted, she saw for a moment the shell of her father's body, filled with flame.

"And finally, we are water," said the Druid, "the waters of the wombs that bear us, of the male seed that quickens us, the blood that flows in our veins. Blood is the water of life; Conmor's blood has fed the earth—may his sacrifice be acceptable to the gods!''

From the dark figures behind Druith came a low ululation of agreement, and Maira shivered. The old women of the clan had taken up position behind her mother like a flock of ravens, and with eyes that seemed to gleam with the same malicious twinkle as they looked at her. Yes, surely they would know about sacrifice—but why, oh why, had Conmor felt required to make the offering? Once more she saw the slow descent of the Selgovan sword and bit her lip, as if pain could banish the memory.

"Fire burn!" Gutuator cried in a great voice, and the people echoed him.

"Wind blow!"

"Flesh consume!"

"Spirit go!"

Sparks exploded upward, challenging the stars, as if the breath of the people had been a gust of wind. The Druid straightened; the swing of his robes as he raised his arms was like the lifting of great wings.

"Windkeeper, I call you! Come from your hallowed home! Over hill, over meadow and the restless grey waters, come to my summoning, now I command you. Send us the wind of your hard-beating wings!''

And once more the wind gusted, then settled to a steady pressure against Maira's right cheek. The flames slanted westward, roaring furiously.

"Conmor!" shouted the Druid, and the hair rose on Maira's arms at the sudden sense of attentiveness in the air. "Conmor son of Ycuit, lord of Din Rhun, I call you to hear me! The funeral feast is laid, your way is prepared. Your new mount awaits you, swifter than any stallion! Soon we will feast you and clean earth will comfort your bones. But your spirit must fare onward. Listen while I show you your road. . . .''

The light beyond the eastern hills was fading, but the

western sky still glowed as if beyond the sea someone had lit a great beacon to guide Conmor home.

"First comes the darkness," chanted Gutuator, "but you must not fear it. You see the dark tunnel through which you must pass. Through just such a passage you emerged into this life, so go forward boldly, as you are a warrior.

"And as you fare forward, you will see brightness burning —a fair light that shines from the form of your Guide. Now you must go to Her; She is your Way-shower. Her beauty like spring water, Her voice like singing birds. So fair, She brings forgetting of all you have known here, and remembrance of the lovely land, your eternal home. . . ."

It was almost dark now. The first stars shone like the eyes of the Lady. The hills bulked dark and featureless against the sky.

"Onward, fare onward, Conmor my brave son. Go boldly over the gulfs that gape for you. The roaring beasts' devouring jaws, you must pass by. You will go safely, for the Lady is with you. All evil slumbers when She shakes the silver bells.

"Onward, fare onward, though the dark wings of ravens may threaten like thunder—for now comes sweet singing, and the white wings of swans. Their song bears you onward, over the sword-bridge to the island of apples whose fruit feeds the gods."

From the circle of watchers came a single sigh. Half-entranced by the chanting, Maira gazed around her. The women's robes were rent in mourning, their hair disheveled, and the moustaches of the men glittered with bright tears. But every eye shone with the light of the lovely land, and it seemed to Maira then that it was not such an ill thing to die—not if you were a warrior, and the people bid you farewell and a Druid guided your soul.

With a brief, distracting triumph she remembered Trost's unceremoniously buried body, imprisoning his spirit forever in the earth unless he should find the wisdom to make his own way home. In Din Carn they would mourn for him, but how could their prayers pierce the barrier Novantae grief had raised between them? She thought they could not—she hoped not! And this was only the beginning of the honor-price she meant to make the Selgovae pay!

"Onward, fare onward to the Isle of the Blessed," Gutuator said slowly. "For there you shall dwell with the gods' own fine harpers to play you their music, and all the fair women filling your cup with mead. Great warriors shall you meet there, and masters of every craft. Fair men and women will be your companions there.

"And then for awhile you will dwell among them, till the time of your transforming, when you are reborn to the Clan."

"Reborn! You shall be reborn!" The cry swept the circle, echoing the Druid's words. "Do not come as a bull or a hawk in the heavens," shouted one, "but return as a man, Conmor, a warrior for the tribe!"

"Come to me, Conmor!" cried Maelor's wife Britta, clapping hands to her belly. "You will be welcome in my womb!"

Maira closed her eyes, feeling the fire's heat dry her tears as quickly as they appeared. If she had had a husband, it was *her* belly to which the spirit of her father must have come—but the manner of his dying made that impossible now.

Not as my child but as your own self I will keep you, she thought then, remembering the stripped skull enshrined above the spring. The west was dark now, except for one bright star that shone just above the line of the hill. The logs of the pyre had fallen into a heap of dully glowing coals. *The flesh is freed, and the eternal spirit knows its road, but your ghost will remain here, my father, and tell me what to do now!"*

Maira's gaze moved from the coals to the faces lit by their glow. In that dim light she had to guess at their features, but she knew that Waric's lined face was twisted with loss, while the chanting had left in Maelor's eyes an afterglow of joy. Calgac the High King's son looked as if he were thinking of something else entirely, and cousin Maelscuit stared blankly, his fingers rubbing absently at the golden arm ring he wore.

Maira marked it, weighing them, wondering what they would do now. She realized that their grief and anger had no focus. They would mourn, but without leadership, that was all they would do.

The chieftain provides that focus for his people, she thought, frowning, *but we have no chieftain now. When the wake is over and the barrow raised over Conmor's bones, they will have to call council and decide who will take his place.*

She had always assumed that Eoc would be the next chieftain, but then she had always assumed that the time of choosing would come years from now, that her father would die old, and by that time Eoc would be a seasoned warrior with a growing family. And now her father was dead in his prime, and Eoc might well die too. Even if he lived, who could tell whether his shattered arm would heal well enough for him to fight again?

Maelscuit map Bituit was their closest kin, and barely within the eligible degrees for election at that, for both of Conmor's brothers had died in the last Roman war, and they left no sons. The idea that the leadership might pass from her line rankled, and the vision of Din Rhun with another lord was like a spear to the heart.

Her gaze moved once more to Maelscuit's smug face. She thought, *If they make him chieftain he will bless the gods and hold to what he has*. And the lands Maelscuit already possessed lay westward. How much would he worry about protecting the people of Scaur Vale from the Selgovae attacks that must come if they appeared defenceless? And what honor would impel him to punish Din Carn for the night's work just done?

The low murmur of Gutuator's chanting ceased. He straightened and paced slowly deasil around the pyre, moving from west to north, to east and south and back to his place again.

"From the land of death to the land of life I come. Now Conmor's body is transmuted and his spirit flies free. Let us go now to feast him and give him strength for the way he must go." With a final salute to the dying pyre, the Druid strode down the hill. Black-robed women flowed like a dark wave around Druith, bearing her after him.

"We will feast to strengthen his spirit and appease his ghost," said Waric in a low voice.

"Only vengeance will do that, and you know it well," said Maira clearly. She shook back her bright hair and stepped in front of the warriors, and something in her carriage held them back while she passed before them down the hill.

They had set up trestle tables in the hollow between the peak of Din Rhun and the step-hill, just outside the remains of the fort's outer wall. The wavering light of the torches on their poles lit the bothies the clanfolk had built for temporary shelter during the funeral. In the center was the fire, and the spit which bore the browned and sizzling carcass of the boar.

It was always boar for a funeral feast—the beast of the Earth Goddess and the Underworld, sacrificed to propitiate the dark spirits who would hold the dead man's flesh and the ghost that clung to it while the immortal spirit winged free.

Maira shivered in spite of the warmth of the grey cloak she

wore. Up on the hill, Gutuator's words had almost succeeded in comforting her. But he did not tell all of the story. The pure spirit was beneficent, but there was another part of the soul that was not so kindly. Conmor's ghost would surely haunt them if his burnt bones were not consigned to the sheltering earth with the proper rituals.

And although earth already imprisoned Conmor's killer, the vengeance would not be complete until the clan from which he came was punished. Surely that was why Maira's belly still burned with the need to see Selgovae blood. She shut away memory of the pain she had seen in Carric's eyes and stared at the boar that burned as Conmor's body had burned. The platter in front of the empty high seat held the haunch of roast meat that would be buried with Conmor's bones to sustain that part of his spirit that the barrow contained.

She tried to eat a piece of bread, but it seemed tasteless. Two tables away Antiochus the trader was telling some of the younger warriors how he had heard the Selgovae gloating over Conmor's death when he was last in Din Carn. The bread crumbled in Maira's clenched fingers. The trader had told her the story when he arrived, full of avuncular concern and flowery expressions of sympathy. If Antiochus was so sympathetic, how could he continue to trade with the Selgovae? she wondered then, but she supposed she should be grateful he brought them news of their enemies. If her father had listened to his warning the last time he came, he might still be alive!

I will listen to you, Antiochus! she said silently, *Feed me all your poison—it will only nourish my determination to be revenged!*

Maira looked at her mother, wondering how she was taking it, and then quickly away. Druith looked *old*, and Maira felt suddenly very much alone. A week ago, she had been worried, but she had been protected. Now in one way or another she had lost father, mother and brother, and her hope of a husband was gone. What was left for her now?

Temella laid a gentle hand on her arm. "Can I get you something else? Perhaps some more mead?" Her eyes were dark with concern and a kind of avid interest as well. For a moment Maira longed for the sweet oblivion that mead could bring; then she shook her head.

"Thank you—are there any berries or apples left?"

Temella got up to look for them, and Maira heard a soft harp-note and turned her head. She saw Tadhg at the lower end of the men's table, his instrument cradled in his arms. His platter of meat sat untouched before him. She wondered if he had eaten since Conmor died; she had not heard him speak at all. His gaze was dull, unseeing.

Are my eyes like that? she wondered. *He is like a struck stag who does not yet understand the death that is dragging him down. Oh Conmor, my father, how could you leave us alone?*

For a moment the harp's painful music came clearly. Maelscuit got to his feet and the music faded to silence as he lifted his hand.

"My clansmen and kinfolk, we are gathered here to mourn the death and to celebrate the life of Conmor our dear Lord. Let us drink to him!" He held his cup high, a movement repeated along the tables like wind lifting the branches of trees.

Maira raised her cup in salute, then set it to her lips with a prayer that his spirit should fill her as she was filled by the mead. Old Idha had settled like a crow beside Druith and was patting her hand, pressing her to drink as well. Druith shivered and seemed to come back to herself from some far land in which she had been wandering. Maira looked at them resentfully. It was she who should have comforted her mother, or rather her mother who should have been comforting her. Confusion held her still, and the moment passed.

"Tonight we are feasting on the funeral boar!" said Waric hoarsely, "But I remember when he and I were lads, and Conmor killed his first boar alone. . . ."

Men stirred and stilled along the tables, settling themselves to hear the tale.

"The beast had been raiding the cornfields and rooting up the young grain. Kennet's son Conn took his dogs to drive it away, but it killed one of the dogs and wounded the other and wounded Conn so that he limped ever after. But Conmor heard of it and thought he would make a hunting. Kennet was oathed to Conmor's father, you see, but they were both off away to Blatobulgium for some meeting of the chieftains they were holding there. That was before the Red Crests pulled the fortress down, you see, and—"

"Go on with you, Waric!" someone cried. "What about the hunt?"

Waric held up a gnarled hand. "I'll not mar a good tale because you have no patience. First you must know why the two of us went out alone."

"No doubt because your sires would have hobbled you like

straying horses to keep you home!'' said his wife. Their three sons were just coming to manhood—no doubt she wished she could stop their ears with beeswax now!

"Well, perhaps we were foolish." Waric grinned. "But we were young and strong, and Conmor would not share the glory. Not even with me," he added, "but that he knew he would need a good man behind him. And I insisted—I did not oath to him to be left behind when there was a fight in store!"

"And so you two set out together," said Dumnoric, Temella's promised man. "Where did you find the boar?"

"Ah—you're impatient. That's not hard to understand. Conmor and I had no patience either, when we were young." Waric smiled benignly, and Maira found her lips twitching in an unfamiliar smile. She had heard parts of this tale from her father long ago.

"It was a grey morning, with the mists lying heavy on the hills as if someone had thrown a sheep's fleece across them to keep them warm. And cold, too—we shivered as we crept out of the steading and through the dew-wet grass to the woods where we had hidden our weapons the night before. We did not want anyone to see us leaving with them and ask what we meant to do."

Yes, that was close enough to the way Conmor had told it, Maira remembered, though he had also said Waric overslept, and he had to wake him without answering questions from the rest of the household about their purpose at such an hour.

"And we made our way to the heart of the forest, where the monster laired—a great beast, black-bristled, with tusks like knives. We had no dogs to ring him, but he had made a trail down to his favorite wallow. The brush was thick to either side, so we lay in wait for him there."

Now that Waric was finally coming to it, the others stilled. Even Maira held her breath, and she had heard the story before. For a moment she could hear her father's voice, telling it, and she fought back tears.

"And then we heard the boar coming, and when he had passed me I jumped out behind him and Conmor sprang to face him with his long lance poised. It was not a proper boar-spear, mind you, but he had bound on a cross-piece, so—"

"In the names of the gods below will you get *on* with the story?" Calgac exclaimed. Waric glared at him, but one did not reprove the High King's son publicly. He sniffed, and after a reproving moment went on.

"The boar gave a kind of grunt and ran straight at Conmor, right onto the spear. You would have thought that would finish him, but the cross-piece broke and he kept going, and I yelled my war-cry and leaped on him, striking with my sword."

He stopped and looked around him with satisfaction. He had had a *reason* to mention the cross-piece, after all.

"And that killed the boar?" asked Dumnoric quickly.

"Oh aye," Waric answered complacently. "There was blood all over, mind you, but when we had washed in the stream Conmor and I realized that none of it was our own, bar some scratches from the brambles. So we gutted the beast where he lay and carried the carcass home on the spear—and a heavy journey that was—harder than the killing had been. But we got it home at last, and then we found out what it was to be heroes!"

Druith stirred a little and Maira turned to her.

"I remember when they returned," her mother said softly. "It was just after that happened that Conmor asked for me. He was as fair as a young god, coming across the pasture with his kill. And now he himself is slain, and his son—" She stopped herself.

"Eoc will heal, mother. Give it time," Maira said automatically.

Druith frowned at the men's table. "But will his inheritance wait for him? Maelscuit lords it there as if he were chieftain already, and if he fails, others will leap to pick up the sword Eoc cannot hold. We have to guard it for him; you must fight for his rights. You have to choose a man who will help you and give the power back to Eoc when he is well."

Maira stared at her. Must she mate herself for Eoc's sake? She saw no one there who was Carric's match, and how could she accept a lesser man? And in any case, would it serve? A weak man could not protect the clan, and a strong one would not want to give up the power.

Maelor had started a new tale of how he had gone as Conmor's armor-bearer ten years before when the Caledonii came down from the north and the tribes rose against Rome. Ulpius Marcellus had brought a great army out from behind the Wall to crush them, but it was not really a victory. The Alban warriors had dispersed like autumn mist, fading into the hills where the Romans' spear-straight roadways did not go. And the fortress of Blatobulgium was still abandoned.

When Maelor finished the men cheered, for many of them

were old enough to remember that fighting, when Conmor had been in his prime.

"A great warrior he was," said Petric. "We will miss him sorely. But his last fight was a good one, I have heard, and he was avenged by one of his own blood." He shifted on his bench and lifted his cup in salute to Maira. The others looked at her uncomfortably, aware that a young woman had accomplished what they considered should have been her brother's task, or theirs.

Maira flushed angrily. The night was wearing on and the feasting was done, but there was another task that they had apparently left for her to do. She got to her feet, and startled, they watched her walk steadily to Tadhg. There had been no proper lament for the chieftain, and if they left it much longer no one would be sober enough to hear.

Tadhg sat, head bowed, agile fingers motionless against the harp's smooth curve. She stopped before him, but he did not move.

"Look at me, man of Eirinn." She kept her voice low. "You ate at Conmor's hearth and slept warm by his fire. Now he is gone, and it is time to mourn. Pick up your sweet singer, harper, and give us a lament for the Lord you have lost!"

Tadhg looked up and Maira flinched from the pain she recognized in his dark eyes. His skin looked even whiter now, as if his blood had flowed with Conmor's into the ground. She had not known he was still in such sorrow. But so was she, and she had played her part in the ritual. Why should he be spared? It was his duty, and his privilege.

"Come—strike the minor chord of mourning," she said gently, reminding him of the time he had tried to explain to her the three measures that brought sorrow, or slumber, or joy.

His answer was a whisper. "If I sing the farewell, then he will be gone. . . ."

Maira felt, like an echo, the ache of loss. Then she remembered the shrine by the spring. "And if I could prove to you that his spirit remains with me here?"

Tadhg stared at her, and she saw his face change and knew a throb of fear. *What have I promised him?* she wondered wildly. *What can I do to justify—*

But the harper's hands were already seeking the taut gut strings, and suddenly the instrument quivered like a bent bow. Maira stepped away and lifted her hand for silence. Conversations stilled, and the first notes of the harp came distinct and

sweet as the call of a bird. Again and again they came, until
men murmured, wondering if the harper was going to sing.

And then at last, when Maira feared that Tadhg would shame
both himself and her, she heard his voice—a raven's croak that
steadied in a moment to a tenor made sweeter by the overtone
of pain.

> *"The sun behind the pointed hill*
> *Goes down; the bird wings to her nest.*
> *In glen and corrie all is still;*
> *The herdsman seeks his nightly rest.*
> *The stars like wild-flowers strew the sky*
> *And all things sleep in peace but I—*
> *My lord is gone. . . ."*

Maira closed her eyes, the beauty of the world around her
piercing her numbness with a poignance all the more painful
for having been suppressed so long. How could the world still
be fair, when her father was no more?

> *"The hall where once he held his state*
> *Is ashes, and the anxious owl*
> *Sits mourning by the shattered gate;*
> *Upon the hills the grey wolves howl.*
> *Oh sing, my harp, of sorrow now,*
> *The painful payment of my vow—*
> *My lord is gone. . . .*
> *When he swung high his sharpened sword*
> *Light scattered bright upon the ground;*
> *Like honey to the tongue his word,*
> *Like gold the justice in him found.*
> *But all his glory now is fled,*
> *His chieftainship is with the dead—*
> *My Lord is gone. . . ."*

The harper's voice grew softer now, and Maira strained to
hear.

> *"Alone and kinless I remain;*
> *Lost is the land where I was born,*

> *And now the lord I loved is slain*
> *And fatherless, his people mourn.*
> *I see the ravens fly once more!*
> *I hear the howling wolves of war!*
> *My lord is gone!"*

Maira shook her head, unable to stop the tears. The harper stared straight ahead of him, his face a mask of pain. His eyes were fixed on some vision beyond the circle of torches and the dim silhouette of the *dun* against the night sky. What did he see?

> *"And shall I change the harp for sword*
> *To slay the kin of those who slew*
> *The one who saved me with a word*
> *When from my own despair I flew?*
> *There is no healing for this pain—*
> *My lord will never come again—*
> *My life is gone. . . ."*

Abruptly Maira realized why Tadhg had not wanted to sing. She recognized the look in his eyes now—that same fey stare that her father had worn when he turned to meet Trost's blade. The assembly was silent, with the deep silence that is a greater tribute than applause, but Tadhg was looking at *her*, as if she alone still connected him to the living world.

I told him that Conmor would still be here, she remembered, and knew that if she could not make it true for him, the harper would die. She felt the weight of the bond between Tadhg and his chieftain upon her, as she had felt the need of the people who came to her as she stood in the mud with her father's blood on her breast and his sword in her hand.

Maira saw the hope beginning to fade from Tadhg's eyes and took a swift step toward him. "Wait! It will be all right. . . . Believe in me. . . ." She was babbling, she did not know what she meant to say.

Tadhg shook his head. "Lady, you are as lovely as the rising sun, but I see only darkness now."

"By the love you bore my father I bind you, Tadhg," she said desperately. "Hold off despair for just a little while!"

He lifted his eyes to hers, and attempted a smile. "What can you do? He is gone."

"Is he?" Determination hardened. "Wait and see."

Someone had struck up an old war ballad. The old women had helped Druith away and others were gathering up the feast's remains. For the moment no one was watching her. Stifling a sob, Maira pulled her cloak around her and slipped away from the circle of firelight. No one called, and in a moment she was stumbling up the track to Din Rhun.

Conmor's pyre was only a faint curl of smoke against the icy stars, and the men who guarded it did not see her pass. Shivering with something more than cold, Maira forced herself along the path to the spring.

There at last she stopped, wondering what to do. The water crooned with its own sweet music, and starlight gleamed softly from the hazel withies that formed the shrine. Maira bent, and saw the white glimmer of Conmor's skull inside.

"Conmor, my father. . . ." Tentatively she reached in and flinched as her fingers brushed the smooth curve of polished bone. She took a deep breath, knelt on the damp stones, and took the skull firmly between her hands.

"Conmor, listen to me," she began again. "The warriors are drinking your funeral mead and telling stories that will grow less truthful as the mead casks grow emptier. Already they are losing the truth of you—some by giving you greater glory, some by trying to diminish what you were.

"What can I do? Eoc still lies wounded; you saved him, but for how long? They will squabble over your lordship like crows on a carcass, and who will keep the leavings from the Selgovae wolves?"

She paused for breath, sure she had heard something, but there was only the gentle voice of the stream.

"Tadhg will die if you have not some word for him! What did you do for him? I have to know!"

Now she heard only the whisper of wind in dry grass. She let the empty skull come to rest in her lap and closed her eyes. And then, in the darkness of her mind, came words.

Daughter, the Bright Land calls me. Let me go. . . .

Maira's pulse pounded in her ears, and for a moment she could hear no more. Then she shook her head.

"No—oh no, my father! I saw you stand to meet that sword, and by that act your people are bereft and I have lost the man I loved! Perhaps your blood bought Eoc's life, but without your counsel, what will we do? You *owe* them, and you owe me, and until the people of Din Carn have paid for your dying, I will not let you go!"

She held up the skull, and in the dim light its shadowed eyes seemed to stare back at her.

By my sacred head and by my blood which runs in you, you hold me here. But I warn you, daughter, you will pay the price of lordship too. Yet if you are determined, then question me, and I will tell you what you want to know. . . .

SEVEN

The Red Stallion

DRUMS POUNDED LIKE galloping hoofbeats, pounded again, and were still. The people of the White Horse Clan settled themselves in a circle according to their callings: in the west the priests and men of learning, in the north the lords and the warriors, the farmers and herders in the east, and in the south all those whose skill supported the great households—the craftsmen, the makers of music and the servants and lesser folk whose contributions were thus recognized. Maira looked around the circle and for a moment felt her heart lifted. She had not seen so many of her people together since her brother's wedding, and never in such an ordered company.

The Vindomarci are a great clan—who shall dare to defy us? she thought proudly, then remembered that they were a clan without a lord, as headless as her father's body beneath its mound, and her face grew grim once more.

The last murmurs stilled as Gutuator came into the center of the circle and thrust the standard with its white horse's tail into the ground.

"This is the law of our people," he said slowly, "that an heir to lands or honors should be chosen from within the four generations of a lineage. Today we are gathered to choose a chieftain for the Clan of the White Horse from the line of Arminorix of Din Rhun."

He bent, struck flint on flint and lit the wood that had been laid ready on the slab of stone. That stone had been there, with the marks of ritual fires upon it, when the Novantae first came into the land. Since then it had been used four times to hallow the choosing of a chieftain. Now Gutuator made the fire as he had made it for the assembly that elected Maira's father. He had been there also in the time of Maira's grandfather, forty years ago, and some said that he had been at the choosing after Arminorix died.

Maira stared at him, realizing that he had never looked any different in all the years of her growing. She looked at the length of his silver beard and the lines in his face and wondered how old Gutuator was now.

I will ask my father, she thought with bitter satisfaction. Her gaze moved past the new mound they had raised over the ornamented bronze bucket that held what remained of Conmor's bones, and his arms, and the food and gifts they had prepared for him. The clan thought they had lost him, but she knew better than they.

Maira saw Tadhg watching her from the other side of the circle and smiled. At least *he* was still alive. That was the first thing her strange companionship with the dead had won for her. She had bound the harper as her father had bound him, by her knowledge of the tragedy that had exiled him from Eirinn. But now that she had his allegiance, what was she to do with it? Was he supposed to play the harp for her while she tended her cows?

"This is the lineage of Arminorix," said the Druid. "In the first generation a son, Brannos, who lived to rule. In the second generation, Brannos' son by his first wife Mandua was Ycuit, and by his second wife Britta he had a daughter, Viduna and a son, Bituit. To make a third generation Ycuit wed with Rhianna the High King's daughter and had two children, Conmor our chieftain and his brother Dagolit who was killed by the Romans along with his two sons ten years ago. Viduna bore a daughter, Maga, who married out of the clan, and another daughter, Druith, who married Conmor. By his wife Ana, Bituit had one son who lived, Maelscuit. In the fourth generation, Conmor and Druith had two living children, Eoc and Maira, and Maelscuit has two little daughters and a young son, Calator."

The litany of names rolled easily from Gutuator's tongue, and the old women ticked them off, one by one, on their fingers. But it was only a formality. Everyone knew that unless they called Maga or one of her children from the north, the only candidates of age to bear the chieftain's torque were

Maelscuit and Druith from the third generation of the lineage, and in the fourth, Conmor's son Eoc, and his daughter Maira.

There was a little pause. A light wind was herding the clouds across the sky, and sunlight and shadow dappled the hills. Maira sat very still, her senses unnaturally sharpened to awareness of the solid earth beneath her, the scent of the grass, the rich colors of the trees and the shape of Din Rhun against the sky. *My land,* she thought, digging her fingers into the soil.

Ambdor map Bron got to his feet and she frowned. He was a big, red-haired fellow, beginning to run to fat, and one of Maelscuit's sworn men. He coughed and looked around him portentously.

"Men of the White Horse, hear me. Tragedy has taken our leader and struck down his son—" He cast a pitying glance toward Eoc, who lay on a stretcher with Tadhg and his sword-brothers beside him. He was bandaged and dosed and wrapped up against the wind, but at least he was *there,* and even Ambdor could not afford to ignore him.

"Only one man of the lineage of Arminorix has both the right and the strength to lead us now. I nominate Maelscuit to be our lord!"

There was a murmur of approval, and Druith gripped Maira's arm. "He will take it away from Eoc—you must *do* something!"

Maira stared at her. Druith herself was of the lineage; why didn't she claim the sovereignty herself, and rule after her husband as Boudicca had done? But her mother was sitting still, shivering, as if that one plea was the most she could do. Her face was as worn and desolate as a winter field, and Maira felt anger mixed with an unwilling pity as she looked at her. *Old woman,* she thought, *you should have died with your man.*

Dumnoric jumped to his feet, with Rosic and Kenow close beside him. "My lord Eoc is descended through the lineage two ways, and from an older line!"

"And he lies there with a shattered arm," said Ambdor. "It is not the lad's fault, surely, but who knows when he will sit a horse again, much less wield a sword?"

He waited while men spoke in low tones and women whispered behind their hands. Maelscuit looked a little white around the mouth. He was sitting very still, trying to conceal his eagerness. *He must have given up all hope of ever seeing this day,* Maira thought bitterly.

Calgac got to his feet, the princely torque glinting on his neck, and the people quieted to hear him. He was a fair enough young man, with light, ruffled hair like the breast of a wood dove, but Maira thought she saw a hint of petulance in the set of his lips and of weakness in the line of his jaw.

"If you cannot agree," the prince said winningly, "the High King will authorize a change in line. Elect a man whom the High King will approve, a strong man to lead you." He smiled complacently, and everyone knew whom he had in mind. There was more murmuring then, for Calgac was an outsider, and it was bad form to propose oneself, however obliquely. His own warriors stretched and grinned, and Maira realized abruptly that there could be worse things than to be ruled by Maelscuit.

"Eoc will recover—let us not reject Conmor's line because of temporary misfortune!" cried Kenow.

"With the Selgovae snapping at our heels?" objected one of Maelscuit's men. "We cannot afford to be leaderless! Maelscuit has already sired children to follow him, and he is a proven warrior."

"He proved how fast he could run when the Romans came," Waric commented softly, but not so softly that those around him did not hear, and laugh.

Maira bit her lip, knowing that if anything were to be done, it must be soon.

Brenna merch Conbrit, a big strong woman who had ridden with the men in the Roman wars rose to speak. Maira remembered having cited her exploits when she asked Conmor to let her train with the sword, but she did not know her well.

"Clan and kinfolk, listen to me—let us remember what is most important here. We want no leader who will seek rule for the sake of glory. We are a border people, and we need to see first to the safety of men and cattle and land. I will not support any candidate now, but I ask you to consider well when you choose. Who has both the courage to lead us in battle and the will to organize our defense? We need a man who will have the patience to conciliate, the compassion to comfort, and the discipline to put the people's good before his own!"

"Where will you find such a man, Brenna?" asked Waric with a short laugh. "Do you think the gods will send us a lord from the Otherworld? Let us hold with the blood of Conmor!"

But not to Eoc, Maira thought suddenly, for it was her

brother's own heedlessness that had crippled him. He was not the man Brenna had described, the man needed to lead the tribe.

"There is another child of Conmor's blood." Calgac stood up again, settling the folds of rich cloak gracefully around him. "Conmor's daughter is of an age to marry. If I were to become her husband, I would have the right to lead you. . . ."

Maira felt the blood leave her face, then rush painfully to the skin. He had never even spoken to her!

"My sister shall not marry any man's son just because he says so!" One could scarcely hear Eoc's whisper in the babble of discussion that followed.

Father, what shall I do? she cried silently, but it was her mother's harsh voice that answered her.

"Do not listen to Eoc—take Calgac and rule until Eoc is well again."

"No." Maira's head was buzzing. "Once he has the power he will not easily give it up again." The buzzing grew louder, as if some inner voice were striving to be heard. She shuddered, and found that she was standing, waiting for the clamor to still. Words came to her.

"As you have reminded us, I am Conmor's daughter." She nodded politely to Calgac. "And since my father is dead and my brother lies ill I must accept or refuse a husband myself, however improper it may be." Her voice was low, clear, and the sheer unexpectedness of her intrusion had gotten their attention. The last time most of them had seen her she had been a child; they were seeing her as a grown woman now. "I do not choose to wed the High King's son and remove the leadership of the people from the lineage of Arminorix. And so it would be, and you know it,"—she gazed sternly around the circle— "despite all his intentions and assurances.

"We are as loyal to the High King as any clan," she went on, smiling at Calgac in a vain attempt to soften her words. "But the Vindomarci are the rim of the shield that protects his lands against the Selgovae. We cannot be ruled from Carbantorigum!" She waited, savoring the murmur of agreement. They were listening to her! She had never before understood what a heady feeling that could be. Eoc seemed to have lapsed into semi-consciousness, but Tadhg was watching her with shining eyes.

"That is very true," said Catulch approvingly. She was Maelscuit's second wife, and very ambitious. Maira did not return her smile. "Do you speak in favor of my husband, then? Be sure he will protect you now that your father is gone."

"Will he?" answered Maira. She threw back her cloak and turned slowly, letting them see that she wore her father's sword. She had kept it by her for comfort ever since the night he was slain. "Did Maelscuit avenge Conmor?" she went on. "No—it was no man among you who did that. I was the one who struck the blow!"

Wind lifted the hair from her neck, and the sun slipped from behind a cloud and shone full upon her. Light flared from the hilt of the sword.

"Let Maira lead us!" cried the harper. "She is as much a warrior as any of you!"

Maira turned sharply to look at him and stopped, dazzled by the sun. *Is this what I wanted?* she wondered desperately. *"You will pay the price of lordship,"* her father had said. Was this what he had meant?

But whatever had been meant or wanted, the struggle for the chieftainship was beginning now. Instinct drove Maira to fight for it.

The mutter of discussion was like muted thunder. The old women had their heads together, and Maira knew that if necessary, the words of the mothers would sway their sons.

"She's only a girlchild!" said Waric.

"She is Conmor's daughter, and she led the defense against the men of Din Carn," responded Maelor.

Urr's deep voice seconded his. "She has been as good a lord to me and mine as any man."

Maelscuit found his voice at last. "Would it be legal to elect this girl? It cannot be!"

"Gutuator," cried a dozen voices, "tell us the law!"

"The law speaks only of the lineage, not of the sex of the heir," the Druid answered impassively. "Maira descends from Arminorix through both grand-daughter and grand-son."

"And through that daughter her right is stronger still," added Urr, "for Viduna was a child of Britta the chieftain's second wife, who was herself a daughter of the Old Race whose rule descended by mother-right and who held this land before ever the Iron People came over the narrow seas."

Maira bit her lip, wondering if that reminder had been wise. But she was not the only one in that assembly who carried the old blood. Men stirred and looked at her differently as ancient tales stirred in their memories.

"It takes more than blood-right to rule a clan," said Maelscuit scornfully, "and, yes—more than a quick arm. Does this girl have the strength to rule a clan of fighting men?"

"Boudicca ruled the nation of the Iceni and more," retorted Maira, "and she made Rome tremble!"

"Boudicca was a grown woman who had borne children and ruled for many years at her husband's side," said Waric. "She had both wisdom and experience. If a woman is to lead us, then better your mother, Druith, should rule."

Maira turned quickly to look at her mother, shaken between hope and consternation. And for one wild moment hope won, and she thought to see her mother straighten and round on them all, making everything right again. And then she saw how long it took Ness to help Druith to her feet, how she struggled for speech. *She cannot do it!* Maira realized. *Her time is done and it is my turn now!*

"The lordship should go to my son," Druith said in a low voice. Tears were running down her cheeks to fall unheeded to the breast of her gown.

"Ah, the poor lady," said Maelor's wife Britta compassionately. "She still grieves for her man."

"Her son is incapable, and she does not want to rule," said Maelscuit triumphantly.

"But her daughter does!" Maira fought to keep her own voice steady. She had said it, now. "And if I am chosen, I will have Druith to advise me, and not her only." She took a deep breath and looked straight at Waric.

"You erred in your tale of the boar, but I can correct you. I can tell you what you shouted to Conmor when the boar came. . . ." Swiftly she bent and whispered into the old man's ear what Conmor's spirit had told her. His face went the color of dough.

"And you, Maelscuit—" Maira took a step toward him. "Shall I tell them how you gained the cattle to win your bride?"

A murmur of awe and fear swept the circle. Men's fingers flicked in the warding sign. Only Gutuator remained unmoved. Maira looked at him anxiously. She dallied now with spiritual things, and with a word he could turn them against her, but he only returned her look with a little smile. Maira took a deep breath and began to pace around the circle.

"Conmor's spirit speaks to me, and as he directs, so will I

lead you! Oh people of the White Horse, awake and look around you,'' she cried passionately, and she did not know if these words were her own or if her father's spirit were indeed speaking through her now. "While you waste time arguing, the Selgovae are arming, and preparing to lay waste our land!

"We must work hard to replace the stores they burned. We must replace the cattle they stole. As they have raided us we must attack them, but cleverly—for gain as well as for glory. Do you think the High King will be able to get compensation from the Selgovae? How many of us will be dead by the time that honor-price is paid?"

"But they will attack us in return!" cried Catulch. "Let us make peace while we can!"

"Indeed, we must have defenses." Maira gestured up the steep slope. "But do we not already possess the greatest of fortresses, far stronger than the mound of Din Carn? Our fathers deserted it by order of the Red Crests, but Rome will not enforce that ruling now. Let us build up the walls and make level the platforms. Let us gather stones and stores, and build shelters to keep ourselves and our animals through the winter snows!"

All around her she saw heightened color and shining eyes.

"And then we will attack the men of Din Carn?" cried Dumnoric.

Maira nodded and drew her father's sword. "Then we will go against them, and their blood will water the thirsty ground!" She remembered Carric's face, contorted in the firelight as he looked down at her. Soon his face would change in fear . . . soon the Selgovae would pay for their treachery. The honor-price for her father's head and the destruction of her dreams could not be paid in cattle or grain or gold. She wanted to see blood flow.

The blood-beat thrummed in her ears. A bitter intoxication shook her. The young men surged to their feet, shouting, and the older men whispered, wondering what she knew. Maelscuit was still protesting, but no one listened to him any more.

"Death to Din Carn!" shrieked Maira, swinging the sword so that it flashed back the sunlight.

"Death to Din Carn!" shouted the warriors.

"The gods are with her," said old Idha. "I see dark wings—the Lady of the Ravens will bring her the victory!"

Yes, I hear the ravens calling! Louder and louder came the

cry, or perhaps it was the cheering of the people she heard.
Maira no longer cared. Some last instinct of caution whispered
that this was not that policy of restraint that Brenna had called
for, that she was no better than Eoc, now. But this dark
intoxication could no longer be resisted, and if it bound the
people to her it would serve its purpose and she could seek
wisdom presently.

"Let Maira rule us and the Goddess will bless us again!"
cried Urr, and his sons roared full-throated approval.

Whatever they had wanted, whoever they had supported, the
whole clan caught fire now. Maira swayed as if she had pulled
back a door-curtain to let in the breeze and admitted the
whirlwind. The people's emotions beat against her awareness;
their passions whirled her out of herself as her own ecstasy fed
theirs.

And in all that throng only two stood silent—Gutuator, who
watched with unreadable dark eyes, and Druith, who was
weeping silently.

Old woman, weep if you will! Maira raged silently. *All my
life you have cherished your son, but your daughter will rule!
Weep, my mother, for I will not pity you!* And Maira turned
away and shouted, and tossed the sword like a firebrand into
the air. As it came down she caught it, and the whole clan
shouted her name.

And if for a moment another thought came to her, she had no
time to consider it before they raised her on their shoulders to
bear her away—and that was that perhaps Druith was weeping
for her daughter, not for her son.

The stallion's shrill challenge cut through the noise of the
encampment like a battle horn. The people who had come to
see the making of the new chieftain listened and laughed
uneasily. The Druids, finishing their preparations, heard it and
nodded, noting the strength and spirit in the sound. Maira
heard it from the enclosure in which she was being made
ready, and half-rose from her carven stool.

"Please sit, Lady—we must comb out your hair. . . ."

Mute, Maira sat down again and submitted to the painful tug
of the comb. She knew that Maelor's wife Britta was trying to
be gentle, but like a horse being groomed by an unfamiliar
rider, she felt the awkwardness and hesitation and twitched at
every stroke. Ness could have done it better; her mother could

have done it more easily. But Ness was only an old servant, too low-born to be permitted here, and her mother sat silent with the other clan-mothers, their dark robes folded around them like black wings.

A little wind rustled in the enclosure's leafy walls. From beyond them Maira could hear Tadhg's harping, but it did not comfort her, for his playing held the one-two-three, one-two-three rhythm of galloping hooves.

Father, help me—you went through this once! Tell me what to do! There was no answer. Perhaps Conmor could not hear her from the spring on Din Rhun. For the ceremony they had come down to the broad plain where Shinnel Water joined the Scaur. All she could see of Din Rhun was its peak above the trees.

Her breathing had quickened as if she were about to begin a race, and she forced it to slow. All the omens had been cast and the preparations made. She could not flee this fate now. To die or to go forward was the only way.

From outside she heard the voices of her guard of honor. She wondered if they realized that through the woven branches of the enclosure every word came clear?

"Is she almost ready?"

"Soon. The women will let us know."

"It's no wonder if she wants to delay it." The first speaker laughed uneasily. "The Druids say that this is the old way—the oldest way, to make a Queen for the land; but it seems strange, and dangerous."

"You're too young to remember when Conmor was made chief," said the other man. "It was the same thing then, only with a white mare. The male is the clan and the female is the land. When the chief weds the mare he marries the Goddess, and when he eats of her flesh he is made one with the land."

Maira realized that her fingers were clenched in the white wool of her gown and forced them to loosen. Most of the clans had given up this way of kingmaking, reserving it for the inauguration of the High King. But hers was the White Horse Clan, and it held to the old ways. Mechanically she smoothed the crumpled wool, trying to comfort herself with the Druids' teaching. This time, the stallion would stand for the people and *she* would be the Goddess, married to all of them, part of the land.

Her pulse was racing and she tried once more for calm.

Tadhg had stopped playing, and in the stillness she heard someone whistling. She jerked and Britta asked if she had hit a snarl. Maira murmured some reassurance and forced herself to sit back again, straining to hear. The whistling continued, and after a moment her mind caught up with her body's awareness and she recognized the tune. Carric had whistled that melody the night he escorted her home from the Selgovae lands. For a moment she was there again, riding in the scented darkness, and tears pricked beneath her shut lids. She told herself that anyone could whistle that tune, but she trembled with a deeper recognition. She knew that it was Carric.

He must be mad to have come here! Why had he come? To mock her, to try to shake her resolution . . . or because he loved her and did not want to let her go? She could not dare believe the latter was true. She could not stop the ceremony now . . . and if she ran out of the enclosure and into his arms, where could they go? The Vindomarci would not accept the leader of the raiders who had killed their chieftain as the husband of their Lady, and the Selgovae of Din Carn who had rejoiced at Conmor's death would never accept his daughter.

And thinking of that, Maira remembered once again why she was here, and felt the quick flush of anger tingle through her. Did Carric believe her to be so weak that the memory of what they had shared would make her forget everything else that had passed? Did he think so little of her honor, or her pride? He was the tanist of Din Carn, and she was Din Rhun, and between them there had never been peace, except for a little while when the Romans came, nor could there be.

The whistling went on for a little while longer, but she made no sound or sign. Then it ceased, and Maira shut her eyes to hide the treacherous tears.

"There, my Lady—your hair hangs down your back like a cloak of red gold!" Britta stepped back and handed Maira the bronze mirror so that she could see. Her golden torque was off-center and she adjusted it, twitched at the amber necklace that had been Antiochus' gift to her. From the dark bronze her shadowed face stared back at her, stiff and empty as a Roman carving in stone.

Goddess, hear me! desperately she prayed. *This must be more than a show for the people*. The People. . . . Vividly, memory showed her the encampment. There were nearly as many folk here as there had been when the tribes assembled for the Lughnasa festival, for not only the householders but their wives and children and bondsmen had come today. How was she to lead them? Even with Conmor's spirit to advise her, how could she possibly be wise enough to choose—

She heard the heavy thunder of drums, and her heart missed a beat. Time enough to worry about leading the clan, she thought, when she had survived the consecration.

"Ah, they are coming for her. Not long to wait now," said the guard.

"Good. I am tired of standing," his companion replied. "Don't worry, lad, she will be lucky for us. The Goddess has already touched her. Wait and see."

Maira heard and shuddered. Britta, misunderstanding, promised she would feel warmer when she was out in the sun.

In the sun, thought Maira, *where my promised husband waits for me. . . .* Carric's tune re-echoed in her memory, and for one anguished moment she forgot her anger and remembered how they had talked when she lay in his arms. That was the wedding she should have been going to. But he himself had made that impossible. She set her face, and went out to meet the drums.

In the center of the field was a long, humped stone. No one knew if it were a natural formation or a menhir that had fallen long ago. But since the coming of Arminorix into this land, every chieftain had taken his oath with his feet upon this stone.

And now it was Maira daughter of Conmor who stood there, fitting her narrow feet into the hollows worn by the feet of her ancestors. And perhaps something of them lingered in the stone, for as the soles of her feet got used to the cold, grainy surface, she found a curious calm spreading through her. She stood very still, letting the wind stir the long folds of her robe and her shining hair, and waited for the Druids to come.

The drumbeat was muffled. Across the field she saw Gutuator and four other priests approaching, cloaked in the hides of sacrificed bulls, and crowned with the wings of sacred birds. The cloaks were painted with spirals, and from their fringes dangled little pieces of metal and plaques of bone that tinkled as they moved. She wondered how they had learned to walk that way, as if they were flowing over the grass.

Around the circle they paced, slowly drawing inward, until Gutuator stood just in front of Maira, focusing attention, and power. The others were younger than he was, but their eyes all held the same ageless calm. The priest who stood in the west took a step forward and lifted his hands.

> *"I invoke the blessings of the West—*
>   *The bounty of knowledge and learning,*
>   *The foundation of wisdom,*
>   *The beauty of teaching and judgement,*
>   *Of chronicles and counsels, of histories and all*
>   *sciences—*
>   *May they be present here. . . ."*

The voice of the Druid vibrated through the air, and it seemed to Maira that the blood burned in her veins; her mind raced furiously, as if in a moment she would understand the causes and meaning of all things.

Then the second Druid stepped out and his voice rang across the field.

> *"I invoke the blessings of the North—*
>   *The glory of battle, the strength of the warrior,*
>   *Steadfast, unyielding, quick to strike his foe,*
>   *Covetous of honor—*
>   *May they be present here. . . ."*

And it seemed to Maira that a chill wind shook her, and with a cold fury she remembered every wrong she had suffered. Her fingers itched for her father's sword.

> *"I invoke the blessings of the East—"*

the third Druid was speaking now.

> *"The prosperity of the householder,*
>   *Rich in treasures, in cattle and fine clothing,*
>   *Generous in hospitality—*
>   *May they be present here. . . ."*

The wind shifted, and Maira felt a breath of moisture on her skin. She thought of rain falling, of the fine stream of rich milk hissing into the pail, of celebrations and feastings at Lys Speiat.

> *"I invoke the blessings of the South—*
> *Sweet music that bears the spirit to the Otherworld,*
> *Craftsmanship and subtlety,*
> *The fierceness of fair women,*
> *The loyalty of servants—*
> *May they be present here. . . ."*

The voice of the fourth Druid lilted and laughed. The scent of meadow-grass crushed by the feet of the crowd was dizzying, but the stone Maira stood on held her with a steady pull that would not let her fall.

Then Gutuator lifted his hands, and all the others turned inward, facing him. Maira breathed in the charged air and felt her skin tingle. Dimly she understood the meaning of the invocations—as the inward spiral of the Druids' circumambulations had focused the consciousness of the crowd on the middle of the field, so their incantations had drawn into consciousness the combined strengths that were the soul of the Clan. But what was their center? What was the strength of sovereignty?

> *"I invoke the blessings of the Center—"*

Gutuator's voice rang out across the field.

> *"The power of kingship,*
> *The renown of the kingdom,*
> *The primacy of all arts,*
> *The reward of warriors—*
> *May they be present here."*

The air throbbed. The sense of pressure was almost too great to bear. She was at the center—she *was* the center now.

"Maira, daughter of Conmor, son of Ycuit, son of Brannos, son of Arminorix, are you willing to stand as chieftain to the White Horse Clan?"

Gutuator's voice focused Maira's awareness. Now she saw only the deep eyes that held her own. But she felt the people's eyes upon her. They were waiting for her to reply.

She tried to answer, but her throat had gone dry. Was this

how Urr and Petric and the others had felt when they swore their oaths to her? Maira had never expected to pledge her own service to any man, but now she would be sworn to all of them. . . .

She wrenched her gaze away from the Druid's and searched the crowd, not knowing who she hoped to find. There were her own men, and Tadhg, with a kind of shining in his eyes that hurt to see. Temella's face was pale with awe. So many faces—she could not tell if Carric were among them. But her mother was in the front, and Druith's face was set like stone. Maira turned abruptly back to Gutuator.

"I am willing." Her answer carried clearly.

"And will you swear now to be as a mother to the people, nourishing them in time of peace, protecting them in war, upholding the rights of the weak and punishing the wrongdoing of the strong?"

"I will swear."

"And by what will you swear all this, daughter of Conmor?"

Maira cleared her throat, afraid again, for from this oath there could be no unbinding while she lived.

"I swear by the gods of our people." Her voice trembled a little, but she forced herself to continue, calling up each divinity in her mind's eye as she invoked it, then letting it go to make room for the next.

"I swear by the Lady: by Earth our Mother, by the Mare and the Sow, by the Goose and the Swan, by the Lady of the Ravens and the battlefield, by the Lady of the sacred flame and by the One who dwells in every pool and stream. . . ." Maira remembered the Presence she had felt in the sacred pool, and joy strengthened her voice. Then the memory of the other vision that had come to her there surfaced, and she went on.

"I swear by the Lord: by the Antlered One, by the Lord of Club and Cauldron, by the God of Sword and Wheel, by the Many-Skilled One who wields the Spear of Light, by the Stag, the Stallion, and the Bull. . . ."

The sense of pressure increased, as if there were scarcely room for all the Powers she had invoked in the space around the stone. Her gaze clung to the Druid, who was standing with the balanced alertness of a man driving a difficult team. Of course, she thought, relaxing a little, Gutuator was no stranger to power.

"I swear by the spirits of my ancestors," she finished, "and if I fail in this oath I have given to my people, may the sky fall and cover me, may the earth give way beneath me, and may the waters swallow my bones.''

Gutuator turned to the people.

''Thus your Lady takes oath to you; will you pledge her your service in return? Your food for her table, your warriors for her following, your obedience to all lawful commands?''

''We swear! We swear! We will!'' they cried, as if the earth itself had found a voice to shout the words. The sudden flood of approval went to Maira's head as if she had swallowed a draft of strong mead.

''Then remember what you have sworn!'' said the Druid sternly. ''For the gods bear witness to what you say, and it is they who will judge any who proves untrue!''

Maira stared at the blur of faces before her. In exchange for the service of Urr and Petric and her other men she had given cattle, but for her people she must give her life—by living for them, and if necessary by dying. She remembered her father's blood upon the ground and for a moment she understood what he had done and why. At this moment she could have welcomed the sword and never felt the pain.

She shook with the force of the love she felt for the people around her; each breath of the weighted air sent power tingling through every nerve. And then Gutuator's supple hands gestured dismissal, and the sense of Presence around her began to ease.

Maira straightened, and as her head cleared and her breath steadied she heard the stallion's shrill neigh.

''Behold, the Lady Maira has been sworn to you and accepted,'' said Gutuator. ''There remains now the consummation of that commitment, for from the union of opposites comes strength and the balanced integration of the Powers that rule the world.''

''Lord and Lady . . . Light and Darkness . . . man and animal. . . . Let the White Mare be united with Her Lord!''

The gods had drawn off a little, but Maira felt that They were still watching her. The Druids began a low chant whose syllables spelled enchantment though Maira could not understand the words. But she was not really listening—she was not looking at the Druids or at the crowd, but at the red stallion they were bringing onto the field.

The stallion was in his first strength; he had never covered a mare. Nor had he ever felt the constraint of a bridle before, and he did not like it. Only the ropes around his neck held him as the men half-led, half-dragged him toward the stone. Maira watched the striking forefeet and understood that her blood might well feed the ground today. This was why the gods were waiting. This was to be her testing.

And when it was over she would be either the Lady of the Land or its Sacrifice.

For a moment the horse caught some scent that startled him. He reared, and the force of the movement sent two men sprawling. Maira supposed she ought to be afraid, but in that moment all she knew was that this creature was beautiful. His chestnut coat had the red sheen of polished bronze; in the light of the westering sun it glowed as the changing leaves were glowing in the trees, so that the stallion seemed to shine from within.

That illumination showed her the movement of every muscle. He reared again with an easy power, as if he were held there not by earth's pull but only by the ropes, and that only for so long as he should choose. He was closer now, and Maira saw the straight strength of his legs, the deep chest with the well-set neck, the powerful hindquarters.

As they brought him to the stone he tossed his head and snorted, more curious than angry now. Maira caught the flash of a dark eye in his fine head, and the flare of his nostrils. The reins were knotted on his neck. She tensed, knowing that she would have but one good chance.

The men fumbled with the neck ropes, ready to slip them free. The stallion pranced and sidled, and for a moment stood fully sideways to the stone. Maira grasped a handful of mane and vaulted onto his back, the slit sides of her robe swirling behind her as she sprang.

She wore nothing under the robe, and for a moment the feel of the smooth hide against her bare thighs startled her. Then the neck-ropes were jerked away, and the stallion leaped forward, trying to get out from under this strange weight on his back.

Maira's legs flexed around his smooth sides, but no strength of hers could hold her there—she must sense his movements and become one with them, forget all but that unity. The world heaved around her as the horse bucked and twisted; then he stretched his neck and with a jerk that almost unseated her began to run.

Maira grabbed for the reins and hauled back, desperate to

turn the stallion before he crashed into the crowd. With the powerful neck at full extension it was like hauling on a log. She pulled and released again, then jerked suddenly on the left rein so that the horse was taken by surprise. His head was pulled to the left and his body followed it.

But that was only a momentary impediment. The stallion could still leap and swerve, and now he was off again. Maira swayed with him, learning his rhythms, making her body an extension of his, and after a few moments she began to smile. But the horse was not beaten. He reared, and Maira held onto the coarse mane and let him rise, ready to resume her pressure on the reins when he came down. She felt the great muscles working beneath her legs and exulted in their power.

And soon she became aware of another thing. The horse was in good condition, but his spine was prominent. With no blanket to pad it the ridge of bone pressed hard against her. His sweat kept the hair from irritating, but with each motion the bone rubbed—painfully, and then not painfully, but setting her to throbbing with an odd pleasure, almost like—

—like the pleasure she had felt when she clasped Carric's thrusting body between her strong thighs . . .

With terror and wonder Maira thought of what she was doing, and what was yet to do. But still the stallion surged beneath her, ever more responsive to the messages of her knees and hands, as if his power was becoming hers.

It was the unity she had craved in Carric's arms—the union so cruelly severed. *Yes!* her heart cried, and she loosened the reins and let the red stallion run.

And the people heard her laugh and began to cheer.

After a time the stallion started to tire. His pace slowed, and obedient to the bridle at last, he cantered in a long curve that followed the line of the crowd. Ahead of them the Druids were waiting, like ghosts against the grass, for they had stripped to their white under-robes. Her heart wrenched with pity and fear, Maira turned the horse toward them and drew back on the reins.

Suddenly, the white-robed figures surrounded her. Ropes snaked out to entangle the stallion's feet, and Maira flung herself free. The stallion thrashed in his bonds, grunting in outrage. Maira stood panting, knowing she must do the hardest thing now. The Druids had gotten a rope on each leg of the horse, and now they pulled them taut, hauling the stallion onto his back while he struggled and tried to kick free. For a moment she shivered with hesitation, then she leaped past the flailing hooves.

There was no possibility of penetration, of course—they had told her that it was sufficient for her to simulate copulation by touching him. For a moment, knowledge of who and where she was vanished; she pressed herself against the stallion, once, again, with the scent of horse all around her and the pulse pounding in her ears like hoofbeats, overwhelming all other sound. A shout exploded from her. "I am the White Mare!" Then the fifth rope tightened around the stallion's throat, and Gutuator pulled her away.

Crimson filled her vision—the stallion's red hide, red blood fountaining as the Druid's knife slashed down. Maira screamed; it was her father, then the stallion again, his great body still fighting the death that sucked his strength away as his blood gushed onto the thirsty ground.

A deep-throated moan of satisfaction rose from the crowd. Gutuator's arms were like iron bands, holding Maira against him while the sacrificial priests went about the bloody work of butchering the slain beast and putting its flesh into the cauldron. Head pressed against the Druid's chest, Maira felt the vibration of a deep humming that became a chant into which her consciousness fled gratefully, no longer able to bear the knowledge of what had just been done. There were green fields in Gutuator's singing, and woods whose bare branches swelled into buds of green. And there were grazing flocks, and fat herds of cattle, and fields of ripening grain. The Druid sang on, and Maira saw the grain being harvested, the withered leaves falling to enrich the soil.

"All things grow, all things die," he sang. "All things are reborn. . . ."

And then there were people in his song—tribes like her own and others, building homes, raising children and dying, to be replaced by others as generation followed generation, race followed race, for untold centuries.

All things grow, all things die, all things are reborn!

She saw her own father, young and strong, standing with wide eyes above the body of a slaughtered mare.

Maira opened her own eyes and saw before her the great cauldron of riveted iron. Unresisting, she let them strip off her stained robe and lift her into it. Horror and understanding warred within her. Her body still throbbed. Now, vividly, she remembered Carric's embrace. But the blood was like her father's—how could she devour what she loved?

"Remember, the acts we perform here only represent a deeper reality."

The voice of the Druid thrust her awareness deeper as her body folded itself into the cauldron and was covered by the broth. The chieftains had eaten the flesh of the sacrificed bull. Offered to the god, the sacrifice *was* the god, and through that symbolic act, the worshipper who consumed it fed upon a spiritual reality.

Images swirled dizzily—she was an infant floating in her mother's womb, surrounded by nourishment. She opened her mouth and salt, sweet liquid flowed into it; food was placed upon her tongue and she swallowed it.

But that could not be right! It was a stallion they had slain—so how could the cauldron be a womb? She had loved the stallion as she had loved her father, loved Carric, and now she had eaten—

Maira's reason trembled on the sword-edge of knowledge; then horror pushed her past all old perceptions, and she understood that her father's death was only the other half of this sacrifice. The stallion had died for the people, and for the land. The brutal expansion of consciousness she suffered now was to prevent the sovereign from ever forgetting the price of power and the meaning of the bond between ruler and realm. . . .

She bent her head and drank again, and remembered a black bowl and a dark pool. She chewed the meat slowly, making the stallion's flesh her own.

"As I consume your flesh, oh courageous one, let your valor become part of me," she whispered. "Now I am both the mare and the stallion—male and female together—the people and the land." She stopped, shaken by a wordless intuition that male and female, woman and animal, she and all the great world around her were one. The gods she had invoked earlier swirled through her expanded consciousness, and she understood that they were One also, that she and They together were part of Something Else whose identity was no sooner glimpsed than gone.

And then the moment passed, but as if she had no skin, Maira felt the presence of the Druids standing around the cauldron, of the people around the field, of the circles of earth and sky. She stood up, coming naked from the cauldron like an infant emerging bloody from its mother's womb. She lifted her hands.

"I am the White Mare and the Red Stallion!" Maira's voice rang across space. "I am the clan and the land! I am the many and the One! I belong to you!"

And the people shouted their response to her. "Rigan! Rigana! Great Queen!"

EIGHT

Din Rhun

MAIRA HEARD THE crack of a whip and a long rumbling and turned, shading her eyes to see. Lod was guiding his father's oxen up the slope of the Dun. The sledge quivered behind them, too heavy with stones to bounce even on the rough ground. Calculating, Maira's gaze moved from the sledge to the half-built wall.

Yes, that would make another course of stone for the northern corner. Lod could haul perhaps two more loads today, which would bring the wall almost to gate-height, and several of Maelor's men had promised to come tomorrow to work on the southern side. . . . She sighed, mind busy with figuring.

The walls were growing. Slowly but steadily Din Rhun was beginning to look like a fortress again. But she could not have dreamed it would be so difficult!

"Lady, Coric's sent word that one of his oxen is lame and tomorrow he can only send you two teams. . . ."

Maira turned, biting her lip in frustration, then saw it was Maelor's young son and managed a smile.

"Did he say how long it would take the beast to heal, or offer a replacement?"

The boy shrugged, and Maira frowned, thinking. The loss of one team would delay the work by days. Perhaps Waric would know someone else with a team. She did not like to disturb him, for he had the best memory of how the Dun had looked before they tore the old walls down, and she was already depending on him too much for advice on its rebuilding. At least Waric was as eager to see Din Rhun restored to its former strength as she was.

Thanking the boy, she picked her way across the slope, whose steepness was made more treacherous by the bits of broken stone that littered it now. By the time she had reached the first gate, three people had stopped her with questions. Two of them could have been answered by anyone with sense; the third meant she must dig into her limited store of gold to get more iron hoe blades from the smith in Din Prys.

Perhaps they could have accomplished the work with tools of hardened wood or stone—their ancestors had moved great masses of earth that way. But it took longer, and she wanted the ditches dug and the banks raised before winter came. It was taking too long anyway. She had been chieftain more than a month now, and the younger warriors were getting restless. They could easily turn on her if she did not give them action soon, no matter what oaths they had sworn. But the whole clan would deny her if they were caught unprotected by Selgovae reprisals.

I wonder what Conmor would do? Perhaps this evening she could manage a visit to the shrine above the spring.

But what she really needed, even more than she did that still voice that made Conmor's wisdom her own, was simply a little time alone. Of all the things she had hoped or feared when she stood up to claim leadership of the clan, this she had not expected—that every moment of her day would belong to others, to command, to mediate, to advise. She could not have imagined this perpetual *busyness*. . . .

I'm like a woman who bears triplets and then the year after, twins! Maira thought wryly. *With all of them wanting my attention constantly, jealous if I seem to favor one over the others, hurt if I simply do not hear*. . . .

She paused to catch her breath next to the wall, and the woman who was helping to pile the stones there saw her, and flustered, began to work faster.

"Yset, isn't it?" asked Maira. "You are doing very well—already more than I expected today," she added soothingly, and was rewarded when the woman blushed with pleasure and slowed to a more sensible pace.

At least she seemed to have handled *that* interchange all right, she thought as she went on. But this sort of thing was the least of the problems confronting her. If only the ceremony of inauguration could have given her some instant wisdom. Her memory of the ritual had the distorted splendor of a dream, and the dreamlike sense of great significance that could not be put into words.

She knew that it had changed her—she looked back at her old life across a gulf as great as that which separated Din Rhun from the eastern hills—but she did not know how. And the hectic drive to complete Din Rhun's fortifications gave her little time for self-analysis. She knew only that the ritual had changed the way the rest of the clan perceived her. She was not just Maira any longer, Conmor's girl; she was the head of her people, their totem and touchstone, the sacred White Mare.

She went on, asked someone where Waric was, and was directed around the side of the hill. Several huts had been erected within the outer wall already, for the weather was turning cold, although there had been little rain. From one of them came singing.

> *"The meaning of number One now say,*
> *That I may learn it well today!"*

Maira smiled and ducked through the door. The children inside did not notice her. Eyes fixed on the Druid who sat with them, they were learning the chant of numbers.

> *"Number One is pure Necessity,*
> *The sin that fathers sorrows;*
> *Nothing before it, nothing follows. . . ."*

The children blinked at him like young owls, but they sang the next question, and this time Maira joined them.

> *"The meaning of number Two now say,*
> *That I may learn it well today!"*

Gutuator answered, "Two oxen yoked to one cart—

> *"They pull, they fall,*
> *That is the marvel!"*

Maira repressed a smile as one of the children saw her, giggled, and stuttered out the next question. Imperturbably the Druid replied,

> *"There are three parts of the world,*
> *Three beginnings and three ends,*
> *For the oak as for men.*
> > *Two oxen yoked to one cart—"*

Repeating the series, the song went on. The familiar words echoed from past to present memory. Four, Five, Six, and Seven and Eight—the numbers she had learned as a child, beguiled by the bright images whose meaning she understood no more now than she had then.

> *"Nine spirits dancing around a fountain*
> *In the light of the full moon;*
> *The wild sow with nine piglets in her lair,*
> *Grunting and rooting, rooting and grunting there;*
> *Little one, little one, to the apple tree run—*
> *The old boar will teach you a lesson. . . ."*

Maira thought she had seen those white spirits dancing near the sacred spring. But the black sow laired with the dead. She wondered, *Does my father understand the lesson of the old boar now?*

The counting finished. The children began to squirm like puppies, pinching and punching at each other. Smiling, Gutuator dismissed them and they tumbled through the door.

Only one hesitated—Maelor's youngest daughter Budica, who was old enough to know that Maira was different now, but did not understand enough to be in awe of her.

"You sang very well, Budica," Maira told her, and when the child grinned, gathered her into her arms. There was something very comforting about the firmness of that small body, and Maira held her close.

"My father is building a great wall!" said Budica confidingly.

"Yes, love—he's doing it very well."

"Will the wall keep us safe when the bad men come?" Budica gazed up at her.

Maira's grip tightened. "Yes, love, it will!" Her intensity frightened the child, and Maira let her go. *It must*, she promised silently. *It must!*

"But it will not, you know," Gutuator answered when Budica had gone. "Not forever. Do you think you can protect everyone always? Death will claim that child someday—will take all of them, and there is nothing you can do.''

"Yes, death will come," hissed Maira, "but if I can help it, not at the point of a Selgovae sword! Do you think I am wrong?" she looked up at him fiercely. "Was I wrong to keep Conmor's head from the pyre? But you preserved it for me; you consecrated me to the clan! Why, grandfather, why?"

"The function of the Druid is to inform, to judge, to advise—but not to decide."

Maira nodded. "And to prophesy! What does the future hold for us here? Tell me, Druid—tell me now!"

Gutuator closed his eyes. His features stilled, and for a moment Maira thought he had shut awareness of her away. Then his lips moved.

"I see the land of Alba. . . . I see a land always at war. When no outland enemy threatens, the people fight among themselves, region against region, clan against clan, family against family. But again and again the alien enemy shall come, first Rome, and then others. And again and again the choice shall be yours—to surrender, to resist, or to assimilate your enemy. . . ."

Maira stared at him, but he said no more, and after a few moments his eyes opened and his dark gaze met hers. She shook her head helplessly.

"It is not my responsibility to decide for all those future centuries. I must make choices for *this* time, this place!" she said angrily. "Am I leading my people wrong?"

"I do not believe so," Gutuator said gently. "Conmor died because he thought his omens bound him. But you are something new. Your father could not have persuaded the people to rebuild these walls, but now that they have chosen you, they seek more changes. Even if change is painful, or fails, it is good to stretch and grow."

Maira stared at him sullenly. She had not wanted to change anything.

"Remember how the Goddess pursued the dwarf who tended Her cauldron, Maira. From change to change She hounded him, until he grew into his power. That is how She teaches Her children." Gutuator's white robes glowed dimly in the gloom, but his face was in shadow.

"They look at *me* as if I were the Goddess," whispered Maira. "But I am not even a mother, and sometimes I am so very tired. . . ."

For a moment there was silence. She felt the Druid watching her and kept her face hidden against her knees.

"Go to your own mother, then," he said finally. "She has lived long enough to gain some wisdom, and she will comfort you."

Maira jerked upright. "No! She hates me because I took the chieftainship from her precious son."

"Granddaughter, do you think that because she is your mother her growing is done? Druith has things to learn too—you can help each other. It does no good to ignore her, you know. You will have to understand and forgive each other before you can be free—if not in this life, then in the next. . . ."

"Well, it will have to be in the next life then!" retorted Maira, "because with the best will in the world, I don't know where I would find time to make peace with her now!"

She heard someone calling her name from outside and stood up. With a bright smile she saluted the Druid and slipped out the door. At least she had asked his advice, though she did not think it had made her much the wiser. And at least, she thought as she turned to answer the call, she was no longer so tired.

"My Lady—" Petric was puffing from his climb. He gasped for breath and she put a steadying hand on his shoulder. He nodded then, and tried to grin, and some of the purple faded from his cheeks. "Maira, you must come—there's a party of Romans riding up the road!"

Maira swore softly. She had expected this, but she had hoped the fortifications would be finished before it came. But someone, inevitably, had told someone else who had carried the word to Luguvalium. . . .

Who was their leader, she wondered, and what under the sky could she say to him? For weeks she had been too busy to worry about her appearance, and it did not matter to those who labored with her here. But these Romans would expect to speak with someone who looked like a leader.

"Quick, Petric, see if Maelor is on the hill." The piper was a bit of a dandy, and in a case at his belt he always carried a comb of carved horn. Maira was already wearing the golden torque and her father's sword, but her cloak was ragged and stuck full of burrs.

"And see if anyone has a decent cloak that I can put on," she called after Petric. He grinned back at her and hurried on.

By the time the Romans had rounded the guard hill and set

their horses up the road Maira was ready for them, her hair smoothed and her stained tunic covered by Britta's russet cloak with the edging of tablet-woven braid. Perhaps she would not look like their idea of a chieftain, but at least she would not shame her people now.

She peered over the unfinished wall, counting them. She saw nearly thirty horsemen—a troop of cavalry, wearing mail over leather jerkins and red scarves knotted at their necks. They carried oblong shields and wore bronze helmets that had a ridge along the top and a kind of brim behind.

It was Roman gear, surely, but most of the riders had British stature and coloring. Maira's glance moved back to their leader, a smaller man on a big horse with a more elaborate version of the armor the others wore and a crest of red horsehair in his helm. Memory flashed back the face of the brown-haired Iberian officer who had talked with her father at Lyn Mapon.

Tiberius Flavius Pintamus, yes—it must be, she thought, and wondered whether he would remember having met her before.

When the Romans pulled up before the rough opening in the wall, Maira was sitting on a boulder with Waric and Maelor flanking her and Tadhg a step behind. The others had been eager to swell the guard of honor, but she would not stop the work even to impress Rome. And indeed, she thought they might find it even more impressive to see everyone working so hard.

And this was the first time in weeks she had had a moment to sit still and look at her land. From here she could see most of the Nova valley. Autumn was advancing, and the grass on the upper slopes had cured to a pale gold. The rougher ground glowed russet with drying bracken or the misty lavender of heather. On the flats and in the corries the plumage of the trees had deepened in color, and the great bowl of the sky was a pale blue-green, translucent as a pane of Roman glass.

She felt a surge of fierce protectiveness and looked back at the Romans. *I will keep this land safe from both Roman and Selgovae! Father, you have dealt with these folk—tell me what to say!*

The Decurion and two of his men dismounted and marched through the gateway, backs straight, strides nicely coordinated to maintain their spacing over the uneven ground. Maira wondered if her own men could have done so well.

She recognized Pintamus immediately, and it seemed to her that something, perhaps surprise, flickered across his impassive features. They would have told him that the election went to Conmor's daughter, but apparently he had not connected that information with his memory of the girl who had brought him beer at Lyn Mapon.

But if he was startled, his reaction was well-controlled. His nod held just the proper shade of deference, and he brought his arm to his chest in a neat salute.

"Lady, for the loss you have suffered I bring the condolences of Rome. I am glad to have known your father, if only for a little while. He was a fine man."

Maira inclined her head in acknowledgement, fighting to keep her face as impassive as his. *It means nothing,* she told herself. *It is only diplomacy.*

"And I bear congratulations also on your election. May peace and prosperity bless your rule." There was perhaps the briefest flicker of a glance to the walls that were rising around him, and Maira repressed a smile.

She had told everyone to keep working, but she had not specified on which parts of the walls. If the eastern ramparts grew faster than those on the other side of the hill it would do no harm, and it not only allowed more of the clansfolk to see what was going on, but created a fine impression of industrious activity.

"Commander, I thank you for your sympathy and your good wishes." Very graciously, Maira got to her feet, knowing that they would stand eye-to-eye. She had his entire attention now.

"I see that you are already busy. . . ." This time his glance at the walls was deliberate.

"Indeed." Her glance captured his, challenging him to disapprove. "We have been working hard. Would you like to see?" She started forward. The Roman nodded and followed her, with his guards and hers a few paces behind, eyeing each other warily.

Waric had counselled her against doing this, but she suspected that the Romans had a plan of the old fortress filed somewhere at the Petriana. And even if they did not, it would be easy enough for Pintamus to spy out the place. So why not make a great show of candor and innocence and show him everything? After all, these walls were not being built to protect them from the Romans—not this time.

"We were somewhat surprised, Lady, to hear of the choice your clan had made," Pintamus said carefully.

"Do you disapprove?" Maira continued walking, her steps sure, while the Roman had to watch his footing.

"We uphold the right of lawful succession in those lands we rule. . . ."

"And even, I trust, in those you do not."

He smiled and evaded the challenge in her voice. "You were chosen legally. Why should we object to that? Our concern was because of your youth, your inexperience. . . ."

And not because of my sex? she wondered dubiously. But perhaps not. The memory of Boudicca must still be vivid in the minds of those who held Britannia for Rome.

"There may be matters regarding the relationship between our governments of which you are not aware," he went on.

"Such as the Roman command that all the Alban hillforts should be pulled down?" Maira shook her head. "I knew it, and even if I did not I have counsellors to inform me. . . ."

"Then why?" With a sweep of his hand he indicated the oxen who were hauling another sledgefull of stone up the hill.

Maira pointed to the charred timbers of Lys Speiat, just visible beyond the guard-hill.

"Do you see that?" Her voice shook despite her effort to control it. "My father died because we had no walls of stone. If you will not keep the peace in this land, you cannot deny us the right to defend ourselves against our neighbors. Fear not, Roman—I shall not give you cause to attack me here unless you try and take this defense away!"

She turned on him and he took an involuntary step backward.

"It was part of the treaty ten years ago," he said neutrally.

Maira made an obscene gesture. "*I* did not swear to it. Young I may be, and inexperienced, but I hope I have as much courage as any man or woman of my race. If you destroy our defenses, what does it matter if we die on your swords or those of the Selgovae? We will still be dead." She looked at him narrowly. "And so will many of you."

He nodded. "I have not threatened to report it." For a moment the words hung between them. "Tell me of your enemies. . . ."

"The Selgovae. The men of Din Carn." She spat out the words.

"Who killed your father," he added sympathetically. "And you believe that your clan has the strength to face them." It was not quite a question.

She stared at him. "If the wolves fight each other what is it to you?"

"If I prefer one pack to the other it would matter to me."

They had walked almost all the way around the outer wall, scarcely seeing it. Maira moved more slowly as she saw the cavalry troopers and her own folk awaiting them.

"No," she said finally, refusing the offer he had not quite put into words. "We will fight our own battles. I have no mind to owe my vengeance to Rome."

Pintamus shrugged. "My scouts and I are always moving, but we have a temporary camp on the site of Blatobulgium. If you change your mind, send a message to me there."

There was little enough feasting at the end of the meager harvest. At best men felt that a distraction had been removed and now they could set their whole strength to finishing Din Rhun. They had insisted on building a house for Maira within the inner wall, though she would have been content with a bed in Maelor's steading. But she understood that the clan needed to see her keep a greater state, and Maelor's household was full enough without her and her following.

And so she became mistress of her own house—no flammable construction of woven withies daubed and limed, this, but a solid round of the same stone as the wall. Temella and Ness were there to attend her, and the three sons of Urr formed her permanent guard, and Tadhg and his harp had their place by her fire. At least it was convenient to the work, and to the well where Conmor's head was still enshrined.

Maira lay warm in her box bed, watching the beam of morning light filter through the space between the wall and the spotted hide across the door and move across her bedcurtain, trying to remember how long it had been since she had sought Conmor's counsel.

Perhaps I no longer need it, she thought drowsily. There was an odd sort of relief in the thought, but reason told her it was too much to hope that this new life of hers should already be settling down to something predictable and understood. And she was not yet ready to let him go.

The light moved an inch farther, blazing through a gap in the weaving like a tiny star. She supposed she should get up. The days were growing shorter and she must not waste the light. But it was warm beneath the covers. The hound puppy they had given her—already the size of a sheep, for he was of the breed that could run down a stag—lay sprawled across her feet, snorting and snuffling as he hunted dreams.

And then she heard a sound that was neither the deep breathing of the other sleepers nor the morning song of a bird. She stilled, recognizing it—the faint, hopeless sound of stifled tears.

Carefully Maira withdrew her feet from under the sleeping dog and sat up, shivering in the chill air. The sound came again, from her left, where Temella lay. She should have known that, she thought. Ness would have wailed aloud or not at all. Frowning, she swung her legs over the edge of the boxbed and slipped through the curtains.

"Temella?" she paused with her hand on the housepost, curling her toes away from contact with the cold floor. "Temella, what is it? Tell me now—"

Abruptly there was silence. Maira sighed, pulled the curtains aside and sat down on the bedframe. "Temella, I heard you crying. Tell me what is wrong." She had put just an edge of command into her voice and was ashamed of it, but the chieftain had the need, and the right, to know things that were denied a friend.

There was another silence, then a muffled sob. "I swore I would not tell you, but if he's dead already I don't care!" Temella sat up and dabbed at her tears with the coverlet.

"Dumnoric?" Maira suppressed a groan. There were only two reasons she could think of for Temella to weep this way, and it would have been so much easier if her friend had simply been carrying some other man's child.

"You don't have to tell me," she said grimly. "I'll say it, and then he cannot blame you for giving him away. He couldn't wait, could he? He and the rest of the hotheads have gone raiding! Doesn't the fool know that the Selgovae will be expecting—"

"He said he'd be back before dawn with enough cattle for us to marry now," babbled Temella, "but the sun is up!"

"Temella, be still!" In the sudden silence they both heard the young dog whine and then begin to growl. In a moment Maira had her ear pressed against the earthen floor, but she could not tell if the vibration she sensed were distant hoofbeats or the galloping of the pulse in her ears. Cursing, she scrambled to her feet, grabbed her sword belt and a spear and pushed through the door.

The air was moist and heavy, and mist still veiled the lower hills. The puppy nosed at her legs, plumed tail slapping the door.

"No, Windchaser," she said softly, "it's not time to play. Be quiet and listen for me, lad—there!" She stopped scolding as the dog stiffened, ears pricked and nose testing the air.

Maira gathered her breath to cry the alarm, and heard, faint through the mists, an anguished call. Muffled but growing louder, she heard horses' hooves.

"Wake, awake! Warriors are coming! 'Ware, Din Rhun!" she yelled, and ran for the gate.

Something moved like a ghost through the fog below, resolved itself into a man lashing a weary horse up the hill. As Maira watched, the beast staggered and fell. The warrior threw himself free and began to run and she recognized Kenow.

Tadhg and Lod and his brothers had taken up position behind her, spears ready in their hands. From the other huts and houses half-wakened warriors were emerging. She heard the sour music of a horn.

More figures moved in the mist. Dumnoric cantered toward them and reined to a halt, shouting, followed by a third man, who shrieked and toppled from his pony's back, chest sprouting the wicked head of a spear. Rosic and another rider followed, and then the hill was swarming with riders as the men of Din Carn surrounded them and bore them down.

"Dumnoric, get in here!" shouted Maira. "Hold the gateway, all of you!"

The enemy warriors swept forward, their ponies slowing as the slope grew steeper. Maira searched the strange faces, looking for the one she feared to see.

Dumnoric wheeled back to face them, shouting defiance and shaking his spear. And then suddenly Carric was there. Dumnoric cast his weapon. The missile grazed Carric's right arm as he jerked to one side and thunked into the chest of the man behind him. Dumnoric swore and kicked his horse toward the gate as Carric began to call his own men away.

The defenders parted to let Dumnoric through. Seeing the enemy fall back, Maelor's son and some of the others darted out after them. A sword flickered and the boy fell. Dark wings beat in Maira's ears and she ran toward the body, her own men behind her.

Carric's bay stallion reared as he pulled him up. For a moment the scene was oddly still.

"Keep your cubs penned, Maira, or you'll lose them!" Carric laughed. "But if you have to go hunting, keep away from Din Carn!"

Face contorted, Maira swung back her arm; muscles strained and released as she flung the spear. Like a black bird it sped toward him and clashed harmlessly against his shield.

Carric laughed again and began to rein his horse away, then pulled back sharply and shouted her name.

Maira, straightening, had only begun to look around when someone crashed into her. She staggered, felt a shock, and grabbed at the man who had run into her as he began to fall.

"I could have had her! I could have brought the she-wolf down!" someone was protesting. "Carric, why did you warn her?"

But Maira, taking her defender's whole weight against her, scarcely heard. She saw his black hair, and the bobbing length of a spear jutting from under his arm. She got him down onto the ground and set her hand to the shaft.

"No," said Waric harshly. "If you move the spear he will die."

Uncomprehending, Maira looked back at the man on the ground. Confusion gave him her father's features, and she felt her gut twist. Then he groaned, she blinked and focused, and set her hands on either side of his face.

"Tadhg, be still," she whispered hoarsely. "I will take care of you."

The dark eyes opened, dilated with pain. "No. . . ." she could hardly hear the words. "Since I killed the harper . . . of the King of Munster . . . my life has been forfeit. *You* know. . . ."

Maira shook her head. "My father took that burden. Now you belong to me."

"I have repaid Conmor," whispered the harper. "I have saved his daughter and seen her made Queen. . . ." He coughed, and Maira saw crimson blood and knew the spear had pierced his lungs. Her people had no craft to cure such a wound, but still she shook her head.

"Tadhg, I need you!" she said desolately. He did not seem to hear.

"Bury my bones in Conmor's mound, but send my heart back to my own country. . . ."

"You cannot die!"

With effort, the dark eyes focused on her face and he tried to smile. "Lady, I have never been more than half alive since I left Eirinn." His eyes closed wearily. He coughed again, more of the bright blood trickled from his mouth, and he lay still. Maira looked down at the supple hands that would never coax music from a harp again and felt her own heart squeezed by a giant hand.

Shivering, she tried to get to her feet, and Lod helped her to stand. She looked at the grim faces around her. *It is my fault.* Anguish crystallized into anger. *I had been hoping defense would be enough; that we would not have to war against Din Carn. . . .*

Her wandering gaze found Dumnoric's face and he flinched and lowered his eyes. A red trickle of blood wound down his arm, but she could not pity him now.

"How many?" she asked hoarsely.

"Fifteen men followed me." His voice was as harsh as her own. "Besides myself, three will fight again."

Maira nodded. "We will have revenge, but it will be hard after such a loss."

"But won't the High King help us?" asked Temella. Someone gave an unbelieving laugh. "But where else can we look for allies?" the girl said desperately.

Maira looked at her, then through her, southeastward toward Luguvalium, remembering the offer Pintamus had made to her. Her voice was the snarl of the wolf the Selgovae had likened her to.

"We must ally ourselves with Rome."

NINE

---❧---

Luguvalium

"YOU ARE MAD, little sister. You cannot even control the warriors, and now you think to call the march with Rome? Ah, if only I were out of this bed!" Eoc swore weakly and winced as he tried to move his arm. Morning light filtering through the open door of the roundhouse showed his face too clearly—colorless and thin.

Maira looked down at him, distantly aware that once she would have snapped back at him without thinking. With a kind of wistfulness she remembered how they used to squabble, like puppies in the straw. She should have come to visit him more often, but there had been so much to do!

"If you had your strength you would likely have led them on that fool's chase yourself, and it would be *your* task to tell weeping women how their sons died—if you returned yourself to tell the tale," she answered evenly.

"How can you say that to him?" exclaimed Beth. "You have stolen his lordship! Must you insult him too?" Beth glared at Maira and the child at her breast ceased to nurse and turned his head to stare at Maira with vague grey eyes.

She sighed. Perhaps it had been a mistake to come here. But they were still her family, and at least their hostility was a change from the pressure of expectation laid upon her by the rest of the clan.

"If you came here to taunt me, say so and be done with it!" said Eoc hoarsely.

"I came here for counsel," Maira said placatingly. "You know the young warriors better than I. How can I calm them long enough to lay plans that will achieve their end?"

137

Eoc began to laugh, then coughed. "Beth, get me something to ease my throat so that I can tell her why she's wrong!" Eoc's head turned fretfully against the linen pillow that his mother had stuffed with sweet herbs and he closed his eyes. Maira met Beth's resentful glare.

"I won't leave you alone with him!"

"Beth, at least your man is still alive! Here, let me take the babe while you do as he has bid you." She held out her arms, and after a moment Beth grimaced and handed her the child.

Maira cradled the baby against her, finding a curious comfort in his fragile warmth. A surge of fierce protectiveness shook her, as if he had been her own. And indeed, this boy-babe might be her only heir.

"I'll make sure you survive!" she murmured into his soft hair. "I will protect you, my little acorn, until you grow into a great tree!" The grey eyes focused on her face and the rosy lips opened in what could have been a gas-bubble or a smile.

"And just how will you protect him, and you yourself still little more than a child?"

Even in a whisper, the voice was not Beth's. Startled, Maira looked up and saw her mother standing there.

"The walls of Din Rhun are already high," she said defiantly. "If you won't come into the fortress voluntarily I'll send men to bring you there."

"And is this boy to spend his childhood behind stone walls?" asked Druith bitterly. She passed Maira and sat heavily on the bench by the hearth. She was still wrapped in her shawl of heavy grey wool and Maira shivered, stirred by a scrap of dream memory—an old woman, old women, draped in darkness with their seamed faces lit by the fretful flickering of a fire. She fumbled to identify the scene, then Druith picked distaff and spindle from their basket and turned to look at her and it was gone.

"He must go outside sometimes," she said. "How will you keep him safe from the Selgovae with so many of our warriors gone?"

Maira shifted the baby to her shoulder and felt him relax against her. She stared at her mother, remembering the escort that awaited her outside the thorn hedge, choosing her words. Gutuator had told her to seek Druith's counsel. . . .

"Dumnoric's folly has left me no choice but to ally with Rome."

Druith stiffened. "You would sell us to the Emperor like

another Cartimandua? Your brother would never do such a thing! Your father—"

Maira cut off that speech with a harsh laugh that startled the sleeping child, and for a moment she was occupied soothing him to silence again.

"How do you know what Conmor would have done, old woman?" she said coldly. "Does he talk to you?" She stopped abruptly, wondering if Druith knew about her nightly visits to the shrine by the well.

"He fought the Romans. He knew that if you give them a drop they will drain the barrel dry. What kind of an inheritance will that be for this child?"

"Better Rome than the Selgovae!"

"Because you are afraid to face Carric of Din Carn?"

"Your husband died on a Selgovae sword! Doesn't your blood cry for vengeance? Did you love him at all, then, or do you only want to sit at the side of power?" Maira took a deep breath, furious at her mother and at herself for losing control. It was only Druith who had this ability to make her scream like a little child again.

The baby began to whimper, and still shaking, Maira laid him in his cradle.

"You cannot sell your people to the Romans, Maira! I will not have it!"

"Would you forbid Eoc if he wore this gold?" Maira fingered the torque at her neck. "You always loved him more! At least you still have your son; Maelor's is dead, and I will do whatever I must to avenge him, to avenge all of them! I have no choice, now!"

Her voice had risen, and Eoc roused, muttering. Druith went to him.

"Make her go away, mother. Her voice hurts my ears. . . ."

Druith glared at her daughter. "You heard him! I will deal with you later, girl. Go now!"

Maira shrugged and shook back her hair. Did her mother think that threat still had power? She had come here hoping for counsel, hoping that there was another way. But the men outside were waiting for her, and worse than her mother's anger would threaten her if she failed them.

Pintamus and his scouts were already at the Stone of Maponus, a finger of granite set into the turf where the River

Leva flowed into the Salmaes, when Maira and her men arrived. They had wrapped their red cloaks closely around them, for the wind off the water was cold, and their horses were picketed in a hollow where they could graze. But their sentry saw the British warriors coming, and they were already forming up to meet them as they came over the rise.

Maira gave a quick glance over her shoulder and Lod grinned back at her. "Get into line," she hissed. "Look at *them*—do you want to shame me?"

"Never mind the Red Crests, Lady," Petric said comfortably. "They know well we've no need to ride in straight lines to fight."

She glared at him, but there was no time to explain why she wanted to meet the Roman with a following which looked effective, and he shrugged and brought his mount back into position. Maira sighed. After three days' riding, some of it through the rain, there was little they could do to smarten up. Perhaps their toughness would impress the Romans.

"My Lady, you are welcome." Pintamus' brown face showed neither admiration nor scorn. "I would offer you some refreshment, but we've a ride of some hours remaining. Can you continue on now?"

Maira nodded shortly. The last time she had been here was the previous year, at the gathering of the tribes, and her eyes had been on Carric, with the sprig of bloom stuck through his cloak pin, wrestling his bay horse down. She forced the memory away.

Despite their scornful laughter, her own men had formed up close behind her as the two groups joined. Were they wondering if they had done well to follow her? Despite her words after the Selgovae attack, this decision to make an alliance was by no means a settled thing. She thought ruefully that despite her message to Pintamus, it was only after her quarrel with her mother that she had decided finally to ride east to Luguvalium instead of south and west to see the High King.

But her men were still behind her. As the thin line of the Wall grew larger Maira found that thought comforting.

And soon enough she could see the red sandstone bulk of the fortress, with the smoke of Luguvalium across the river beyond. She realized that Pintamus was watching her and schooled her features to give nothing away, hoping he had not seen her eyes widen at the first sight of those high walls.

She heard a murmuring behind her and silenced her men

with a look. But she understood. Din Rhun was a fine fortress, but it owed its strength to nature more than to the work of men. The walls of the Roman fortress called the Petriana rose uncompromising from a gentle rise in the ground. Through the serrations at their tops she saw sentries passing from tower to tower.

The great gate was itself a fortress, with more sentries, and the road was crowded with soldiers, supply-carts and a bewildering collection of town- and country-folk in the mixed Roman-native dress of Britannia. For a moment she stiffened, thinking she saw Antiochus of Tarsus, but when she looked again, he was gone.

Maira straightened and took up her reins, and Roud, feeling her tension, tossed her head and pranced excitedly. Face proudly expressionless, Maira rode beneath the great arch of the gate and into the Petriana.

But the place made her nervous. A thousand men might hold this fortress, plus artisans and servants and native wives, but she had seen more at Lyn Mapon. Was it all the uniforms? They passed into the square before the Praetorium and she realized abruptly that what made her so uneasy was all the straight lines!

The houses of her own people were usually round, surrounded by circular walls. Even when they gathered, their encampments followed the lie of the land. But these Romans had imposed their own order on the landscape with no more care for its natural lines than their rulers had for its people's ways. . . .

But it is no matter. I don't have to like them, only to use them! she told herself, then frowned, for it seemed to her she could hear her mother saying that you were bound to get muddy if you walked through the mire.

Above the Praetorium's huge doors was set a bronze medallion with the face of a man; Maira had seen its like carried as a standard and leaned over to ask the Roman Commander what it was.

"Commodus, the Emperor," he said with a somewhat bitter smile. "Still with us though he's been dead for three years." Her face must have shown her confusion, for he sobered. "The medallion is the standard of the Ala Petriana—the cavalry wing stationed here. It is supposed to bear the features of the reigning Emperor."

"But you have a new Emperor now, do you not?" Maira

stopped, embarrassed because she could not remember the name.

"More or less—depending on who you ask." The bitterness had returned to the Roman's tone. "Septimus Severus wears the purple, and he has proclaimed our old Governor, Clodius Albinus, to be his heir." A Tribune and two other officers passed and Pintamus broke off abruptly, returning their salutes respectfully.

Maira eyed them warily, noting a certain well-fed elegance that contrasted with the lean intensity of the man beside her. Now she was beginning to remember the gossip that had set the tribes to buzzing three years before. The Emperor Commodus had been assassinated, and his death had launched a power struggle among the three greatest generals. The Governor of Britain was one of them, and he had pulled three legions out of the island to support his claim.

And now one of the contenders was dead, and Severus had made peace with his other rival. It should have settled the matter, but Albinus still kept his men in Gaul, and some said that perhaps the warring was not over after all.

She glanced sidelong at Pintamus, wondering where his sympathies lay. He was a junior officer, and he did not seem to be wealthy. But he must know that the people of the White Horse had no gold, so what could he hope to gain by helping them? She frowned.

It had seemed simple, when he offered her Roman help at Din Rhun, but here she saw him as part of something much larger and more alien. She looked around at the swarming people, the uncompromising stone walls, and fought the impulse to wrench her mare's head around and run. This must be what the cattle felt when they first saw the bars of the pen after a summer of freedom on the hills!

If she ordered her men to turn and ride out again would Pintamus try to stop them? Could they even find their way? Reason told her that Rome had no grounds for keeping her, but it also failed to explain why Rome should court her in this way.

"Does it seem very strange?" asked the Decurion. "I felt much the same when I first came to a city, for I grew up in the Iberian hills."

Maira managed a smile. "Where are you taking me?"

"To stable our horses and then to the Praetorium." He motioned toward the large building they had just passed. "The Prefect would like to meet you."

Maira did not ask why. She would learn soon enough, and she did not want him to think she was afraid. She did not seem to be in any danger so far, and she told herself that if she kept her head she should be able to gain more from this meeting than she gave away.

The corridors of the Praetorium were floored with worn wooden boards, but there were painted designs on the walls. The Prefect's antechamber had red tiles, however, and Maira felt warmth rising through them even through her heavy shoes and woolen braes. She looked down for a moment, amazed. She had heard that the Romans had devices for heating their homes this way, but it was only mid-October—hardly cold at all.

Then the carved door with its gilded fretwork opened, and Pintamus took Maira's arm and led her toward the inner room. For a moment Maira held back, thinking, *This man holds the power of Rome. . . . But he is only an officer, and I am a Queen!* Her thought went on, and she lifted her chin and with a long stride preceded Pintamus inside.

"Sir!" Pintamus took a step to one side, stiffened and brought up his arm in a smart salute. "I present to you Maira daughter of Conmor, Lady of the Vindomarci." He turned to Maira. "Lady, you are in the presence of the Tribune Lucius Ostorius Rufus, Prefectus Alae and Commander of the Wall."

"But my dear," the Prefect exclaimed in British, coming out from behind his table and offering her his hand, "you are so young!" Whatever he had been expecting, he was already relaxing, discounting her. Maira managed a sweet smile and let him take her hand. He was a big man, beginning to run to fat a little though his fingers were still calloused and strong, with skin reddened by years of exposure to a sun much hotter than that of Britannia, and thinning reddish hair.

Maira lowered her eyes. "My father died very suddenly and my brother was injured. My father should have ruled for many years, but I must take his place now." She lifted her head and he stepped back a fraction as if she had brought up the blade of a sword. For a moment his eyes measured her, then he glanced quickly at Pintamus and smiled. He gestured, and a slim, dark-skinned man moved forward with a silver tray.

There were three goblets on it, already filled with purple wine. The Prefect picked up one.

"Drink with me." He handed it to Maira and offered another to Pintamus, then took the third. "Let us honor your father's shade." He poured a few drops from his goblet onto the floor, then set it to his lips.

Warily, Maira drank from her own. She had tasted wine only once before and was not sure she liked it, but this stuff was smooth and sweet, and its fire soon settled to a gentle glow. She could understand why some of her people paid so highly for it.

Her fingers caressed the delicate silver filigree of her goblet.

"Do you like my cups?" asked Lucius Ostorius. "They come from Syria, where I served for many years."

"But your British is very fluent," said Maira politely. Even if she had been willing to reveal her knowledge of Latin to Pintamus, she would not have dared try to speak it to this Roman nobleman. She had expected Pintamus to translate for her.

"I was born in Britain," the Prefect said with a smile. "My family has called it home for four generations, and my grandmother was a great lady of the Dobunni in the south. Many officers would consider it a penance to be assigned to this frontier, but Clodius Albinus was doing me a favor when he used his influence to get me transferred home."

Maira stared at him, trying to read the mixture of Celt and Roman in his face. An old Roman-British family, he had said. She wondered what it was like to have such a heritage, and how that lady of the Dobunni had felt, married to a Roman overlord.

The Prefect's bland gaze moved from her to the Iberian officer who stood a little behind her, and she knew abruptly what he was thinking. Perhaps another alliance between Roman and Briton could win Alba as Brittania had been won.

Her own gaze went to the Decurion, assessing him like a horse she thought she might buy. Pintamus had none of the sheer physical presence that haunted her when she thought of Carric, but he was well-built and coordinated—a good man on a horse and probably with a sword. But to marry a Roman—an alien who would not understand the meaning of the sacrificed stallion or the sacred pool! How could she even consider it?

To save my people and avenge my kin I can consider it, she told herself. *I can do whatever I must!*

"And so your High King has given you no help against your enemies?"

Maira realized what Lucius Ostorius was saying and all her attention focused on his words. An offer of help—that was what she had come here to obtain.

"We have treaties with Segovis, and with Buan of the Selgovae too," said the Prefect. "To help one against the other would destroy the peace we have made. But I can officially approve the rebuilding of your defences, and supply you with funds to replace the food and animals you have lost." He saw her stiffen and lifted a hand. "And I will send to King Buan and put pressure upon him to discipline his people. That is all I can do for you, you understand, but it should enable you to protect your clan. . . ."

Maira started to protest. She wanted safety not just for a season, but for the coming years, a safety that only a crushing and final defeat of the warriors of Din Carn could provide. But the Prefect's face had closed against her. This was all that she would get from this man, now.

And at least it was something. She managed a smile.

The Prefect was making marks on a wax tablet, which he handed to Pintamus.

"Thank you for your generosity, sir, and your time," said the Iberian.

"Indeed, the mothers of little children will bless your name this winter, when hunger stalks the hills," said Maira, putting real warmth into her smile. His eyes narrowed appreciatively, but already another officer was coming in with a message in his hand. Maira and her problems were only a minor distraction in a very full day.

Pintamus took her arm and drew her back, saluting once more as he reached the door. Outside, the light was fading. The high edges of the buildings cut sharp lines against the ripening gold of the sky, and there was a pungent smell of cookfires in the air.

"It is too late for you to set off again today," said Pintamus quietly. "But there is a house in the town where I often stay. Would you like to go there? There will be a comfortable room for you and accommodation for your escort, though I doubt they will use it. I suspect they would not mind seeing something of the taverns of Luguvalium!"

Now that she considered it, the fatigue of the day's riding and the stress of meeting the Prefect weighed on Maira's bones. Yes, it would be good to rest, to eat a meal.

And when she had recovered a little, perhaps she could learn more about this one Roman who seemed to have some sympathy for her, though nothing in his manner suggested any attraction, and who might yet be persuaded to stretch the limits of Roman policy.

By the time they had crossed over the river to Luguvalium it was almost dark, and Maira had only dim impressions of a town of wide streets and buildings built from the same red stone as the fort. They passed the bulk of the basilica and the temples of the gods, the walled villas of the wealthy merchants of the town where hanging lamps glimmered among the trees, and continued on into a narrow street redolent with the smell of cooking and echoing with song.

The house to which Pintamus brought them was an inn— Maira had heard of such places, but had never seen one before. The ornamented doorway had a certain faded elegance, a charming foreign air that reminded her of the wares the Greek traders sold.

When she had made sure that her men were settled happily, Maira let herself be persuaded to try the luxury of a Roman bath. It was a small one, not like the great public pools that served the town, but in addition to the cold bath and the warm one, it had a hot tub and a slave girl to assist one to bathe.

Maira lay back in the hot water, letting it soak away her weariness as it washed the soil of her journey away. Suddenly she grinned. Was this the secret of the Romans' power? After they had conquered a country they introduced their captives to this incredible dissipation that softened the body and sapped the nerve. *And it might almost be worth it*, she thought drowsily.

She was used to bathing in icy mountain streams that left the skin glowing and every nerve alive. But just for once, it was very good to lie in warm water while someone soaped your hair. To let yourself be cradled, to be supported as gently as by a mother's arms.

Abruptly Maira sat up, remembering her mother's last words to her.

"Domina, have I pulled too hard on your hair?" the slave girl's soft voice distracted her. "It is so beautiful. May I rinse it now?"

Apologizing, Maira sank back to let the girl finish the job, but much of the pleasure had gone. She refused a concluding plunge in the *frigidarium*, got out and let the girl dry her with a soft towel.

"Here is a gown the officer has sent for you. He says the room where you will dine is very warm. This is a *tunica* such as the Roman ladies wear. . . ."

Maira suppressed a smile. She did not know if Pintamus wanted to win her to Roman ways or only to have a dinner companion who would do him credit, but she certainly had no desire to put back on a heavy tunic that smelled of horses and the sweat of the road. The gown the girl was holding up was of fine linen, dyed a lovely misty blue like a spring sky. And Maira had always wondered what she would look like in a Roman robe. . . .

Maira stood in the doorway to the dining chamber, smoothing the folds of the *tunica* and summoning up the courage to go in. The gown was so light—she felt half-naked, wearing it, and oddly, more diffident than she had ever been when the men of her own people saw her half-stripped for games or ritual. Perhaps it was because they understood just what her exposure did and did not mean. Or perhaps it was only that she feared these foreign garments made her ridiculous.

Pintamus was already lying on the dining couch, staring into the coals of the brazier that heated the room. There was a little table in front of him, bearing a pitcher and two cups of red Samian ware. They used couches something like that for the great feasts at the High King's house in Carbantorigum, but Maira had always eaten with the women of the Queen. Perhaps that was what seemed so odd—there were only herself and the Roman officer in the room.

A cold draft from behind her stirred the folds of her gown and she sneezed. Pintamus turned, and Maira came slowly into the room. She was watching his face anxiously, and despite his control, she saw the widening of the eyes that betrayed astonishment, and the growing glow of appreciation as he continued to look at her.

"The dress of my people suits you very well," he said at last. He eased over on the couch and motioned to her to recline beside him.

She eyed it dubiously. "Do Roman ladies dine with their men this way?"

"Sometimes," he said blandly. "Do not be afraid."

Her chin lifted. He must not think he had frightened her, and besides, there was nowhere else to sit in the room. Rather stiffly, she settled herself upon the couch by his side. He had bathed too, and his hair had been dressed with some pleasantly scented oil. Maira was very aware of the perfume, lying there beside him, and of the warmth of his body so close to her own. He clapped his hands and a serving lad appeared at the other door.

"We are ready now for the dinner I ordered, and more wine." He poured a cup and handed it to her, then lifted his own in salute. Maira sipped gingerly. She had already had more wine to drink today than she had ever tasted in her life before. She wondered if it were more potent than heather beer.

"This is not so good a vintage as the Prefect serves." Pintamus seemed to sense her thoughts. "His comes all the way from Greece in great amphorae, while this stuff is from Gaul."

Maira smiled. "I think I like this better. It is not so strong."

The Roman shook his head and grinned. "Don't count on that—it's sweeter, that's all!"

"Your Prefect was very gracious," she went on. "Will he do all he promised for me?"

The boy brought in a bowl of lentils cooked with onions and spices and a basket of soft bread. There was a blue glass flask of *muria* on the tray as well. Maira's nose wrinkled at the pungent fishy odor and she waved it away, but Pintamus seemed to enjoy it. He poured some out and mopped it up with a piece of bread, then washed it down with a swallow of wine and turned to her.

"He gave me the order for the money, but it was too late to go to the pay master. We will pick it up in the morning, and you may find it easiest to purchase grain in bulk from the merchants here."

Maira nodded. "And what about his messages to the High Kings—did he say that only to humor me?"

The Decurion shrugged. "He meant it, and he will do it—when he has time. But I do not think you should depend too much on its effectiveness."

"I understand. If my own King would not act on my appeal, why should he pay attention to a suggestion from Rome?

Especially since—" She stopped herself, wondering whether she should say what she had heard. But surely he must know. "The word among the tribes goes that your Governor sent gold to the northern princes before he took the Legions out of Britain to fight for the Emperor's power."

Now it was the Roman's turn to look embarrassed. It must be a hard thing for him to know that the British beyond the Wall were held in check by treaties and gold instead of by the arms of Rome.

The servant brought them a dish of venison cooked in a sauce made with honey and preserved fruit in wine. Maira's head was already buzzing, and though the feeling was not unpleasant, she was afraid to drink much more. She reached for the water flask to dilute what was in her cup.

"Do you think they will keep those treaties?" Pintamus said baldly. Maira wondered if the wine he had drunk was affecting him too.

"Why not?" she answered bitterly. "It is easier to be paid than to fight, and as long as we are fighting each other, we cannot fight you."

There was a sudden alertness in the man beside her. Maira turned to look at him and was startled when he took her hand.

"Such a white, shapely, hand to hold a sword," he said softly. "Why do you fight each other, Maira?" He was still holding her hand, his hard fingers moving gently across the calluses made by the hilt of her sword and caressing the tender skin in the center of the palm.

The boy took away the venison and replaced it with a brace of roasted pigeons seasoned with garlic and thyme, but Maira no longer felt hungry. Pintamus did not eat much either. He was still waiting for her to answer, still stroking her hand. She felt that light touch all the way up her arm.

"For glory . . . for cattle . . . or perhaps for excitement . . . ," she answered slowly. "It has always been our way. But for me it is different now. My father is dead and my people are in danger because—" She broke off. She had been about to say, *because of the weakness of one I thought I loved*, but that was not a thing to tell another man. "Because the Selgovae have made it more than a game!" she finished, and hoped he had not noticed the pause.

"And you hate them?" he said softly. Now he was touching her arm. His hand moved delicately over the soft skin of her shoulder, pale where it so rarely felt the sun, and to her neck where her ruddy hair had been fastened up with pins. The servant replaced the fowl with honey-cakes and poured them more wine. Then he retreated to the corner of the room and began to play upon a wooden flute.

Maira remembered how Tadhg had played for her, and her eyes stung with tears. Then her body remembered Carric's touch, and she felt the hot blood flush her fair skin. Carric had said that he loved her, and Tadhg had been killed by Carric's men. . . .

"Yes," she whispered viciously. "Yes, I hate them."

Pintamus' hand came back down to the clasp at the shoulder of her tunica, and she remembered how Carric had unpinned her dancing gown. She lay still as the Roman's clever fingers manipulated the bronze fibula and let the two pieces of the tunica fall free so that her breast was bare.

She whispered, "Din Carn must be destroyed. . . ."

The Roman bent over her, kissed the words from her lips and moved down her neck to her breast. Shuddering with hatred and arousal, she lay back in his arms.

"My Commander will never authorize an expedition, but he cannot know where I take my men once we ride out of the Petriana," he murmured against her hair. The pins were loosening and she could feel the silky mass of it cascading down.

"Will you fight for me?" She pushed the folds of his toga away and gripped his shoulder, feeling the hard muscles move beneath his smooth skin as his hands searched her body.

"My men and yours together, disguised so that the Selgovae do not know who we are. . . ." His sword-hardened fingers slipped under the skirts of her gown and found the softness between her thighs. Maira gasped and held hard to his shoulders, for there was no strength in her legs now. The serving boy was still playing in his corner, a sweet sad piping like a memory of love, but she did not care.

She thought that perhaps Pintamus had not intended to seduce her until he saw her clean and dressed in the Roman gown, but ever since the Prefect had offered such minimal aid she had hoped for this opportunity. She lifted her head and her lips brushed Pintamus' neck and the smooth-shaven chin; she drew him down to her and found his mouth, nibbling, biting, until she felt him trembling too. Then she pulled away.

"With our combined numbers, all trained fighters, we will outnumber the warriors of Din Carn," she whispered breathlessly. Pintamus was pulling at his toga, and she loosened her grip so that he could get free. Then she reached down to arouse him, but he was already stiff and ready for her.

"We will fall upon them with torches to burn their homes as they burned mine."

His fingers found the heart of her pleasure and she moaned as her flesh seemed to burst into flame.

Pintamus' voice came harsh in her ear. "Their flesh will sheathe our thirsty swords!"

And then his weight crushed her and Maira cried out as he thrust into her, in pain, in passion, in triumph.

And the darkness that came after was like death, in which her only memory was the sorrow of the flute-player's song.

TEN

The Circle Between The Worlds

THE MISTS WERE still smoking off the dark waters of the lake when Maira came out of the house on the crannog. The compacted brush mat upon which it was built gave slightly to her step, and she reached out for balance to one of the pilings that rose from the lakebed below. After three days with Neithon of Lyn an Gêi, she was still uneasy at living upon the water, but he had agreed to join the warparty when she went against Din Carn, and that was the important thing.

She took a deep breath of the damp air, stretching cramped muscles and trying to clear the mists of sleep from her mind. She had not slept well here, but she did not know if that was because of the strange setting, or from some lingering reaction to her night with Pintamus a week ago. . . .

Only a week! Maira shook her head in wonder. Sometimes what had happened between them seemed an unlikely dream. But when she heard a flute or felt the bruises on her breasts and arms, the feel of his hands upon her was as vivid as if it had happened a moment ago.

She bit her lip angrily. It was not the bruises that disturbed her, for she had left her mark on him as well—it was the persistence of the memory. She had meant only to bind the Roman to her until her vengeance was done, and if now there were a link between them, then her night of love with Carric might still bind her to *him* as well. . . .

When he is dead the link will be broken, she thought. *Then I will be free.*

"Lady, the boat is ready now."

She turned and saw Neithon himself beside her, drops of mist glittering in his iron-grey hair. He was a big, sturdy man, limping a little when the damp pained the leg he had broken years ago, but hearty and energetic still. She was amazed that he had agreed to follow her, for his lands were at the southeastern boundary of White Horse territory, and the crannog, set in the midst of its lake, was as safe a retreat as Din Rhun.

"Thank you." She reached out and pressed his hand. "And thank you for the word you have given me."

"Aye—well, it's been long since I took the war trail, and I loved your father." Neithon led the way to the edge of the platform and held the boat steady for her to get in. Urr followed her, and she saw more of the flat-bottomed craft drawn up ready to take her other men.

As the long strokes of the pole sent the boat surging over the water, Maira wondered if that was why the other warriors she had visited on this journey had agreed—for the game and the glory rather than from her sense of grim necessity.

But it does not matter why they do it, she told herself, *so long as they come to me when I send word!*

Mist hid the tree-tops, but the air was clearing nearer the ground. The horses penned beneath the trees lifted their heads as the boats neared, ears flicking and nostrils flaring as scent and hearing identified the strange moving shapes on the water.

Maira slapped Roud's neck and staggered as the mare shoved back at her. She stroked the soft muzzle and picked up the bridle; Roud tossed her head coquettishly and Maira cuffed her.

"You're glad to see me but you aren't ready to go back to work? Is that it?" Maira laughed as the roan head dipped penitently, and deftly slipped the bridle on. It would be good to be on horseback once more, and on the road for home. There were several other housesteads they could visit on their way, but these were close enough for a later journey from Din Rhun. Right now all she wanted was to see the pointed peak of the fortress against the sky.

Soon they were all mounted, and the pack ponies were protesting the weight of the sacks of grain. But as they moved out along the muddy road something flickered among the reeds as if the mist itself had taken a form. Roud shied and as Maira reined her down the bird blazed white in the sunlight and flew away.

"A crane!" Urr made the Sign against evil and the other men began muttering. But Maira set her heels into Roud's sides and drove her onward. She did not care what omens appeared—she was *not* going to spend another night on the crannog.

Neithon had predicted that the mist would burn off by noon, and Maira was relieved to see the air grow brighter. They rode single-file through a beech-wood that steamed with moisture as the sun grew stronger; the leaves were mellowing with the rich tones of autumn, and the whole world seemed fashioned of silver and gold. Somewhere above was a hint of pale sky.

To reach Lyn an Gêi they had crossed the River Nova and swung westward. Now they were heading east again, toward the road by the river that would lead them home. But within an hour of their nooning the air thickened suddenly. Everything beyond a few horses' lengths ahead dimmed as the veils of mist dropped down once more. Even sound seemed deadened. When the path branched the light had no direction to tell them which way to go.

Urr pointed to the left. "Lady, this road seems more travelled. Whether it is the right road or no, surely it is more likely to lead us to some dwelling where we can get directions."

Maira sighed. She had strained her ears with listening and her eyes in peering through the gloom. And it was her own fault—if she had had the sense to ask Neithon for a guide there would have been no difficulty. In the silence all she could hear was Roud's gusty breathing and her own pulse thudding in her ears.

"Very well." She lifted the reins to urge Roud forward, heard something and reined in sharply. Confused, the mare tossed her head. Yes, surely she heard someone singing— something that was harmonious without having a melody.

She turned to ask Urr what he thought it was, but he was waiting for her to lead on with a patient unconcern that stopped the words in her throat. Couldn't he hear it? Then perhaps it was a delusion, or a sending to her alone.

But if she could not understand it, neither could she withstand its call. Schooling her features, she turned Roud onto the path.

Very soon they heard the sound of the river, and sighed in wordless gratitude as the trail dipped down to follow it. Maira had thought the Nova was broader here, but it had been a dry summer, and she could not claim to know its whole length well.

They went forward and the singing grew louder. There were words now, in no language that Maira knew. Then the road descended the riverbank, and before they realized what was happening they were splashing through a shallow ford.

This *could not* be the Nova. Maira tried to stop, but the singing compelled her. Her men were muttering behind her, but their mounts imitated Roud's eager jog up the hill and through trees that opened out into a broad meadow.

Maira's heart thumped abruptly. She saw a circle of grey shapes humping out of the mist; a paler shape in the midst of them from whose swirling robes the mists seemed to flow. It was from this central figure that the singing came.

"The circle!" exclaimed Urr. "The circle of the Old Ones and their sacred stones! How did we get here?"

Maira felt something contract in her breast as she recognized them, but at least now she knew where they were. The stone circle lay on one of the Nova's principal tributaries—they must have turned upstream when they should have continued down to its junction with the river a few miles above Din Prys.

And still the silent singing rang in her ears.

"Do you see nothing else there?" she whispered finally.

"But Lady—" They shook their heads. "What else would there be but meadow mist swirling around the old stones?"

"There is something else," she said. "It calls to me. The necessity is upon me—I must go in." After she had said that, they could do nothing, though their faces showed their fear. If a compulsion drew her it was her right and her duty to obey it. She was the Queen.

Maira dismounted and handed her reins to Urr. Roud whickered anxiously as she walked toward the circle, but she kept on, and as she passed between the stones the mist seemed to thicken behind her. When she looked back she could see nothing but a flicker of light that darted from left to right around the circle, sealing her in.

She was shaking, and her hand closed on the cold grip of her useless sword. She came to a halt before the white figure in the center of the circle. Its face was hidden by a deep hood, but nothing covered the flowing silver beard. Fractionally Maira's fear began to ease. He lifted his head and she met his eyes.

"So—you have come."

Maira did not know if she heard him with her physical ears. Not that it mattered. He had called her out of the world she knew to the place *Between* where only the Druids walked at will. She straightened proudly. She knew that Gutuator could read her fear if he wished to; it was herself that she needed to fool now.

"I have come, grandfather, but why have you called me here? Surely you could talk to me in Din Rhun without making such a mystery!" She tried to laugh.

"Perhaps, though in the Middle World it is harder to speak true," he answered her. "But that is not why I have summoned you." He took a deliberate step to the side and Maira gasped as she glimpsed another figure behind him.

"Only here would you talk to *him*," said Gutuator. He gestured, and life leaped in the statue's eyes. Carric's eyes, in Carric's hated face!

"Traitor!" she hissed at the Druid. "I thought you had some love for me! How could you do this?"

"My child," Gutuator said softly, "I have loved and will love you longer than you can know. . . ."

But Maira hardly heard him. Carric was straightening; his lips moved—

"Trost? I thought I saw Trost beckoning from the old standing stone. . . ." He rubbed his eyes, focused on Gutuator, and took an involuntary step backward, his fingers flickering in the warding sign. "How did *you* get here?" He stopped, looking around him, then tried to laugh. "No, not here, for the stone is gone. How did I get *there*, wherever. . . ." His wandering gaze found Maira, and his hand went to his side. But he had no sword, only the long-bladed hunting spear.

Maira stared back at him, for a moment too shaken by his physical presence to think of hate or fear. Had he grown taller, or was his face thinner, with lines where there had been none before? He looked older, harder, and wrenchingly, more beautiful. Suddenly she saw what he would be in full maturity.

"This Circle lies between the Worlds," came the deep voice of the Druid. "And what is between the Worlds transcends the world. We come to this place from three realities, but there is only a single Present now."

Maira shook her head in confusion. What other reality could there be but the doom that lay between her and Carric?

"Have you brought him to me so that I may take my vengeance? Or to claim the honor-price for your daughter's husband?"

"What good would wealth or vengeance be to me?" Gutuator bowed his head.

"Then why bring us here?" Carric exclaimed.

The Druid's gaze fixed each of them in turn. "I serve the Truth—always and only. I have brought you here to find the Truth you share!"

"Then its name is Love!" cried Carric, his gaze kindling.

"It is Death!" Maira's reply crossed his and hung, echoing, in the still air. The mist seemed to thicken; for a moment Gutuator and Carric were only shadows, as if her own words had cut her off from them.

"But why, Maira—why?" As Carric turned to her his figure brightened. For a moment the glow in his face made her want to hide her eyes.

"Why?" Her voice cracked. "You killed my father, and Tadhg!"

"Maira, *I* did not kill your father," Carric said gently. "And the man who did died at your hand, have you never considered what that meant to me?"

Maira blinked, for where Carric had been she saw now darkness and the leaping light of a fire, and then herself, standing above Trost's empty body with her father's bloody head cradled in her arms.

And then she saw another scene—a girl whom she remembered seeing at Lughnasa, weeping and rocking back and forth, murmuring Trost's name. Her body was rounding in pregnancy, but her child would never know its father or honor his grave.

At least I had my father's care until I was grown. . . . She thrust the thought away.

The visions faded. Maira coughed. "If you had kept your warriors away from Lys Speiat, both Trost and my father would be alive today," she said bitterly.

"They are not *my* warriors! Only my friends! My father is still chieftain, and I only command the men who are oathed to me!"

"Then why did you come with them?" she cried suddenly, remembering his face in the firelight, reliving her pain.

"I thought I could control them . . . ," he answered with such a weight of sadness that she wanted to go to him, to tell him that it did not matter anymore. "I thought I could keep it from going too far."

She took a step toward him and his head came up suddenly. "And have you done so much better, Maira of Din Rhun, that you can scorn me? If you could not keep your hotheads from trying to raid us, what did you expect *us* to do? I tried to draw my men off when we reached the *dun*. I am sorry for the death of your harper—but if you had not run out from behind your defenses like a fool he need not have died! You *are* the chieftain, Maira, cannot you control yourself, or your men?"

Maira felt swift color flame in her face. She had not stopped them—she could not stop them now.

"Oh Maira, Maira, I have tried so hard! If I could only make you *see!*"

And abruptly she did see—the tense faces of the Selgovae underlit by a council fire. She saw Carric summoning unsuspected eloquence to plead with them, saw some of the older men nodding, saw the clan mothers agree. But the young warriors jeered at him and then he dared to say no more. It was their chance at glory that all this talk of conciliation would steal.

"But at least I got Cador to agree to wait. Haven't you wondered why no attack in full force has come, when all the country is buzzing with talk of your fortifications and preparations for war?" Carric turned to her and held out his hands.

In this clear light his hair shone like red bronze. He was wearing a laced leather tunic that left his arms bare— there was a pink scar on one of them and she wondered if he had gotten it in the fight at Din Rhun. Muscles moved beneath his skin and she remembered the strength of his arms, holding her. . . .

All of her senses resonated to that memory. She fought to keep her knees from trembling, but there was nothing she could do about the aching emptiness she had not known existed before they lay together; that void that nothing, not even her night with the Roman officer, had been able to fill.

"You understand, don't you?" Carric cried. "You need me as much as I need you. Oh Maira, do you know what I'm feeling, girl?" He was very close to her now. He reached out and touched her cheek gently. "Maira—" His voice was hoarse. "Your skin is like the breast of a dove. . . ."

She shut her eyes as his hands closed on her arms. She felt as if only his strong grip kept her from falling. *Blessed Goddess,* she thought desperately, *I cannot allow my body to master me.*

"Carric," she managed to say his name at last. "What can I do?"

"Make peace for us both, my love." His breath was warm against her ear. "Your strong walls will keep your people safe. Swear peace for them and come marry me! You are their Lady—they will have to accept what you do!"

Visions flowed from his mind into hers—fat cattle grazing, fair-haired children wrestling with puppies in the bracken beside the fire, herself, with him beside her, cantering over the moors.

And the sight of his bay stallion reminded her of the horse whose death had made her Queen. Vividly she saw that fine head poised as they brought him to her, and his blood crimson on the ground. Shuddering, she pulled away.

"Carric—that is just it. I am their Lady. Can you imagine what that means? I am married already. By the Great Rite. Married to *them!*" She paused and saw his face change and knew that he was seeing her memories as she had seen his, understanding what the ritual had been like for her. "What will they feel if I abandon them to live with their enemy? And I must tell you this, too—chieftain though I be, I can no more hold my warriors forever than you can. They will have blood, and if I do not lead them to it they will have mine! It is my death you are asking for when you ask me to come to you, for I can be released from that bonding no other way. . . . ."

"There must be a way!" he said passionately. "We'll both leave—I'll take you north to the country of the Caledonii. We will find some far glen where we can pasture a few cattle and make love through the long nights until spring comes again."

Exile. . . . Maira stared at him, wondering that he would accept that worst of punishments for her.

"And do you think we can live thus forever, out of the world?" she said at last, blinking away tears. "The word will wing its way here somehow, and then they will come after us." The mists around her seemed to swirl with crimson shadows.

"Then we will go south!" he said cheerfully, reaching for her again. "Even the most vengeful warrior will not follow us into the arms of Rome!"

Maira flinched away, staring at him in horror. The arms of Rome! She had lain in the arms of Rome through a night of passion that was more hate than love. Desperately she tried to shut away the memory, lest Gutuator's magic should show it to Carric as it had shown him the rest.

"Very well, I should not have said that—I know how you hate them. But there must be some place we can go!" Carric threw his hands wide and turned to Gutuator. "Tell her—tell her that she must come away with me!"

Gutuator did not move. "I do not *tell*," he said softly, "I mediate, I show—but you must decide."

Carric turned back to Maira, his face flushed and eager in that uncompromising light. "Maira, say you will come to me somehow—promise me!"

She stared at him, and the face of Pintamus appeared between them, so clear to her that she could not believe he did not see it too. Would Carric look at her with such longing if he knew that she had used her body to buy his death from Rome?

"If you do not," his face grew as hard as the stone from which he took his name, "if you do not, then this is the end for us. I can bear this struggle no longer; I can seek no more ways to save both your people and my own!"

Maira bit her lip to keep it from trembling. If she looked at him she would be undone. It was over—over! And it had never really had a chance to begin! She must not let him see the grief that was twisting her belly. She forced coldness into her voice as she replied.

"Carric, it ended when my father died. . . ."

"And so you will cling to his corpse instead of opening your arms to a living man? What children will he give you?" he asked bitterly. Then his face changed. "Or perhaps he was always the rival. It was not the clan nor the land that held you from me, but a love for your father that went beyond a daughter's loyalty!"

Maira remembered Conmor's headless body sprawled on the bloody ground. Conmor was her father—of course she loved him, but not as Carric had said! The thought brought bile to her throat. It was not true; she kept Conmor's head because she needed his guidance. She could not rule the clan with her own wisdom alone!

"You told me I was the first, but was that true?" Anguish, and anger, carried Carric on. "Or did your own father have you long ago?"

Emotions she could not name exploded Maira's awareness. Without volition the sword sprang into her grasp and she leaped for him, shouting obscenities.

Light flared around her; dimensions shifted dizzily and the world disappeared. Maira's sword came down on nothing; there was no earth beneath her—she was falling, no, she had fallen—she lay, breathing in hoarse gasps, feeling the moisture from the wet grass beginning to seep through her clothes.

After what seemed a very long time, Maira forced her body upright. Beyond the stones she could see her men. Urr was trying to persuade the others to come into the circle after her. The stones had seemed grey in the mist, but she could see that they were actually a kind of pink now. She looked up. The mists were disappearing, and pale sunlight slanted through the trees.

Petric shouted. Maira lifted one hand, then got to her feet. There was no one else in the circle; no other footprints on the wet grass. But she had not really expected there would be. Wearily she rubbed her eyes, then walked back to her men.

"Lady, what happened?" Urr asked when they had retraced their steps to the road that followed the Nova northward and home. "You disappeared into the mists and then suddenly they swirled and began to break up and we saw you lying on the ground!"

Somewhere to the north and east of here, Carric would be finding his feet, still hearing the rustle as the animal he had been pursuing fled away.

"Was it the spirits of the Forest, or ghosts of the Old Ones seeking your soul?" asked Lod. "Is it danger for the clan?"

Maira shook her head. There was always danger—no more now than there had been before.

"It was a message from Gutuator, but it was for me alone." Her whole body ached with loss, but she had one bitter consolation. . . . At least Carric knew that it was war between them now.

Her men, accepting that what had happened was Druid business, followed her home in silence. And if they saw the tears that would trickle down her cheeks no matter how she tried to master them, they did not dare to ask her why.

ELEVEN

Samain

SAMAIN WAS FIRE and darkness, as the sun faded earlier with each day. The Romans divided this season between the eighth and ninth months of their year, but for Maira's people it was the moon of the ivy's flowering, whose spirals signified the beginning of the winter's rest and the new year. Yet Samain itself was something different, belonging neither to the old year nor to the new. It was a time when the doorway between past and future, between life and death, was set ajar.

And which of the dead will visit us this year? wondered Maira as she came out of her house. *Will Conmor appear as a presence for all to recognize?* Her meeting with Carric had shaken her, and perhaps she had put less passion into her persuading when she returned to Din Rhun. She had many promises of support for the war party from down the valley, but here, in her own place, many looked at the high walls she had compelled them to raise and replied that with such defenses there was no need to go to war. Perhaps Conmor's ghost could persuade them where she could not!

The others, like Dumnoric and Maelor, chafed at every day of careful planning that kept them from their revenge. Maira was using all her authority to hold them, leashed and straining like hunting dogs eager to be after their prey. But there would be no more irresponsible raiding of the kind that had killed Tadhg and Maelor's son. This was war, not a day's hunting, and when Maira struck, the blow would be a final one.

She saw Antiochus trudging up the path and lifted a hand in greeting. The trader had driven his wagon up the Vale earlier that afternoon and had made camp just outside the walls. She had sent word to him to come to her when he was settled in.

"I liked it better when you dwelt down by the water," he said, panting. "When I was young I was like a goat upon the hills, but such a climb is hard on old bones. I'll be glad to get back to my own country, where the ground is flat as a summer sea." His face was still flushed above the black beard.

She smiled. "But isn't the view from up here worth climbing for?" The last light of the dying sun glowed rosy on the Selgovae hills and lent a deeper luster to the fading leaves of the trees in Scaur Vale. The air had the peculiar crisp clarity of early winter, hazed by the wood smoke whose aromatic scent teased at her memory.

Antiochus grunted and wiped sweat from his forehead with a corner of his cloak. "I just came from there," he said, gesturing eastward.

Maira grew very still. "Do you have a message for me?"

Antiochus shrugged. "You must not blame me, Lady. Young men are hotheads. You must not allow yourself to be upset by the form of the words."

"What did he say?" She knew her voice was too loud, too hard, and fought for control.

"He says that wolves mate for life, but if one partner goes rabid, even its mate will flee from it, lest it infect the pack and all die. Death lies between you now!"

Maira stared at him. She had said the same to Carric at their last meeting, why did she feel as if a sword was twisting in her breast?

"He says—forgive me—that you wear power like a child trying on its father's robes. You want to be a legend, and you have betrayed your own people as well as his love!"

The wind shifted and Maira's nostrils flared at the lingering stench of blood from the autumn slaughtering. For a moment blood filled her vision as well—Conmor's blood, the stallion's blood, Carric's blood. How *dare* he say such things of her!

She realized that she was trembling, and forced herself to calm. She must not let this foreigner see her fury. She must think of something else—of the Samain feast, of butchered beef hanging in the smokehouses, turning gently as the air currents nudged it, packed in salt, or pickling in brine. It went hard to slaughter cattle, but there was never enough fodder to keep all of them through the winter, especially this year, and every autumn they must choose which beasts to sacrifice to the good of the clan. What they had now should be enough to keep them, if the winter was not too long or hard.

Blood and fire—we die by it, and we live, thought Maira. She wondered if Carric were standing somewhere, breathing in the same scents on the autumn breeze, despising her. In Din Carn, as here, each family would be baking special bannocks and preparing the flesh of the dearest of their cattle, the "mortal one," to welcome the spirits of the dead back home. Would Trost's spirit be able to find its way back from his unhallowed grave by Lys Speiat to Din Carn? Damn him— damn them all!

"Thank you," she said tightly. "Will you join us tonight for the feasting?"

"I am too tired with traveling." He shook his head, his eyes moist with regret. "I would fall asleep with my feet in the fire. I will rest in my wagon, and in the morning lay out my wares for any of your folk who wish to see."

Maira stayed where she was after Antiochus had left her, striving for calm. Suppressed, her anger turned abruptly to sorrow.

Suddenly she wished she had returned Trost's body to his kin. It could have been Dumnoric, or Eoc, who was lying in alien soil. Perhaps next spring, when winter had cleansed the bones, she would send to the Selgovae to claim their son.

If I am still here to send word to anyone! Her thoughts sought their logical conclusion. She fought well for her strength, but war was chancy even for the strong. Perhaps by next spring she herself would lie among the stones of Carric's stronghold, forever exiled from the friendly shadow of Din Rhun.

"Maira, my Lady, what are you doing? I thought you came out to light the torch!" Ness bustled past her and snatched the flints from her hand. Maira shook her head in self-mockery, realizing how her mind had wandered, and let the old woman strike sparks into the tinder and coax the little flame to grow.

"Thank you, Ness. The evening is so lovely I was distracted." She lit a splinter from the fire and touched it to the head of the torch bound to the pole before the door, taking a quick step back as the torch burst into hungry flame. The woman of the house always lit the Samain torches, one for each ghost the family was calling home.

One torch for Conmor—she saluted it, then turned to light the other flame for Tadhg, though it was likely enough that his spirit had winged like a homing gull across the grey seas to Eirinn.

Fires were blossoming before the other dwellings of the Dun as well, and in the steadings up and down the vale, as if some of the early stars had fallen to the earth and were burning there. The little lights made the shadows seem darker, suddenly. Maira shivered and followed Ness back to the friendly glow of the hearthfire.

The feast was ready. She settled herself on the bench to the right of the place of honor behind the fire and facing the open door. There was a carved chair there, her place, usually, but tonight it waited for an invisible guest. Maira lifted the cup of polished oakwood bound with silver and made the sign of blessing across the beer it contained, then set it on the bench.

"For Conmor." She raised her own cup in salute.

"For Conmor." From the Women's Side Temella and Ness echoed her, while across from them the voices of Lod and his two brothers provided a deep harmony.

Ness hastened to set a platter beside the cup, laden with the chieftain's portion of the beef she had cooked that afternoon garnished with onions and apples, the late greens and the barley bannocks dripping with fresh butter, and the chunk of white cheese. Then she served the others.

"Eh, Temella—next year you'll be keeping the feast in your own house, no doubt, and asking the spirits to fill your belly with a child!" Ness grinned at Temella, who nodded and tried to control the blush that was reddening her fair skin.

Maira stared at her, realizing how long it had been since anyone had embarrassed *her* by such teasing. Of course the Clan gossiped about whom she would marry, and after a time they might become uneasy if she showed no signs of taking a man and bearing a child. But they had all seen her married to the Red Stallion; they would not joke with her about weddings now. She was aware of an absurd pang of loss.

Temella was babbling on about Dumnoric. He had given away some of his cattle to families who had lost men on his raid, but he would get more, and then they would be married. She gave Maira a quick glance, half hope, half apprehension, and Maira suppressed a bitter smile. Only by risking his life again in battle with the Selgovae was Dumnoric likely to win more wealth soon.

The dog poked his cold nose into her palm, and distracted, she fed him a morsel of meat with the crisp fat still on.

Windchaser was still clumsy in the house, but fleet as a deer on the meadows; the beef disappeared as if he had inhaled it and he sat, trembling with eagerness, his eyes fixed hopefully on her face.

It had grown quite dark and Maira felt a breath of cold wind brush her cheek as the wind found the open door. Light from the torches outside flickered crazily, chasing the shadows until it seemed as if it was not the torchlight but something moving before it that made them. Something, or Someone. . . .

Maira felt some shift deep within her and put out a foot to brace herself—but it was not the bench that had moved. The feeling was oddly different, but now she recognized it. She had felt it within the circle of stone.

The Otherworld is drawing close to us now. The hair on her arms and the back of her neck lifted with a chill that was not cold. Had her consecration given her this perception, or her experience in the circle between the worlds? Or was there something different about Samain this year— something dangerous?

The dog unfolded his gangling limbs suddenly to stand beside her. Had he sensed something? But no—it was her own movement off her bench that had alerted him. With a sigh she sat down again. She had been about to go down to the spring to commune with the head of her father. But what answer could she have looked for on this of all nights, when Conmor's spirit could be anywhere? Her uneasy gaze sought the empty chair and Windchaser whined, sensing her anxiety.

"Do you see something there, lad, or do you only want that bone?" Maira smiled ruefully and gentled the dog's silky ears.

Temella and Ness were roasting nuts in the fire, laughing as the cooking meat inside made them pop and skitter on the hot coals. Ness was renowned in the Clan for her skill in interpreting their motions, but as usual, the prophecies seemed to be all of children and marriages. And perhaps that was inevitable on this night when all the spirits seeking reincarnation came home. At Conmor's funeral they had prayed, *"May you be reborn to the Clan!"* Once more death and birth confronted her as two halves of a whole.

Maira set her half-empty platter among the bracken fronds for the dog to polish and gazed into the coals as if she could read her future in the play of light and shadow there.

Then Windchaser lifted his long, mouse-colored muzzle, flopped ears pricking. His lanky body stiffened, and after a moment the beating of his plumed tail rustled the bracken.

"What is it lad? Who's coming?" Like the dog, she strained to hear.

But she felt it first, as a tremor in the earth beneath her, a pulse-beat transmitted through the living rock of Din Rhun, and recognized the rhythm of the Samain drums. She stiffened, then laughed at her own anxiety, but still something deep within her resonated to that subliminal pounding.

Presently her ears heard it too—the sound of deep drums, of rattles made of bladders filled with stones and of voices chanting the Samain song. Temella jumped up, with Lod and his brothers close behind her. More slowly, Maira and Ness followed them.

Torches were bobbing on the slope below. The procession always started at the farmsteads farther down the vale—they would just be leaving Maelor's housestead now. The torches came to an uneven halt before the cluster of huts at the first gate of the Dun. She saw shadows moving, and something pale that dipped and swung in the uncertain glow. For a moment the chanting ceased, then there was a burst of laughter.

Temella grinned. "Is the beer ready? If everyone is being equally generous, I wonder that the dancers had the wind to climb the hill. They had more time to sober up between stops when we were spread all over the valley!"

Maira smiled and gave her friend a swift hug. Last year they had danced with the procession all the way up Scaur Vale. It seemed like another lifetime now.

The torches started moving again. The drumming grew louder as they progressed from house to house in the outer circle, clockwise around the hill. The words of the chant came intermittently, with the householders' replies.

> "Behold, here we are,
>   Come from afar,
>   Your gates, friends, unbar—
>   And hear us sing!"

They were at Waric's house now—as large and well-built as Maira's own. They heard his voice answering, hoarse with age but still loud.

> "Wise ones, tell me true,
>   How many are you?

And give your names too—
That we may know."

Maira and Temella peered over the inner wall. The singers were anonymous under coverings of animal skins trimmed with bits of colored wool, scraps of cloth, bright bits of metal and rattling bones. Their faces were hidden behind masks. Boar and bull, stag and ram, bear and wolf and wild-cat cavorted in the torchlight, now making as if to rush the house door, now splitting apart to dance with the girls who followed them, bodies arching suggestively until their antics sent the girls in giggling retreat to the protection of the crowd.

Their names were the names of the beasts whose semblances they bore—the totem animals of all the families. But above them loomed a flapping, clacking, monstrosity—the White Mare—with the bleached horse's skull wired to its pole so that the jaw could be opened and shut, and the worn pale horsehide flowing down to conceal the man who bore it.

A simple head-count let one guess which men of the Clan were in the procession. But they were all equally anonymous. No one knew in advance who would carry the Mare.

There was a great shout as the final verse was chanted and the procession crowded into Waric's house for bannocks and beer. Then they came out and moved on to the next place, and the next, spiraling up the hill. Maira watched the lurching image of the White Mare with mixed anticipation and something else, perhaps recognition, or fear.

And then, it seemed very suddenly, the flat space before Maira's doorway was filling with people, for half the Clan seemed to have followed the procession up the hill. Ness and Temella retreated back into the house and Maira stood, blocking the doorway, wishing absurdly that she had her sword.

Abruptly the White Mare loomed over her. The discs of polished bronze set into its eyeholes glinted evilly in the firelight. The bits of metal that fringed the horsehide jingled as it moved. Maira flinched and heard laughter, then stood, biting her lip as the pale skull swung down and toothed jaws snapped beside her ear.

The masked dancers launched into the first verse of the song and Maira summoned enough presence of mind to answer. The Mare butted at her, setting off a volley of obscene comments, then tried to nose past her to Temella. The give and take of the chant continued as the beasts demanded beer and Maira's rhyming denied them.

> *"You must give us to eat*
> *Both barley and wheat,*
> *As the spirits you treat*
> *So shall you prosper!"*

Maira shook her head and struggled to recall the answer. Grotesque shapes crowded around her like figures from a nightmare. She cleared her throat.

> *"The Druid shall say*
> *What shall send you away,*
> *As the night yields to day*
> *And is banished!"*

As if she had evoked him, Maira glimpsed Gutuator's pale robes. For a moment there was silence, as if the people thought he might indeed say the word of dismissal, but he only smiled, and the drums throbbed triumphantly.

The spectral horse bobbed forward. Alone this time, it chanted loudly,

> *"The White Mare will sing;*
> *The spirits will bring*
> *New life and blessing*
> *To everyone . . ."*

Maira lifted her hands as if in surrender and stepped aside to let the masquers pour past her to the hearth where Ness waited with the platter of "soul-cakes"—bannocks made specially with honey, and a heavy skin of beer.

The "Mare" was too big to fit into a dwelling, so Maira took a cup of beer out to it. A calloused hand darted from beneath the horsehide and the cup disappeared. The people had drawn back to form a semi-circle around the doorway, and the acid sweetness of the hornpipes shrilled and warbled above the pulse of the drums. More torches dyed the scene with ruddy flickering light—it was impossible to count the people, hard even to recognize them.

Fortified by the beer, the masquers came out again, steadying as they reached the colder air, and began to dance.

It was an old dance, full of intricate stepping and punctuated by grunts that were more and more like the calls of the animals whose skins the dancers wore. Overlaid upon the scene before her Maira could see others, in which men dressed entirely in skins danced before little round huts like those the herdsmen built for themselves when they summered in the hills, and scenes even stranger, where naked men copied the motions of a priest with head-dress like the Antlered God.

Then the tune changed and the dancers began to draw the women into the circle—the young women especially, married or maiden, all who were capable of bearing a child. They blushed as the comments from the crowd became franker and more personal, but there was an odd, vivid brightness in their eyes. It was not sexual excitement, but some other need that impelled them to unpin their tunics so that the dancers could rub soot across their bare breasts and lift their skirts so that the dance-leader's wand could strike their thighs.

In a moment, thought Maira, *I will understand*. But it was so hard to think in this tumult, and the beer she had drunk was buzzing in her head—no, it was not the beer, but the music that pulsed in her blood and set her feet to moving with the rest.

Past and present wavered in and out of focus around her, and it was the dance that was causing it, the dance that linked all times and all realities. With a shout she abandoned herself to the music, stamping and twirling in place until the others fell back to form a circle around her. Now only the White Mare remained with her in the center. Together they danced, mirroring each other's motions, while the beast-maskers spiraled around them. The old women were watching her, whispering behind their hands, but Maira did not care.

The faces of her people flickered by her as she spun—Temella and Dumnoric, Waric and his wife who had died two years ago, Urr and Lod and a young man who looked like Eoc dressed in the tunic Druith had made for the first of her sons. Without surprise, Maira understood that the dead of the Clan had accepted the invitation to join in the Festival. But though she searched their faces, she did not see Conmor.

Someone shouted. Turning, Maira saw a point of light flare upon the distant peak of Craig Duw. Laughing, she seized a torch and dashed up the steep path to the crown of Din Rhun. Panting, she stopped before the wood heaped there, and then, with a brief prayer, plunged the torch into its heart.

The crowd below grew still, waiting for the flame to catch. Then light exploded from its heart and they shouted as if the fire itself had found a voice for its triumphant birth.

The blast of heat drove Maira backward, but she bore it until she saw another flicker in the high place above Din Prys. And there would be a fire at Carbantorigum too, lit by the High King—a chain of fires from one end of Novantae territory to the other. She knew that throughout Britannia and Alba the bale-fires were burning tonight, welcoming the friendly spirits and keeping evil at bay.

Carefully she descended, and the cheering people brought her to the circle again. But deprived of its partner, the White Mare had found another task.

Gutuator was sitting on a bench with the drummers beside him. As they throbbed softly, the Mare danced toward him, then retreated as if afraid. The Druid sat very still, eyes closed, hands open upon his knees. But every line of his body showed alertness, as if he listened for something no one else could hear.

There is one other who sees both worlds, thought Maira, knowing herself for the old man's true descendant even while she hated his attempt to manipulate her and Carric in the stone circle. Biting her lip, she watched the White Mare mince up to the Druid, and then bend and lay that monstrous head in his lap.

Gutuator jerked, shuddered, and opened his eyes.

Temella darted forward and knelt beside him, keeping well clear of the Mare. "Prophesy!" she cried. "Master, tell me what my future will be!"

Gutuator looked at her, then through her. The crowd hushed at the sound of his deep voice.

"A storm shakes the apple tree and blows all its blooms away, but another year comes, and the tree bears fruit in abundance and the baskets are full. . . ."

Maira supposed that meant that once the present troubles were over Temella would have a fruitful marriage, although, she realized with a tremor, the Druid had not said to whom. Gutuator's prophecies were always cryptic, and she had never known if these were the images he really saw, or the imagery in which he cloaked his meaning lest his words should constrain someone's free-will.

Petric stepped up and got a prophecy which seemed to promise him prosperity. Waric's answer was less certain. Ness tugged at Maira's arm and she knew that she would have to take her turn too, however reluctantly. A prophecy for her was also an omen for the Clan.

But she could not bring herself to kneel. Proudly she stood before Gutuator, and the people quieted.

"Speak to me of the future, Druid," she said clearly. She waited, and saw with irritation that his expression did not change.

"The White Mare is borne by the Red Stallion;
The White Mare devours the Red Stallion;
The White Mare bears the Red Stallion. . . ."

Maira's breath caught as she saw standing with the people the chestnut stallion who had been slain to make her Queen. She blinked and he was gone. Gutuator drew breath to speak again, but the words never came. Instead, the silence was filled by a confusion of noises from down the hill. Maira ran to the wall and saw torches moving jerkily upward, heard frantic speech with an edge of terror. But she saw no blood and heard no screams. Whoever was coming had not been frightened by any human enemy.

She motioned to Lod. "Get down there and find out what's going on. Bring the calmest person you see up to report to me!"

Lod moved quickly, but he had barely reached the outer gate when the torches surrounded him, and the babbling lot of them rolled back up the path and the circle opened to let them in. Maira recognized the family from down the valley who had taken Eoc and Beth in. Fear gripped her belly. Had something happened to Eoc or to her mother?

All the torches streamed sideways in a sudden wind. The newcomers pressed around the Druid like children hiding behind their mother's skirts and he stood up, his stern gaze piercing the darkness. More footsteps—Maira stiffened, then saw it was her mother, barefoot, with her hair escaping from its braids. Druith stood in the gateway, commanding all attention, then pointed down the hill.

"Druid, prophesy!" her voice was shrill. "Tell us who has sinned, to keep the dead from their peace!"

Slowly she backed across the circle toward Gutuator, still pointing, so that all eyes remained fixed on the emptiness behind her.

For a moment the only sound was the crackling of the torches and the moan of the wind through the stones. Then

Maira heard something else—they all heard it—the rapid drumbeat of a horse's hooves, galloping up the hill. Maira's skin prickled, and the sense of disorientation she had felt earlier abruptly grew stronger. It was like a sound just beyond the limits of hearing, or something that the focus of her eyes could not quite see. Her senses struggled to interpret her perception. Around her men shifted uncomfortably, and she realized that they were sensing it too.

The hoofbeats grew louder; beyond the gate Maira saw a kind of curdling in the air. She blinked, focusing, and her breath caught. From all around her came a collective sigh.

The figure of a horseman was precipitating from the darkness—the sturdy dun stallion that had been buried in Conmor's mound and on its back a warrior bearing Conmor's long spear and whorled bullhide shield. As it approached, the apparition grew steadily more substantial, but even when it was near enough for Maira to recognize the boar-scar that twisted up one arm there was no head that she or anyone else could see.

"It is Conmor!" came a man's voice, hoarse with fear.

"Have mercy on us, Lord—what must we do?" a woman echoed him.

The horseman reined in, and though his head remained invisible, every line of his body showed that he was listening. For a moment no one breathed.

What are you doing here, my father? You are frightening them! Maira's throat worked, but she could not voice the words.

Then the dun horse shook his head impatiently and half-reared. The rider eased his restraining grip on the reins and the animal paced slowly around the circle, and men gave way before him like wheat bent by the wind. He turned back toward the gate, and as man and horse moved away their figures appeared to thin until Maira could see through them to the torchlit stones of the wall. Then the apparition disappeared, but for what seemed a long time they heard the retreating echo of hoofbeats going down the hill. . . .

"Read me this omen, my father," Druith said finally in a voice that was almost steady. "Conmor's head remains unburied, and his spirit cannot lie at peace. Now he rides Scaur Vale— what does it mean?"

The people had drawn back, leaving Maira and her mother to face each other across the bent back of the White Mare. There

was a murmur of fear and someone made the Sign against Evil.
Druith looked at Maira with challenge in her eyes.

"Of course Conmor rides!" Maira said clearly. "This is the
night when all the dead return, so why not Conmor? He is
visible because he was powerful, and newly-slain. He is
headless because of the stroke of a Selgovae sword!"

Those near her quieted, then Gutuator stirred and all
attention snapped back to him.

"War," the Druid said slowly. "War and the death of men
are omened when the headless warrior rides. This is the first
time, but it shall not be the last. When you and your children
are forgotten, the men of Scaur Water shall tremble when the
horseman rides down from Din Rhun. . . ."

Druith wheeled and pointed at her daughter accusingly.
"You see? Your own father's ghost proclaims it! If you lead the
men of Din Rhun to war disaster will come! You, and you—"
wild-eyed, she pointed from one warrior to another, "if you
follow her you are doomed!"

Maira stared at Druith, more horrified by this screaming
fury with her mother's face than she had been by her father's
ghost. Once more she scented hysteria around her. She could
have dispensed a chieftain's justice immediately on anyone
else, but she could not order her own mother seized or slain.
Even if she had commanded it, she did not think anyone would
obey.

Men called to Gutuator to say more, but he remained silent.
Windchaser pressed against Maira's leg, growling softly, and
Maira knew he was sensing the nascent panic of those around
her, and her own response. In a moment they could turn and
rend her, desperate to exorcise their fear.

She stared helplessly around her, almost without will to
resist them, for it was her own mother who had betrayed her.
Her spirit cried again and again, *How could you do this to me?*

Then the Druid lifted his head and caught her frantic gaze
with his own. He was watching her expectantly. The flames of
the torches danced in his eyes.

Suddenly Maira shook herself like a horse coming out of a
pool, took a step forward and lifted her head.

"People of the White Horse!" she cried, "you have chosen
me and bound me by the holy sacrifice. My life is yours at any
time—but first you must listen to what I say!"

She took a deep breath. Stillness spread around the circle
until the only sound was the growling of the flames.

"War," she began slowly. "The Druid speaks of war, but why should that surprise you? Have we not been at war since the Selgovae attacked us more than two months ago? Has there been a day since then when we have not planned our revenge? Are you men and women or only babes, that you flinch at the name of war?" Scornfully she looked around her and saw reddened faces and eyes that would not meet her own.

"It was not I who led the last ill-fated raid a month ago, but I have sworn to those who rode against Din Carn to lead them against it again—when we are ready—when the time is right! I am no hothead to run heedless into danger, but neither will I allow my honor or that of my Clan to be mocked by our enemies!

"And if my father's spirit rides armed through the valley then I rejoice," she went on, "for surely he will ride before us when we claim our vengeance. He is only wondering what is taking us so long!"

Someone gave a tremulous laugh, and someone else began to cheer. Maira felt the knots in her belly loosen. She had them—she had caught them by invoking that lust for glory that was never far from her people's souls.

"But he said there will be death," a woman offered a last uncertain protest.

"There will be death indeed!" growled Dumnoric; "the death of our enemies!"

"Do not believe her, she is deceiving you!" cried Druith. "She seeks vengeance not for her father but for her own pride!"

Maira jerked as if her mother had struck her, hearing an echo of what Antiochus had told her, but everyone else was speaking so loudly now that no one seemed to have heard. Druith raved on incoherently and Maira pushed through the crowd toward her, horrified that people should see her this way.

"Grandfather, help her! Calm her somehow!" cried Maira. Druith saw her coming and started to back away. Gutuator turned.

"Daughter, master yourself," he said in a low voice. "Right or wrong, you cannot change what will be. . . ."

Druith stilled, staring at him, then shook her head with a bitter smile. "Old man, old man—you should have been a spirit yourself long ago! You have forgotten what it is to be a parent, to see your children being destroyed. And you— all of you—'' Her gaze fixed the others and they began to listen again.

"Do you think me driven mad by grief? Beware lest the same grief come to you. You cry out against the Selgovae, but they are our cousins; you would do better to fear the alien invader who has tried to destroy both us and the Selgovae before and will again. But I see that you will not believe me," added Druith with what was almost her old dignity. Maira wavered between relief and a new fear that she would sway them.

"Mother," she began, "please!"

"No!" Druith said sternly. "I will not support you just because I bore you. Why should I, when my own father will not second me?" She turned back to the Druid, and Maira sensed from her the same feeling of frustrated longing for a parent's love that she herself was feeling now. The thought was strange enough to replace all others for a second or two, then she realized that Druith was speaking again.

"You think you know so much, with your chanted philosophies and your tables of the stars," said Druith grimly into her father's silence. "You know nothing of the darkness at the heart of things! I have seen it, old man, and if you cannot interpret it for me then I must seek those who will. . . ."

At last Gutuator's monumental calm was troubled. He stepped toward her. "What will you do?"

"I will go to the Wisewomen of Craig Duw."

It was a simple enough statement, but it struck silence into the crowd. Legend said that seven cailleachs lived on the Black Mountain, or perhaps they were spirits, or if they were only old women, they were sorceresses. Or perhaps there was nothing there but the nests of the ravens whose wings darkened the air. It had been long since anyone dared go see.

And to go now, at Samain when the doors were open between the worlds—who could tell to what unearthly realm the path might lead?

"Mother, you can't!" cried Maira, but already Druith was pushing through the fearful crowd.

"Chieftain you may be, but you cannot order *me!*" Druith flared. "Follow me if you dare. If your courage matches mine then maybe I will listen to you!"

TWELVE

———❦———

Craig Duw

THE WIND WHIMPERED across the hillside, shook the twisted branches of the pine trees, and sobbed to silence. Maira shivered and added another stick to her little fire. The wind sounded like a lost child, crying itself into exhaustion, then beginning again.

But this time it is the mother who is lost, thought Maira bitterly, *and the child is looking for her*. . . .

Firelight reddened Roud's grizzled flanks as the mare lifted her head, ears swiveling and nostrils flaring to test the air. Then she snorted softly and went back to gleaning the dry grass from between the stones. Windchaser's ears twitched, but his head remained solidly upon Maira's foot.

Maira looked down at the dog and unwillingly smiled. When the first search for Druith had yielded nothing, she had shouted down Waric and Urr and the rest of them who wanted to send out a full warparty. She could not leave the *dun* undefended, but it would be safe enough in Waric's dependable, if unimaginative, care. And something within her knew that she would never find Druith unless she sought her alone.

But no command of hers had been able to prevent the hound from following her. Maybe that was just as well, thought Maira as the wind began to whisper again. She had not expected the journey to be so lonely. She put more wood on the fire and tried to pick out enough stones from the space beside it to make a reasonably level and comfortable bed.

Where does my mother sleep tonight? she wondered, torn between anxiety and anger. Druith's horse had been missing,

177

and she had taken a cloak and food as well. Perhaps she was warm and safe in some herdsman's hut, or perhaps she had simply hidden for a day or two and then turned homeward, and was sitting there laughing at her daughter's gullibility.

But the only way to find out was to pursue the quest to the end. And it was that, not the uncertainty and discomfort of the journey, that bothered Maira. Whether or not she found her mother at Craig Duw, she was going to find *something*. . . . Imagination conjured up a vision of the seven crones of Craig Duw, as if every old woman who had ever frightened her had been distilled into this terrible flock with eyes like birds of prey and cloaks like ravens' wings.

Angered by her own fear, Maira tugged at the rocks and threw them crashing into the tangle of junipers below the pines. And then her fingers closed on something large and smooth, but too light to be a stone. She looked down and almost dropped the thing, for it was a skull.

It was no wonder that she had taken a moment to recognize it, for long burial in the peaty soil had left it as brown as a stone. The jawbone was cracked but the crown seemed intact— well, nearly so, for as she turned it she saw the bronze blade that had given the death-blow still embedded there.

Staring, Maira felt the world shiver suddenly. There was shouting and movement and the bright crimson gush of blood, then silence broken only by the quarreling of crows. She trembled with awareness of the land around her—the steep, tangled slopes of hills where birch and ash fought for space with the enduring pines, and the bare peaks above them where ferns and grasses clung to the stones. And everywhere was the murmur of trickling waters and the incessant whisper of the wind.

Maira grimaced and set the skull carefully on a stone, then filled her wooden cup with water and placed it with the remains of her bannock and cheese in front of the thing as an offering.

"Stay there, old warrior, and guard my sleep," she said softly. "In the morning I will lay you to rest once more."

She pulled enough bracken to make a bed, wrapped herself in her heavy cloak and lay down. Windchaser curled up against her back, his warmth like a second fire. As the coals faded, the eyeholes of the skull filled with shadow, until it appeared to be watching her.

But the shadowed gaze was not unfriendly, and why should

she fear, whose father's skull was her favorite counselor? Perhaps this was the head of an ancestor too.

"Watch over me," she murmured once more as sleep drew its grey blanket across her consciousness, "and if you have any wisdom to offer me, I will gladly hear."

And like ravens manifesting from an empty sky to descend on some dying prey, the dreams came. Maira dreamed of the battle in which the owner of her skull had died, when little brown-skinned men in fur kilts stalked each other across the hills. She dreamed of her own people fighting the Romans and among them a woman who looked like Druith, but young. She dreamed of men in bright helmets and tunics of linked mail fighting, and of men in armor like metal shells under banners bright as flowers. She dreamed of a long line of men in tight red tunics and white braes that marched through the hills while others wrapped in chequered cloaks like her own threw lightning against them from the shelter of the glens.

Endlessly, it seemed, the pageant went on. This was a lonely land, and one of little use to men, but a breeder of battles. Maira felt herself sinking to some deeper level of dreaming, but still she saw warfare. Only now it was not men she watched, but something other—exquisite, attenuated forms that flickered in and out of human semblance as they fought. With what awareness remained to her Maira wondered if the constant warring of men had left these echoes in the Otherworld, or if the human battles were a reflection of some perpetual conflict among the older powers?

The next day Maira continued her journey through hills which grew ever higher and more desolate, chilled by a wind that carried the bite of snow. She passed from upland forest to the high moorlands where only an occasional birch or pine found shelter from the wind.

The track wound upward through an empty landscape. Except for the path she followed, there was no sign of man, nor indeed of much else at this season, save only an occasional hare startled from the heather or the slow circling of hawks in the sky.

By the third day the silence had swallowed Maira's soul. She no longer spoke to Roud or Windchaser. She only rode onward, squinting into the wind. Sometimes she wondered if she were lost—if anyone had ever come this far. But there was

the path, and now and again horsedroppings no more than a
day old. Someone else had passed this way, and who but her
mother would be so crazed as to seek Craig Duw in the dead
time of the year?

A dull but growing anger fueled Maira's journeying. Druith
had challenged her in front of all the Clan; she had no choice
but to follow her. But she had not thought the journey would
take so long. She had little over a week before she must join
Pintamus with her men. She had to find Druith and get back to
Din Rhun!

And so she pushed herself and her mount upward, ever
upward, while the grey light faded, fighting despair. And then
there was a sudden sound, a horse's neigh, from somewhere
near. Roud stumbled, lifted her weary head to test the breeze,
then stepped out with an energy she had not shown since this
journey began.

"Ah, lass—are you lonely too?" Maira patted the shaggy
neck. "I think we will both find company soon." Something
stirred within her—not excitement, for she was too cold and
weary for that. A dull satisfaction, perhaps, that became more
tangible when the path dipped into a little grassy hollow and
she saw her mother's grey mare tethered there.

Stiffly Maira dismounted and looked about her. The place
was protected by a mighty outcrop of granite, perhaps the
highest part of the mountain, for from here all slopes seemed to
lead down into shadow. And if this were the peak, then the
cavern must be here. . . .

She led Roud into the hollow and tied her to a small birch
tree, knotting ropes together so that the mare could reach the
trickle of water that flowed down from a crack in the rockface
and seeped across the grass, its undulations marked by the
brighter green of mosses studded with liverworts and starry
saxifrage.

The western sky still glowed with the sun's dying fire, but
with every moment the light in the hollow dimmed. Even if the
entrance to the cavern had been obvious it would have been
hard to see.

If indeed the doorway were visible to mortal eyes. . . .

Reason told Maira to make camp and build a fire, to look for
the cave when morning came. But she could not bear to be
thwarted now, so close to her goal. Druith had found the way
in—whoever guarded it must admit her as well!

Angrily Maira stripped pack and saddle from Roud's back and dropped them. Windchaser was lapping noisily from the pool at the base of the waterfall, and suddenly aware of her own thirst, Maira picked her way across the tussocky grass and knelt stiffly beside him.

The water was like crystal in her cupped palms. It flowed from the heart of the mountain, she thought, and there must be some virtue in it, for as the cold sweetness filled her she felt her weariness ease. With a sigh of pleasure Maira sat back on her heels, wiping her mouth with the back of her hand.

In mid-motion she stopped. The water falling into the pool had flickered suddenly with a light that came and went as if it were catching the glow of the setting sun. But the rock faced east, and Maira had not yet lit her fire. Excitement dried her mouth and she got to her feet.

"In the name of the Lady Who is Mother of All I command you." Maira stretched out her arms. "Open to me!"

The red glitter brightened, as if someone had put more wood on a fire somewhere within. Maira stood very still, letting her eyes unfocus until the surface of the water disappeared.

"In the name of the stallion whose sacrifice made me Queen," she whispered, "let me *see*. . . ."

And from somewhere impossibly close to her came a single pure note like the ringing of a silver bell. Maira's sight cleared, and through the curtain of water she saw the doorway into the hill.

Windchaser whined as Maira started toward it, and she looked back over her shoulder. He was shivering, standing with one paw lifted as if he could not quite summon the courage to take that next step after her.

"It's all right, lad," she said softly. "Go guard the horses, Windchaser—guard, lad! Stay!" She pointed toward Roud, and with head and tail both drooping the hound moved away from her and lay down between the horses, whined once more, and was still.

Maira turned back to the waterfall. The door was still there, waiting for her. Biting her lip, she took a deep breath and went through.

The passage led downward through the rock, its turnings alternately revealing and blocking the glow of the distant fire. The way grew steeper and more slippery, and though a fire might burn in the depths of the mountain, the air was chill.

Maira felt as if she were being drawn back into some cold and terrifying womb.

And then the path levelled abruptly and the entrance to the cavern was before her. Through the opening Maira could see a rock wall polished by the lapping of some long-vanished lake. The triple spiral pecked into its surface was limned in light and shadow by the fire that burned beneath the great cauldron in the center of the cave.

Maira blinked and took a careful step forward, then stopped short as black shadows flapped toward her. They were birds— no, something larger. She thought of the dark cloaks worn by the old women of the Clan. They stilled, her vision identified three near the cauldron and others clustered behind them. Were there seven of them, waiting for her?

Her heartbeat shook her chest, but she straightened and walked toward the cauldron.

Eyes gleamed from the shadows. Words formed from the crackling of the fire.

"Maira daughter of Conmor—why have you come here?"

"If you know my name then surely you know that too," said Maira defiantly. "I seek my mother."

A ghost of laughter stirred the shadows. *"I* am your Mother," the Voice replied.

Anger moved Maira nearer to the fire. "I seek Druith daughter of Gutuator," she echoed sarcastically.

"I am *her* Mother," came the answer, or answers, for surely more voices than one were in those words.

"What, all of you?" Maira glared at the faces the firelight showed her—the faces of all the old women who had ever frightened her. "Why are you playing with me? I know Druith came here—where are you hiding her?"

"Why are you looking for her?" The simple question reverberated in the chill air.

A quick answer came to Maira's lips. *Because she challenged me before all the Clan!* But was that the only reason? Would her authority have been undermined if she had simply dismissed her mother's words as grief's insanity and commanded men to search for her?

She had thought that she had simple, logical reasons for coming on this chase, but now she began to understand that another need had impelled her. There were things she and her mother must say that no man of the Clan should hear. Their private battle had gone on too long, and she knew now that she could not ride out against Din Carn with this unresolved behind her.

But if her own people were denied her true reasons, what right had these—*creatures*—to ask? Eyes glinted back at her through matted, age-bleached hair; bony hands clutched twisted staffs. They were mocking her, laughing at *her!* Maira's lips drew back in a snarl.

"The answer to that question is for Druith, not for you!"

"Ah, she is so ferocious, this little one," said one of them.

"Like a wolf cub defending its den while its mother is away," another replied.

"What shall we do with her, eh, sisters? She is so trapped by her own illusions! If we told her the truth she would swear it was a lie!"

Maira's fists clenched. Furious phrases rose to her lips and stopped there, for how could you curse creatures already doomed to an eternity of age and ugliness?

She rushed toward them. "Tell me what has come to my mother or I will drown you in your own cauldron!"

"Oh—ho, ho, ho!" Cracked laughter blended into the harsh calling of birds. Bony fingers became talons and black wings bore seven ravens swooping through the cave. One of them dove for Maira's head and she flinched in spite of her anger.

And then the cries of the birds resolved themselves into laughter again and the old women were standing where they had been.

"We do not tell you because the truth cannot be confined in words," one of them said more kindly. "But if you have the courage to drink from our cauldron, you will see—"

Maira recoiled, remembering the last time she had drunk from a sacred cauldron. But the cailleachs challenged her with their bright birds' eyes. Dark wings beat in the shadows of her soul.

Slowly she went forward. Slowly she reached out to take the bowl of black jet that one of the cailleachs held out to her in a withered hand. The cauldron was huge, made of riveted plates of black iron. Wisps of steam rose from the dark surface of the liquid within it, as if it were almost ready to boil.

Maira thought, *The Goddess devoured the dwarf who had tasted only three drops from Her cauldron. What will a bowlful from this one do to me?* She cast a swift glance at the shrouded figures on the other side of the fire. Vapors from the cauldron blurred their faces and softened the harsh lines of age, dissolved their sharp shadows into each other until she could no longer tell if there were seven of them, or only three, or perhaps a single Face whose features changed too swiftly to be seen.

However you come to it, the Cauldron is the same, said the crackling of the fire. *Drink, my daughter, and understand.*

The broth in that cauldron was as black as the river that flows through the underworld and never sees the light of day. Maira dipped it up with her bowl, drank, and found it so bitter it seared the tongue.

She gasped, and gulped more involuntarily, but this time the liquor was as red as blood, with blood's salt, sweet taste and that tang of iron she remembered only too well.

Slowly she swallowed the second mouthful, then looked into the bowl again. Now the liquid it held was as white as milk from a heifer that has just birthed her first calf. Trembling, Maira let its smooth sweetness soothe her wounded tongue, and her sore spirit, separating her from all her pain.

The world whirled around her. The bowl slipped from her hand and she tried to catch it, but she was the one who was falling in a slow spiral through the mists between the worlds.

The mists swirled around her, then thinned, and as she had *seen* Carric's memories in the stone circle, scene after scene played itself out before her wondering eyes.

She saw Conmor her father before the silver had frosted his hair, riding a dun horse at full gallop across the fields. He bent over the black mane and slapped the horse's neck to urge it to more speed, and then Maira saw there was someone ahead of him, a slim girl with hair as red as copper who rode her grey mare as if they were one being.

But as she watched, the girl straightened, gentled her horse to an easier pace and let Conmor catch her. And when he reached her he grasped her wrist, and sliding off his horse, pulled her down with him. And they lay together, there in the field, while the horses grazed peaceably nearby. And as the girl looked up at Conmor, Maira saw her face, and her eyes were like those of Gutuator, but the lines of the face were a mirror of Maira's own.

The scene changed. Maira saw Druith and Conmor mourning their first family—the children who had died before she and Eoc were born—and felt the echo of that rending pain.

And after that there was a glimpse of battle in which Conmor and Druith fought side by side. She was good, Maira realized with a curious detachment. By then Druith's body had already begun to thicken, and she used her weight to add force to her blows without letting it slow her down. Her vision widened, and for the first time Maira got a good look at the enemy, and saw that it was Rome. . . .

And then the scene of battle wavered and was gone. Now she peered through the shadows inside a house where a woman tossed on a bed of straw. Other women hovered around her, sponging her sweating body, steadying her, encouraging. Maira saw the muscles of the distended belly ridge and relax again and realized that the woman was in labor. As the contraction passed the contortion of her face eased and Maira recognized Druith once more.

Then the great muscles squeezed again, and Druith's face set in a mask of concentration. For a long moment she strained, and then came a deep shout like a battle cry. Once more her body convulsed, there was something wet and bloody between her thighs. Ness lifted the thing and laid it on Druith's belly— a female infant, squalling furious protest against her forced entry into the world.

The cord was cut, and Druith reached for the squirming child and offered her breast. For a moment the baby struggled, then began to suck greedily. Maira saw Druith lie back with a triumphant smile and heard her words: "My daughter. The line of Britta goes on!"

And only then did Maira realize it was her own birth she had seen. *She was proud of me then,* she thought in wonder. *She was glad when I was born. . . .*

More scenes followed—Druith watching Maira straddle her first pony, Druith presenting Eoc with his first sword, Druith watching Maira tag after Conmor and turning away, and later, her mingled joy and sadness when they laid Eoc's little son in her arms.

And after that came scenes that Maira remembered herself, though they were different, seen from this other point of view. She had not thought how her mother must have felt, seeing the body of the man she had loved sprawled headless on the ground; she had not realized that her own eyes had held that hint of madness at Conmor's funeral.

And there was one final scene, when the old women of the

Clan offered Druith initiation into their secrets, and Maira felt her mother's anguish as she realized finally that her youth, her beauty, and the power of her maturity were gone. . . .

You have seen the life of the woman who bore you, said a still voice. *Do you wish to know what your own life will be?*

"No!" cried Maira instinctively, and then, more softly, "No." Druith had begun with all life could offer, and the thought of her sorrows still made Maira shudder.

The beginning of my life has been blasted already, she thought grimly, *and I can see no good ending. I will endure what I must, but I do not want to know the way of it beforehand—not now. . . .*

Then what else would you ask of Me? that still voice said.

What else? What else *could* she want to know? Maira spoke into that silence.

"Only the reason for all of it—only for you to tell me the reason why!"

The mists thickened around her. Images appeared and vanished before she could name them—the gleam of the bitch-hound's teeth as she tore the hare; the swift pounce with which the she-otter jerked the darting fish from the stream; the falcon's terrible stoop as the pigeon struggled through the air; and finally, the hen's beak, snapping up the hidden seed. . . .

But it was not a seed, but herself, Maira—seized by that great beak and sliding down into shadow as she had descended into the cave. Knowledge struggled within her as she had struggled to emerge from her mother's womb, but she could not name it. And then the darkness engulfed her completely and she knew no more.

Somebody was cooking stew. Maira's nostrils flared, she turned toward the scent, touched wet grass and sneezed. Startled, she opened her eyes.

The grasses next to her were pearl-edged with dew. Beyond them the bleached green of the turf blended into mists that swirled like those of the place between the worlds. She could see nothing beyond it, but the place Between had not included the humped shapes of horses nosing at the grass, or a warm weight against her back that a moment's thought identified as Windchaser, or that wonderful smell of simmering meat and crisp bannock baking on hot stones.

After a moment of struggle with her cloak, Maira sat up. She saw a small fire burning on a hearth of flat stones beside the stream. A clay pot was resting on two of the larger stones with its round belly over the coals. On the stone beside it she saw the bannocks she had smelled, just beginning to turn a delicate brown.

Someone wrapped in a heavy cloak of black wool crouched over the fire, stirring the pot with a wooden spoon. Maira sneezed again, the figure turned, and Maira gazed into her mother's eyes.

She curled her feet under her and rewrapped her cloak, for the morning air was chill. She cleared her throat.

"Where did you get the pot?"

"I brought it with me," Druith said calmly. "One needs something to cook in, even in the hills. Why?" Her eyes narrowed and she looked at Maira appraisingly. "What have you been eating?"

"Cold bannock and cheese, mostly. I suppose you brought the seasoning herbs with you, too?" Maira grinned.

"Of course." Druith raised one eyebrow, but Maira realized that her mother's competence did not anger her anymore. She began to laugh and both Druith's brows went up this time.

"And here I was imagining you wandering lost and hungry in the hills," Maira said finally. "I was *so* angry with you!" There was a short silence. Maira looked at the solid rock face behind the waterfall, then back to her mother again. "How long have you been here?"

Druith shrugged, and for a moment something unreadable flickered in her eyes. "Who can tell? I woke up, and you were there, sleeping like a log of wood. I saw a coney by the stream, and I had my sling, and with rabbit for a stew, I thought I might as well put breakfast on."

She picked up the wooden spoon and tasted the broth, then moved the pot from the stones to the grass between them, using the folds of her cloak to shield her hands.

Maira rummaged through her saddlebag for her horn spoon, wondering how she had had the sense to bring it when she had obviously forgotten so many other useful things. By the time she was settled by the stewpot again, her mother had piled the bannocks on a little mat of woven grass.

For a little while their mouths were too busy with food for words, and Windchaser gnawed happily upon the bones. But as Maira swallowed the stew she began to digest the implications of her mother's presence here. The grey horse had been in the hollow when she arrived the night before—Goddess, she *hoped* it had only been last night! But there had been no sign of Druith. Her mother must have been in the cavern, therefore—it was much easier to believe they had both been there without seeing one another than that she could have missed seeing Druith here in the open.

But that meant her descent into the cavern must have been *real.* . . .

Maira coughed. "Mother, in the cavern, what did they show you?"

Druith finished rinsing her pot in the stream, filled it with clean water and put it back on the fire to make tea. Then she sat back and met her daughter's gaze.

"I saw you," she said slowly. "And myself. . . . And you, my daughter, what did you see?"

"The same." Remembering, Maira felt the betraying flush warm her cheeks and looked down at the grass. "I saw you. I never knew that you were proud of me. . . ."

Druith flinched, then sighed. "Perhaps I was afraid to spoil you, or perhaps—to praise you seemed like praising myself. My pride in you was something I did not know how to show."

Maira nodded. "Now I know that you loved *me*. Did you love Eoc more?" The question hung between them like a thrown spear. For a moment Maira wished she could recall it, then she felt the emptiness where that fear had been and realized that it was time to be free of it, no matter how she feared what the answer would be.

Druith's gaze had turned inward. After a moment she frowned. "Yes," she said slowly, "or at least, he was easier for me to love. I have been trying to understand why. Perhaps it was because my own mother died when I was young, and Gutuator was both father and mother to me." She shrugged. "You can imagine how I loved him—who else had a father who could charm the wild birds to feed from his hand?"

The water began to boil and Druith dropped dried sprigs of chamomile into the pot and took it off the fire. Soon an aromatic vapor was scenting the air and Maira breathed in appreciatively.

"And then suddenly Conmor had become a man, and he loved me, and there was never a fairer warrior of the White Horse Clan. If he had not my father's wisdom I did not care—at least I could win an argument sometimes! After a time, of course, the first splendor wore away, but the death of our children made a bond between us—I thought nothing could break it. Eoc's birth, and yours, were like a promise of new life to me.''

Druith blew on the tea, took a careful sip, then passed the pot to Maira.

"And then?" Maira asked gently, holding the steaming pot hard to still the trembling in her cold hands.

"And then you grew up. Eoc was always my pride, always turning to me, but you followed your father from the time you could walk. How could I vie with him for your love, or with you for his? And there was always so much for me to do—with the cattle, or the crops, or helping Conmor to govern the clan. Eoc seemed likely to be Conmor's heir, and though I loved him I know his character—he needed all the training I could give. I think perhaps that a mother is always harsher with her girl-child, knowing she will need to be strong. Men seem so very vulnerable!''

Maira stared at her, remembering how angry she had been with Conmor for giving in to his despair. But Conmor was not the issue now. She shook her head.

"But the choice for chieftain fell not on Eoc, but on me! My mother, do you resent that still?''

"The choice 'fell'?" Druith echoed mockingly. "You sought it, my child. You went for it like a horse to the stream. But how shall I judge you? I did what I thought right. Perhaps Eoc would be no better as a chief than you. At any rate, it is done now, and too late for me to try to change you. The hardest of a parent's tasks is to know when the task is done. Gutuator knows it—he is only himself, not 'my father' anymore.'' She smiled painfully. "Now it is our time to learn.''

For a moment Maira was silent. The mist was lifting now, shimmering like a silver curtain in the morning sun.

"You did what you thought right," she repeated at last. "Mother, that is what I am doing now. I need your counsel, but I have to be the one who decides, and if I make mistakes—'' She swallowed, thinking of Tiberius Flavius Pintamus and Carric of Din Carn, remembering the complex net of love and hatred in which all of them were tangled now.

"If I make mistakes," she went on, "then I must be the one to pay the honor-price. Will you come home with me?''

Druith replied with a rather crooked grin. "I will lose my temper again.''

"I would worry if you did not," said Maira. "I suppose I will, too. But if the anger goes on for too long, you must make me another pot of your stew. . . ."

Druith looked at her, and Maira saw with wonder that her mother's eyes were filling with tears. It hurt her in some deep place she had not known she had. Hastily she set down the tea and scrambled over to take her mother in her arms. But somehow, it was Druith's arms that went around *her,* Druith's broad breast against which she lay, and held so, and for a moment she knew peace.

After a time she saw the sky burning blue above her, and remembered who she was and what she had to do.

"At Samain," she began with difficulty, "when we all saw my father, you swore it meant doom. To me your words seemed a final treachery. You have to understand—even if what you said is true, the men are sworn to attack Din Carn and I cannot change it now. There is no way out of this but through. . . ."

She closed her eyes to keep back the self-pitying tears. *No way out but through,* she repeated to herself, *And I do not think I shall reach the other side.*

"A madness was on me," said Druith slowly. "I had lost so much, and to see your father's apparition like that made all I had denied come real. Conmor was without his head, and it seemed to me that the rest of us were too. There was a wrongness to it, and I was afraid I would lose you, too. . . ."

Maira felt Druith take her hand, but she dared not seek the haven of her mother's arms again. After a time she blinked, and squinted at the sun. A kestrel slid across the sky and sailed out over the rumpled hills that stretched into blue distance below. At least it was still the world she knew.

"The morning is passing." Maira got stiffly to her feet and held out a hand to help her mother. "We had better go."

THIRTEEN

The Sword Dance

"THERE—DO YOU see the hilltop with the broken stones?"

Maira strained to follow Waric's gesture. The moon had not yet risen, and she wondered how he could tell one hill from another in this twilit gloom. It was not raining, but gathering clouds had brought an early darkness. The damp air that lifted Maira's hair felt oddly warm for winter, but why should she expect the weather to be normal when so much else in her world was strange?

She blinked, thought she saw an irregular silhouette. "Is that the Roman fort?"

Waric gave a growl of laughter. "That was our fort, once. The Red Crests made the tribe dismantle it in my grandfather's time, and without it we could not hold the land."

Maira nodded, forgetting he could not see the movement, then grunted acknowledgement. Waric's mother had come from Lyn Mapon, and he had visited her people often. And surely for them to have a man who knew these hills was a good omen, for only darkness could cloak their movement through the territory of their enemies.

She cast a quick glance over her shoulder, though it was hearing, not vision that confirmed that they were following. Urr and his three sons came after her, as they did always, with Maelor, hot-eyed with grief for his dead son, close behind. Dumnoric and Kenow had sworn vengeance for the men lost in the last raid, and after them came Neithon and the other warriors from down the valley, close to fifty in all. It was not the full fighting strength of the Clan, for she would not leave her people undefended, even when so many were safe behind the walls of Din Rhun. For the most part those who followed her were young men and a few young women who wished to garner a dowry of glory before settling down to found families.

"But the Red Crests found a use for the ruins," Waric added with a kind of grim humor. "When they built Blatobulgium on the next hill over they used the remains of our fortress for ballista practice!"

Maira could just make out the shape of the land beyond the hill they were passing, a dim mass against the banked clouds. There, then, lay her goal, or at least the first step to it. Pintamus would be waiting there with his men, and then it would no longer be her nerve alone that held them to this task.

"Well, the Roman fort is in ruins too," she said soothingly, "so we are even now!"

"I laughed when I heard they were pulling it down!" said Waric, "As if we would ever *want* to use a place where the dogs of Rome had laired! Someday perhaps their famous Wall will crumble as well!"

Maira remembered the knife-line of masonry she had seen and shook her head in the darkness. Even if the world should change entirely, she thought, something of that achievement must remain.

She heard a heavy flapping overhead and stiffened, waiting. An owl called from the trees beside the road, but she could not tell if it were the same bird. She heard someone behind her muttering a protective charm and smiled bitterly. If the corpse-bird called to wish them well why should anyone be surprised? And night was most fit for this business they were on, for it was surely the dark face of the Goddess that watched over them now.

The track dipped down, they splashed through the stream at the bottom of the hill, then turned upward again. Here the land to each side was clad in thick second-growth, for the Romans had felled all the timber when they were here. She hoped that Waric knew where he was leading them. She had no desire to spend the night blundering about in hostile territory. And then someone grunted surprise, and looking up, Maira saw the pinprick glow of a fire.

She felt a change in the men behind her, as a shift in the wind will transform a forest by lifting the undersides of leaves, or all the dogs in a house will lift their heads at once, ears pricking toward a sound their masters cannot hear. An impulse stirred in her—why not attack the Romans, now? They were the ancient enemy! Her throat ached with the unuttered battle-cry, for in that moment she could have done it, and without remembering oaths or plans they would have followed her.

Then Roud neighed in greeting and like the calling of a distant horn Maira heard the Roman horses answering. Without conscious intention, her legs tightened and the mare moved more quickly, sensing food before her and a rest from journeying.

I could stop it—I should stop it—I could stop it, even now—Hoofbeats on the stony trail beat out the litany whose echoes resonated in Maira's skull. But her lips did not move. She seemed to watch herself ride up the hill into the glow of the firelight, into the power of Rome.

"My Lady." Pintamus rose to his feet as Maira reined in. For a moment no one moved—the Roman with his Brigante scouts around him and Maira and her men, like a frieze of warriors on the Triumphal Arch of some Emperor. Then the Decurion lifted his arm in the salute to a sovereign, and the scene came to life again.

"You had no difficulty?"

Maira shook her head. "We gathered just north of Din Prys, and came on by night. Waric son of Dumnor knows this land well." She held out her hand toward Waric and the old man nodded to the Roman, proudly, admitting no inferiority. "We came as swiftly as we could in the dark," she went on. "We met no one, and I do not think we were seen."

"Very good." Pintamus came a step closer and looked up at her. Maira kept her own face expressionless, unwilling to acknowledge the complicity she read in his smile.

"It is a pattern of travel we must continue to follow, I fear," he went on. "There are too many folk in the Vale of Anan who would wonder at the riding of so large a company. Half this night is already gone. There is some shelter here, and we should rest while we can. Tomorrow, a little before sunset, we will ride north."

Maira looked around her. Part of a stone wall sheltered the fire, and dim shapes showed where other walls had once been. But no buildings stood here now, only the square, high-peaked, leather tents of the Roman Commander and his men.

"Where shall we camp, then?" she asked softly.

"In the south square, I think, next to my men. Rufus will show you." A sharp gesture brought a young man from the group of Scouts—red-headed as any Briton, but with dark eyes. He sketched a salute for his Commander, then turned to Maira and Waric with a grin.

"Come on then. You'll want to get what sleep you can. The horse lines are down the hill and the privy trench nearby." He spoke with the quick sharp accent of the south, the grin still on his face so that she wondered if he were mocking them.

"Very well," she answered coldly. "Waric, do you take the men along with him and settle them. In a few moments I will follow you."

"Yes, Lady." Waric's respect rebuked the Brigante's off-handedness. He turned in his saddle and motioned to the rest of the warriors. "Come, my brothers, and let us see where these Romans would have us lair."

Maira watched them disappear into the darkness. *The times are strange when the wolf and the dog lie down together,* she thought. But if the world were as it should be she would not be here.

Pintamus took her rein and laid his hand on her knee. *"Cara,"* he said, very softly. "Come down off that horse and let me greet you properly. You must be tired and cold after your ride, but my tent is warm, and there is room and enough for you there. . . ."

An involuntary touch of Maira's heel set Roud sidling away. A turmoil of memory showed her the Roman's face, contorted in passion, and Carric's anguished eyes. She would kill him—she must—but coolly, as a warrior. To mix the pure passion of her vengeance with lust dirtied it somehow.

"What passed between us at Luguvalium was a private thing," she answered in the same low tone. "On the war trail I must live like my men." She tried to soften her refusal with a smile. "They must think of me as a warrior, not as a woman, now."

Something flickered in his eyes—anger, or only disappointment? Then he shrugged and smiled ruefully. "Perhaps it is as well. We will both need our strength for this journeying. But at least you can sit with me by the fire for a little and share a jug of spiced wine!"

It was barely mid-afternoon when they woke and began to prepare for the night's journey, but already the sun was slanting across the western hills. Maira packed up her meager gear, then wandered through the rubble that had been the fort's western wall, gazing idly at the patterning of sunlight and shadow on the hills. Trees hid the slopes below her, giving way farther on to scattered fields and then the pale glimmer of the lakes of Mapon. Beyond the low hills surrounding them lay the valley of the Nova. A bird could have flown in a straight line across the water and on to Din Rhun.

In the western sky, clouds were building up in great masses that filtered the rays of the setting sun into sheets of golden light. Those clouds held rain, or snow. But no breath of wind stirred her hair. If they were lucky, perhaps the storm would remain only a threat on the horizon.

With a sigh she turned and began to pick her way along the line of stones. The fort had been built in a rectangle, running roughly southeast to northwest. Ten years had barely blurred the gouges of the five ditches that surrounded it, and though young trees were springing between the stones of the old barracks, the outlines of their walls was still clear.

"More than nine acres were enclosed by these walls," said a voice behind her. "The fortress had shelter and support and stabling for the horses of nearly a thousand men . . ."

Maira recognized the liquid accent of the Roman Commander and waited without turning as he joined her on the wall.

"Who were they?" she asked softly.

"Nevians, at first, from Germania, and later the Second Cohort of Tungrians. Their home was the low sandy land beside the north sea."

Maira nodded, wondering what they had thought of this hilly land of Alba, so far from their home.

"Why did they come here? Did the Empire force them?"

Pintamus laughed and offered his arm to help her down from the wall. She jumped down without taking it and followed him along the broken pavement between the long foundations of the barracks.

"The Army is a good life for a young man who is healthy and wants to make his way in the world. The son of a tribesman who fought against Rome may find himself fighting *for* her on the other side of the world. If he does well and fulfills his term of service he may make Centurion and retire with a pension and land. They will make him a citizen then, and if his son follows him into the Legions he could become a Tribune and eventually a senior officer. . . ."

Some quality in his voice made Maira look at him. Pintamus was staring at the ruins of the fort without seeing them, but there was a kind of shining in his eyes. Abruptly she remembered other things she had heard him say.

"That is what *you* want." It was not a question.

He nodded, and let his breath out in a long sigh. "My father's father kept sheep in the Galician hills. My father died fighting in Parthia. But my sons will have a purple stripe on their togas and be rulers of men."

How, wondered Maira, by camping in these ruins and sneaking off to help her fight her war? But she said nothing. What mattered was the fact that he was helping her. She did not want to know why.

"It must be a hard thing to die fighting for a foreign Empire in a foreign land," she said softly.

He shook his head. "You do not understand. It is all Rome, and a man who loves fighting does not care where he dies if he has tasted glory. There are Legions of your southern Britons now serving on the Rhine, and your people also will someday serve a foreign lord in foreign lands."

Maira shivered, as if he had spoken prophecy. "No, I do not understand. I do not understand fighting when it is not for your home."

"Ah," Pintamus said gently, "but you are a Queen. Men without standing may feel differently."

She shrugged and looked away, unable to explain why it was not the same. A man in an alien army might fight for glory, but never with the ferocious passion of people who were defending their homes. She gazed with longing toward the northwestern hills that stood between her and Din Rhun.

It is for you I am doing this, she thought bitterly, *for the sake of the sweet green hills of my own dear land, and its fat cattle grazing, and its silver rushing streams. . . .*

"Look there—" Flavius Pintamus touched her arm and pointed to the foundations of a large building near the center of the fort. "There was the hospital. It had double timber walls for warmth and insulation from noise, and separate corridors."

Maira smiled slightly, understanding that he was trying to impress her with the care the Army took of its men. It was impressive, she agreed, but how much consolation would it be to die in comfort if you must do it far from home?

She thought, *When death comes to me I hope it will be within sight and smell of my own hills*. And perhaps it would be soon. The idea brought a little twist in the gut. Then Eoc could be chieftain as he desired and there would be an end to all this pain. Somewhere on the journey home from Craig Duw she had begun to understand that if she killed Carric of Din Carn it would be very hard to live after him.

For a moment the thought of Death lapped at her awareness like a black lake into which she might sink until even the memory of pain was left behind.

"And here they had their shrines. . . ." The voice of the Roman recalled her to the present. It was almost dark now. In the dusk she could see little beyond the shapes of the stones. Pintamus moved among them, peering at the inscriptions.

"See—here is an altar to Minerva, who the Brigantes say is the same as their Goddess."

Maira went to look over his shoulder as he traced out the Latin characters on the waist-high column of reddish stone.

"*Dedicated by the Second Cohort of Tungrians, Caius Silvius Aspex, Commander,*" he translated. "Someday, perhaps we will rebuild this place and I will command it. Shall I dedicate an altar to your Brigantia then?"

But Maira had moved past the altar and was kneeling beside something whose contours her fingers were reading, though she could scarcely see. It was a head, with smooth carved features and bound back hair. She lifted it into the last of the light.

She heard the Roman's indrawn breath. "It looks like you!"

Maira stared at the smooth curve of cheek and forehead, the straight nose, and the slightly down-slanted almond eyes, trying to relate them to the face she saw in her mirror of polished bronze.

Not my face, she thought, touching the hard surface of the stone, *but my skull. Perhaps when I am dead they will put my head in a shrine like Conmor's. . . .*

Very gently she set the stone head on a level slab that had fallen outward from the wall, wedging smaller rocks behind it to hold it upright. In the dimming light the carven features seemed to soften; for a moment the curved lips appeared to smile. Maira took a piece of bannock from her pouch and laid it as an offering on the stone. Then she sat back on her heels, lifting her hands in homage.

Sweet Lady, if You have power in this place then hear me! I do not ask for power or glory or even that my own life be preserved, only for a victory that will preserve my people.

Lady, I ask for a final end to this warring between Carric of Din Carn and me.

The blood roared in her ears, darkening her vision, and she swayed as if the ground had shifted. She strained to hear the words that were distilling from the chaos of her soul.

What you have asked you shall be given, daughter of Din Rhun, but first you must drink from My cauldron one last time. . . .

In her mind pictures were forming. Maira moaned, striving to pierce the confusion of vision. . . . And then someone took her arm and began to shake her. She opened her eyes to Pintamus' alien face and the vision was gone.

From the camp behind them came a horn call, and Pintamus stood up. "The men are ready, and the light is almost gone. It is time for us to ride."

They made less than fifteen miles that night, for the new moon rose late and gave little light, and when they passed dwellings they drew rein and went quietly. The dale of the Anan was a rich and gentle land, and populous, so their progress was slow.

At dawn they turned into the woods east of the road where the rising ground of the hills met the richer bottomland. They divided into small groups scattered among the trees and posted lookouts to guard against discovery by some hunter or herdsman chasing a stray.

The day had remained still, with a heaviness in the air that deadened sound, but it was damp, and Maira shivered and burrowed deeper among the leaves. She found it hard to sleep, and when she did, her rest was haunted by dreams. There was something she must tell Carric, but she could not get to him, and when she did find him she saw only the terrible lifting of his sword. Then dusk fell and they woke her. She could not remember what she had dreamed, but her cheeks were wet with tears.

The second night's journey was more difficult, for here the land rose sharply toward a pass into the high dales that sheltered Din Carn. The main road continued along Elvan Water, but Pintamus led the war party along a lesser trail that led up the headwaters of the Anan, and from thence aside along a brook that had carved a deep cleft through hills that glowed like blood in the light of the rising sun.

Above them the sky had brightened from rose to a misty

blue by the time they emerged into the shadowed depths of a grass-covered bowl carved out of the hills.

"Dis Pater's Cauldron," said one of the Brigantes with a grin. "It is a very secret place. We have camped here before." His companions laughed, and Maira frowned, sensing some hidden meaning behind their amusement.

"We will rest here today and eat at sunset," Pintamus said sternly. "If we leave here close to midnight we will reach Din Carn a little before dawn."

Maira nodded. It was the way they had planned it—to strike the Dun at the darkest hour, when everyone would be most deeply asleep, and to make their own escape westward through the Dalvean Pass in daylight, when the light would help compensate for their enemies' greater knowledge of the countryside.

As we were asleep when they came upon us, thought Maira grimly. *We will take them naked in their beds and let them fumble for their swords!* The thought had filled her with dark joy when first it came to her, but now she was only tired.

I need sleep, she thought as she wrapped her cloak around her. *I did not rest well yesterday, and I will need my strength for the fight.* She lay down on the bracken her men had piled for her and exhaustion dragged her into the dark.

And again she dreamed. She was fighting Carric, but she did not want to. She tried to call out a warning, but his face was a mask of hatred, and then it was not his face at all, but her father's, turning with lowered blade to meet the slow swing of Trost's sword.

Maira awoke aching in every muscle, her mind shadowed by a lingering dread no determination could dispel. The Romans already had fires going, and someone had been hunting and brought back two deer. Maira stood beside the fire and held out her hands to the grateful warmth, for the chill seemed to have settled in her bones.

To the south great towers of cloud were billowing up beyond the hills. Even in this cup in the mountain she could feel the changing wind—now almost warm, like the breath of some great animal, and now cold as the kiss of death. Higher and higher rose the clouds, pregnant with storm. It was early winter, and too much to hope that the weather would wait on men's convenience, but she hoped that if a storm must come it would be over swiftly, before they started on their way.

"Here, Lady—drink with us!" Rufus held out a skin of

cheap wine. Maira smiled at him and took it. The sour stuff burned her throat as it went down, but heat was what she wanted now—an internal fire to dispel the cold and drive her inner darkness away. She drank again and felt a welcome warmth in her belly, the beginning of a buzz in her head that would keep all this dismal thoughts at bay.

One by one the others awakened, stretching, cursing, going to the brook to splash themselves with cold water, then back to the fire. The venison was beginning to cook and the rich scent of roasting meat made mouths water. Some of the Romans had got out their cookpots and were boiling up dishes of porridge. Maira thought of the cheese in her saddlebags, but it was too much trouble to dig it out. She would wait for the venison, and meanwhile, console herself with more wine.

More fires were lit, and as the evening darkened, men gathered around them, checking their weapons, tightening the straps of a shield or putting a better edge to a sword. And they were talking, Brigante and Novantae united by a common enemy, happily sharing tales of ancient battles that grew more marvelous as they shared the wine.

Maira gnawed on a rib bone, then tossed it into the fire. She would be sick if she tried to eat more, but there seemed to be plenty of wine, and it tasted sweet to her now. She was vaguely aware that she was a little drunk—that was what she had intended. She had to get through this time of waiting, and perhaps the haze of alcohol could veil her visions and make them go away.

She stared into the leaping flames and saw Carric's face, but it did not matter anymore. *My love, my only love,* she thought with a detached sorrow; *will I destroy you, or will you kill me?*

Better if he killed her, she reasoned muzzily, for surely if she slew him his ghost would haunt her. And yet if she died and Carric lived who would defend her people from the men of Din Carn? There was no help for it—they must die together! Maira smiled in satisfaction and reached for more wine.

"We fought the Selgovae in the east four years ago, when they were harassing the Votadini," said Rufus. "They were good fighters, but we were better."

"I remember the women of Curia—they were glad to see us when we were done!" said Haterius, a dark man who looked more than half a Roman despite his British tongue.

"Ah, my own wife will be glad enough to see me return!"

said Petric. He picked up the sharpening stone and began to slide it along the edge of his blade with a cold, scraping sound like the iterative cry of some strange bird. "I'll have a tale or two to tell her then. I got to Lys Speiat just in time to see the tails of their horses when they hit us before, but they won't be able to run from me this time!"

There was a shout of laughter from the next fire. Maira saw that Dumnoric had jumped to his feet, waving his sword as he demonstrated his favorite parry. She grimaced, remembering how he used to argue that move with Eoc, neither of them ever convincing the other. For Temella's sake, she hoped it was as effective as Dumnoric believed.

A blink of light drew her eye to the hills. Had that been a torch? No—now it came again, a flare of white light against the underside of the clouds. Lugh was shaking his flaming spear and sending lightning across the sky. Some of the men murmured and pointed southward, wondering if it were an omen.

"If we are getting ready for battle, why should not the gods war too?" Maira asked gravely. "This must be a good night for fighting—there's no cause for us to fear!" Suddenly that seemed very funny and she began to laugh, and the men around her were drunk enough so that they laughed too.

"Ah—when the cries of battle fill the air the strength of a god is in me!" exclaimed Rufus. "I will kill, and kill, and no weapon will be able to touch me!"

"I am an old fox, and I know tricks these Selgovae dogs have never learned," said Urr. "I will send the heads of my enemies rolling across the ground like hazelnuts shaken from a tree!"

A growl of agreement came from his three sons. Through the haze of wine Maira felt the excitement building among them as the tension of the approaching storm built in the air. Lightning flashed more frequently now, but the gusts of wind were intermittent. The storm was still far away. She watched in wonder as light played back and forth across massed clouds, as if every time Lugh cast his spear some invisible opponent cast it back at him.

Petric finished sharpening his sword and sheathed it. The wine went round again and someone pulled out a pibcorn and began to play. After a little the tune resolved into a simple, hypnotic melody. She did not recognize it, but Waric and Urr

and the older warriors stiffened like wolves hearing a distant
howl. Men began to beat out the rhythm with a clashing of
swords against shields.

"Since we have wine, let us sing the war song of our fathers
who came from Gaul!" shouted Waric, getting up a little
unsteadily and drawing his sword. He began to sing—

> *"The dance of blood and wine,*
> *Sun, is Thine—*
> *The dance of blood and wine!"*

The others chorused after him,

> *"Fire, fire, steel, oh steel!*
> *Fire, fire, steel and fire!*
> *Oak, oak, earth and waves!*
> *Waves, oak, earth and oak!"*

And the fire leaped up as if to answer, or perhaps it was only
in response to the freshening wind. Lightning danced across
the sky, and she heard distant thunder like an echo of the beat.

> *"And the dance and song,*
> *Battle-strong,*
> *And the dance and song!"*

The warriors drew their swords and began to circle Waric
with a slow, prowling step that grew quicker as the song went
on.

> *"By the dancing blade*
> *A circle's made—*
> *By the dancing blade!"*

The circle closed, and as the chorus ended the swords swept
up, flashing fire and lightning.

> *"Song of the blue steel*

> *That loves to kill,*
> *Song of the blue steel!"*

The dull pounding of blade on shield resounded in Maira's bones. Fire crisped along each nerve. Now she was on her feet too, with her father's sword gripped tightly. Pintamus sat watchfully next to the other fire with his own long cavalry sword lying across his knees. Maira grinned at him, beckoning. Did not the wine burn in his blood as well? Could he not hear the music? She laughed and called to him, but he remained still, looking back and forth from the dancers to the sky.

> *"Fight, whereof the sword*
> *Is the Lord—*
> *Fight of the wild sword!"*

This was what she needed—this wild inebriation more powerful than wine. Thunder rolled across the heavens; a bolt of lightning forked and crackled through the clouds. The flashes grew closer as the dance swirled more wildly, and Maira laughed.

> *"Fire, fire, steel, oh steel!*
> *Fire, fire, steel and fire!*
> *Oak, oak, earth and waves!*
> *Waves, oak, earth and oak!"*

The music bore them around and around again. Lightning split the sky and for a moment cloaks and faces flashed into daylight color. Then it was gone and dazzled eyes reversed images so that she saw dark figures dancing against a sheet of light. A warm, moist wind gusted across the meadows and set the leaves to dancing in the trees. Pressure weighted the air.

> *"Sword, oh thou great King*
> *Of battle's ring—*
> *Sword, oh thou great King!"*

The words ripped from a hundred throats in a mighty shout. Swords hurtled glittering into the air and were caught again. Pintamus shouted inaudibly, gesturing wildly and pointing to the sky.

> *"With the rainbow's light*
> *Be thou bright—*
> *With the rainbow's light!"*

They sang of the rainbow, but it was the lightning whose brilliance flared from their brandished swords. Maira whirled in place, and her blade sent light glimmering around her as the flashes of lightning chased each other across the sky.

"You fools, put down your swords!" cried the Roman. "The lightning will strike them—the gods will strike *you!* Put down the blades, curse you, until they pass!"

Thunder cracked, deafening them. Startled, men seemed for the first time to see the fury approaching them and cast their weapons away. Only Maira still stood beside the wind-whipped fire with sword raised in homage to the skies.

"Maira, are you mad, girl? You'll be killed! Put that thing down!"

Pintamus' voice seemed to come from very far away, and his words were meaningless. Maira shook her head. If the gods wanted her they would take her, whether or not she had a sword in her hand.

"Don't you see them?" she cried ecstatically. "They are coming—they all are coming now!" She jabbed at the heavens, pointing out the bright figures she saw emerging from the clouds. "See—there is Lugh, the Lord of Lightnings! He leaps, he laughs, and ah—now he launches his bright spear!"

And as she spoke the bolt seared the skies. Men stilled, stared, waiting for the thunder.

"Taranis—now I see him, swaying in his chariot. Shining in his hand I see a sword of fire! Foam flies from the bits as his grey horses gallop—now do you hear them? Hear the hoof-beats rattle, and the rumble of the spoked wheels across the ground?"

Taran . . . Taran! came the voice of the thunder, in a long roll that traversed the skies.

"The Good God, he is following! Now his great club rises—now it strikes!" On her words, the air exploded around them in a great clap of sound.

"Dis Pater has come for us!" wailed Rufus, dropping to his knees as if he would burrow into the ground.

"Oh, they are coming, they are marching above us," chanted Maira. "All the dead warriors are rushing to the war! The heroes are advancing—do you hear their tramping footfalls, the hoofbeats of their horses, do you see them marching there?'' She stretched out her arms to the heavens, turning as the vanguard passed over her and Lugh's lightnings flared beyond.

Light limned their stern faces and glittered on their armor. She saw the flower of all the world's armies—warriors of her own people and men arrayed in gear she had never seen before. And then, among the last of them, she saw a face she knew.

''Conmor!'' her shriek startled ears grown deaf with thunder. ''Conmor, oh my father—take me with you now!''

But he neither turned nor looked down, and he did not answer. Only one final Power rose up behind him; Maira saw the face of a woman whose bright hair flared and whose eyes were dark with sorrow, who drew across the skies behind her a raven's wing of rain.

Thunder rattled in the distance, the drumming of hoofbeats in the heavens faded and was gone. Once, twice, lightning flickered on the northern horizon, and then there was only darkness and the sudden, icy rain.

FOURTEEN

The Lady Of Ravens

THE RAIN STRUCK like the buffeting of mighty wings. Men struggled to soothe the terrified horses and to cover weapons and armor.

"Be calm, lads—it will soon be over," came Pintamus' even voice. "Feel how the wind is blowing. The clouds will soon be gone and then we'll have a bit of moon to light our way. Be grateful you're not archers. You can strike just as hard with a wet sword as with one that's dry!"

This brought general laughter. The rain began to slacken, and in the west one could see the occasional glimmer of a star.

But Maira sat on the wet grass where she had fallen when her exaltation left her. Her visions had driven the last fumes of wine from her head, and now she was left alone in the darkness, cold and rather sick, and suddenly very tired.

And there's a cold hard ride and a battle to fight before morning, she thought despairingly. *Goddess, why couldn't the lightning have struck me and saved me all the pain?*

After a time her gut began to cramp painfully. She wiped her sword dry and sheathed it, then forced herself to stand up and stumbled toward the privy trench, drawing her cloak over her head against the rain. Nausea overcame her twice before she got there, and she stood gasping, wondering whether she should crawl away into the woods and vomit her guts out in privacy. Surely they could win the fight without such help as she would be now!

But it was not her prowess they needed, but her presence. She had gotten her men this far; dead or alive she had to lead them now. And there was the trench at last, with two shapes already huddled at the other end of it, talking softly. With a sigh of relief Maira pulled away her clothing and squatted down.

"Who's that?" came a voice through the darkness. The words had the accent of the south. Maira tried to summon the strength to answer.

"Never mind—it's only one of the Novantae," his companion cut in. "But we can speak Latin if you want privacy. None of those barbarians know our tongue."

Maira could have told him differently, but what did it matter? Her body's inner convulsions were all that concerned her now.

"Think you we can find the way to the hillfort in this darkness? We came from the west, before."

Something in the final words penetrated Maira's awareness. Was the man talking about some routine visit by the Roman troop, or was there indeed some secret here?

"Ah, that was a good trick to play! It set the pot boiling nicely! But where did the Commander get the Novantae cloak?"

"From the trader Antiochus at the Lyn Mapon Fair, after that Selgovae boy died. He had been looking for a way to get things moving here, and the natives played right into his hand. . . ."

Antiochus! Had the trader betrayed them? And if so, in what else had they been deceived?

Maira froze, waiting for them to say more.

"It will be time for us to move soon," the first man said. "We will take them by surprise, leave one or two alive to tell the tale, and once more the Novantae will get all the blame. When the news reaches the other clans there will be war. The Caledonii will find few to listen to their talk of a campaign against us then, and surely the government will rebuild Blatobulgium under the Decurion's command."

"May the gods grant it!" said his companion. "I am tired of this wandering life, with the ground for a bed half the time, and no regular meals."

Maira recognized the voice now. It was Haterius, the dark-haired man. *I will kill him,* she thought dimly, *but the sword-death will be too clean—I will use my bare hands!* The first man laughed, and now she knew him as well—Rufus, who had shared their fire. *I will kill both of them.. . .*

"Ah well, I am babbling," said Rufus, "but it is a relief to speak, now that it's almost done. Remember, we are to try to keep that gangling Novantae bitch alive."

"Why?" Haterius' laughter made Maira feel unclean. "Does he want to fuck her again or does he plan to sell her to the Arenas in Rome?"

"Maybe both—who cares? Anyway, I have yet to see her use that sword!" Rufus stood up, lacing his leather breeches and pulling his tunic down.

You will see me use it, I promise you, said Maira silently.

"I think the rain is easing up, at last." Haterius got to his feet. "And the commander was right—there is the moon! We'd best get back to the others. We'll be moving out soon."

Feet squelched on wet grass as they came toward her. Maira pulled her cloak over her face and huddled closer to the ground. The feet came closer, stopped. She could feel them looking down.

She felt for the cold hilt of her knife. *If I leaped now I might take one of them, but the other would spread the alarm!* She felt her tensed muscles tremble and forced herself to relax. *No,* she thought bitterly, *I can't try it now. I'm not sure I could even kill the one.*

"Hey lad—was our wine too much for you?" said Haterius in British. "If you like, we'll just roll you into the ditch and bury you here!"

Maira forced a groan and the two Romans began to laugh. One of them poked her with a hobnailed toe; then, still laughing, they went off toward the fire.

And then there was silence, broken only by Maira's harsh breathing and an occasional pattering as the wind spilled water from the bare branches onto the ground. Maira allowed herself to sag, and retched the last of the wine and venison she had eaten onto the ground.

I have to stop them, she thought dully. She heard the summons of the Roman horn and staggered to her feet, wiping her mouth with a twist of wet grass. The horn blew again. A horse neighed and metal jingled and clashed.

They would be mounting up now, Romans and British all mixed up together. How could she tell her men what she had heard? They were used to arguing out every order and plan—the Romans could slay them all while she was still trying to explain what was going on!

Maira made her feet carry her forward, flogging her weary

brain. She would have to face Pintamus as if nothing had happened—as if she was only sick because of the wine. She felt sick enough, surely, though she could not tell if it were the body's weakness or despair.

I have been used, she thought dully, *and I walked into the trap like a calf to the slaughtering pen. How Pintamus must have laughed at me! I thought to seduce him into aiding my revenge, and all the time he was tricking me into serving his own plans.*

Urr had saddled Roud already and held the mare while Maira settled the iron-bound leather cap on her head. He helped her up and handed her the lances and her long shield. She opened her mouth to speak to him, but there were too many people around them. Later, she told herself—when they were on the road.

The men seemed subdued—by their drinking, or perhaps by the storm or the knowledge that battle was near. She could not tell which, and as they set their horses at the twisting pathway through the gorge she needed all her attention to help Roud negotiate the slippery trail.

She had tried to use the Roman and instead he had used her—the shameful truth of what she had heard echoed and re-echoed in Maira's memory. *Carric was right,* she thought dismally, *if I had been willing to take the risk I could have stopped this war. But my father's blood must still be paid for, and the men are ready for battle now. If I ordered them home now I don't think they would obey!*

The mare slipped on a loose stone and for a few moments Maira's attention was all on steadying her, for the rain-swollen torrent was rushing loudly down its stony bed not far below. Then at last they came out onto the track, turned south for a little and then west to join the road up the Elvan Water to the pass.

It had begun to rain again, but not heavily. If the road was clear, less than two hours would see them to Din Carn. She had less than two hours to decide what she must do.

The horses' hooves beat out an eager rhythm on the stones. *A Selgovae killed my father, but I slew him . . . Selgovae stole our cattle, but we have taken theirs . . .* the inner dialogue ran on. *And what we do tonight is not a simple raid, but war. Rufus was right—if we destroy Din Carn the whole north will be set afire, and in the winter too, when the homeless will die from the cold.*

A thought came to her. She had heard that the Roman Governor had paid the northern princes in gold to keep the border peaceful while he was away in Gaul. But rumor said his star was falling now. If the three Legions he had taken were gone forever, then there was only a thin line of soldiers left to defend the Wall. How long would the tribes hold themselves back from such a rich and poorly defended prey?

Pintamus had said he was acting without the Prefect's knowledge, but she wondered now. To divide and rule was Rome's way, and surely with tonight's work the splitting of the Britons of Alba would be well begun. The Decurion's command numbered fifty men, and he had only led thirty before. Despite their mixed British-Roman dress, she wondered if all of them were even Brigantes.

But even if her warriors knew with whom they rode would it make any difference now? With every step that Roud took, with every thought that came to her, her anguish grew.

I have wrought too well to persuade them to this battle. But I did not think where it would lead. I sought vengeance for my wounded heart, and now my nation is betrayed!

The waning moon slipped through the clouds toward the western horizon, carrying with it all the time she had left to choose. Eastward she thought she saw a pallor—was it sunrise, or only false dawn?

Her head drooped, but her hands were clenched on the reins. *Goddess, help me!* came her heart's cry then. *Take my life if you will, but save my people—show me what I must do!*

At the top of a hill they drew rein to rest the horses. Maira pulled Roud aside and turned her face to the thin rain. The heavens were weeping too, she thought, in anticipation of the day.

If she had been at home she would have asked the Druid to make a sacrifice, but she had nothing to offer here, except— abruptly she pushed back her woolen sleeve, and drew her dagger. She winced as the sharp blade bit her arm, then felt the hot blood begin to flow and sighed.

"Cathubodva, Cathubodva, Raven of Battle," she whispered, "by my own blood I summon Thee! Dost smell it? Dost see it? Look, it nourishes the ground. . . ." She stretched out her arm, letting the wound bleed freely. Roud caught the scent and threw up her head, snorting uneasily, but Maira reined her in.

She heard a sharp order and the sound of hooves as the troop began to move. Petric called to her and she gave her arm a last shake and loosed the rein, holding her arm pressed tight against her side. Hoofbeats clattered on stones, but she thought she heard an echoing rattle of thunder in the sky.

Oh Great Queen, I call Thee; her lips moved silently as they rode on. *Mor-Rigan, hear me! As the red mare of battle and the white, red-eared cow, as the wolf-bitch and the raven now do I call Thee; I call Thee by Thy cauldron, and by Thy flowing stream!*

Come to me—aid me, and Thou shalt have slaughter, men crying in agony, blood soaking the ground! Let the gods fight without Thee, here is more bitter battle. Dogs of Rome I will give Thee, and Britons who betray their land!

The beat of horses' hooves set the rhythm for her litany. Her wounded arm throbbed in sympathy, and a gust of wind brushed her cheek like a dark wing.

Images from old tales pulsed in her memory—the fair maiden who tempted the hero; the mighty Queen who drained men of seed in her bed and of blood on the field; and finally, the dark winged hag who prophesied disaster, and who stole strength from men's arms and courage from their hearts with her terrible cry.

And like a vivid dream knowledge came to her. She saw scenes from tales she had never been told, mouthed names she had never heard. Had she gained this dark wisdom from the blood of the red stallion, or from the crones' cauldron, or was this some deeper awareness, always inherent but never accessible till now?

And so they rode on, and further on, hearing beside them the rush of the swollen stream, until a light grew around them that was too bright to be the vanished moon, the silver, shadowless radiance of a cloud-shrouded day. Mist drifted across the moors; vapors rose from the wet ground until the earth seemed as insubstantial as the sky. The men were murmuring. This was uncanny weather for a fight, but they would not turn back now.

And then the track wound down to the ford in the stream, and on the rising ground beyond it they saw the defending ditches and granite rampart of Din Carn.

Pintamus held up one hand. "This is the plan, then," he said in a low, clear, tone. "We will ride for the gate and hack through it, and then kill all we can. Rufus—do you have the torches? Memor—get your axe out now."

Maira straightened in her saddle. Around her, men were adjusting shield straps and re-settling their helms.

"Men of the White Horse, form up behind me," she began, ignoring the Roman's frown. Perhaps she could separate them into two parties, and then—

"What's that?" asked one of the Brigantes suddenly. The wind had drawn down a veil of rain between them and the Dun, but something dark was stirring at the ford. Without order, the whole party moved closer, straining to see.

"It's only an uprooted tree brought down by the rain," said Rufus.

"No, it's a body!" one of the Brigantes contradicted him.

Maira's own men remained silent, but she felt them closing up behind her. For the first time since the storm, hope began to stir.

The dark thing at the ford raised itself. Water splashed with a sound that was different from the rushing of the stream. Maira urged Roud forward, staring.

"It is a woman." Words came to her, focusing their vision. "An old woman in tattered black robes. . . ."

Now they all saw her ravaged face, her lank white hair, and the bloody garments that she was washing in the stream. The terrible eyes fixed them; the Hag saw them and smiled.

"Men of Din Rhun, the Romans have tricked you. . . . Men of the White Horse, beware!" Her harsh whisper curdled the thick air.

Pintamus swore and started his horse down the hill, and the dark figure blurred into motion—three great ravens flapped heavily upward, deafening them all with their cries. The horses plunged frantically as the three birds passed over them. Maira saw the cold glitter of jet-black eyes as the last bird went by, and a dark feather falling from its beating wing.

She reached out with her wounded arm and caught it. Her lips opened, the breath rushed out of her in a terrible cry. It seemed to go on forever; it came not from her, but through her, a cry that was all the world's terror and anger and pain, the distillation of all her own agony.

Hearing it, men felt their bowels loosen, felt a sharp despair that darkened vision, felt panic and confusion and a desperate fear. And men heard it in the sleeping *dun* as well, and came awake screaming from shattered dreams.

A sharp order from the Roman Commander brought the

unthinking response of long discipline. His men urged their mounts forward, and the hysterical Novantae horses began to run too.

Maira did not try to stop them. Her heels drummed against Roud's wet sides as they splashed through the ford.

"Treachery!" she screamed, "Awake, you are betrayed!" She reined Roud away from the Romans, and some of her own men followed her, their faces working with uncomprehending anger.

"I heard the Romans talking," she shouted, hauling her mare around to face them before one of those swinging swords found her back. "It was they who raided here after Conon died and threw the blame on us. They would use us to set all Alba at war!"

She began to rein Roud around, to lead them all away from the battle, but Waric had already set his mount back toward the Romans, snarling with rage. And now the wicker gate of the *dun* crashed open and Selgovae warriors began to boil out like ants from a broken hill. When Carric's father heard of Din Rhun's rebuilding he must have strengthened his walls and brought his people in. She had not expected so many to be there.

In a moment the battle became an incoherent welter of individual combats—Novantae who had understood her were fighting Brigantes or Romans while the others attacked the Selgovae, and the furious Selgovae warriors struck at any stranger they saw.

Maira felt a dark lust stir within her. *"Blood, blood!"* it shouted, and she remembered her vow. *Let it be blood, then,* she thought, and she slipped the first of her lances free of the strap that held it, let the reins fall to Roud's neck, and kneed her toward the Dun.

She saw Haterius on his dark bay horse, swinging his long cavalry *spatha*, and shouted his name.

"I heard you boasting of your betrayals, Roman—and dishonoring me! Turn, and you shall see if I can fight!"

He jerked at his horse's head and flung up his oblong shield. Maira turned Roud with her knees as if they were running cattle down the glen, drew back her arm, and threw. She heard the lance clatter harmlessly off the Roman's shield, but Roud was already swerving in a tight circle while Maira jerked a second weapon free.

The Roman was almost upon her. His sword exploded toward her and she took the blow on her own shield, her legs convulsing around Roud's belly as it rocked her back. The horse half-reared, Maira bent over her neck and shifted her grip on the lance, using the momentum as the horse came down again to strike downward into the man's exposed side.

The shock as it hit his ribs nearly tore the shaft from her hand. She grunted with the effort to hold onto it, and then the Roman horse lurched forward and the movement drove the wickedly barbed lance head the rest of the way into its rider's side. Maira kicked Roud away, still holding the shaft, and the lance head tore its way out again, bringing half the Roman's guts with it, and screaming, he fell.

A thrown lance grazed her thigh. She turned, saw a Selgovae warrior reaching for another and cast the weapon she held at him, leaving a red trail through the air. She thought he fell, but men and horses surged around her. It was too close for lance-work now, and she brought her father's long sword whining hungrily from its sheath.

From the corner of her eye she saw Urr trading blows with Rufus. She thought she saw him falter and began to turn Roud, just as the Roman's flashy swordwork brought his blade under Urr's guard and across the old man's chest.

Now, when she could have used another lance, she did not have one ready, but Lod had seen it too, and his spear darted like a serpent toward Rufus' back, bit through linked wire and leather and bone, and jutted out through the Roman's chest. For a moment Rufus stared down at the spearhead, crimson now with his own heart's blood, and then his face changed and he toppled from the saddle.

Urr was still clinging to his horse, clutching at his slashed breast. Maira met Lod's anguished gaze and pointed down the hill.

"Get him out of this, Lod, and save him—go on!"

She drove Roud between him and the other Romans, was buffeted by a storm of swords for a few furious moments before more of her men came up to defend her and she could breathe again.

She had to stop this, she thought, before they all died without ever understanding what had gone wrong!

"Carric—Carric of Din Carn, come out to me!" Her scream pierced the confusion of men's shouts and the clatter and clang of blows. Across the melee she saw Carric's bronze-brown hair; someone fell back before him—she could not tell if it was a man of Rome or one of hers, and he stood clear.

"Selgovae, Novantae!" she shrieked, "I call for a contest of champions. Let me and Carric decide the issue now!"

Fractionally the noise abated. She saw Carric striding toward her, Pintamus drawing off with his men. Biting her lip to hide its sudden trembling, she swung her right leg over Roud's withers, held out shield and sword to keep from getting tangled, and slid to the ground. Stiffened by so many hours in the saddle, she landed badly and nearly fell. But the men had drawn back into a circle, eyeing each other warily and watching her with a kind of avid curiosity.

"By the dancing blade, a circle's made—by the dancing blade!" The words of the sword-dance echoed in her memory. *I should have made them give Carric a mount and met him on horseback,* she thought, desperately flexing her cramped legs to get the circulation going. On foot, Carric's height and reach would give him the advantage.

But Roud still stood where Maira had left her, flanks heaving, neck white with flecks of foam. *She's tired too,* Maira realized, *so perhaps it is just as well.* She smiled bitterly, remembering that her purpose was not to survive the battle, only to end the war.

No—not even that, she corrected herself. It was simply to find a way to talk to Carric. But seeing Carric approaching her, naked as he had leaped from his bed and splendid as Caractacus with his shield of painted hide and his lances in his hand, she understood that it would not be easy. There was no love for her in his face, no reminiscent softness, only an adamantine determination to win.

She sheathed her sword, unstrapped her last three lances and set them one beside the other point upward in the damp earth. Carric stopped, facing her, and set three of his own spears ready, handing the others to one of his men to take away.

"I am Carric son of Cador, and I stand to champion the folk of Din Carn today. You have dared to come against me armed for war, but you will not go home to boast of it!" His gaze was implacable, but curiously unfocused, as if he were trying to look through her.

"Carric," Maira began, "wait a moment—there are things I must say!"

"No." He jerked a lance from the earth and lifted it. "When we spoke in the stone circle, you had your say. I will not listen to your deceptions again."

"Carric, the Romans—"

Something blurred through the air toward her. Horror, anger, exasperation, all warred in her, but her body was already moving. Her shield came up, she turned and felt his lance tear its way past.

"The next spear will pierce your breast. Foolish girl, you should have stuck to your spindle!"

Somehow Maira's own lance was already in her hand. "I have ridden the red stallion and faced the crones of Craig Duw—do not question my courage! I am the Lady of my people, and their protector!" Her arm swung back, weight shifted to propel the lance outward. At the last moment she remembered that she did not want to kill him and a twitch of her strong fingers shifted the aim so that the lance flew harmlessly past.

Carric barely bothered to step out of the way. He laughed, but there was no amusement in the sound. Then he moved, and Maira saw the second spear speeding toward her, faster than the first one had come. Her dodge this time was awkward. She grabbed for her lance and threw, aiming for his legs, hoping that she could get him off-balance long enough to speak.

But his shield dropped, almost negligently, to deflect the missile. He reached for his third spear. But this one he did not throw immediately. He was watching her. Maira remembered how her father used to watch an approaching deer, lance ready in his hand.

"You should never have come here, Maira," he said softly. "The women of Din Rhun will rue this day!"

And that was certainly true, but even as Maira struggled for an answer he moved. She blinked and tried to see where the lance was coming, but there was only a shiver in the air to warn her.

Goddess! Stark terror held her motionless; she heard a *thrumm* and felt a wind on her cheek as the lance flashed by.

I must respond . . . I must respond . . . she told herself. Her fingers felt nerveless; her skin was cold and she knew she must be as white as the mist that still clung to the hills.

"Carric," she whispered. Dark wings were beating in the caverns of her soul. She struggled with the temptation to let them free. *Just a little*, she thought, *just enough to scare him, please!*

Her sight cleared; her hand closed on the smooth wood of the lance shaft. In a single smooth motion she whirled and cast the spear.

This time it flew true. Perhaps it did not have Carric's power, but she could see he had not really expected it to come near him, for his shield was down. Now it was his turn for an awkward scramble, and the thunk as the lancehead pierced his shield echoed around the ring.

For a moment Maira thought she had struck Carric as well. But after a moment he turned the shield, wrenched the lance out and tossed it aside, inspected the hole and evidently decided that the shield had not been seriously weakened, and then drew his sword. His face was contorted in a grimace, and Maira realized that he was angry now. She would have to hold him somehow until action had released some of his rage. Perhaps she could get through to him then.

He moved toward her with little soft steps, like a stalking mountain cat. Holding her own sword ready, Maira edged away. Then suddenly he was upon her. She got up her shield to receive his blow; without willing it her own sword swept around and she staggered as it was deflected by his blade.

The blades clanged and parted; Maira forced weary legs to carry her out of reach, but she was almost to the limits of the circle now. Panting, she dodged beneath his blow and righted herself. She swung her sword up to guard again, but her arm was trembling.

"A brave lass she is, surely, but no match for our young Lord," said a Selgovae regretfully.

In the eternal second before Carric came at her again Maira knew it was true. She might have been able to give him a good practice match when she was rested, but not after all she had been through in the past three days. More strongly now she heard the dark laughter of the Mor-Rigan, but she did not dare unloose that power against Carric, and for her, there was no middle way.

He paused, long blade poised and angled slightly behind him. She cast up her shield as it blurred toward her, too late saw it twist down, tried to move her shield back again and cried out as his blade caught its edge and tore it from her arm. There was a long, indrawn gasp from those watching, then a murmur of approval as Carric straightened and with a negligent grace threw his own shield away.

The scorn in that gesture sent a quick flash of anger through Maira. Without the weight of the shield to slow her, she felt some strength returning. With a harsh laugh she dragged the helm from her head and tossed it after Carric's shield. She saw men on both sides grinning. They did not understand that a full head-blow from Carric would knock her senseless even with the helm, and without it at least she could see!

Carric did not like that admiration, or perhaps it was the shining of her bright hair in the sunlight that reminded him who he was fighting. He grimaced, and Maira knew that if there had been any restraint in his fighting before, he would show none now.

Two-handed, she poised the sword before her. He struck, her swift angling of the blade parried it, but the force of the blow knocked her backward. She stumbled and found her feet again, standing wide, trying to find some solid footing on the muddy ground. Carric's blade flashed again, dazzling as the sun broke momentarily through the clouds. Maira struck at the light, felt her edge score flesh, then a jerk as his sword twisted and neatly slid under hers, tapped her exposed fingers numbingly and lifted it from her grasp.

Once more instinct carried her back out of range, although reason told her she was finished now. Her dagger came into her left hand.

"Do you think that little knife can hurt me?" said Carric softly. "Maira, you must surrender now."

She looked at him, realizing that for the first time he had spoken her name. Then she shook her head and with a swift movement reversed the dagger, resting its cold point at the hollow of her own throat.

"It is still my defence against you, Carric," she fought to keep her voice steady. "I will not shame my people by living as your captive here. I only ask that they be spared. They were misled, as I was, but the responsibility was my own. . . ."

Something broke in his face then and he gestured around them with his sword. "But why—Maira, *why* did you come here?"

From the corner of her eye she could see Pintamus and his men drawn up in formation a little up the hill, waiting like vultures.

"Ask the Romans," she said bitterly, nodding toward them.

She wondered now if they had intended to pull out of the fight all along and let the British kill each other. "You were deceived by their trickery, and I by my own grief and pride." In a few moments it would be over, and she could go down into the friendly dark.

"Well, then," Carric grinned suddenly like a wolf catching sight of his prey. "Let us strike a blow at our common enemy!" He turned to his people, pointing his sword at the hill. "Did you hear her? Will you let these dogs of Rome return to their stone kennels to boast of how they have driven us for their sport?"

Selgovae and Novantae together responded with a snarl, a cry, a roar of soaring rage. Maira blinked as they exploded into motion, and the strengthening sun struck flames from their already reddened swords. Carric snatched up Maira's fallen weapon and held it out to her.

"Come on then, woman," he shoved the hilt into her hand. "Don't you want your revenge?"

He was grinning, curse him—grinning! Maira gulped once and then found herself laughing. Hands that felt as if they belonged to her once more sheathed the dagger and closed on the sword.

"To horse—to your horses—they're getting away!" cried Maelor. Already mounted, he grabbed Roud's rein and dragged her toward Maira, then turned her loose and kicked his bay into a gallop up the hill. Someone had brought out Carric's big stallion. He leaped onto its bare back and shouted to her, and Maira found strength she did not know she had and pulled herself into the saddle.

The Romans were pushing their horses up the slope on the far side of the stream while the Novantae who were still mounted struggled after them. The Selgovae were delayed by the need to catch and bridle their horses, but once they were up on fresh beasts they made better time. Maira slapped Roud's neck, trying to keep up with Carric, and the tired mare stretched her neck and ran.

Now the Selgovae were outdistancing the Romans as well. Shouting, they circled and closed in, driving the enemy back upon the slower Novantae. Like a herd ringed by wolves the Romans drew together, fighting with a disciplined efficiency that almost compensated for their inferior numbers.

For a few moments the battle was even, and then, just as Maira and Carric came up to them, a barked order formed the

Roman troopers into a column that punched through the ring of
warriors and down the hill. With a shout Carric kneed his
mount toward them, Maira at his side. The big bay shocked
into the first rider, sending the smaller horse sprawling. Two
others charged Carric then, swords swinging frantically to get
him out of the way before the rest of the British caught up to
them.

Maira dug her heels into Roud's flanks and the little mare
made another valiant effort and blocked the third rider's
escape. Maira's sword rose and fell, striking the Roman blade
away and continuing on into the man's side. She saw a spear
speed toward Carric's back and shouted; then one of the
Brigantes attacked her and she maneuvered Roud frantically,
trying to dodge his blows while he caught hers on his shield.

But she had the strength for it now—the black wings were
beating, and she did not have to hold them anymore. It was not
battle that had bested her, but the strain of fighting Carric! She
felt a cry building in her chest and let it tear free, and even the
men on her own side faltered for a moment before a new fury
spurred them on.

The Brigante's guard slipped then, and she had him. As he
fell her eyes met Carric's, and she laughed. Then Carric's
glance fixed on something beyond her; as his face changed
Maira whirled and saw Pintamus bearing down on her with his
spear poised in his hand. Desperately she hauled on Roud's
reins. She could feel the tired mare's muscles bunching
beneath her, but it was not enough, or perhaps it was too much;
Roud half-reared, turning, and the spear that had been aimed at
Maira took the mare in the chest.

There was a long scream of agony, and Maira never knew
whether it came from the horse's throat or her own. She threw
herself free as the mare lurched and toppled in a tangle of
thrashing legs that brought the Roman horse down too.

When Pintamus managed to extract himself from the saddle
it was to see his men taken prisoner, grim-faced warriors
surrounding him, and Maira standing over him with drawn
sword. He lifted one hand in a gladiator's gesture of surrender.

Maira knelt by Roud's head then, murmuring meaningless
words of comfort while the mare's bright blood gushed onto
the muddy ground. There was no need for a mercy stroke, for
the soft eyes were dulling already. Maira remembered how the
blood of the red stallion had flowed and thought, *Now the mare
as well as the stallion has died for me*. In that moment, she felt

their loss more sharply than she did that of her men. At least
the warriors understood why they died.

And then no more breath distended the laboring nostrils. The
crimson river dwindled and ceased to flow, and after a few
twitches, the long, lovely legs were still. Her throat aching too
painfully for tears, Maira got to her feet again.

The warriors had watched the mare's dying in the silence
they would have accorded one of their own. Now they turned
to the Roman, who straightened, staring back at them with
almost steady eyes.

"And what do you intend to do with me?"

Carric laughed shortly. "For what you tried to do to us?
Surely you can guess the penalty!"

Pintamus attempted an answering smile. "If you kill me,
Rome will not rest until this heap of stones you call a fortress is
leveled to the ground."

"I do not think so," said Maira harshly. "I think that the
Prefect will try to forget that you ever lived. Was that not your
agreement, Roman? That he would have no knowledge of you
if you failed?"

Once more Pintamus looked around him, reading his death
in the faces he saw. Then his angry gaze returned to Maira and
he spat.

"These were not the words you had for me, my lovely,
when you lay in my arms and swore the death of that barbarian
who stands by you now! Does he know that? Does this noble
chieftain know you were my whore?"

Maira heard the little murmur of speculation ripple around
the circle, and Pintamus laughed.

"I do not think you will dare to judge me!" He stared at her,
challenging.

Afraid to look at Carric, Maira lifted her sword. "I *thought*
that Carric had betrayed me, but you have tricked us all. Yes, I
will judge you, knowing that the Goddess judges me. Prepare
to die."

The pride came back into his eyes then, and he loosened his
breastplate and set his sword hilt-first into the mud, facing the
blade. "You will at least grant me this honor." His gaze dared
them to deny it, and before any of them could move, Tiberius
Flavius Pintamus slipped the tip of the *spatha* beneath his
armor and threw himself forward onto the blade.

From those who watched came a little satisfied murmur, as
if something, at last, had been well done. Maira looked at

Roud's blood upon her hand. The Roman's body was still twitching. She stepped forward, struck his head from his trunk and set it upon the body of the mare.

"You have had your honor, then," she said coldly. "But you should not have slain Roud!"

Then, finally, she turned and looked up at Carric; but he would not meet her eyes.

FIFTEEN

The White Mare

LIKE A WOLF that waits until his prey is weakened before he pulls it down, winter struck as the war party returned from Din Carn. They had barely time to bury their dead before the snow fell, and stayed. Men huddled in their houses, listening to the wind plucking their thatch, and wondered if their salted meat and stored grain would last until spring. There was sickness too, and Maira was kept busy helping one household after another, getting supplies to those who needed food, finding folk to feed stock and nurse those who fell ill.

Others shivered and complained of the weather, but Maira hardly noticed the cold. When her heart was frozen what did her body's pangs matter? She worked until she was exhausted, and then slept a few hours and rose to work again, with Windchaser following devotedly at her heels. Only in the week when snow fell so thickly that no one could leave Din Rhun did she suffer, for then there were no duties to keep her from thinking about Carric and all she had lost.

He had not spoken to her after the battle. The Novantae had taken their own dead and wounded and left the men of Din Carn to bury theirs and the Romans they had killed. Carric's father had promised to raise a mound for Roud and to set up the head of the Roman commander for her monument, but from Carric himself had come no word.

And there had been no news since then, either. Reason told Maira that no one would send messages in such weather, but her heart did not believe it. She had told Pintamus that the Goddess would be her judge, but she was judging herself, day by day. She took food to Urr's family, or stood on the mound they had raised over the dead and thought, *I have lost Carric finally,* and, *It was for my folly that my people died!*

Even when cold and inactivity set the other women to pecking at each other like penned hens, Maira retained a kind of distant courtesy that killed the hot words in their throats. Druith had moved up to the *dun* from Eoc's house in the valley and tried her best to cosset her, but Maira smiled gently and continued as if her mother were not there.

But Temella learned early to wait until Maira had left them before she discussed her wedding plans.

"She is fey," said her people, watching her pace the pathways of the *dun* with Windchaser like a gaunt shadow at her side. "But surely winter will not last forever," one would say to another. "Perhaps she will be comforted in the spring. . . ."

After the end-winter feast of Oimelc the weather began to break, and the ewes dropped their lambs in all the most inconvenient places on the cold hills. Everyone was busy then, getting the sheep to shelter, helping ewes whose young died and feeding orphaned lambs. And then it was the turn of the cattle to give birth, and everyone began to breathe easier, seeing a promise of new wealth for the coming year. When next the moon swelled, the hawthorn bloomed white in the hedges and the mares foaled and were ready for breeding again.

Maira walked down to the new house they had built for Eoc on the ruins of Lys Speiat. Beth's belly was rounding with the child she had conceived that winter, and Acorn was pulling himself up on everything and everyone within reach in his efforts to stand. At least they had gotten him through the winter, she thought as she detached his fingers from the skirts of her tunic and set him in her lap. In such cold as they had endured, many small children died.

He butted at her breast for a moment, then realized there was nothing there for him and grabbed for the shiny hilt of her sword.

"Acorn—take care, love, and don't drive your Aunt Maira to distraction as you have me!" exclaimed Beth. She rubbed at the small of her back and sat down with a sigh. Her new pregnancy had gentled her, thought Maira, or perhaps she was simply growing more secure.

"I don't mind," said Maira softly, kissing the baby's plump cheek. "He grows more beautiful every day." Acorn was going to be a fair man when he was grown, she thought wistfully. Perhaps he might come to look like Conmor. He made another try for the sword, and she captured the little fingers in her hand.

Patience, patience, small hero, she said silently; *perhaps this blade will come to you one day!*

Beth was laughing. "You will spoil him—your mother has warned me!"

Eoc's tall shape filled the doorway. He was still pale and far too thin, but he was on his feet, and the sulky look was beginning to leave his eyes. For some things, at least, he could even use his right arm again. He beckoned to Maira.

"Snowfoot's had her foal finally—do you want to come see?"

"Go ahead," said Beth. "When I have *my* next foal I hope he will be just as excited about me!" She reached for her son, and Maira got up and followed her brother outside.

"How long ago?" she asked as they reached the field and she saw the shy creature peering at her from behind the shaggy rump of its dam. It was a horse colt, promising to be red roan like Roud. She supposed Eoc would sell her the foal if she asked him, but the thought faded almost as quickly as it had come. Her mother's grey mare was good enough if she had to ride. What did she need another horse for?

"Two weeks and a little over—it has been some time since you were here," he answered her. "Snowfoot is just coming into her foal-heat now. See—" He pointed, and beyond the group of mares and foals Maira saw Eoc's chestnut stallion trotting toward them. "We had better get the little one safely out of the way!" He shouted, and Coll dashed up with a soft rope and led the protesting foal aside.

For the moment the mare seemed to have forgotten her offspring. She tossed her head coquettishly and pranced sideways, tail lifting then dropping again. It reminded Maira painfully of how she had danced for Carric at Lughnasa.

But the stallion was not in the mood for foreplay. He quickened his pace, every line in his body quivering with power, and as the mare started to sidle again he lunged at her, knocking her off-balance and nipping at her neck until she stood with legs braced and tail held stiffly to one side to let him mount and enter her.

Maira closed her eyes, unwilling to witness that powerful joining. She had known one coupling in hatred and one in love. She did not expect to know either again. To live had been bearable in the cold of winter, when the world was as dead as her heart. But now the sun was warm, and the scent of blossoms drifted on the soft air. She had not expected to feel so much pain.

"Well, what do you think?" said Eoc.

His business finished, the stallion trotted away. The mare shook herself, nosed for a moment at the grass, then nickered for her foal.

Maira kept her face turned away as if she were watching them, not wanting Eoc to see her tears.

"Snowfoot is a good breeder. She will make you a wealthy man," she answered him. "Is that what you were wanting? Eoc—are you happy now?" Now she looked at him, watching his face as he searched for an answer. Both of them knew that she was really asking if he had forgiven her.

After a moment he shrugged and smiled, flexing his weak arm. "When this is strong and I am a warrior again, who knows? But for now I am happy. I have learned to appreciate some things I never had time for before. . . ." He looked up the slope toward the *dun* and then back at his sister. "I still feel the desire for power—I was bred for it, Maira, we both were! But I can promise you this much—I will not do anything to endanger the Clan!"

And that is more than I can say for myself! Maira thought bitterly, nodding acknowledgement. Eoc would do now—she stopped herself. Do for what? She was still the chieftain.

It was then, as she gazed blindly at the stallion and his placid mares, that she knew she could not go on with it any more.

Maira sat in the shrine that housed her father's skull, listening to the cheerful gurgling of the spring. Someone was playing on the pibcorn away up the hill; the bittersweet melody drifted down to her, harmonizing with the music the waters made.

She had not been here for some time, she realized. In the winter it had been too cold, and more and more often she had instinctively known what her decisions should be. *I suppose I have been learning,* she thought then; *or perhaps I simply no longer care.*

But none of her new wisdom could help her with the problem she faced now, which was how to lay her burden down.

"Listen to me, my father," she whispered into the gloom. "I have done my best for the people. I thought they might claim my life when we returned from Din Carn, but they mourned the dead and celebrated the victory—the victory!" she exclaimed, remembering the silent faces of the dead. "Now I am beginning to wish that they had killed me too! What shall I do, Conmor? What wisdom do you have for me now?"

She stared at the smooth dome of his skull, barely visible in the gathering darkness. The eye-sockets were shadowed as if Conmor were watching her.

She closed her eyes, breathing deeply to still her spirit, and waited for him to speak to her. But this time images came instead—shadowed trees that rustled softly and the patient whisper of deep waters.

Peace—Words came to her at last. *Give me peace and let me go*. In the silence that followed she did not know if the thought had been Conmor's or her own.

After a time she opened her eyes and sighed, for she had recognized the place she saw. "I understand, oh my father," she told him. "I understand and I will do what must be done."

Maira slept lightly, and woke when the first light of morning was edging around the hide that covered the door. She could hear the regular breathing of the other sleepers in their box-beds, and smiled, identifying them one by one. She dressed and looked around her for something in which to carry Conmor's skull. She saw a leather bag in which her mother sometimes kept spinning wool—that would do, but she did not want to wake Druith to ask.

I will leave her something in exchange. One of the southern steadings had given her a length of crimson wool which Druith had admired. Maira put it down where the bag had been. It would be good for Druith to wear bright colors again.

Only, as she stood up again, Maira found her eyes blurring with tears, and fought an absurd desire to part the curtains and crawl in beside Druith and let her mother soothe all her anguish away. But she knew that it would change nothing. She and her mother must each live her own life now. Surely Druith would understand. Softly Maira eased past the hide curtain and made her way like a ghost through the mists of morning to the wicker shrine by the spring.

When she came out, Conmor's head hidden in the leather bag clasped in her arms, she met Gutuator coming down the hill.

"Where are you going, daughter of my daughter?" His deep eyes held her gaze. Maira felt herself coloring, but could not look away.

"I am going to serve the Goddess at Lyn Duw," she answered a little defiantly, wondering if he could read intentions in her heart of which she herself was not entirely aware. "Is it a fortunate day?"

For a moment the Druid seemed to look through her, and his eyes reflected her pain. They then cleared and he focused on her face again.

"It is a good day for birth or death, for giving or gaining," he said slowly, "for in the end they are all the same."

She stared at him, wondering why he did not question her or tell her what to do. But that had never been his way.

"I cursed you when you brought me and Carric together at the Circle of Stones," she said abruptly. "I am sorry. If I had been wiser, many might have escaped suffering."

Gutuator's eyes searched her, and then, very faintly, very sweetly, he smiled. "What makes you think that the worst thing in this world is pain?"

And then, without seeming to move, he had gone past her and was continuing his smooth progress down the hill.

After a moment Maira shrugged, took the short path down to the east gate and from there to the pen to saddle the grey mare. Windchaser wanted to follow her, but she ordered him back to the *dun*. He sat down just outside the gate, whining softly, and watched her ride away, and it seemed to her that his obedience was an omen.

As Maira jogged down the track beside Scaur Water she cast a critical eye across the newly sown fields. She saw red wheat and white wheat and barley, and oats just beginning to fuzz the furrows with green a few fields away. If the rains behaved themselves this year the harvest would be a good one.

Maira realized then that she was checking off dangers as if she did not expect to return, and understood that if she did come back this way she would be changed. She was going to the sacred pool to serve the Goddess, and to wrest from Her some answer to her pain.

She felt curiously lighthearted now. The sky had never looked so delicately blue, and the rising song of a lark seemed a distillation of the beauty of the day. The thorn trees were heavy with blossom, and she leaned out to cut a spray of flowers, carefully trimmed the thorns away and twined them into a wreath for her hair.

Even Lyn Duw seemed bright this morning. With the sun almost overhead, its still waters mirrored the sky. Maira unsaddled and unbridled the old mare and left her contentedly cropping grass at the edge of the trees. Then she picked up the leather bag and followed the trail through the birches to the water's edge.

It was very quiet here. Maira found herself regulating her breathing lest she disturb that peace. On her way she had wondered if she did wrong to bring her father's head to the pool rather than burying it with the rest of his body in the mound. But her vision had shown her deep waters, and as she sensed the stillness she knew that here Conmor's restless spirit could be at peace.

And what about my spirit? she asked herself then. She set down the bag on the stony shore and began to remove her garments, folding them carefully. She thought, *Perhaps the sacred waters will wash away my pain*. . . .

Then she picked up the leather bag, and hesitating only a moment when she felt the chill of the water, she walked into the pool. The deep water where the offerings were placed was on the other side, where the trees came to the edge of the sheer bank. But Maira did not want to toss her father's head into the water like a ball too worn out to be played. She could at least do him the honor of carrying him to his rest.

Her skin tingled with cold, and then after a time she felt only a warming numbness. She moved slowly, seeking new footing carefully before she went on, so carefully indeed that her passing barely disturbed the surface of the pool.

She put out one hand to grasp the growing reeds and pulled herself along the edge of the deep water. Here she had stood, she remembered, on the day of Beth's purification, when she thought she had seen the Antlered One. It seemed very long ago.

Now she turned with her back to the shore, and balancing carefully, held out the bag.

"Blessed Lady of the Waters—" She spoke softly, and the stillness around her seemed to become deeper. "Here is my father, who is also Thy child. Too long have I clung to him. Now I give him back into Thy keeping. Oh Sweet Lady, receive his spirit, and in a happier day may he be reborn."

Maira took a deep breath, then cast the bag outward, teetering for a moment on the smooth stones, then finding her footing again. The bag was a dark blur against the bright air, then it shattered the water's smooth surface into a sparkling circle of spray. The waters fountained around it, for a moment it floated, then water poured in through the gathered top and pulled it under, and the pool settled to stillness once more.

So—it was done, and she felt a weight lifted from her, as she had when Carric knocked her shield away. And what now?

Goddess, I stand within Thy cauldron, she said silently, *as I stood when I asked Thee to choose my way for me, and again when I was made Queen. Oh blessed, bitter Mother—have I drunk enough of Thy wisdom? Wilt Thou give me a new birth now?*

A fragment of memory came to her—sunset at Blatobulgium and a stone goddess-image to which she had made her prayer. And there had been an answer—she must drink from the cauldron once more.

Maira sighed and bowed her head in acknowledgement, then bent to taste the dark waters one final time.

She tasted bitterness, coughed and lost her footing, and when her feet reached for new purchase she could find nothing on which to stand. She struck out with her arms and the movement thrust her head out of the water. She gasped in air, but now the shore was farther away and she went under again.

Panicked, her body struggled, gasping and gulping until the water tasted as salt as blood. Again she sank, flailing, into cold darkness. Her ears buzzed, awareness retreated inward until she could no longer feel her limbs.

And now the water seemed to bear her gently upward into a blaze of light. Brilliance filled her vision, in radiance she floated, and the taste of it was sweet to her tongue. Time expanded down a long tunnel of light. Words formed in her awareness, though she no longer knew if she were the thinker or the thought.

Not her father, but she herself was the sacrifice, the willing offering. This was the Lady's judgement, and her merciful release from pain. . . .

Maira's vision cleared. A new world came into focus around her. She saw broad meadows starred with pale flowers, and trees whose leaves were singing birds. Bright figures were coming to greet her—there was Urr, grinning, and Tadhg carrying his harp. And with them came another, Conmor her father, with a smile she had not seen on his face since she was a child. She moved toward them, gazing wide-eyed around her. Surely Roud must be here somewhere too, galloping happily over the emerald fields!

She saw someone else before her, white-robed, and recognized Gutuator. But her grandfather was not dead. . . . He shook his head as if he had heard her thinking, and she understood that the Druid could walk at will in either world.

It was Gutuator who accompanied her onward, for Maira felt something drawing her, like a breath of a scent or a fragment of a song. Then a Presence emerged from the glory around her like an opening flower.

Maira stared, for the face was familiar—she saw the Lady of the storm and the ford, the full beauty of a face she had seen carved in stone, her mother's face, and finally a face she had seen in a bronze mirror once, when she wore the sovereign's sacral gown—a face that was her own.

My child, you have served Me. . . . The Voice seemed to come from everywhere. *What is it that you desire?*

A choice? But how could that be? She had thought there was only pure existence here. She found her voice.

"What choices dost Thou offer me?"

To go back now, or to stay here, to rest, to rejoice in the Glory, until you are ready to return again.

Maira blinked, for the feel of the Voice was different. And there was a difference to the shape that mediated the Light to something her eyes could see—it was a man's form now, crowned by a graceful sweep of branching horns. She bowed to the Lord as she had bowed to the Lady.

"To return," she repeated slowly. Images swirled in her awareness; beauty all the more poignant because it was somehow *familiar*, like a half-remembered lullabye. "Yes, I *have* been here before!"

And now she remembered how even ecstasy had become unsatisfying—not for any lack in its perfection, but because her own spirit was not large enough to comprehend it, and so she had accepted incarnation again.

And yet, it was very good to be home. Here she could swim

in seas without stain, and run through woodlands that had never a thorn. Horses never tired here, or went lame, and music was everywhere. Even the air here was like a balm to give her bruised and aching spirit ease. Surely she had suffered enough for one lifetime and deserved the time to heal.

But as she thought of the pain just past she remembered the people for whom she had borne it.

"What will happen to the Clan if I stay here?"

Each soul will earn the fate its own will wins it, came the stern answer. *What is that to you?*

"I am the White Mare! I am bound to them! How can I bide with the Blessed knowing my people need my help?"

Is this your choice, then? The Lady spoke to her once more. From somewhere nearby came a call like a stallion's neigh, and Maira remembered the vows she had sworn at her consecration. But those oaths had only been for a lifetime— what she chose now would be for eternity.

"What will come to me if it is?"

You will return, and you will serve your people and their land, as conquered and conqueror, in poverty and in power. New tribes will come and seem to swallow up the old, but your blood and your spirit will endure. You will return to serve them again and again until the borders of Alba know peace. . . .

Maira shuddered, unable to comprehend so many lifetimes, so many centuries. "Leave the future to its own pain!" she exclaimed. "Only tell me if my people are in danger now!"

Yes. The Lord and the Lady spoke as one, and Their word shattered the peace around her into a thousand visions of destruction and war.

"Send me back—I must go to them!" the soul that was Maira cried.

The Faces before her dissolved into a blaze of Light. For a moment she seemed to glimpse some unimagineable Unity beyond them, but the brilliance grew and grew until it engulfed the Lord, the Lady, and all the Lovely Land. Now there was only light, and Maira was whirling, spinning dizzily upward until she burst into a blur of shadows and breathed in pain.

"Maira, my Maira, *breathe*, my love! Come back to me!"

Something within her responded to that voice; Maira focused, followed it, felt her body once more. She coughed convulsively then, as if she had swallowed the whole of Lyn Duw, and gasped for air again. *Lyn Duw*— but she had been *in* the sacred pool. Now cold stones were under her and warm arms around her. She shuddered, coughed again, and managed to turn onto her back.

She saw blue sky overhead, and a netting of fragile birch leaves. Slowly Maira focused closer, and realized that it was Carric whose arms held her, who stared at her with panic in his eyes.

Wondering, she reached up to touch his face and saw quick tears blur his eyes. His arms tightened painfully around her, and with a sob he dropped his face against her breast. For a moment he lay there, not speaking, listening to the rasp of breath in her lungs and the slow, steady beating of her heart.

His hair was wet. As her fingers closed on it she squeezed out more water, and she sighed.

"I don't understand," she whispered hoarsely. "Were you in the water too?"

Carric's head came up then. "Where do you think I would be, woman, when you were floating face down in the pool?"

"But you could have drowned. . . ."

He managed a shrug, still holding her. "I'm taller than you are—I could still touch bottom when I got to you. But do you think I would have cared, if I could not save you? Maira, did you *want* to die?"

"No!" she exclaimed, and then, "Perhaps—I no longer know what I intended, only that I couldn't keep on as I was."

"But you *knew* that I would come for you in the spring!"

Maira tried to sit up, gasped, and subsided back into his arms. "How should I know that?" she flared. "You sent me no word!"

"Who should I have sent to you—Antiochus? That trader will never show his face in these hills again, but even if everything he told me was a lie, there were things you had said, and the Roman. . . . I had to think, Maira."

"I wanted to kill him too," Maira sighed, "but there has been too much killing. And he distorted our words—he did not invent them. How could you still love me?"

His arms tightened around her. "I still loved you—that was the one thing I did know. But by the time I had sorted things out, the snow was too deep to send a messenger. This winter was terrible on the moors, Maira. Many of my people died. My father was one of them."

His face had gone grim, and Maira reached up to touch it. "Then you are the chieftain now?"

He nodded. "You can understand how much had to be done. I understand more of the needs that constrained you, now. But I should have made time to come to you, or sent someone to speak for me!" He shook his head in pain. "But it had been so long—I think I was afraid!"

"My poor love," Maira said gently. "Who am I to judge you? Oh Carric," she went on, "we have had enough loving and hating already for a dozen lives!"

"The hating, maybe—but we have a long tale of loving yet to tell!" Carric grinned, and Maira's breath caught in her throat. His hands moved down her body as if seeking assurance that she was indeed alive, and where his fingers passed she felt new sensation, as if he were bringing her to life again.

"You are cold!" he said accusingly, pressing her closer against him.

"Then you will have to warm me." Laughter bubbled through her as his grip tightened and the movement of his hands became more purposeful.

His body covered hers, and she felt as if her flesh had caught fire; surely her wet hair must be steaming upon the stones! And then she stopped thinking, for the flame within blazed like the light that had so recently surrounded her, only this time she was no longer alone.

When Maira became aware of herself again the sun had moved westward and the pool was in shadow once more. But it was the neigh of a horse that had awakened her, coming from somewhere beyond the trees. The sound came again, she stirred, and Carric opened his eyes.

"The horses!" he sat up suddenly. "I should see to them." He stood up and began to search the strand for his scattered clothing. Maira found her own clothes still neatly piled where she had left them and put them on.

"Horses?" she echoed him. "You were not alone? Or have you found a way to ride more than one?"

He glanced at her and grinned. "You'll see." He pulled his damp tunic over his head and picked up his belt.

Maira shook her head and followed him through the woods, wondering if her mother's mare were still waiting there. Her mind was beginning to function again; she could see problems, questions, waiting like wolves to spring. But she found her stride quickening, her back growing straighter, her heart readier to fight than to fear. And that was surely a change from this morning!

Was it Carric who had turned the world around for her, or her escape from death in the pool, or—Memory clutched at stray images, there had been light, she remembered, and song. But what she had seen in that light eluded her, and she could recall no word of the song. There were only the echo and afterglow of some great emotion that was at once a distillation of longing and of joy.

But surely *something* had happened to her, and Maira thought that even this much knowledge would be enough to carry her through whatever was to come. Only it was strange that Carric had come just now—

She hurried to catch up to him. "Carric, how did you know to look for me here?"

"I met your grandfather at the ford below Din Carn this morning, and he told me to come and meet you here." He stopped to look at her. "I thought you had sent him to me."

She shook her head and Carric stared at her. "Then how did he know?" he asked.

Maira took his hand and shrugged. "Gutuator is a Druid," she said simply. "And I think that perhaps I will take his advice from now on!"

Carric sighed, then pulled her to him as if he were still not quite certain of her reality. For a time, time stood still.

"Carric—we understand each other now, but some things have not changed," Maira said at last. "You are bound to Din Carn, and I am still the Lady of Din Rhun."

"I know . . . all that time I sent no word to you I was thinking about that."

"But what are we going to do?"

"We are going to be married, and spend a lot of time on horseback, my love." He grinned and pulled her after him through the last of the trees.

Maira blinked at the sudden blaze of the sun. Squinting, she saw the old mare and two other horses grazing in the meadow. No, there were three—Carric's big bay stallion and a dappled mare nuzzling a foal whose coat had the dusky sheen of a cygnet swan's.

She took a step forward, staring.

"A filly-foal," said Carric softly. "She'll be white as a swan's wing when she's grown. The mare dropped her near

Roud's mound, and I thought that in time to come this little one could carry you between Din Rhun and Din Carn.''

"But your people," Maira said softly, her eyes still on the foal. "Won't they resent me?"

"Not once they know you. Now that your walls are finished surely your people do not need you every day!" Carric answered her. "You can spend part of the year with me, and I will spend part of the year with you. There will be times when we must be separated, surely, but it will be better than the way things have been!"

Maira bit her lip, thinking hard. What he had said was true, and perhaps Eoc, as he recovered, would even be glad to act as her deputy.

"I don't know if what we will have will be more like a marriage or an alliance!" Carric said then, "But Maira, I need you! I am too quick to joy or anger—I need you to make me think and plan!"

The foal, intrigued by these two-legged creatures and their noises, had gradually moved closer until her velvet muzzle brushed Maira's hand. Maira stood very still, afraid of frightening her.

"You think that I can help you, after all the mistakes I have made?" she asked softly.

"I think we will need whatever wisdom we can find, and all our courage too." Carric's voice grew grim. "More riders have come to me from the princes of the north. They should reach you soon. They say that Clodius Albinus' star is falling, and if he is beaten in Gaul then all the oaths of peace we swore will be as the wind. . . . Even I can see that war is coming, Maira, and it will be such a war as will make our raiding look like children's games!"

Maira stared at him. To be together—yes, that was the answer. As she and Carric could not survive if they fought each other, neither could their land. She stepped toward him and set her hands on his shoulders, and he stood still, waiting, head bent a little so that he could meet her eyes. For a moment the sun, shining through the branches behind him, laid upon his head the shadow of horns.

"My oath to you then, my Lord, to fight beside you until our lives end!" *And perhaps beyond*—a stray thought came to her, but that did not matter now. Perhaps all their pain had been only a hard training for what was to come, but they were united now.

"And my oath to you, my Lady," he whispered, "to serve you as I live!" His hands came up to cup her breasts, not in lust, but in homage. His hair, as he bent to kiss her, was as red as the coat of the red stallion had been. But Maira knew that there would be only life between them now.

For a few moments longer the filly watched the two humans, waiting for some noise or motion, for another touch of that soft hand. But Maira and Carric did not stir, and after a time the foal, losing interest, snorted and picked her way back to her dam, nosing at the dappled mare's firm bag for the sweet milk she knew she would find.

Background

Like the paleontologist who reconstructs a dinosaur from fragments of bones, my task in writing this novel has been to extrapolate backward from archaeology, history, and the scattered survivals of European folklore to the original forms of early Celtic culture. The scarcity of material and the uncertainty of interpretation provide considerable scope for disagreement even among the experts. I am prompted, therefore, to present some background on my research for those who are interested in such things.

The Land.

White Mare, *Red Stallion* takes place in what is now Dumfriesshire, Scotland. This region has endured some of the more colorful chapters in Scottish history, being blessed with excellent farmland, and cursed with one of the main invasion routes into Scotland. As the Scottish West March, it was as renowned for murder and mayhem as the rest of the Border. Even in the Roman period it was sufficiently lively so that fortresses were built specifically to keep the local tribesmen in line. They were only intermittently successful.

Luguvalium lies beneath the modern Carlisle. The ruins of Blatobulgium may still be seen at Birrens near Lockerbie, as can the remains of the Iron Age hillfort which the Romans used for ballista practice at Burnswark. Some of the finds from Birrens are now in the museum at Dumfries. The site referred to in the book as "Dis Pater's Cauldron" later became known as "The Devil's Beef Tub", and was a favorite spot for the Border Reivers to hide stolen cattle (cattle rustling is an old Border custom too).

Most important, of course, is Din Rhun (the Lance Fort), a remarkable pyramid shaped hill near Penpont which is now somewhat redundantly called Tynron Doon. Below it is a circular mound with a few scattered thorn trees around it which suggested itself as the site for Lys Speiat ("the enclosed housestead of the hawthorns"). Excavations indicate there was an Iron Age hillfort on the Doon, whose stones were later recycled for use in the local church. Dow Loch (Lyn Duw) is said to be nearby. According to local legend, at times of stress a headless horseman rides down from the peak to terrify the countryside.

The People.

The unconquered, unconverted Celts of the British Isles were far from being the mistily melancholic folk who often appear in "Celtic" fantasy. They were a lusty and often violent people, fond of bright colors and colorful deeds, venerating the human head, the horses which were their pride, and the cattle by which they lived. Their gods were the tutelary deities of the tribe, their goddesses the territorial guardians of watersheds who resided in the sacred wells and springs. Like every other culture of that period (including the Romans) they practiced blood sacrifice. Along with the Vedic peoples of India, they were the most culturally conservative of the Indo-Europeans, and the two groups appear to have retained in common certain cultural patterns long after peoples occupying the territories between had learned other ways.

Racially, the people of Alba were probably the product of several waves of Celtic immigration. The last group of conquerors would have been closely related to the Belgic settlers who ruled southern Britain when the Romans came, and who were still allied with their cousins in Gaul. Physically, this last wave was tall and fair of hair and skin, although brown-haired people were common, and eventually became genetically dominant. The western lowlands of Scotland were ruled by a tribe the Romans called the Novantae. The River Nova, or Nith, seems to have been the border between them and their Selgovae neighbors, though the exact boundaries are uncertain and probably shifted periodically. It should be noted that the term "Pict" was first used (by Roman writers) in the third century, in reference to tribes north of the Edinburgh line who had earlier been labeled Caledonii, while the southerners had been called Maeatae.

As close relatives of the Celts of Gaul, the Celts of southern

Alba would have spoken some variant of the proto-Brythonic tongue which developed into medieval and modern Welsh, Cornish, and Breton. The Goidelic language of Ireland (Gaelic) was brought to Scotland by the northern Irish Scotti in the fourth century, who eventually settled in such numbers that their tongue replaced the native British, and the area became known as the land of the Goidels—Galloway. Personal and place names used in the book are either Roman or an extrapolation of second century Brythonic, with the exception of the Festivals, where Gaelic names are used because of greater familiarity.

Folklore.

The only extant account of the inauguration of a Celtic chieftain was written by a shocked English monk (Giraldus Cambrensis) in the twelfth century. According to Giraldus, the king-elect of one of the northern Irish tribes copulated with a mare which was then sacrificed and cooked, the king being bathed in the broth and eating and drinking it as well. Interestingly enough, in India, a ceremony in which a Queen mimed copulation with a dead stallion was preserved into the nineteenth century.

Horses were prized and venerated by both ancient and modern Celts, and often appeared on coins and in art. The "hobby-horses" of later folk tradition may be a survival of this veneration. Students of folklore may be surprised to find the "Mari Lwyd"—the "grey mare" of Welsh Christmas custom, appearing in the novel at Samain, however the white horse procession seems to have been a New Year's, rather than a Yuletide, custom. It therefore seemed appropriate to move its appearance to Samain, which was the Celtic New Year. Irish folklore cites at least one instance of the "horse" making its rounds at Hallowe'en. The procession of oddly dressed creatures escorting the horse represents spirits who are seeking food from the living, and should be familiar to anyone who has ever put out treats at Hallowe'en!

History.

In A.D. 192, the Emperor Commodus, son of the great Marcus Aurelius, was assassinated. His death precipitated a power struggle among three generals, C. Pescennius Niger, D. Clodius Albinus, and Septimius Severus. Niger was quickly disposed of, leaving Severus, who held Rome, and Albinus, who had pulled three legions out of Britain to fight for him, and who kept them in Gaul. Severus named Albinus as his heir, but this solution was only temporary. In A.D. 197, approximately a year after the events covered in *White Mare, Red Stallion*, the two armies battled it out near Lyons, and Albinus was killed.

Soon after, the allied tribes of Alba attacked, and did considerable damage to the Wall. The new Roman governors attempted to deal with the situation, but it was not until A.D. 208, when the Emperor himself mounted a major campaign in Alba, that the tribes were "pacified". Indeed, the Emperor seems to have dealt with the northern British so drastically that they gave no more trouble until near the end of the century. He himself died while preparing to finish the campaign, but that cannot have been much consolation to the people of Alba.

Sources.

The following works were of particular value in the writing of *White Mare, Red Stallion*:

Violet Alford, *The Hobby Horse and Other Animal Masks*, London: Merlin Press, 1978

Lloyd Laing, *The Archaeology of Late Celtic Britain and Ireland*, London: Methuen & Co., 1975

Françoise LeRoux and Christian-J. Guyonvarc'h, *Les Druides*, Rennes: Ogam-Celticum, 1982

Maire MacNeill, *The Festival of Lughnasa*, Dublin: University College, 1982

Trefor M. Owen, *Welsh Folk Customs*, National Museum of Wales, 1974

Alwyn & Brinley Rees, *Celtic Heritage*, London: Thames & Hudson, 1974

Peter J. Reynolds, *The Iron Age Farm*, London: British Museum Publications, 1979

Anne Ross, *Pagan Celtic Britain*, Columbia University Press, 1967

Graham Webster, *The Roman Imperial Army,* New
York: Funk & Wagnalls, 1969

and the series of monographs published by the City Museum of Dumfries.

The Lughnasa harvest song in Chapter Two is adapted from material in *The Lughnasa Festival;* part of the chant in Chapter Three is adapted from the *Ancient Laws of Ireland;* the invocation of the quarters in Chapter Four is based on a schema given in the middle Irish text of *The Settling of the Manor of Tara,* as analyzed in *Celtic Heritage;* the songs in Chapters Eight and Fourteen are translated and adapted from ancient Breton chants in the collection *Barzaz Breiz,* edited by Villem-arque; and the masquers' song in Chapter Eleven is adapted from a traditional song quoted in *Welsh Folk Customs.* The other poetry, for better or worse, is my own.

Diana L. Paxson
Samain, 1984

JACK L. CHALKER

LORDS OF THE MIDDLE DARK

Across the galaxy and beyond, the Master System ruled. Once the product of human intelligence, it now far surpassed its creators. All understanding of it was lost and any attempt at rediscovery ruthlessly suppressed. The rule of the Master System was unchallenged.

Yet there was a key, long forgotten, that would break that control and it happened by chance that two people, an American and a Chinese woman, stumbled across the secret of the five gold rings that were the key.

Now their only hope lay in finding the rings themselves for the Master System was at their backs, hunting them down . . .

First British publication of the huge US Science Fiction bestseller.

POSTALITTLEHAPPINESS

Post·A·Book

A Royal Mail service in association with the Book Marketing Council & The Booksellers Association.

Post-A-Book is a Post Office trademark.

MORE FANTASY AVAILABLE FROM
HODDER AND STOUGHTON PAPERBACKS